THE
PECULIAR PEOPLE

JAN DE HARTOG

THE
PECULIAR PEOPLE

A Novel

A Cornelia & Michael Bessie Book
Pantheon Books, New York

Library of Congress Cataloging-in-Publication Data

De Hartog, Jan, 1914–
The peculiar people / Jan de Hartog.
p.   cm.
"A Cornelia & Michael Bessie book."
ISBN 0-679-41636-6
1. Quakers—Indiana—History—19th century—Fiction.
2. American Indians—Fiction.   I. De Hartog, Jan, 1914–
Peaceable kingdom.
II. Title.
PR6015.A674P4   1992
823'.914—dc20   92-11682

Book design by M. Kristen Bearse

Text is set in Janson.

Manufactured in the United States of America
4 6 8 9 7 5 3

Contents

Author's Note

This is a novel, a story about people who lived a century and a half ago. Like all of us, they had ancestors whose lives shaped them, and descendants whose lives they molded. The salient difference between them and the majority of humanity is that they were Quakers and lived at a dramatic time for the Society of Friends and for America.

It was over three hundred years ago that the name 'Quaker' was first used; the founder, George Fox, sentenced to six years in prison in England for interrupting a church service in 1660, said to the judge: "One day thou too wilt quake before the Lord," to which the judge responded: "Take the quaker away." For some reason, the name stuck; when William Penn landed in Pennsylvania with one hundred of his coreligionists, the accepted epithet for members of the Society of Friends was Quakers.

The 'peace testimony' of the Quakers served them well during their first century in America. It brought peace with the

Indians in Pennsylvania at a time when, elsewhere in the colonies, massacres and revenge raids were common. It also brought about a climate in which trade and business flourished.

During the War of Independence, however, their very peaceableness became their downfall, as they refused to bear arms for either party. The British expressed their displeasure by turning Philadelphia, that most staid and orderly of all American cities, into a 'recreation area' for their Hessian mercenaries, with brothels, gambling dens, bars, and alehouses. There were fights in the streets, women were raped, shots were fired; Friends withdrew into the safety of their homes, behind bolted doors and barred shutters, and prayed for deliverance.

After the British had been defeated, the Hessian troops were replaced by the Congressional Army which, jubilant in its victory, had acquired a taste for battle. When its commander received the order from Washington to arrest 'forty merchants known as Quakers for treason and trading with the enemy,' his men welcomed the opportunities this presented.

The result was wholesale persecution. Quaker houses were ransacked, Quaker farms put to the torch; of the forty arrested, thirty were banished to Virginia, all their possessions confiscated; two of them were hanged on the Philadelphia Commons. Quaker farmers in the interior took shelter among the Indians; one Friend, whose farmhouse was set on fire, begged the Indians who came to defend him 'not to use violence, for the sake of their souls.' He was severely beaten by the mob.

Finally, the persecution in Philadelphia petered out. No more houses were looted, no more women brutalized, Quakers were no longer jeered in the streets. An orderly society was reestablished; but there had been a change. Friends who refused to swear the federal oath of allegiance, because of their testimony against oaths, found to their dismay that this meant exclusion from all official and quasi-official functions. Not only could they no longer take part in the government of the colony they had founded, they were barred from virtually all other positions which, historically, had been theirs; only in commerce and farming could they find employment.

The result was a closing of the ranks. The Society, excluded from public life, turned inward. It was clear that 'the Holy Experiment' had failed; contrary to their expectations, the Peaceable Kingdom of Isaiah, where the lion will lie down with the lamb and the wolf with the fatling, was not about to be realized. They felt it their duty to nurture that concept in what they called 'the remnant,' so that when times changed, their children would be ready to take up once more the 'motion of love' that had almost, almost brought about the ideal society. It was in fact a withdrawal from the world, but they did not see it as such. They saw it as creating an intimate, protective community for their offspring, 'a garden enclosed,' a place of tenderness and unity. A time of soul-searching began, a purification of the Society from worldly endeavors.

They decided on a series of reformations. The first was the decision, arrived at unanimously—Quaker fashion—to adopt greater simplicity in dress, in their homes, in behavior, in speech, even in gravestones: from that day on, all gravestones were banned as 'creaturely activity.' They started their own schools, where their youth would be protected and kept unspotted from the world. Gradually, without their being aware of it, the garden enclosed turned into a fortress under siege.

The flock needed shepherds, so the elders took it upon themselves, in all humility, to serve as overseers who would guide those in error or confusion. Before they realized what they were doing to themselves and their Society, they became inquisitors, and the committees for Ministry and Worship star chambers. The overseers visited Friends at home and 'labored' with the family, meanwhile sniffing the air for the smell of tobacco, glancing about for glasses that might indicate the use of spirits, frowning at portraits and miniatures as 'inducing a spirit of vanity'; they checked the table linen for lace edging, which constituted creaturely activity, and if the table itself had curved legs it had to be removed as being too worldly. Singing, dancing, balls and garden fêtes, clubs, associations, and even non-Quaker charities were 'severely discouraged.'

Soon, the American Society of Friends seemed to have withdrawn from the world forever. From a living religious and moral force in society they had turned into a quaint, xenophobic sect who called themselves 'the peculiar people,' wore peculiar dress, used peculiar speech, and were concerned only with themselves and their peculiar shibboleths. They had become virtually a secret society, and the garden enclosed a prison; in the year 1827 they went stir crazy.

It was a time of sweeping reforms in other religions, a time of revivals and schisms, of established churches splitting apart into young offshoots, usually in response to the fervor of individual evangelists. Every church had that problem; so too the American Society of Friends. Outside evangelists started to stir up trouble; in 1827 five 'ministers' from England were active in Philadelphia Yearly Meeting's territory, and they created mayhem in the garden enclosed. On theological grounds that now seem byzantine and obscure, the Society of Friends split into two warring camps: orthodox and 'activists,' later called 'Hicksites' after their spokesman Elias Hicks. Rather than 'holding one another up with a tender hand,' the members of the two fractions, named after their Meeting Houses 'Arch Street' and 'Cherry Street,' went for the jugular. Intermarriage between the two Yearly Meetings was punished by excommunication, in Quaker terms: 'being read out of Meeting.' All contact between the two Yearly Meetings was banned; each behaved as if the other did not exist, each called themselves the only true Quakers, and woe to those who said otherwise.

As a result, Friends involved in the great 'concerns' of the times felt suddenly bereft of the spiritual support that had, over the centuries, been the source of their strength. The Underground Railroad, the secret route by which escaped slaves were smuggled from farm to farm on their way to Canada and freedom, was suddenly declared to be 'in error' because it did not 'minister to the slaveholders.' Other concerns which depended on the support of the Quaker community were considered to be 'a source of uneasiness' by one or the other splinter group. Those out in the field lost the sheltering arms of the Society of Friends, which had been both their inspiration and spiritual refuge down the ages.

It is in these years of darkness and doubt that we take up the saga of the Quakers in America. But first, a visit to Birmingham, England.

The
Peculiar People

CHAPTER I

BIRMINGHAM, ENGLAND

December 1832

The atmosphere in the sickroom was stifling. Mordecai Monk, a portly, middle-aged cherub in Quaker garb, stared in horror at his mother dying on the fourposter bed. The old woman was breathing haltingly, in gasps and pantings, as if climbing a hill: stumbling, recovering, clawing herself toward higher ground where she would be safe. The room smelled of vile medicinal potions. The doctor at the foot of the bed rummaged in his bag of instruments, unaware of the fact that he had become more a hindrance than a help to the panicking woman battling her way up the hillside.

Suddenly Mordecai decided that everyone had to leave, himself included. It was obscene to stand there and watch her torment. He put his hand on the doctor's shoulder and whispered, "Out!" The doctor bridled in proprietary pride; birth was his, death was his, this layman was the intruder. But, being the son, Mordecai had the authority. "Out!"

He opened the door. The doctor and the nurse obeyed; he was about to join them when it occurred to him that this constituted a flight on his part. He was her son, he should not leave her alone in her terror, panting, trying to scramble up that invisible hillside. He closed the door and went back to the foot of the bed.

She had kicked the quilt aside. Her feet, toes cramped as if to gain a foothold, looked young. He had once shared the life of the body now expiring. He had been part of her, like those feet. He leaned over and said, "Mother?"

She halted briefly, looked about her in confusion. When her eyes found his, she gazed beyond him with a look that made him turn around to see who it was, standing behind him. There was no one; yet she lay scarcely breathing, eyes wide, staring beyond him. "Basil, love," she whispered, out of breath after her frenzied effort to escape, "how wonderful of thee to come . . ."

He did not know what to say. There was no Basil in the family. He knew no Basil; neither, he was certain, did she. Who did she see in her last moments?

"Basil who, Mother?"

"Thy father," she said, panting, but no longer in panic. It was as if she had reached her mysterious sanctuary.

"Father's name was Amos, Mother," he said, reduced to an obstinate child by the enormity of death.

"No," she said, "his name was Basil. Don't tell! He loved me." She smiled. "He is here now."

Who was she talking about? In what secret room, what adulterous bed— His thoughts fell silent at the stillness of her smile. He realized that she was dead.

He stood looking at her with an abstract sense of loss. He had never truly loved her. She had been a tiresome old woman, scatterbrained, sentimental, a silly spoiled widow who loved pugs and fed them chocolates till they died. She had had no sense, and loved only the snoring little dogs she was killing with her brainless tenderness. After his daughter Becky had died at birth, and his wife Emily a month later, Mother had tried to take their

place in his life with a greed that had, at the time, filled him
with revulsion. Now her frozen smile filled him with guilt.

He turned away and opened the door. The doctor and the
nurse came in to take possession of what was no longer a person
but a thing.

"Sir?"

He became aware of young Hodgkins, the parlormaid, curtseying. "Tea is served in the drawing room, sir."

"Thank you, Hodgkins." As an afterthought he added, "Go
and tell cook that Madam has died."

Back in the security of his study he gazed out the window.
Snowflakes were drifting through the halo of light around the
streetlamp across the road. He was born in May '88. It must
have been summer '87 that his mother had spread her adulterous
thighs to receive the mysterious Basil. He gazed at the falling
snowflakes with growing anger. Basil's seed had squirted, life
had leapt into the warm darkness of his mother's secret depths;
nine months later Amos Monk, the cuckolded husband, had
cradled a squalling infant, the son, Mordecai, he would love
above all others until he was felled by a stroke.

Anger turned into pity. How lonely she must have been.
Lost, helpless, not knowing what to do with the gift of love God
had granted her and which no one would accept, except little
dogs.

How could he find out who his real father had been? Better
not even to try. Let her rest in peace. He drew the curtains and
went to bed.

Four days later, a memorial service for Hannah Monk was held
by Birmingham Monthly Meeting of the Society of Friends. As
the only next of kin, Mordecai Monk was granted the privilege
of joining the elders on the facing bench. There he sat, unmoved,
staring at the hall full of faces. It was a combined gathering, the
partition between the men's and the women's sections had been
hauled up for the occasion. It seemed a lot of people for the

slight body in the coffin. It bore no connection to the living Hannah Monk, who had gone to join her lover in the great beyond.

One of the elders to his right began to speak. 'O great mystery of death.' 'Darkness, which awaits us all.' 'God's love.' He was irked by the man's professional piety, and grew aware of boredom settling over the meeting. Ten minutes later the second ministry came. He recognized the voice: Sarah Moremen, clerk of the Women's Meeting. 'Hannah Monk—farewell to a courageous soul.' 'Remembered with affection.' 'Good works.' 'Ready hospitality—example to us all.'

Silence. Then the third voice: Barbara Harrison, the women's chairman of Ministry and Worship. 'Hannah Monk—dear soul—always ready to help—pure and chaste—radiant.'

Silence. Waiting for the fourth voice to start a pious paean for the newly proclaimed saint, he suddenly felt outraged. Her soul was gone but, my God, the body still lay among them in a coffin, dead to all passion. Late summer '87, thrusting, arching, it had surrendered to a power vastly superior to the small flickering flame of her will; now she was being remembered for 'hospitality,' 'good works,' 'love of dogs.' At the time she had been swept away by a hurricane of passion; to deny that now seemed a degradation. Insufferable!

He had never spoken in meeting, never risen during worship to spout some fatuous thought. Now he suddenly found himself on his feet, saying, "Is this all Friends have to remember her by? Hannah Monk, never been on earth before, never to be seen again?" He tried to end it there, but something stronger than his sense of decorum or even his own will made him press on. "Is this all we have to present at Hannah Monk's death? Will no one say, 'She was a helpless, lonely woman, at the mercy of passion, a victim of forces crushingly superior to her slim, gilt soul'? There can be no love without truth. If we want to honor Hannah Monk's memory in the spirit of love, we must say, 'Hannah, thou wert a fool. Hannah, thou didst not have any sense. Hannah, thou wert at times an embarrassment because of thy muddled emotions, thy rudderless tenderness trying to find a harbor.' But we must add also, 'Hannah, dear Hannah! If only we had loved thee in return, without conditions, without the implied suggestion that thou shouldst calm down and organize thy feelings first, so we might converse in rational terms!' Damn us! Yes, damn *us*! *We* are the damned, not she! *We* are the ones who did not recognize in the generous, scatterbrained woman the essence of God, the force of love, the force to which we all owe our presence in this world. Now we carry the burden of a guilt that came too late, decisions that can no longer be made, a belated insight into Hannah, now home, we hope, with God. But even if she is not with God, even if she is out there somewhere in the void, cast out into darkness and damnation, she will have a person, a *man* on whom to spend the gift that all of us rejected." He suddenly realized he had been indiscreet. He must get out of this! A final phrase, something that would enable him to stop, gracefully. "Truth and love. They are inseparable. That is the essence of our Friendly persuasion. Farewell, Friend Hannah. Forgive us, love. Farewell."

He sat down and hid his face in his hands. He had made a spectacle of himself. He had said things about his mother that were slanderous. He prayed to God to free him from this situation, which he had brought upon himself. Then a hand entered his field of vision. Meeting was being broken. He shook the hand. Then another, on his left. He rose; together with the elders, he shuffled out of the facing bench, head bent, praying to be gone, never to set eyes on them again.

As he walked up the aisle he became aware of voices around him. Whispering. Coughing. Out, out. He was almost there when he found his way barred by a woman. He felt like turning to flee: it was Sarah Moremen. She looked at him with eyes full of crocodile tears and gushed, "Friend Mordecai! That was the most *moving, marvelous* ministry I have *ever* heard, in *any* meeting for burial! Thou wert *truly* in the power of the Lord! Thou hast spoken for us *all*, and by us *all*, I mean us *women*. Bless thee, beloved Friend!" To his horror she reached up for his head, pulled it down and planted a wet kiss on his forehead. He turned to flee, but another woman barred his way. Women, women everywhere, grabbing his hands, gushing, "Thank thee, Friend! Thank thee! *Wonderful!* How *true!* Love and truth! Inseparable! Friend . . . *Friend!* . . ." Frank Henderson, chairman of Ministry and Worship, came to his aid, taking him by the arm and escorting him into the open.

"Can I drop thee anywhere, Mordecai? Thy mother's house?"

"Thank thee."

They spent the short journey in silence, listening to the muffled footfalls of the horse's hooves in the snow. Frank Henderson's silence said it all.

That evening Hodgkins, the parlormaid, curtseying, brought him a letter on a silver salver. An official invitation, signed by Sarah Moremen, clerk, and Barbara Harrison, chairman of Ministry and Worship of the Women's Meeting, for him to address the Meeting next Friday at eight P.M., on the subject of 'Truth and Love.' *Refreshments will be served in the interval after the lecture, before questions.*

The young maid, apple-cheeked and with wide blue eyes, looked like someone living in a world of sanity.

"Thank you, Hodgkins," he said. "That will be all for tonight."

The girl whispered, "Yes, sir. Good night, sir," curtseyed, and made off with the silver salver pressed against her bosom as if to shield her virtue. What was the matter with women today? 'Truth and Love'? What in the world could he say about truth and love that he had not already said in that emotional outburst this morning? How could he get out of it? *Refreshments after the lecture, before questions.* Somehow, that seemed to strip the last vestige of sincerity and spontaneity from his outburst.

The small impulse of curiosity as to what he might have said about truth and love made him go to his late father's bookcase and take out a tome he would never have expected himself to consult: a concordance of the Bible. He took it to the desk, lit the gas lamp over it, and looked up 'love.' There turned out to be many kinds of love: *Love (verb); Love of God; His Love; In Love.* He turned the page and found a small square of newsprint, yellowed with age, pressed between the pages. It did not say which newspaper, but it must be old: the letters were old-fashioned, with *f* for *s*. He wondered what it was doing in this book; then he saw a name and started to read, his heart in his mouth.

INVITATION

to an afternoon of Scripture, Prayer
and Worship, on July 8th, A.D. 1787, at 3 P.M.,
in the annex to Birmingham Town Hall.
The Meeting will be led by the Reverend
BASIL GOODLOVE
from
Maryland, America.
Hymns! Testimonies! Laying on of Hands!
Speaking in Tongues! Glimpses of the Future!
Admission 3 pence.
All proceeds to go to the Rev.
GOODLOVE'S
Fund for the Suffering Poor.
Families welcome! (No dogs, please.)
Nota bene: the doors will be closed at
3:15 P.M., sharp.
Praise the Lord!

He put the piece of paper back between the pages. Basil Goodlove. His true father. Why else would Amos Monk have put the cutting in this book, in this precise spot? *'Clave unto these in love.' 'Be without blame before Him in love.' 'Father in truth and love.'*

Father in truth and love! This awful man, this mountebank

with his 'glimpses of the future' and 'all proceeds to go to the Rev. Goodlove's Fund for the Suffering Poor'!

He took out the newspaper clipping again. July 8th, A.D. 1787. He was born May 14th, 1788. The lecherous false prophet! The dates could be a coincidence. Coincidence? The name, the fact that Amos Monk had hidden this clipping in a tome that no one but himself would ever open? Under the heading 'love'? It added up to an awful sense of truth. This man, this sanctimonious salesman of hymns, testimonies, and the laying on of hands had lured his love-starved mother to his bed, or, God knows, the floor, and—

He closed his eyes; he shut the book and put it back on the shelf. He returned to the window and watched the snowflakes float through the halo of the gas lamp across the street.

'Father in truth and love.' The real sorrow, the deepest, was that after reading the clipping, he had called his father 'Amos Monk' in his thoughts instead of 'Father'.

Father in truth and love. He should accept the invitation. But what could he say to those women? For the moment there was nothing but held-back tears at the death of the father he had loved and the emergence of one he loathed. He loathed the foul, slimy swindler with the greasy hair, the lecherous lips, the bulging trousers—how did he know, for God's sake? Maybe Basil Goodlove had been a dashing, handsome preacher, who inspired . . . Inspired? Lured women into his bed and squirted his foul seed and—

It was simple: he was a bastard.

Out of it all came the strange conclusion: thank God Becky died at birth, before the capacity to know that she was a tainted child. A bastard father had tainted her. And sainted Emily, her mother, so thin and worn. The two of them: Becky beautiful and perfect, Emily thin and worn. And now his own mother had gone. And his father. All there was left was the knowledge that somewhere inside him, somewhere within the successful chocolate manufacturer, the proud inventor of the patented liqueur-filled bonbon Heavenly Smiles, within the soul of the good Quaker, the honest trader, the pillar of Birmingham Society, slumbered another self: the seed of Basil Goodlove, layer-on of hands and lifter of skirts, speaker in tongues, benefactor of the suffering poor, fornicator of helpless, lovelorn women—

Enough! *'Truth and Love.'* Next Friday, Women's Meeting, eight P.M., with refreshments before questions. What part of him was Basil Goodlove's? Who had spoken at her meeting for burial? *'Is this all we have to say about Hannah? Will no one say, "She was a helpless, lonely woman, at the mercy of passion, a victim of forces crushingly superior to her slim, gilt soul"?'* He had not said that; he had been in the power of the Lord, as the saying went. Could it be that he had spoken in the power of Basil Goodlove?

He turned away from the halo of the street lantern and covered his face with his hands. Truth and love. But the greatest of these is love. Goodlove. O God, give me Thy power, only Thine, come Friday night!

What nonsense. He did not believe in God. Hush! Not to be repeated, his well-kept secret for over thirty years. He would be insane to do it, insane. Back to chocolates, my friend! Back to the safety of the factory. Lecture the foreman about too much sugar in the last batch of Heavenly Smiles; or get thyself a dog to talk to, nights. A dog. Lecture a dog about truth and love, then give him a ham bone.

Truth and love. Women!

He rang for Hodgkins and ordered some port. Still snowing, outside. Too snowy for walking. And too late, to go to Liza.

He tore up the invitation and tossed it into the fire. He was watching the flames leap and devour when Hodgkins came in with the port. Virginal breasts. Nice little bottom. Good night, Hodgkins.

"Good night, sir."

A dog, Mordecai. Get thyself a dog!

CHAPTER 2

BIRMINGHAM, ENGLAND

December 1832

He arrived at the hall half an hour before he was due to speak: a portly middle-aged man out of breath, already sweating, cherub's curls going limp over his ears. He took out his notes before entering.

To his astonishment, every seat was taken; women were standing in the aisles. Was there another speaker? He was received by the gushing Sarah Moremen. "*Never* seen such a turnout for *any* speaker before!" she cried.

He must have struck a chord in women with his emotional outburst; to be expected to do the same thing twice was ludicrous. He had spent the week earnestly preparing for this speech. '*Love and truth*,' '*Truth and love*'—he suddenly realized that he was the last person to hold forth on any subject other than the manufacture of chocolates or the running of a factory. Please, God, let me lecture on Heavenly Smiles! *One day, as I inspected the bonbon section, the foreman said—*

He was taken to the facing bench and seated between the meek Barbara Harrison and the aggressive Sarah Moremen. The hall was full of women, standing room only; obviously, they were expecting another emotional sitz bath. Did they not realize that the funeral of one's mother was a one-time occasion? If he were to carry on in the same vein, God forbid, he would reveal that he was a closet atheist! *'Sir,' the foreman said, 'I'm afraid that this batch may have to be remelted, all chocolates have an air bubble inside.' Then the thought hit me: what if we filled*— Sarah Moremen rose beside him with a rustle of skirts, her mere bulk imposing silence. She asked, bassoon-like, "Friends, may we have a moment of worship to enable this meeting to center down?"

She thudded down beside him and continued breathing. He prayed, not to the Creator of the universe but to a chairman of the board in the sky, that this cup might pass from him and be handed to someone else, like the female Minotaur by his side. But after what seemed a condescendingly short period of worship, the Minotaur rose once more. "As Quakers, we are not given to false praise," she bassooned, "but I *must* laud this evening's speaker for the sensitivity, the fulsomeness of feeling with which he spoke at the meeting for burial of the late Hannah Monk, his mother. All of us who witnessed that occasion were united in the desire to hear him develop more fully the concept of the relationship between truth and love. Friend Mordecai." She sat down, propelling him to his feet as if they were sharing a seesaw. He took to his notes, looked up, and saw a hall full of white faces turned up at him in anticipation. He gazed at the back of the hall, looking for a way out; then, suddenly, he was met by something unexpected: a source of strength. It was not his, it was his audience's. They seemed to fuel him by their expectancy. He opened his mouth for a squawk, then heard himself say, "Friends, good evening," in a conversational tone, as if they were gathered in front of a fire and not in a hall with moths swirling around the gaslights. "Now I face you, I realize that my labored preparations for this evening were fatuous. Allow me to dispose of them." He found himself tearing up his notes, slowly, demonstratively, dropping the snippets on the

podium. He thought: 'Impostor! Con artist! All thee is doing—'
But he silenced the panicking, still small voice, took a deep
breath, like a draught from that well of power, while the women,
their white faces turned upward, waited in innocent surrender.
Then he said, with a shudder of sudden exhilaration, "Truth!
Let's start with the truth. Who am I, to claim the right to address
you tonight? A rich man's son who inherited at the age of thirty
a successful factory which runs itself. Only child, married at
forty. Had a stillborn little daughter a year later. Wife died within
a month thereafter; moved in with his mother. A solid member
of Birmingham Monthly Meeting, who never opens his mouth.
A contributor to worthy causes. A lonely reader, during firelit
evenings, of Byron, Shelley, Blake. *Ah, moribus vacuum vires
consilium declamavunt!* Ah, thou vacuum, while other men hold
forth in wisdom!"

There was a nervous titter of laughter, growing into a ripple.
An inner command demanded that he turn the laughter back
into silence at once. "What right have I to hold forth at you
tonight? God knows! I don't." The silence became stillness. In
the stillness he said, "Yes, only *He* knows. And He is here, now,
tonight, in this hall, in Birmingham, vibrant, awesome, among
us. So let's ask Him." An impulse made him let the stillness last,
until it was released by his saying, "No answer? That was 'truth.'
Now for 'love.' Let me tell you what I know of love. I loved my
wife. I courted her in the accepted manner. We were married
under the care of this Meeting. We were happy in a self-conscious
way until our first child was born, little Rebecca, expected with
tenderness and awe. All I really know about love is what I felt
when the midwife placed into my hands the cold, white, perfect
little body from which all life had gone. All I know about love
has its origin in that one brief moment, when I looked down
upon the perfect little body of Rebecca Monk, aged three minutes, dead."

He had a moment of awareness that this was awful. He was
telling strangers about something he had not even told Emily.
Then the power of those in front of him fused with the power
within, and he cried, "That moment, I *hated* God. I spat on God!

I tore my heart out and flung it at the sanctimonious mug in the sky and cried with all the rage within me: 'I hate you, you cruel monster!' "

The silence was still with shock.

"I never recovered. Neither did Emily. We lived, briefly, in melancholy tenderness, beset by tears. Then she died, and a meeting for burial was held during which I said nothing. I moved in with my mother. She too died, and there was another meeting for burial. Then, at last, something within broke in me and I spoke. I do not believe I can ever speak like that again. The funeral of one's mother is a one-time occasion."

He remembered thinking of that; it made him falter. He had broken the spell by introducing an element of planning into something that was totally spontaneous. Grasping at a straw in his confusion, he took a sip from the glass of water on the lectern. When he looked at those faces again he was overcome by the strangest feeling: a motion of love. Suddenly he loved them, all of them, because they were women. Women who lived by their emotions—like himself, he now discovered, after years of unemotional horse sense. He became aware that he was actually saying this, to that hall full of faces: that he loved them because they were women, because they lived by their emotions, because he did too, which he had discovered only recently, after years of priding himself on his calm common sense.

Now what? He almost expected a group of them to come and grab him by the collar and toss him out into the street. What was this wild, passionate nonsense he was spouting? But they remained as still as the leaves of a tree, waiting for the breeze. "Forgive me," he said. "You asked me to speak the truth about love. It is a dangerous, narrow road we are treading, lined on both sides with snakepits, shrieks, howls of frenzied passion. But we can only begin to understand the love of Christ by loving one another as men and women, not as neuters. I speak to you in the terms of a man. We Friends have always considered equality between man and woman to be the cornerstone of our persuasion. We must adhere to that, we must hold one another up with a tender hand so that, together, we may experience the presence of God. All I can do, myself, is stand before Him with, in my hands, the white, perfect little body of dead Becky, and weep. That is the truth about *my* love. Now, I hand you over to yours."

Suddenly faced with a lack of words, he sat down, his head in his hands, exactly as he had during meeting for burial.

The silence seemed to last and last. Then he realized that it had turned into worship. He sat motionless, empty of all thoughts, until Sarah Moremen reached out and took his hand, and Barbara Harrison the other; there was a rustling of crinoline, meeting broke. But a feeble voice came from the audience.

"Would the Friend who just spoke please speak again?" Barbara Harrison asked. "We are unable to hear thee."

The voice called out, "Is Friend Mordecai prepared to answer questions?"

Barbara Harrison looked down at him. He rose to his feet, waited for the silence to settle, and said, "No."

There was a moment of stunned surprise, then another woman's voice in a corner of the hall said, "Amen."

There was laughter, applause, a great shuffling and rustling. Sarah Moremen, with unexpected tact, managed to shepherd him out a side door into an alley. Snow was falling. In a daze he walked toward the gaslit street, where his carriage was waiting. Suddenly a woman stepped from the shadows, barring his way. He halted, startled; she kissed him on the lips. Before he could recognize her, she was gone.

At home, he found that Hodgkins had set up a cold supper for him in the empty dining room. He still felt bemused by what had happened: the brief emotional speech full of embarrassing confessions, the refusal to answer questions, the unknown woman's kiss. All of it bewildering, dreamlike: it could not really have happened to him. Everything seemed a dream, except for the power that had come to him from the audience. But had it? Or had it been, again, his old devil father?

"Have you all you wish, sir?"

He looked up.

The girl curtseyed and whispered, "Sorry, sir."

"I have all I wish, Hodgkins, thank you," he said kindly. "You may turn in now."

"Thank you, sir." She curtseyed and turned to go. He watched her leave without mental comment. He had to stop blaming his father. Ridiculous. He should be his own man.

He took his glass of port up to his study. One thing was obvious: if he were to open his mouth again in front of an audience, he should have more to offer than this incoherent outpouring of raw emotion. He should have a message, a concluding thought, a theology. Looked at coldly, '*We can only begin to understand the love of Christ by loving one another as men and women, not as neuters*' was hogwash. He could not believe he really said that. He had better come up with a rationale for advocating copulation in order to receive revelation. He needed dogma, a structure to his emotional rantings. He should address people's minds rather than cause women to leap at him from the shadows and kiss him on the mouth. Who on earth could it have been? He did not even know if she had been young or old. A bereft mother, perhaps? No, it had not been a motherly kiss.

Suddenly he experienced an overwhelming carnal urge. Liza. It was time he visited Liza again. How was it possible? After speaking of love and truth, however garbled it might have come out—to end up feeling the urge to visit a whore?

He went to the window to look at the street. It was still snowing. The lantern across the road had been turned off by the lamplighter. As in a glass darkly he saw the reflection of his face on the windowpane. A strange face. He, yet not he. Basil Goodlove? He had not looked like his mother, at all. Whose face was this? Pudgy, ringlets, innocent blue eyes . . .

Suddenly it scared him beyond words. He fled.

It was a long walk; he ran part of the way. When finally he rang the bell of the sleeping house he had to wait a long time before shuffling steps approached on the other side of the door; then it opened a crack and a voice asked, "Who's there?"

"It's me," he said, "William. Is she free?"

"Oh, Mr. William." After a brief hesitation the door opened wider. The Negro maid, who had obviously retired for the night, reluctantly let him in.

"Is she alone?"

"Yes, Mr. William—but she's asleep. Do you realize what time it is?"

"Never mind."

He pushed her aside, made his way upstairs, knocked on the door and went in. The room was dark and smelled of a woman. Her little lapdog, in a delusion of grandeur, barked and attacked his right trouser leg, but its tiny jaws could not get hold.

"Who's there?" her sleepy voice asked in the darkness.

"It's me. William." He undressed in a frenzy, threw off his clothes, tossed them on the ground; the little dog barked and barked, prancing around him. He threw his trousers at it, his underwear; naked, frenzied with lust, he found his way to the bed, tore the cover aside, groped, felt her softness, the silken slickness of her hair, muttered, "I love thee, I love thee," and mounted her like a bull.

She cried out, he did not know whether in lust or pain or anger; he possessed her with a fury that destroyed all illusions of tenderness, and collapsed with a sob when, in an instant, he was spent. He found himself ashamed, abased, lying on top of the half-clad body of a woman he had treated as a commodity, a receptacle for his seed. "I'm sorry," he said. "I'm sorry, Liza. I just— I'm not myself." As he lay there, in the depth of self-loathing, he felt her hand calmly, kindly stroking his hair. Then her voice said, "Aren't you the cheeky one! You waited too long, love. You should have come sooner. Now, of course, you jump in through the window."

"It wasn't me, it was—"

"Nonsense," the voice whispered while the hand stroked his hair. "You talk as if you were two different people."

"I am! I am! That's what I came to tell you! Part of me—"

"Hush." The hand pressed on his lips. "Not tonight. I was fast asleep, and suddenly there you were, right inside me; tonight we are not going to talk about the other parts of you. We're going back to sleep together, all of a piece."

"No, we are not!" He sat up and swung his legs out of bed. "We're going to talk."

"Then let's talk in comfort. Come." She pulled him down, he toppled awkwardly onto his back. She rose beside him and pinned him down with her opulent, warm weight. "Talk," she whispered, and kissed his nose. "Talk, wild Willy." The hand stroked his hair with humiliating motherliness.

"I want to talk about *my soul!*" he cried, ridiculously.

She said, "Good," and kissed his lips. Somehow, the kiss lifted him out of his confusion, self-loathing, fear. "I have to hand it to you," he said, when her lips left his, "there you were, fast asleep; in comes a man who first rapes you and then wants to talk about his soul, and—"

"Hush," she said. "It's all right. You're a nice man. I like you. Stop pulling faces at the mirror."

Pulling faces at the mirror? Was that what he had been doing? Was that all there was to his frenzy, his desperation, the flight from his father's ghost?

"How about a cup of tea?" she asked, toying with a little curl above his ear.

"God," he sighed, "is that all there is?"

"What else do you want? Champagne?"

"I want to talk about my soul!" he cried obstinately. "I want thee to tell me who I *am!*"

"You're a sweetie," she said matter-of-factly. "I'm going to make the tea." She climbed across him, arousing his lust against his will. She struck a tinderbox and lit the lamp by the bedside. She was ample and homely in her nakedness in the soft light.

"I swear I will never abuse the word of God to seduce women," he said to the ceiling.

"Bully for you," she responded. "Just lie there and be good

while I make the tea, then we'll talk." A moment later, tinkling with spoons and crockery, she asked, "You didn't frighten Harriet, did you?"

"Maybe I did. I just asked if you were in, and alone, and then I went ahead."

"You're a dear man, William," she said with unfeigned kindness. "I know nobody else who worries about himself so desperately. Why do you want to? You're a sweetie, you'd better know it."

"My name is not William," he said, after a decision.

"Of course it isn't. But to me you are. Now, if I bring you a cup of tea, will you promise not to upset it?"

She came toward him in the lamplight, all globes and glossy hair, carrying a cup and saucer like a lighted candle. For a brief moment, in an ecstatic flash of recognition, he knew that this was salvation: a wife like her, who told him to be himself. But which self? The moment passed, and there it was again: the frenzied lust, the sin of the father visited upon the son, the curse of Basil Goodlove, the demon within. "Come here—here!" he cried, reaching for her.

"Just a tick!" She put cup and saucer on the night table, careful not to spill; then she let him grab her, pull her down into the bed, roll her on her back, thrust inside her with a howl of passion and rage. When it was over, he groaned, "God—dear God—" and once more collapsed on top of her.

She briefly stroked his hair again, kissed his earlobe, then pushed him off her and reached for his teacup. "Be a good boy, drink it nicely. There now. Better?"

"My mother died since we last saw each other," he said. "Before she died she told me that I was a child of love."

"Good," she said. "I'll be right with you." She climbed out of bed and went to get her own teacup.

He continued grimly, "Not 'good'—bad! The man I have taken to be my father all my life was not my father. She gave herself to a charlatan, a lecher, an evangelist who used his powers of persuasion to bed her and put her with child before he pranced on to preach some more about Jesus and topple more virtues as he went."

"Hush," she said. "Let me get settled first. Move over." She climbed back into bed with her teacup. How could a man bare his soul, uncover the truth about himself, in bed with tea?

"Liza," he said, in a final effort to achieve truth, "tonight I started to minister. I preached to a hall full of women. They opened like flowers to me. I have the feeling it was not I speaking to them, but . . . God, I can't face it. *Am* I like my father? *Was* it my father?"

There was her soothing hand again, toying with the curl above his ear, the other ear this time. It was impossible to achieve truth under the circumstances, it was as if everything she said and did conspired to break down his will to know and made him slump back into the comfort of being a nameless male nuzzled by a woman who knew her job.

"I felt pure, and clean, full of power and light. But then, as I came out of the hall and hurried to my carriage down a dark alley, a woman jumped out of the shadows and kissed me."

"Poor sweetie," she said, twirling his curls.

"You don't understand! It wasn't 'poor sweetie' who spoke! It was I, yet not I. It was 'poor sweetie' who had himself kissed and fled."

"Good," she said. "Now kiss *me*."

"You don't want to hear," he said—unreasonably, for it was not her function.

"You talk too much." She pulled him down into the warm nest of no-thought, no-words, the tactile world of the rutting mammal.

He stayed the night. The bill handed to him the next morning by the black maid was one shilling and sixpence, 'for breakfast.' It was Liza's one small sin of hypocrisy.

He set out for home, determined never to preach again. Then, as he stood in the cold morning, the glassy dawn, he found himself thinking: 'the warm nest of no-thought, no-words, the tactile world of the rutting mammal.' It sang; it lifted mindless lust out of its darkness. But men would never stand still to listen to that kind of thing; they would think it offensive, a shock to their womenfolk who would hide their faces in shame. He knew now that this was not so. Women would love it, open the flood-gate of their power to him, the power of a hundred white faces turned up, radiating love.

'God,' he wondered, theatrically, 'what is happening to me?'

As if he cared. He was beyond caring. Since when? When had he changed?

Whenever it had been, there was no turning back now.

CHAPTER 3

LONDON, ENGLAND
March 1833

Meeting for Sufferings—the ruling committee of London Yearly Meeting—gathered on Third Day, Third Month, 1833. It was a hazy day with a promise of spring, the still air spiced with the smoke of fires.

A large amount of business had to be dealt with; Obadiah Woodhouse, visiting young lawyer from Pennsylvania, thought it an inordinately long list. He had come out of curiosity, to observe how English Friends handled their business in a public meeting open to interruptions and questions from the floor. In Arch Street, Philadelphia, committees met behind closed doors; none of their members would tolerate discussing business in front of an audience at liberty to throw a wrench into the holy works.

The clerk, a ponderous banker called Horatio Barnes, dispatched the items with measured speed. Then, when the patch of sunlight on the floor beneath the high window had reached the committee table, he handed the meeting to the chairman of

Ministry and Worship and sat back to listen. There was a sudden tension in the audience, which was made up mainly of women.

The chairman, a mousy elder with a high collar, read from notes: "I have been requested to put to Friends present a sense of unclearness experienced by many Meetings nationwide, at the ministry of Friend Mordecai Monk from Birmingham. Friend Mordecai has taken it upon himself—with the best of intentions —to put into question the spiritual origins of Quakerism and its social concerns. Friend Mordecai has voiced this concept on several occasions in terms that have given offense to many—"

He was interrupted by a woman rising to her feet in the audience: "I protest! Friend Mordecai has not given offense to 'many,' he has given offense to *men!*"

Horatio Barnes said, in a calm voice that brooked no contradiction, "Will Friends please restrain their ministry and give this meeting a chance to center down?" He closed his eyes and folded his hands, creating a silence that lasted a few minutes, then he opened his eyes again and nodded at the committee chairman, who resumed in a strained voice: "The committee for Ministry and Worship, burdened by the concern to present a solution, or an advice, has given long and prayerful thought to this situation, in the spirit of love . . ."

London Meeting for Sufferings, Obadiah decided, was as adept at the use of sanctimonious Quaker jargon as was its counterpart in Philadelphia.

"After long and arduous seeking after truth," the chairman concluded, "our committee has finally achieved clearness. Friend Mordecai's unique ministry should be tested in other Meetings than English ones alone. We therefore suggest that said Friend be given a traveling minute to America, so he may present his message to our beloved brethren across the ocean."

For a moment Obadiah remained openmouthed, then, without thinking, he rose to say, "How dare you! How dare you export a destructive element like this man to your 'beloved brethren across the ocean'? Is it to nip in the bud a schism among you, like the one that has destroyed the American Society of

Friends? Many American Friends, myself among them, believe that there would have been no schism but for the Quaker evangelists from England whom *you* sent across the ocean to your beloved brethren, and who fanned the fire of dissent! Now you seem to be about to expel another firebrand to cause havoc in my country, to rid yourselves of his divisive ministry! May I ask: Is it Quakerly to foist upon us this person, about whom there appears to be a nationwide sense of unclearness? Why not deal with him yourselves, at home?"

Horatio Barnes gazed at him, stunned it seemed. Obadiah decided to take it as an invitation to proceed. "By the way—my name is Obadiah Woodhouse, Philadelphia Yearly Meeting, Arch Street. Have you any idea what you have done to us? What you are about to do to us again? Right *now?*"

"I wonder if the subject is timely," the chairman of Ministry and Worship commented in a small voice.

"Let him speak!" a woman shouted from the center of the meeting; she rose, a statuesque Brunhilde, swathed in what looked like a toga with a cloth helmet like the goddess of the French Revolution. There was a stir in the audience; she obviously represented an important body of opinion.

"Bathsheba Fugat," Horatio Barnes said stonily, "we would appreciate to hear the opinion of the Women's Meeting on this matter presently, but right now—"

"Never mind our opinion!" the massive woman bugled. "We want to hear *him!*" She pointed at Obadiah with a commanding finger.

For some reason, it took the steam out of his fervor; suddenly, he felt he had been making a fool of himself. But now he must plow on for a bit, alas. "Let me take myself as an example," he continued. "The schism has led to a breakup of American Meetings into two hostile camps headed by Arch Street for the orthodox, Cherry Street for the activists. We not only no longer speak to each other, we behave as if the other simply does not exist, except when it comes to intermarriage. I was engaged to be married to a girl I have known since childhood. When the madness of the schism took hold, we suddenly could no longer pass meeting together, as she belonged to Cherry Street and I to Arch Street. Both of us would be disowned if we married out of Meeting, and as a lawyer representing mainly Quaker clients I would commit social and economic suicide. So we turned into the Pyramus and Thisbe of Philadelphia Yearly Meeting, and we are by no means the only ones. A young couple who were appointed teachers in a rural area in Pennsylvania had a stillborn child and discovered that the local Meeting, which belonged to Cherry Street, refused to bury the child because the couple belonged to Arch Street. This epidemic of insanity now rages nationwide; you, here in England, would find yourselves in the same situation if you had not rid yourselves of your religious fanatics by giving them traveling minutes to America. You are about to do it again today. If you had kept previous Mordecai Monks at home, I would have been able to marry my beloved, the young teachers would have been able to bury their baby in a Quaker cemetery, and American Friends would be living in peace with each other, as before. In the name of God, keep your carriers of glad tidings at home! Stop this man, here! Thank you."

He sat down, knowing that he had presented his case with a passion unworthy of a professional advocate. There was a whispered exchange among the committee members at the table; in the audience people muttered and coughed. Horatio Barnes rose once more in corpulent splendor and said, "I am sure every-one present has been moved, as I was, by this cry from the heart. How would it be if the Friend who spoke so eloquently were asked to accompany and guide Mordecai Monk in the early stages of his mission, so as to keep him mindful of the sensitivities of those who might feel victimized by the ministry of an evangelical English Friend? Before I ask for the sense of the meeting on this, may I have the reaction of Friend—er—our American Friend?"

Obadiah was struck dumb by the cunning of the move. In the face of such political acumen, upstarts like himself were helpless. He should have seen it coming; it was an old Quaker trick to turn the weapon around and invite the member who urged action to lead the way so others might follow.

"I shall, of course, be happy to offer assistance as far as I am able," he said feebly. "But, as a lawyer, I have many commitments—"

"Why don't we stop this nonsense?" the woman in the toga shouted, silencing all others. "To call Mordecai Monk divisive is ludicrous! May I ask the American gentleman—sorry: Friend —if he ever *heard* the man in question? Has he ever been present at one of his lectures?"

"No, I haven't," Obadiah had to respond.

"May I suggest that thou dost so, Friend, before shooting off thy mouth? Mordecai Monk is speaking tonight to the Women's Meeting, Westminster Square. Thou art invited to be present. See me afterward." She swung her gun turret on the target behind the committee table. "As to you, members of Meeting for Sufferings, all I can say is: *Phooey!* Just because the man speaks like an angel and appeals emotionally to women, something none of you can hope to achieve, all you cowards can think of is to send him packing! I won't let my emotions run away with me, but let me tell you that all this is an embarrassing example of chicken-livered politics!" She turned to sit down, then fired her final broadside: "I speak in the spirit of *love!*"

Never before had Obadiah heard the word 'love' used as a projectile. She sat down to a cheerful murmur of women. Horatio Barnes stared at her, then said to the recording clerk at the far end of the table, "Would thee, Barnabas Knuckles, please surpass thyself and provide us with a minute which expresses the sense of the meeting?"

In the silence that followed, the quill of the recording clerk scratched. Obadiah wondered what Barnabas Knuckles, a dry little man, could come up with; he wished, fervently, that he had kept his mouth shut.

The recording clerk sanded what he had written, shook the paper, rose, and read in a seedy voice: "Minute 63, Third Day, Third Month, 1833. The meeting labored over the sense of unclearness created by the ministry of Friend Mordecai Monk of Birmingham Meeting. After a lively discussion in the spirit of love, it was suggested that Friend Mordecai be granted a traveling minute to America. After a spirited intervention by (name to be verified), a visiting American Friend, it was suggested that said Friend be appointed Virgil to Friend Monk's Dante." He sat down with a self-satisfied smile, as well he might.

"Does this minute express the sense of the meeting?" Horatio Barnes asked.

The helmeted woman rose once more like an angel of wrath. "After Pyramus and Thisbe, now Virgil and Dante! Would it be possible to describe in contemporary terms what exactly our American Friend is supposed to do with Mordecai Monk, other than drown him at the earliest opportunity?"

Horatio Barnes gave the recording clerk at the far end of the table a pleading look. The quill scratched again, the silence deepened; everyone must be curious as to how a truly professional scribe would summarize this. The quill stopped scratching, the paper was sanded, shaken, and Barnabas Knuckles rose in self-confident neutrality. "After a good-humored intervention by Bathsheba Fugat, which liberated the meeting of untoward solemnity, the conclusion was affirmed that Mordecai Monk shall travel to the United States and that our American Friend (name to be verified) will assist him in his ministry as way opens."

"Thank thee," Horatio Barnes said blandly. He surveyed the meeting and asked, "May we take it that the minute is now accepted as written?"

The combative woman Friend realized that she had been checkmated; she remained seated in stolid silence. An obliging soul rose somewhere in the back and piped, "I unite." A few others followed, all men. Horatio Barnes concluded by asking, "May we now unite in worship?" and demonstratively closed his eyes.

The silence of battle fatigue descended upon the meeting. During the twenty minutes of motionless silence that followed, the patch of sunlight groped up the folds of the tablecloth like a male hand.

The lecture by Mordecai Monk was given in the hall of Westminster Square Monthly Meeting. The audience consisted mainly of women; Obadiah tried to make himself inconspicuous in the back. Someone on the facing bench rose; instantly the meeting centered down in the obligatory silent worship. After a few moments, with a sigh, as of a huge animal stretching, they relaxed.

In the meantime, a plump man in his forties with ringlets over his ears had appeared on the podium. His manner was apologetic, unsure, not the type of firebrand Obadiah had expected. He seemed disarmingly harmless.

The audience fell silent. The speaker began in a quiet, almost casual tone. "Time? What is time, in the world of the planets, the stars, the rings around Saturn, the moons of Uranus? Time, in the mind of God, means nothing. The man who eighteen hundred years ago stood under a tree in a Levantine garden and prayed, 'Father, if it be possible, let this cup pass from me,' did so only yesterday, in God's time. Last night, the world lay sleeping. Everyone slept: Jesus' followers, even the disciple He loved above all others. They had seen Him enter the garden, watched for a while as He stood under a tree; when nothing happened, they dozed off, except for a little dog which peered through the bars of the gate, anxiously, wondering why it had not been allowed to follow its master inside."

Obadiah realized that he had made a fool of himself that afternoon. This was no rabble-rousing evangelist. A dog? In scripture there was no talk of a dog. Or *did* Jesus have a dog . . . ?

"A bobbing lantern approached in the night. The little dog yapped. A clatter of armor; a horse whinnied. It was a patrol of Roman guards, not menacing, not aggressive, moving in the calm security of a power that had ruled the world for five hundred years. The disciple Jesus loved above all others leaped to his feet and tried to bar their way as they headed for the garden gate; the little dog yapped; the gate squeaked on its hinges. The Romans proceeded to arrest Jesus, kindly. They led Him out of the garden with no more than a hand on his shoulder. He went along meekly; then one of the disciples who had been asleep drew his sword. There was a skirmish, a clumsy, almost comical one; Peter, who was no swordsman, sliced off one of the guardsmen's ears by accident. The blood changed the mood; the prisoner was dragged away, so was Peter. After sniffing at the ear lying in the road, the little dog lolloped after them."

The storyteller had thrown a spell over the audience, no one stirred.

Then, suddenly, he shrieked with startling shrillness, "*Ayee!*" and cringed in agony. "The first pain! The first terrible, muscle-locking pain! They had made Him lie down on a cross, again almost kindly, as if putting Him to bed. They had spread His arms wide, crossed His feet, then—'*Ayeee!*'—drove a nail through His wrist. An eternity later, an eternity of blue and green pain, the cross was raised to the cheers of the crowd, and the crucified man cried piteously, 'Father! Why hast thou forsaken me?' "

To Obadiah, the hackneyed words, set to music countless times over the centuries, acquired a heartbreaking immediacy because of the extraordinary evocative power of the speaker. A man, nailed through his wrists to a cross, shrieked in pain, abandoned by his father; it was so graphic that he saw it happen.

"Where *was* the father?" the speaker cried. "Where *was* he? Where among the stars, the planets, the streaking comets, the rings of Saturn, the moons of Uranus, *was* he? Did he not hear the shriek of his tortured son? '*Help, Father! Help!*' "

Extraordinary: the man was not acting out the story but living it; he lived through Christ's Calvary himself, and his audience with him.

"Why did the father not save his child? Why did he

allow him to be flogged, spat upon, gored by a spear, taunted by jeers as he cringed in mortal pain and terror? Why? Why? God, for the sake of our peace, our souls—answer! *Answer!*"

The cry echoed and died. Nothing moved in the hall, except the huge swooping shadows of the moths circling the gas lamps. Then the answer came, in a whisper. "For thee . . ." The man opened his eyes, slowly raised an arm, and pointed at a woman in the first row of the audience. "*For thee!*" he shouted, with spine-chilling force.

The woman sat transfixed, stunned at being singled out.

"And for me . . ." The tone had changed back into a whisper. "Why thee? I do not know. Why me? That I *do* know. Because I am steeped, soaked, drenched in sin, from the moment the seed sprang into the womb that gave me life!"

It did not seem to shock anyone; yet it must be the first time in any Quaker meeting, Obadiah thought, that the moment of impregnation was described in such graphic terms. Then he realized what the man was. Quakers were historically inartistic; sculpture, painting, music, literature, all forms of art were lumped together as 'creaturely activity' and therefore shunned. The cuddly man who stood there flushed with exertion, his curls lank with perspiration, was a poet. The first Quaker poet in captivity. His passionate, stirring speech was not a sermon, it was art.

"In the solitude of damnation," the man continued, "there is only one consolation: a hand reaching out in the dark. A hand that assures: Thou art not alone. A friend, a woman who recognizes thy desperate condition and comes to join thee and kneel in prayer. But that, of course, is a dream . . ."

To Obadiah's startled surprise, the woman in the front row who had been singled out suddenly rose, climbed onto the podium, and kneeled by the speaker's side in prayer. She did so spontaneously, and seemed to embarrass no one. On the contrary, all over the hall women rose to join her, two, four at a time. A number of others rose to leave, mainly men. Fascinating, never seen before in any Quaker meeting—of that Obadiah was certain.

Finally those who wanted to join the women at the preacher's feet had done so, those offended by the spectacle had left the hall. Now the poet started the second act of his one-man drama: an impromptu, intimate reverie on 'love and truth.' He spoke with such artless intimacy that there no longer seemed to be a division between audience and speaker, it became a shared experience.

Obadiah's attention wandered as he tried to envisage what it would be like to take this phenomenon on tour in America. He relished the prospect of watching his father's reaction, and that of his uncle Bernard, clerk of Arch Street Meeting, to the little dog sniffing the ear in the road before lolloping to catch up with Jesus. At the seed springing into the womb, Aunt Agatha's eyes would turn into saucers. Would it result in the same love feast of women clustered around the poet's feet?

Suddenly, meeting broke. Obadiah let the crowd pass. Eventually, he came face to face with the artist himself. At close quarters, Mordecai Monk looked even more harmless, and surprisingly short.

Obadiah introduced himself. "I am supposed to be thy Virgil, Friend Dante. Remember me?"

After a moment of confusion the poet said, "Ah, yes, of course! Excuse me, I wasn't there, but I was told about thee. How kind of thee to come! We must have supper together."

"With pleasure, thank thee."

"It's not for thee to thank me, Friend," Mordecai Monk said, smiling. "It was generous of thee to offer to act as my guide in thy country. I want to hear more about this schism in America. How sad, how very sad for thee and thy bride! Is there anything at all I might do to help?"

Obadiah's answer was cut short by the assault of about a dozen women, throwing themselves on the succulent man with less piety than when, virginal and subdued, they had kneeled at his feet. Supper might be late tonight.

There was to be no supper. Half an hour later, after managing to detach himself for a moment from the crush, Monk suggested, "Maybe on some later date . . ."

It was as far as they got, that first night.

As a matter of fact, there was no further contact until they met on board ship two weeks later, destination Philadelphia.

Chapter 4

Philadelphia

May 1833

The young American lawyer turned out to be a charming traveling companion. The weather was pleasant, the sea lenient; the
voyage easier than Mordecai had foreseen. He tried to form an
impression of American Quakerism by questioning Obadiah
Woodhouse; weary of the unrelenting curiosity, the young man
gave him a book to read, *The Journal of Boniface Baker, 1754–1766.*
"This," he said, "will tell thee more about early American Quakerism than I can."

"Who was this man?"

"The first Pennsylvania Friend to free his slaves and give
them his plantation. He went west with two daughters—three,
for he had adopted a slave girl as his own. His eldest daughter
Becky was raped and murdered by Indian marauders, his youngest he sent back to Philadelphia. He stayed behind in the wilderness with the black girl, Cleo. They started a Friends' Meeting
of Indians, whites, and Negroes, his ex-slaves, who had joined

him of their own accord. It was a utopian community, until the wave of new settlers hit them. Read his journal, his motivations remain at the heart of American Quakerism. Or did so, until the schism of '27.'"

The young man had schism on the brain. Nice chappie, though. Helpful, and as keen as mustard. 'Quaker poet!' Would anyone have called Basil Goodlove a poet? Not in the circles where his father reaped his harvest. All he was, himself, was a luxury edition of the sins of his fathers; God knows, there might have been more silver-tongued rapists in the family tree. Enough of this!

He settled in a deckchair, out of the sun, and opened the book on his knee with a mug of porter beside him. After the first twenty pages he almost gave up; the blessed Boniface certainly took his time getting into his stride. Then, suddenly, it came. *'That night, I discovered I was not the grandson of Boniface Baker, martyred stableboy of Swarthmoor Hall, but the offspring of an unknown rapist who assaulted my grandmother on board the ship that brought her to the New World. She was twenty, and alone.'*

He could not believe it! Yet there it was, in black and white:

'I was utterly shaken. It had been important to me that I was the grandson of a saint, it was the foundation of my self-respect. The truth struck me with such force that I sank to my knees and asked God, "Why? Why has this been revealed to me? Why now?" There came no answer; only the chirping of a cricket in the night.'

How was it possible! A brother, an American brother!

'The discovery changed the course of my life. Until that moment I had accepted circumstances which I considered to be beyond my control. Both my grandmother and my father had been slaveholders. They deplored slavery, but accepted it as a commercial necessity. They had assuaged their consciences by being kind to the slaves, educating their children. My father justified his keeping human beings in bondage by thinking of himself as a member of a spiritual aristocracy, offspring of a Quaker saint who tried to give them humanity, a soul. I, in my turn, thought that God had placed me in a position of dominance because my ancestors had earned that position by their godly lives. The discovery that my

grandfather was an unknown rapist who had violated a helpless girl in mid-ocean on a pile of rope shattered my arrogance. Far from being a member of any aristocracy, spiritual or otherwise, I was simply a slave-owner. That night I was forced by God to decide to free my slaves, give them my land, and strike out into the wilderness to start a new life.

'There is a plan underlying our lives which is not ours. Our fates are predestined without our being aware of the hand that guides, the wind that propels, the tides that carry our souls to their predestined goal . . .'

It was a revelation! The miraculous contact with a kindred soul, whose words seemed to be directed straight at him!

During the rest of the voyage he read the journal, over and over again, until he had become as familiar with Boniface Baker's life as with his own. Obadiah Woodhouse was right: now he understood American Quakerism, totally. He discussed it at length with Obadiah, until the eyes of the polite young man glazed over. No wonder! How could a city lawyer understand the reality of being a bastard, outcome of rape, redemption, passion, and glory that had gone into the making of the life of Boniface Baker, his soul mate, four generations and a world apart? In America, he would not minister about himself, not about Rebecca's perfect little white body, fount of eternal tears, but about Boniface Baker, knight in shining armor, John the Baptist of the American Society of Friends!

On arrival in America, Mordecai Monk was received into the rich, patrician Woodhouse family. The next day he met Simon Weatherby, chairman of Ministry and Worship of Philadelphia Yearly Meeting, Arch Street.

At the Meeting House, a brooding pile of red brick in a courtyard lush with the green of trees, he was given a guided tour. He was shown William Penn's treaty with the Delaware Indians and a number of other historical treasures before Simon Weatherby took him to the clerk's office, a white room with high windows and nothing on the walls.

'Make no mistake,' Obadiah Woodhouse had warned him, 'Friend Weatherby is chairman of the committee for Ministry and Worship, but not the way thee understands it: a star chamber.' It seemed a dramatic exaggeration; Simon Weatherby was a sweet, doe-eyed man in his early fifties with an endearing tuft of baby hair on an otherwise bald head and a mouth almost feminine in its vulnerability. Obadiah must have suffered a delusion; whatever this man was, he could never be the head of a secret thought-police, regimenting the lives of thousands with absurd edicts against pianos, tables with curved legs, the drinking of tea, contact with activists, balls, games, intermarriage between the two Yearly Meetings. The man proved to have an endearing propensity for touching those with whom he spoke; during the tour of the Meeting House his delicate hand sought Mordecai's sleeve whenever it was within reach. This was not a fanatic but a man full of eagerness to understand, full of gregariousness, love.

The first hint of a darker truth came when, back in that white, high-windowed office, Mordecai began to talk about Boniface Baker. Simon Weatherby listened, his moist brown eyes tender with attention, his feminine mouth soft and trusting. Then he said with a smile, "I am sorry to disabuse thee, Friend Mordecai, but the truth about Boniface Baker is somewhat different from the image thee has formed of him after reading his journal."

"Different in what way?"

"In his relationship with his adopted daughter Cleo, the young slave girl he took with him into the wilderness."

Was this where the schism began to show its ugly face? Mordecai had expected to be told that Boniface Baker's theology had erred; instead, Weatherby asked, "Thee knows they had a child?"

"The foundling the Indians put on their doorstep? Certainly."

There was a pause. Then Weatherby said, "I'll tell thee this only if I can be absolutely sure of thy discretion. There are still a number of Bakers around, I don't want to cause them distress."

Some tawdry family secret? How unfortunate.

"The boy was not a foundling, but their natural child. Born from the loins of the black girl, begot by Boniface Baker, her adoptive father."

Mordecai Monk stared at him, shocked.

The delicate white hand touched his sleeve. "I know, dear friend, it came as a shock to us all, the few of us let into the secret. There is overwhelming proof, alas, that Boniface Baker cohabited with his adoptive daughter. They made quite a spectacle of themselves, it seems. Roistering in the reeds around the lake in summertime. Swimming in the nude, chasing one another like otters. In several letters and diaries of the time, written by men who visited them, and whom we trust, there are references to—well—shrieks of lust. A feminine voice screaming in ecstasy inside their cabin after dark. Most unfortunate."

Mordecai Monk stared at the delicate face, the doelike eyes, the smile, and rose. "Excuse me. I'll have to digest this at my ease." A cowardly way of saying: This is foul gossip, evil, rank with deception!

"Of course," the soft voice said, full of understanding. "The truth is not always comfortable."

Outside, in a graveyard empty of tombstones in accordance with one of the most cruel testimonies of American Friends, Mordecai sat down on a bench in the shade of a tree. Instead of feeling betrayed by the mystical brother he had revered, he felt the reverse. Another fumbler in the dark. Another failure at virtue and godliness. A real twin soul, after all, as unworthy of God's grace as he himself.

Under that tree in the burial ground, that morning, with birds twittering in the foliage, he understood at last why God had sent him to America. Suddenly his future ministry became clear: he would be an apologist for Boniface Baker.

Two days later he was asked to address a joint session of the Men's and Women's Meetings in Arch Street. He did not mention Boniface Baker by name. He spoke, with sincerity and the power of truth, about sins of the flesh, the blood-red darkness in which men grab and thrust, groan and cry out, rutting mammals in a primeval forest of the soul. He spoke about his bewilderment when facing the truth about himself, the chains of lust, greed, ambition, heartlessness weighing him down. Only after those chains had been slaked by the grace of God did the Light begin to shine, the blinding light of the Thought behind it all, behind men's ruttings and grabbings, women's plotting and beguiling, behind lust, greed, dreams of riches, power. The Thought underlay the tides of Man, the same Thought that revealed itself in the starry sky, the rings around Saturn, the moons of Uranus . . .

The mighty music came in profusion: images, alliterations, poetic descriptions, soaring language, passion, love. At a particular moment, he became aware that no power was coming to him from the audience, this time. Closed white faces listened to him with, it seemed, mounting disapproval.

Not a single person came to meet him afterwards. The only one overflowing with praise was Simon Weatherby. His delicate hand touched Mordecai's arm and shoulder in effusive admiration.

Well, no one could say he had not asked for it. What now? He remembered the cry from the cabin in the wilderness, and wondered if Boniface Baker and Cleo were watching him from hell or heaven.

"Come," Simon Weatherby said, touching his arm. "Let's have some sustenance and talk about the future."

During a closed meeting of the committee for Ministry and Worship, Arch Street, at which Mordecai Monk was not present, it was decided without dissent that the English evangelist should be kept away from all urban Meetings. *Rutting mammals*, indeed! All in that insufferable English accent. *Grab, thrust, groan, cry out*—in the presence of women! It was disgusting. The man must be mad. Let country yokels get the benefit of his asylum ministry; maybe he would speak to the condition of those who reared cattle and milked bulls to sell their seed. Maybe their women would relish hearing their menfolk referred to as rutting mammals. Make up an itinerary for this madman that will take him as far away as possible from civilized Meetings and, maybe, lose him somewhere in the wilderness. Sell him to the Indians as a saltimbank, for their entertainment. The clerk was requested to record this in less emotional terms and omit all untoward levity; but it was good for the soul to speak one's mind after such an outrage. Obadiah Woodhouse was charged with spiriting the man away, Simon Weatherby delegated to write a note to his opposite number in London Meeting for Sufferings, asking what had possessed them to export this rutting mammal to their brethren across the ocean.

It was left to Obadiah to explain to Mordecai where they would go and why. Pendle Hill, Indiana: the settlement started by Boniface Baker in 1755, now a small town on the edge of the prairie between the Wabash and the Mississippi. There was a personal reason for Obadiah's visit at this particular time. The Friends' Boarding School for Indian Children, founded by Boniface Baker and Cleo, was no longer worthy of its name, for there was only one part-Indian child left, a girl called Himsha, last of the far-western Woodhouses, an orphan. Obadiah, her guardian, went there every year at this time for Founders' Day.

"How appropriate," Mordecai said.

Warthell, Croydon, Croydon and Havers were situated on a busy street in the heart of Philadelphia, among shops displaying a wide selection of worldly goods. Mordecai had chosen the law firm because it was clearly not part of the Quaker establishment.

The inside of Warthell et cetera's offices was less worldly. Three peruked clerks stood with their backs to one another behind high desks; there was no sound except for the scratching of their quills and the occasional rustle of paper. Behind a wall, male voices mumbled. The street noises seemed louder: the pistol shots of cracking whips, the shouts of coachmen, the to-and-fro of rattling wheels. After ten minutes of waiting under the occasional sidelong glances of the clerks, Mordecai was ushered into the office of Mr. Henry Croydon, Junior.

If this was Mr. Croydon Junior, his father must be decrepit. A dry old hand touched his as if in test and withdrew rather hastily. Washed-out blue eyes peering at him over half glasses, mouth hidden behind piously folded hands, Mr. Croydon Junior waited for him to state his business.

It was a matter of legal research, Mordecai explained. An ancestor—well, an uncle: Goodlove. Basil Goodlove. Intimidated by the nerveless eyes and the folded hands hiding the mouth, Mordecai produced the yellowed newspaper clipping from his wallet and put it on the solicitor's desk.

Mr. Croydon Junior did not pick it up. He observed it, owllike, from above. An old owl, waiting to make sure the prey was dead before he swooped. Finally, he picked it up. "H'm. I see. H'm." For some reason he looked at the back, as if something essential might be found there. He did not find it.

"Who recommended us to you, Mr.—er—Goodlove?"

"Monk. Mordecai Monk. Mr. Goodlove was an uncle on my mother's side."

"H'm. Indeed. One might have expected your—er—coreligionists to recommend a Quaker firm. There are several in town."

"Mr. Croydon, do you want my business or don't you?"

The old man lowered his hands to fold them on his desk. Then he said, "It may be expensive."

"I am prepared to pay you an advance, sir."

"Yes, of course. Of course." He picked up the clipping again and looked at the front of it this time. "Quite costly, if it involves research in another state. Was your—er—uncle from another state?"

It became unnerving that, despite his repeated scrutiny of the clipping, Mr. Croydon Junior still did not seem to have read it.

"He was from Maryland. As you will find if you look at the clipping."

"Clipping?"

"The newspaper clipping. On your desk."

"Ah! I see. Maryland. Well, that *is* another state."

"Please name your price, and I will give you an address where to send your report."

"H'm. May I ask you a question, Mr.—er—"

"Monk."

"Ah, Monk. Yes. Would this by chance involve a birth out of wedlock?" The washed-out eyes suddenly turned out to be uncomfortably perspicacious.

"Why do you ask?"

"Because in that event it would not appear in the records of either parish or community."

"I simply want to know more about the man. Who was he? What did he do?"

"Well . . ." the old hand picked up the clipping. "It would seem fairly obvious what he did."

"Quite."

"Do you have any reason to suppose the—er—Reverend led a double life?"

"Why?"

"That might involve an alias, not listed in the records of either parish or community. Was he a Quaker?"

"I do not know."

"I see . . . Twenty dollars, to start with. You'll be asked to pay by the hour, plus expenses."

"I would rather pay in sterling, if it's the same to you."

"Very well: five pounds advance, one shilling an hour, plus expenses."

He counted out the money. "The address where to send your report is—"

"Tell my clerk," Mr. Croydon Junior said, pocketing the coins. "He will take down the details."

"Thank you, sir."

At the door, Mordecai was stopped by the cracked old voice. "Are you prepared for—er—unpleasant surprises?"

"Should I be?"

"Traveling clergy, you know. In this country, there is chaff among God's wheat."

"A crook, you mean?"

Mr. Croydon smiled. "We will let you know in due course, God willing."

Mordecai gave the clerk the address of the Rebekah Baker Friends' Boarding School, Pendle Hill, Indiana, and asked for a receipt.

For that he had to wait another ten minutes. But he was certain: if anyone could put salt on Basil Goodlove's tail, it was the canny old man behind that door.

CHAPTER 5

PENDLE HILL, INDIANA

June 1833

The warm wind of summer came sweeping down the slopes of the Rocky Mountains at dawn. It gathered speed as it stormed unhampered across the empty prairie, growing in power; by the time it reached the wooded hills of north Indiana it had grown into a gale and hurled itself against the highest building in the little town of Pendle Hill, the Rebekah Baker Friends' Boarding School.

In the assembly hall, students, parents, faculty, and guests of honor were gathered in silent worship prior to the highlight of the celebrations for Founders' Day: a historical pageant presented by the students. Dr. Leon Rossini, circuit-riding physician of Baker County, was seated among the nodding elders on the facing bench, sweating blood. *Why* did it always have to happen like this? You organize everything according to a well-planned scheme, and suddenly: chaos. The arrival of the slaves had been planned for *after* Founders' Day and Quarterly Meeting. Everything would have been ready for them by that time: transport, food, hiding place under cover of the school's daily routine. Now, an hour ago, an amateur tragedian had burst into his room crying, "Doctor! Doctor! They're coming in tonight! The station before us has been betrayed! They'll be here in a few hours!" Without pausing for a rational explanation, the half-wit had cried, "I must run!" and indeed had run off. Nobody here seemed to understand that in this operation you could not change plans at the last moment. The slaves would arrive in a school bulging with parents and guests of honor; its grounds, normally deserted, would be swarming with people. Some underground railroad! At times like these, everybody involved in it seemed insane. Take that ravishing Lydia Best, for instance: putting on a historical pageant, today of all days! Although not a Quaker himself, Rossini knew enough about them to realize that 'historical pageants' were 'creaturely activity' the moment they became a play; anything that smacked of the theater, music, or art was the snake in paradise. If the children on the stage, now waiting in their costumes to enact a historical event, actually spoke lines and pulled faces, they were certain to cause 'a sense of unclearness' in parents who had entrusted their precious offspring to this school, thinking they would be educated according to the testimonies. They would suddenly see them being turned into mimes indulging in make-believe, lies; as a result, parents would be walking the grounds and traipsing up and down the corridors of the school into the small hours, congregating in excited clusters to discuss the heresy, while he was expected to take fifteen slaves, as black as the night, through the teeming crowd to the potato cellar. He wished he had realized in time that he was dealing with a staff of innocents in this school, who had no idea what danger they were courting by using the children as a smoke screen for an illegal activity.

The school was the last place he should have selected as a station. But maybe the fact that it was so obviously unsuitable would prove advantageous; maybe some security might be found in its very unsuitability. Maybe there was a God for the barmy.

The ravishing Lydia Best putting on a play was not the only minor disaster; her brother Abner, the henpecked principal, and his icicle of a spouse were another. The only one who was any good—

A sheet of paper appeared in front of his face. Abby McHair, the old matron of the tribe, was handing it to him with a toothless grin. Meeting for worship had ended; now was the moment for him to make his getaway. But it might be too obvious. Better wait until everybody rose and started to move around.

The paper turned out to be a program of the festivities. *'Two* P.M.: *Presentation of the Founders' Day Pageant: "The Martyrdom of Rebekah Baker," words by Lydia Best, costumes and scenery by Lydia Best and Bathsheba Tucker (6th grade). The action takes place in the spring of 1755, on Pendle Hill, Indiana, then territory of the Miami Indians.*

'Dramatis personae, in order of appearance: Abigail Baker: Elizabeth Martin (4th grade) . . .'

Rossini remembered the fact that the old woman by his side was the *original* Abigail Baker. Must be a bizarre experience to watch a reenactment by children of the most bloody, horrendous episode of your life, seventy-five years later. Yet old Abby was beaming, lips parted, watching the stage with eager anticipation, innocent again in her second childhood.

Lydia Best rose, facing the audience with boldness. After the death of both her parents and three little brothers in the '18 flux epidemic, she had, bizarre enough, turned into a daredevil, full of reckless mischief, but this was insane. They were all insane, truly.

"The Baker family," she began, "first arrived on this very hill in the fall of 1754. Boniface Baker—" She indicated William Martin, the midget, grotesque with his wizened old face among the child actors. "Rebekah Baker, his eldest daughter—" Little Lucretia McHair, flushed with excitement in a white organdy dress, curtseyed. "Cleopatra Baker, adoptive Negro daughter of the founder—" Himsha Woodhouse, the last of the Indian children for whom this school had been founded, bowed. They had blackened her face with burnt cork, unnecessarily, she was an exotic creature as it was, a tropical bird among the crows. "His great friend, Chief Running Bull—" Little Boniface Baker, great-grandson of the founder, his baby face full of war paint, wearing an Indian headdress like a feather duster. "The play begins on the day our beloved school was founded by Boniface Baker and his adopted daughter, Cleo. Boniface Baker, as we all know, was a saint: pure, selfless, a man transformed by grief after the murder of his daughter Becky—"

Suddenly, a loud male voice bellowed, "*I protest!*"

'Here we go,' Rossini thought, 'battle commences.' He looked around to see who the first protester was; to his surprise, it turned out to be the English evangelist.

The cry was torn from Mordecai against his will; he found himself on his feet before he knew it. He was about to sit down again when he sensed the mysterious energy flowing to him from his audience: they wanted him to continue, to express their inarticulate emotion in words. He did not know exactly what their emotion was, but it must be like his own. He let them have it, pulling out all stops. It was their will.

"In the name of truth, for the sake of the memory of Boniface Baker, *stop* this mockery!"

On the podium, the children stood rigid with shock. The wanton young woman stared at him openmouthed.

"We cannot suffer any longer this mealymouthed travesty of a godly man's tormented life! Listen!" He pointed at the ceiling; the storm rumbled in the silence. "Outside, the power roars that created the world, the primeval force that Boniface Baker had to do battle with during his years in the wilderness! He was no saint, no ethereal spirit, no golden-feathered neuter swooping through the forest on celestial wings! His was a soul blown about the sky by the gale that now shakes this building! He had *not* achieved freedom of sin by freeing his slaves and giving away his possessions, or by adopting a black girl as his daughter. Before receiving salvation by repentance, he had to crash into a thicket of carnal passion, lost in the forest, drunk, bedeviled by lust; grab his black daughter from behind like a tiger, sink his teeth in her neck, making her scream in the night with the shriek of the cheetah. The child of love born—"

"Stop!" an outraged woman's voice shouted. "Stop this, you madman!"

Breath caught, he looked about him. It was the wanton young woman on the stage. She stood glaring at him, eyes blazing, bosom heaving. "How dare thee? How *dare* thee slander a dead man in the presence of his daughter?"

The old woman! He had forgotten that Boniface Baker's youngest daughter was here. There she sat, hiding her face in her hands.

Someone touched his shoulder and said calmly, "Let's go outside for a moment, shall we? A breath of fresh air."

"I did not intend—" he started. The man cut him short: "This way."

He let himself be led away; halfway up the aisle he shook himself free and ran to the lobby. It reverberated with the thunder of the gale. He pushed open the outside door with difficulty because of the pressure of the wind, stepped into the open, and was nearly blown off his feet.

The gale surged like the surf; trees groaned, wildly waving their arms. He struggled, leaning into the gale, as far as the monument in front of the school, a huge rock with the inscription: *Rebekah Baker, 1736–1755. Now let us try what love can do.*

He had prepared his ministry about Boniface Baker during the interminable stagecoach rides down wilderness trails, in wolf-haunted nights, lying awake in overcrowded dormitories of roadside inns. Now it had burst forth at a totally inappropriate moment, triggered by a word . . . 'Dear God', he prayed, his face in his hands. 'Lead me! Lead me, Lord!'

He felt suddenly lost, alone in the vastness of this continent, confronted with bewildering awareness of his mortality. A thought forced itself upon him: 'I will never go home to Liza. I will die somewhere in this hostile emptiness . . .'

The spell was broken by a bell tolling. What did it signify?

Food? He should go back inside, seek out the young woman, apologize, explain the screech of the cheetah, the lovers' cry heard in the night. In his journal Boniface Baker described, in detail, the nature of the temptation, not its consummation. He had written an impassioned paean on Cleo's carnal attraction, as lyrical as the Song of Songs; then, suddenly, a child was found on their doorstep. After that, no more intimate descriptions of his emotions, only of his good deeds: the school founded, the Meeting organized. One moment he had been leering at black breasts inside a loose smock, breathing the scent of her body, drunk with wild, irresistible desire; the next moment he wrote a school curriculum, a dry report of committee meetings, full of pious platitudes. Why his sudden silence? What had *really* happened?

Loneliness crashed upon him once more, like a wave; loneliness and homesickness for Liza. A cup of tea; her soothing voice saying, 'Don't spill it now, sweetie. Drink it nicely, there's a good boy.'

What had Cleo said to the tiger, after the cheetah's cry? How odd, to feel closer to the dead of this place than to the living. 'I love thee, Father.' Was that what she had said?

'Well, well,' Obadiah Woodhouse thought, 'this time Mordecai has surpassed himself in extravagance.' How explain to these rural innocents that the man was a poet? Or even what a poet was? That 'the shriek of the cheetah' was poetry, a verbal exuberance trying to express the intensity of an emotion, like 'Tyger, tyger, burning bright in the forests of the night'? They probably had never heard of William Blake.

He watched the faculty of the school file into the principal's study: abashed, in a state of shock, stunned by the impact of a meteor slamming into their stagnant pond.

The principal, Abner Best, closed the door, unable to hide his outrage. "You all know Obadiah Woodhouse from Philadelphia? Himsha Woodhouse's guardian. Let me introduce you, Friend Obadiah: my cousin Jesse McHair, who runs the school farm—" A rugged young man with a scowling face, definitely not forthcoming.

"My brother-in-law Uriah Martin, housemaster boys—" The grossly obese creature averted his eyes. His limp hand was damp with perspiration.

"My brother-in-law William Martin, assistant principal—" This was the dwarf who had impersonated Boniface Baker in the afternoon's pageant, or tried to. He was the size of a ten-year-old; a wizened face with an amused smile.

"My wife, Saraetta, housemother girls—" Obadiah remembered her from the facing bench; again he was struck by her oddly sepulchral quality. She looked at him without interest as they shook hands.

"My sister, Lydia Best." Now, this was a different story! On the podium, the young woman had evoked his instant sympathy; face-to-face she reminded him of Charity, whom he had tried to forget, without success. Maybe it was just her un-Quakerly dress. Very pretty.

She shook him warmly by the hand. "Nice to meet thee, Friend. I hope thee will be able to give us some guidance."

"And these are Adam Higgins, the gardener, and his wife, Margaret, the school's cook." The stolid Negro couple wore plain dress; they must be descendants of the slaves who had followed Boniface Baker into exile.

There was a knock on the door. Whoever it was did not wait for the principal to call 'Come' but barged straight in. It was the doctor, to whom he had been introduced earlier. "Old Abby is all right," the man said, as if in answer to a question. "I put her to bed, she's being looked after by her daughter. Mr. Monk has been directed to his room. You are traveling with him, sir?"

"Yes, I am."

"Does the man normally behave this way, or was it an emotional crisis on his part?"

"Yes and no," Obadiah started. "To begin with, he is not an evangelist but a poet, a Quaker William Blake . . ."

"Come now!" the doctor snapped. "I doubt Mr. Blake would

have made a Quaker patriarch grab his black adoptive daughter, sink his teeth in her neck, and set her screaming like a bobcat. Given the circumstances, I would certify Mr. Monk insane without a qualm."

Obadiah laughed in an effort to make light of the whole thing; it was not easy. 'Rutting mammals' was mild compared to lecherous Quaker saints biting the necks of their adoptive daughters.

"It is difficult to describe Mordecai Monk," he soldiered on, manfully. "I appreciate that he must seem unhinged to you, but after traveling with him this last month I have come to the conclusion that he is indeed a Quaker poet, a flower in the desert. Do understand me, I am not trying to excuse what he did today. I have no idea what brought it about. He is an ardent admirer of Boniface Baker. He has a rather personal concept of the man's witness—"

The doctor patted him on the shoulder. "High marks for loyalty, dear sir, but I am a physician. I know a madman when I see one. Your friend is as crazy as a coot; any experienced physician would realize within five minutes that he was dealing with a borderline lunatic. Take my advice: bundle him into the next stagecoach and take him back to where he came from. People in his own world, assuming such a place exists, presumably know how to deal with him."

"Well?" Abner Best asked after a silence. "Anything else we should discuss at this point?"

"Yes," Dr. Rossini said. Then he added, "In private."

Obadiah responded cheerfully, "Well, in that case I think I'll go and have a chat with my ward, Himsha."

"I'll take you to her," said the black cook.

Following her out the door and down the corridor, Obadiah had the feeling that they were not altogether concerned about Mordecai Monk. Something else was going on, something they wanted to keep from him.

It worried him. Himsha was his responsibility; as her guardian, he had to know what was happening in the school.

What on earth could it be?

• • •

"Out with it," Rossini said, trying to keep the anger out of his voice. "What the hell happened—excuse me."

"I don't rightly know," Jesse McHair answered. "Farnham chickened out at the last moment, so now they arrive twenty-four hours early."

"Not twenty-four hours, dear friend, two whole days! It was agreed that we would wait until everybody had left!"

"Well, what do you want me to do?" Jesse asked.

"Do not speak to Viola without having talked to me first, that's what."

"You may want that, Doctor, but Viola has a mind of her own. She jumped me with this. Can *you* handle her? Can you tell her no, if she says yes?"

"I certainly can," Rossini said, confident he could handle the violent black woman. "I have an appointment with her—" he glanced at the clock on the mantlepiece. "Don't do anything, don't decide anything, let me have a word with her now. I'll be back within the half-hour." He left them abruptly and set out for the spot on the grounds where Viola and he usually met.

Dusk was gathering, he had to make a detour with the buggy to avoid attracting the attention of the parents milling around outside the school, in shock and outrage. They hadn't heard anything yet; once they found out that their children had served as cover for an illegal operation there would be hell to pay.

The woods belonging to the school were virgin forest; darkness fell early under the ancient trees. When Rossini arrived at the arranged spot, Viola was not there. Maybe she had slipped out of sight at his approach. He waited, his anger deepening; then a shadow materialized beside him, like a ghost. Without the uncanny knack of rendering herself invisible, the woman would have been captured long ago.

"All right, Viola," he said, "I'm impressed. How did you arrive this time? On a broomstick?"

But she was not in a joking mood. "What the devil's going on?" she whispered, hoarse and urgent. Above them, the wind surged in the trees, her voice seemed part of the voice of the forest.

"We can't put them up tonight, Viola, it's impossible. The place is full of angry parents, and tomorrow people start arriving from all over the county for Quarterly Meeting. The school won't be safe until three days from now."

"Can't do it," she said angrily. "My niggers must be moved tonight. The town is swarming with slave catchers, all I need is this!"

"Maybe so, dear, but I cannot take fifteen Negroes through a crowd of parents and expect nobody to notice."

"I'll bring 'em late tonight. Three o'clock? Surely everybody is in bed by then, no?"

He sighed. "Viola, listen. Try and listen carefully."

"Piss on you!" she hissed in a sudden outburst of violence. "My niggers are stashed away in the swamp! It's driving them crazy, they're afraid of hounds! If I keep 'em there any later than tonight three o'clock, God knows what they'll do. You tell Adam and Penny that I'll bring 'em in tonight, three o'clock."

"Viola," he said, "something happened today at the school that makes it likely parents will still be around at three o'clock, arguing—"

"If I don't take 'em out of that swamp tonight I lose 'em! I can tell 'em a hundred times that hounds are no good in swamps, they won't believe me. If I don't take 'em out of there, they'll go off half cocked and run straight into the slave catchers."

"Very well," he said, weary of the argument, "on your head be it." As he turned away, she grabbed his arm. "Here," she said, "you better take this." She found his hand in the dark and pressed something warm and sleek into it. "Hang on to it for me, in case the paddyrollers get me. Stick it in your medicine bag. I'll be back for it later." She vanished as abruptly as she had come.

Rossini looked at what she had given him: a small package wrapped in oilcloth. She must have carried it next to her skin, for it to be warm. He wondered what it contained.

• • •

Abner was standing at his study window. Night was falling. The wind still whisked the tops of the trees; heavy clouds, pregnant with rain, were massed over the prairie. He did not hear his brother-in-law come in; the voice startled him.

"It is going to be tonight, Abner," Little Will whispered, "three o'clock in the morning. I guess everybody will be settled down by then."

"Oh? Yes. Would thee watch out for them? Take them to the hiding place? I should stay around. Be available, just in case."

"Right," Little Will said, without a smile. He was a man who took everything as it came.

"How many are there, Will?"

"Fifteen. Full house tonight. What about the mad Englishman?"

"What about him?"

"Is thee going to lock him up, or what?"

"By three o'clock he'll be asleep."

"Please God," Little Will said.

In the upstairs guest room next to the boys' dormitory, Dr. Rossini lit the candle on the bedside table and looked at the small package wrapped in oilcloth Viola had given him. Curiosity got the better of him; he unwrapped it.

Some money. A paper envelope with a small lock of black hair. A folded letter which, after a moment's hesitation, he opened and read by the light of the candle.

'Dear wife, a kind person is writing this down for me at my dictation. I find myself on free ground and wish that you were here with me. But you are not here. When we parted I did not know that I should come away so soon. I hope that you will try to come. Do not be descuradged. I was sory to leave you. Keep trying even if you are afraid and I will take care of you and treat you like a lady so long as you live. The talk of cold in this place

is all a humbug. It is warmer here than it was there when I left. Yours in body and mind, and if we do not meet on earth I hope that we shall meet in heaven. Your husbern. Good night.'

Folded inside the letter was a newspaper clipping from the *Bourbon County Eagle*, Kentucky, May 12th, 1832. *'Fifty dollars reward: negro woman named "Viola," about six feet tall, slim build, long face, black gums, long crooked teeth, white eyes and braided hair. Wore white linsey dress and took along red changeable silk and black dress, also a white robe and striped gingham dress. Viola is the biggest devil that ever lived, having poisoned a stud horse and set the stable on fire, also burned General R. Williams' stable and stockyard with seven horses and other properties to a value of $1500. She was handcuffed and got away at Ruddles Mills on her way downriver, which is the fifth time she escaped when about to be sent out of the county. She has a scar on her right cheekbone, several on her breastbone, one on her arm occasioned by the bite of a dog, and her back is badly scarred with the whip.'*

Rossini lowered the paper, then put it all back in the oilcloth wrapper.

After hours of tossing and turning in the unfamiliar bed, with its hard school mattress, Mordecai Monk was on the verge of sleep when the sound of distant thunder wakened him. It shook the bed—could it be thunder? There it was again: a deep, shuddering rumble, rattling the windowpanes. An explosion? Someone had warned him before he turned in not to be alarmed by explosions, it had to do with blasting for the canal and seemed to go on twenty-four hours a day.

Candlelight trembled on the etched portraits of George Fox and Margaret Fell on the wall above the bed, making their eyes look alive; they seemed to stare down on him in disgust. He was disgusted himself. What had got into him, to scandalize that hall full of country bumpkins with his lurid defense of Boniface Baker's incestuous passion? To appreciate his argument demanded a degree of sophistication he should not have expected from a crowd of rustics and a stageful of children. The wanton young woman had done it; her brazen challenge had aroused him to the point where he unleashed on her the full blast of his oratory. It had been in response to her haughty, high-breasted, slim-hipped, flat-bellied defiance of Quakerly maidenhood that he had sallied forth into his Birmingham Song of Songs, culminating in 'the shriek of the cheetah.' Nice metaphor, that. Well, to hell with it. He had blotted his copybook. He had fired a broadside at a Quaker maiden out of pure randiness. This country did it to him; the moment he had set foot in the New World he had been hit by an energy, a vitality in the air which in his case, alas, had become sexual energy. He wanted to go home to Liza. Let's leave for Richmond, right now, and—

But, no, he had to speak to Quarterly Meeting the day after tomorrow; he wondered what reaction awaited him there. The whole trip had been a disaster, so far as audience reaction went. The curse of the schism? Were people no longer open to beauty, spirituality, because the atmosphere was poisoned with hatred? Could he say something about that in his ministry to Quarterly Meeting?

He asked himself what exactly had triggered his outburst that afternoon. The challenge of the wanton young woman had caused it, but the trigger had been a name. The name of one of the characters in her pageant: Rebekah. It had evoked an image, the perfect little body of newborn Becky, dead in his hands. A sacrificial lamb, demanded by a man-eating God.

Hit by guilt, regret, he slid out of bed to pray for forgiveness, but all he could come up with was a cry of pain.

"Becky!" he bellowed, with the full power of his mighty lungs. "Becky! BECKY!"

In the room next door, Abby Baker heard, in a dream, a man shout Becky's name. She and Cleo, in the storm cellar, listened, horror-struck, to Becky's screams as the Indians raped her. Then she surfaced in the present: the wild wind outside, the distant rumble of blasting in the prairie. She was lying in bed at the school, her heart thumping in her throat. She sat up, threw back the quilt, climbed out of bed, and opened the door to the passage. Trailing the horror of her dream, she wandered in her nightgown down the corridor, down the stairs to the lobby, opened the front door at a crack; the wind tore it from her hands and blew it wide open. Then she saw the Indians.

They were coming out of the forest in single file, headed straight for her. She must flee, or they would do to her what they had done to Becky; she stumbled outside, felt her gown ripping as she fell, scrambled to her feet and went for the Indians, her hands made into claws, crying, "Boo! Boo!" When she was a child it had frightened other children; and now it worked again. They were murderers, who had raped and murdered screaming Becky, but as she went for them, claws bared, they turned on their heels and ran back into the forest. Sick with terror and relief, she collapsed, sobbing. Then someone put an arm around her; she looked up: a black face. "Cleo!" she cried. "Please, Cleo, please, please!"

Cleo said, "Hush, baby, hush," and rocked her soothingly, like a child. There were men's voices, but Cleo did not let go of her. Steps hurried away, Cleo lifted her in her arms and carried her away, whispering, "All right. All right, baby. Everything's all right." She had always been strong, Cleo. How she had hated her as a child! Now Cleo was full of love, and tenderness, and understanding.

"Cleo," she whispered, "I was afraid."

"I know, baby," the black face said. "I know, but all's well now, they's gone, all gone. Hush, baby, hush." Cleo kissed her forehead; it made her want to go to sleep.

As Viola held the exhausted old woman in her arms, she knew a rare moment of weakness. God only knew where those crazy niggers of hers had run off to in their terror of the white ghost;

maybe straight into the arms of the slave catchers at the school gates. For a moment she felt like running in the opposite direction and leaving them to their fate; then the doctor and Jesse McHair joined her. She got a hold of herself, left the addled old woman in their care, and set out to look for the fugitives. Maybe nobody had spotted them yet; they might have crossed the road to run back into the graveyard. Or she might find them huddled together on the boat dock. They would not dare take a rowboat across the ghostly lake without her. At least, she hoped not.

Chapter 6

Pendle Hill, Indiana
June 1833

The girls' wing of the school had the hush of a convent when Obadiah visited his ward, Himsha, the next morning. The children looked demure as nuns in their gray dresses, white pinafores, and bonnets. Himsha welcomed him with an adult smile and sat down beside him on the visitors' bench in the lobby, her hands in her lap, as good as gold. But he had read her report card: 'At times, Himsha can be a handful, indeed.'

He talked, self-consciously, about Philadelphia, asked about the pueblo where she lived, life at school. Her demure composure began to get the better of him; she was a disconcerting child, full of mysterious dignity. Where did it come from? Her parents had been the last representatives of the Society of Friends among the Hunis, before being overwhelmed by the Roman Catholic Church. Seventy years ago his great-uncle Joe, together with his Indian wife Himsha, had started a Quaker school in the pueblo. The Hunis had adored his celebrated great-aunt Gulielma, the traveling physician; the family talked about the pueblo Wood-houses as 'the branch that went native.'

"I suppose thee knows all about thy great-great-aunt Gulielma?" he asked, for want of a better subject.

"Of course," the girl said. "She is still with us."

He thought it was just a pious platitude, until she continued, "She sits on a chair in the cave of the bats."

"Excuse me?"

"She looks pretty gruesome now, of course. We hold services in front of her, with dancing and silent worship. People say she was once a beautiful woman. Well, the thing she is now looks like a scarecrow." She gave him a smile.

"I—er—still *sitting* there?"

"Her mummy. In her deerskin suit, and the hat with the arrow. Her hands have gone very brown and look eerie. Her face has gone off too. What they could not keep when they embalmed her were the eyeballs, so they put in moonstones instead."

"Did they really . . ."

"When I'm home I sometimes go and sit at her feet, especially at sunset, when the back of the cave catches the light. Her eyes look almost real. As a child I used to tell her everything, and sort of pray to her. Now I just go and sit and think of nothing. Like in meeting for worship."

"I see."

There was a silence. She smiled, waiting for him to continue. Thank God, her teacher turned up and joined them.

"Having a nice visit?" she inquired in her educational voice.

"Yes, teacher Lydia," the child said with gloomy patience, "I guess so." He felt the urge to escape. 'Face gone off' was a bit much, really. "May I have a word with thee, teacher Lydia?" he asked, rising.

"Of course. If it's all right with thee, Himsha?"

It was not all right with Himsha. The girl stared at them with regal contempt.

"Well, I'll be seeing thee before I leave," Obadiah said. "We still have lots of things to talk about, haven't we?"

"I guess so." A handful, indeed.

"Well . . ." He left it to the teacher to take the lead.

"Let's go to my office," the young woman said. "This way."

He thought she would take him to one of those little offices where teachers had conversations with parents; to his surprise she led him out of a back door, walked to a vegetable garden behind the school, opened the gate, and said, "I thought it best if we talked somewhere undisturbed. A little further still would be best, if that's all right with thee?"

"Of course . . ." He became conscious of the fact that she was a strikingly beautiful young woman.

He followed her deeper into the vegetable garden. She halted between two rows of runner beans. "Now," she said, "this is serious. Mordecai Monk must on no account be allowed to address Quarterly Meeting day after tomorrow. He should be taken home, or wherever, as fast as possible. Would thee take charge of that?"

Suddenly he had enough of imperious women. First a girl aged twelve treating him like a queen receiving a minor ambassador, now a woman teacher telling him to tuck England's most obstreperous prima donna under his arm like a ventriloquist's dummy and make off with him. "I'm afraid my power of persuasion has its limits," he said with a lawyer's smile. "And isn't this going a bit far? I know Mordecai Monk has committed a social offense, interrupting your pageant, but—"

"As a result of that social offense, Friend, a convoy of escaped slaves was scattered in the forest and may be captured any moment by slave hunters who are swarming all over the place."

He looked, bemused, at her blue eyes. "I'm afraid I don't understand."

She waited a moment, listening, then she said, her voice low, "I should not be telling thee this, but this school is a station on the underground railroad."

"Excuse me?"

"Surely, Philadelphia Quakers have heard of the underground railroad? Or are you so wrapped up in mutual backbiting that you are no longer aware of any Quaker concerns?"

He realized he was in court. "Dear Friend," he said, in the tone that went with a wig, "I would be obliged if thee could see thy way to enlighten me. What railroad is thee talking about?"

She gave him a look which, supposedly, was meant to express condescension; but she was too pretty for it. "Friends, from Kentucky to Canada, have organized a secret escape route for runaway slaves," she said. "It is made up of farms, safe houses in towns, and places like this school, called 'stations.' Passengers are transported from one station to the next hidden in farmers' carts, mainly at night. This section of the railroad is under the care of our school. When thee and thy friend arrived, a convoy of fifteen escaped slaves was on its way here. Thy friend's ministry so upset Boniface Baker's ninety-two-year-old daughter that she, either sleepwalking or in a hallucination, wandered outside in her nightgown just as the convoy was coming out of the forest. The slaves took fright and are now in the process of being gathered up, at great personal risk, by their guide. The slave catchers have noses like bloodhounds. So I beg of thee, for the sake of our concern, to remove that idiot Monk from the scene. If thee cannot do that, prevail on him to fall sick or have a sore throat, but don't let him stir up more trouble at Quarterly Meeting. The railroad can only function if there is peace, preferably boredom. I will be holding thee responsible for his removal."

He vacillated between admiration and outrage at her bossiness. "It would mean my telling him the reason why. Would thee want me to do that?"

"No," she said firmly.

"Look, Mordecai Monk is a sincere, compassionate Friend. Because thee did not allow him to finish what he was saying, thee missed the point he was trying to make: that despite Boniface Baker's transgressions he was a paragon of virtue."

"I don't care. If he speaks again he is going to cause excitement and controversy when this place is full of people from all over the county. It couldn't happen at a worse time."

"Nonsense," he said firmly. "The man is a poet, an artist.

He is not a troublemaker, he is the voice of the Society's heart, if it still has such a thing."

Suddenly, to his anger and dismay, she burst into giggles.

"I was not aware of any levity on my part," he said in his courtroom voice.

She looked at him with bewildering amusement. "I'm sorry," she said, "I must have sounded self-righteous. Look, Mordecai may be a Quaker William Blake, but he is the wrong man to address five hundred stodgy farmers from the backwoods at this particular moment. He won't be able to resist the temptation of having a few more saints sink their teeth into a few more necks—"

"Friend Lydia, I am not his keeper. I cannot tell him what to do, no one can. He is a force of nature. Can't I get that through to thee? Thee cannot snap thy fingers and say, 'Off with him!' The least amount of upheaval would be not to thwart him. Unless thee wants me to put before him the whole story of the underground railroad."

"Are you crazy?" a rough, male voice said harshly behind him. Obadiah turned around and saw it was the keeper of the farm—or whatever his function was—Jesse McHair. "What do you mean, bellowing 'underground railroad' for all to hear as far as the school?" the man snarled. "The fact that you're hidden from view doesn't mean that nobody can hear you!"

"I'm sorry if this disturbs thee," Lydia said meekly, "but—"

"Come," the man said, pushing Obadiah aside and getting hold of Lydia's arm.

Obadiah tried to intervene.

"What do you—"

"Shut up," the man said, with such bluntness that Obadiah turned on his heels and marched off between the runner beans, muttering "Yokels! God protect us from rural yokels with a concern!" But he was not exactly proud of himself; he should have stood up to the brute for the way he treated that delicate, pretty woman. But he was out of his depth: a city slicker in hogland. Home, home! Damn Mordecai Monk and his solos for kettledrum!

• • •

Lydia was furious with Jesse. She pulled her arm free and turned to go; but he grabbed her by the shoulder and hissed, "Stop that! Listen to me!"

Her anger collapsed. His grip exuded strength, maleness; tension gave way at his touch. "Is this how thee treats all thy hussies?" she asked, in self-defense.

"I'm asking thee to take a rowboat, this evening, and deliver a message to the slaves on Nightingale Island."

"Is that where they ended up?"

"I got a message from Viola that she will collect them at nine o'clock at night, day after tomorrow, when everybody will be in the Meeting House. She wanted to go to the island herself today, but I told her she cannot risk being spotted in one of our rowboats out on the lake. The place is alive with slave hunters."

"But I don't understand . . ."

"All right," he said with a sigh. "Let me explain. Last night, after old Abby scared the slaves on their way to the cellar, they took off and ended up in the graveyard. Viola took them across to the island in two rowboats, towing one. She brought both boats back to the dock, and I have padlocked them and taken away the oars, because we don't want children at Quarterly Meeting ending up on the island while the slaves are still there. Now, thee will have to take the message to them, from Viola, that they'll be picked up after dark, day after tomorrow. To-morrow there'll still be many people arriving for Quarterly Meeting. Got that?"

"Why doesn't thee do it thyself?"

"Because," he said with strained patience, "I have to go to the next station to arrange for their transport. So, this evening, when everybody is at dinner, take a boat, go to the island, and tell them."

"Tell who?"

"Come on, Lydia!"

"I'm serious. Thee wants me to just holler? Surely I have to give the message to a person. Who?"

"Give it to Jake. Got that? J-a-k-e. He's their leader. A large buck with crooked teeth."

"Buck?"

"A Negro male, sweetheart."

"Charming. How Quakerly."

He walked off; then he stopped and added, "By the way, I'll unlock one boat and put oars in it. When thee is through, shove them under the porch of the Meeting House." Without waiting for her reply he stepped through the beans and was gone.

Row to Nightingale Island at dusk? She had done it often enough, but always with someone else, a friend or—well, a friend. Nightingale Island was the standard outing for courting couples; full of bundling nests and winding footpaths. She had never gone there alone, not after dark. Well, it was the least she could do now for the cause.

She set out for the school. She should find Himsha Wood-house's uncle, apologize for Jesse's boorish behavior; he would never do so himself.

After she arrived, she looked for the man, but he was no-where to be seen. The dinner bell sounded; she waited for him in the lobby between the two dining rooms, but he did not appear.

Where was the man? Was he not hungry?

Obadiah, in his room at the school, heard the bell but decided to ignore it. He was writing to Charity, something he had not done since they had given up all hope of ever being allowed to marry. He could not join Charity's Meeting without committing professional suicide; Charity would never be accepted by his Meeting unless she abrogated her errant ways and cut herself off from family, friends, her entire life. Too much to ask of either of them, so they had separated with a chaste kiss and managed so far to abide by their decision not to communicate in any way. His encounter with Lydia among the runner beans had, for some reason, opened his eyes to the fact that, with their decision, Charity and he had turned their backs on life itself. He was not interested in other women, not about to select a suitable bride from the right family with the right connections and the right dowry. Here, in the wilderness of the frontier, Quakers had retained their essential testimony: the 'underground railroad,' with all the risks it involved, represented the essence of the Friendly persuasion. In her fearless dedication to escaped Negro slaves Lydia Best was like Margaret Fell. Mordecai Monk ministered, like George Fox had, about 'the power of the Lord thundering among us,' but it was thunder for thunder's sake, for the benefit of swooning women. The notion of the man being a Quaker poet was a seductive one, but a poet worthy of the name Quaker had to sing about more than his stillborn daughter and Jesus' little dog.

Obadiah gazed out the window at the treetops, still and serene now against the empty sky swept clean by the gale. What could he write her? If they wanted to live a normal married life, they would have to flee beyond the reach of their Meetings to a place like this: a rural outpost. Alas, there was no employ here for a lawyer. Charity might find a post as a teacher, maybe even in this school, but he? Was he prepared to give up the career he had worked for so long and so hard in exchange for teaching history? Or English?

'*Dear Heart,*' he wrote. '*I know we agreed not to take up contact again, but I have come to the conclusion that our decision was wrong. To me, saying farewell to thee has meant saying farewell to life. I suddenly realized this a few hours ago. The reason for my change of heart—*'

He wavered. If he wanted her to understand why, he would have to write about the underground railroad, the slaves being helped to escape to Canada, the passionate young woman among the runner beans who had suddenly burst into giggles. How odd: her giggling had somehow thrown open a door, made him understand the reality of Margaret Fell's dictum 'Service unites, theology divides.' For centuries this concept had determined the nature of their Quaker witness to the world; before the schism, to be a Friend had called for deeds, not words. Words . . . Was his change of heart all words? Had he been struck by a momentary emotion, seduced by the excitement of being involved in a concern? To turn his decision into reality called for deeds.

His education, his family tradition had prepared him for words, certainly not deeds without words. Take away words, and as a lawyer he would be useless to man or beast. He and Mordecai Monk turned out to be of the same ilk. Compared to Margaret Fell and the giggling Lydia Best, they were gasbags of the Lord.

Chuck it all and join the underground railroad? As what? Engine driver? Crazy. But then, they had all been crazy, the saints upon whose godly lives the corporate witness of the Society of Friends rested. Margaret Fell, wife of a Lord Chief Justice, joining condemned children in the dungeons of Lancaster Prison. Boniface Baker giving away his plantation to his slaves and setting out with two pampered daughters and an adopted slave girl into the wilds of what was then the Far West. Craziest of all had been his great-aunt Gulielma, the circuit-riding physician in men's clothes with an arrow for a hatpin and a freight-mule carrying her pharmacy. For forty years she had trudged the trails of the American wilderness as far as Mexico, hobnobbing with buffalo hunters, Indian medicine men, and French *voyageurs* on the Mississippi, to whom she had been known as 'Pissing Gulie' because of her propensity to relieve herself in plain view of the campfire. And how had she ended? As a mummy in a bat-filled cave in an Indian pueblo, where she sat staring glassily through moonstones, a goddess to the locals.

In the end, he wrote the letter all the same, asking her to join him. Then he put away the quill and went down to dinner, looking for Lydia Best. But she was nowhere to be seen. Where was the woman? Was she not hungry?

Abiding by Jesse's instructions, Lydia waited until the last of the crowd in the graveyard had trooped into the Meeting House for the opening of Quarterly Meeting. There might be latecomers, and they might notice a solitary woman setting out in a rowboat across the lake, so she hung around a while longer in the lengthening shadows. The first mist of evening began to form over the water; that was the danger of setting out in a boat at dusk. She had known this ever since she was a child: if you waited too long, the island would be hidden from sight by fog and all you had to go by to find your way there was the song of the veeries. She swung her legs over the edge of the dock, jumped into the boat, cast off, and struck out, rowing fast, in the direction of the island.

The shore quickly disappeared from sight, the mist was thicker on the lake. She rested her oars and listened. There was only silence. She waited, suspended in a darkening cloud, for the rippling rills of the veeries' song to guide her. Then it occurred to her that the veeries never sang when disturbed. There were people on the island! The veeries would not sing tonight. She started to row again, hoping she was heading in the right direction.

It was farther than she had thought; then, suddenly, the bow of the boat hit the shore with a crunch. She sat listening for a while, motionless, certain someone must have heard her. She thought she heard voices, then it became silent. After a while she heard them again. She felt a shiver of apprehension, overcame it, took off her shoes, swung her legs over the gunnel, lowered herself into the water, and tied up the boat in the reeds. Standing in the water, skirts gathered, she hesitated. Her feet were slowly sinking deeper into the ooze; she waded ashore. She could not see far because of the mist, but it was light enough to make out the beginning of a little path into the brush, one of the many that crisscrossed the island, made by fishermen and lovers, the only visitors to this innocent little wilderness. The path was soon choked with nettles; she put her shoes back on. Standing still, one foot lifted behind her while pulling on the second shoe, she heard a child cry.

The cry was so forlorn, so frightened, that, not thinking, she hurried toward it, jumping across logs, rustling through brambles, catching her skirt. She broke out of the undergrowth with a suddenness that almost made her lose her balance.

She was standing on the edge of a trail, much wider than she had ever seen on the island. It could not be the island! She had missed it in the fog! This must be the wagon trail through the wood across the lake! But where was the child she had heard? Were the slaves here, in the wood?

A secretive but massive sound drew nearer from the darkness of the forest. Down the trail she discerned a row of weary people, five abreast, who came stumbling toward her. As they drew closer, she realized there were not just five. A whole column of people, dazed, their faces frozen in despair, were emerging from the darkness. Prisoners? As they drew level with her, she realized they were Indians. But there were no Indians left anywhere near! Their faces were masks of sweat-caked dust; impossible to distinguish men from women. Never before had she seen such utter hopelessness; they stumbled by, staggering under loads on their heads or shoulders; some of the women carried babies on their backs. Hundreds of them, scores of rickety wagons pulled by emaciated horses, an unending procession of misery and despair. But apart from the creaking of the wagons and the thudding of the horses' hooves, the only sound was the crying of one child.

She found it lying by the side of the trail. An Indian couple were bending over it. Lydia kneeled beside them; when she saw the child she was struck with horror. The little face, ghostly in the mist, was like the ones that had haunted her ever since the epidemic when she was a girl. She knew, before she took the child's hand in hers and felt its burning heat, that the child was dying.

She looked at the parents. Their faces were expressionless masks of resignation. Then, beyond them, she caught sight of a horseman cantering their way, a white man.

She rose, stepped into his path, lifted her hand and cried, "Stop! There's a sick child here!"

The horse reared, the rider cursed. He was an army officer, in his twenties.

"What the hell do you think you're doing!" he shouted, bringing his animal under control. "You damn nearly—" He saw she was a white woman, and his face went blank with amazement.

He touched his hat and said, "Sorry, miss. I didn't see—what can I do for you? Are you lost, or something?"

"There's a child here that needs help," she said. "It must be taken to a doctor at once. Has thee a cart or a buggy?"

"Miss," the officer said, still in a tone of apology, "we've had many of them dying by the roadside. I can't—"

"What does thee mean, many?" she cried. "Who are these people?"

"Mahanoy, miss. They're being removed to their new reservation in Kansas territory."

"Why?"

"Because of the Indian Removal Bill, ma'am. They have to make room for civilization."

It seemed unreal, a nightmare. "How *can* thee?" she asked.

"Excuse me?"

"How can thee do this to *children*? Is thee a Christian?"

"Well, yes . . ."

"Then get off that horse at once and behave like one! Pick up this child and take it to a doctor! I'll tell thee where to go."

"But, ma'am—" He gave up and dismounted. He was tall, lanky, and smelled of sweat and of the honeysuckle he'd brushed against as he rode through the forest. He looked down at the child. It had stopped crying and lay, still and spent, between its parents, who had not moved.

"Ma'am," the officer said, "I've been on this trail for months . . ."

Ignoring him, she said to the parents, "We are going to take your baby to a doctor. We're going to help your baby. Do you understand?" They did not respond. She lifted the child and carried it to the officer. "Get back on thy horse," she said. "I'll hand it up to thee."

The young man looked down at the child, then at her. "Sorry, ma'am," he said, apologetically. "Even if I could, it's too late."

Startled, she looked down. He was right. The child in her arms was dead.

"Better put it back, ma'am," the officer said.

She looked up at him, his image blurred with tears, then gently put the child down in the weeds between its parents, who had not looked up when she took it away. She heard the officer tell someone he would be right back, then he touched her shoulder. "Come, ma'am," he said. "I'll take you home, if you don't mind sitting in front of me."

She let herself be helped up onto the horse. Then the officer swung into the saddle behind her, put his arms around her, and took the reins.

"Where to, ma'am?"

"The Quaker boarding school, in town. I don't quite know how to get there from here."

"The little town across the lake?"

She nodded; unable to control her emotions any longer, she burst into sobs. He said nothing: the horse started to move.

After a while he asked, "Would this be the turn-off, ma'am?"

She opened her eyes and saw that they had reached Lovers' Lane. She nodded. "To the right . . ." The horse turned and walked down the soft center of the road. The air was fragrant with the scent of honeysuckle. Startled thrushes called shrill warnings. A crow swooped down on them, cawing.

"I'm sorry about this, ma'am," the officer said behind her. "I'm a soldier, obeying orders. It wasn't my decision to remove the Indians. It's a law, passed by Congress." When he understood that this made no impression, he added, "They're not human beings like you and me, ma'am. They don't feel things the way we do. They—"

"Shut up!" she cried. Startled by the violence of her own voice, she added, controlling herself, "I'm a schoolteacher. I have taught Indian children. I have Indian children in my school now."

He said politely, "Yes, ma'am."

They rode on in silence; at the junction the horse stopped. He asked, "Ma'am, where now?"

"Turn left here, please. Follow the pike."

"Yes, ma'am."

They said no more until they arrived at the gate to the school. She said, "This will do, thank thee," and slid down the horse's flank. Her feet hurt when they hit the ground; she winced. The officer landed beside her with a clank of spurs and put an arm around her shoulders. She shrugged him off. It was unkind, but she could not bear him to touch her.

"Please, miss," he said, concerned. "You are in no fit condition to walk, let me take you there."

She shook her head. "No, thank thee," she said, trying to keep the tears out of her voice. "I'm all right. Thank thee for thy kindness. Thee had better be on thy way back now."

He hesitated, then blurted out, "Look, miss, in case you should be tempted to come back: don't. Captain Stewart, who's due with the next convoy tomorrow, is not of the same mind as I am. I have three sisters, you see, I know about women. I also know Quakers, I'm from Pennsylvania. But Captain Stewart is from the South, he's likely to act different, should you come back and mess with his Indians. What's more, I wouldn't want for one of my sisters to have any truck with Captain Stewart. If you see what I mean."

"Thank thee," she said.

He saluted. "So long, ma'am. A pleasure, I'm sure. Should you ever need me: Second Lieutenant James Goodall, at your service. Jim Goodall. Good night, ma'am." He climbed back in the saddle, turned his horse around, and cantered off.

She walked up the driveway in a daze. *'In case you should feel tempted to come back . . .'* Would she? Should she? What could she do other than stand helplessly by the roadside and watch them file past?

If she wanted to go back, it should be with a specific purpose, not just to stand there, wringing her hands, berating men who were following orders. But to what purpose? She was not a nurse; even if she were, there was nothing one could do other than give them food and a drink of water. *'They don't feel things the way we do.'* What had been the power in which Margaret Fell confronted

the jailers who hanged children? How had Boniface Baker managed to stand up to Philadelphia Yearly Meeting on the issue of
slavery? What power had they possessed? For one thing, they
had had courage. She had none. The mere thought of watching
another child die made her want to run.

Only as she was about to open the front door and slip inside
did she remember the slaves, the rowboat in the reeds. She could
not go back now, it was too dark, the lake was shrouded in fog.
There were committee meetings all morning tomorrow, at which
she had to be present; the only time would be after the general
meeting had started, which was at two o'clock; and she must be
back before the keynote speech, visibly present on the facing
bench . . .

Jesse would have to do it, first thing in the morning.

Mordecai Monk had a dream—a daydream. One night, after his
ministry, while he was alone, exhausted, in his hotel room, there
would be a timid knock on the door. He would think at first that
he was mistaken, then there would be another knock, firmer this
time. He would open the door, and there, trembling, shy, terrified, yet helpless in her passion, would stand one of the women
who had come forward at his call and kneeled with him in prayer.
A woman like the one who had kissed him on the lips in the
alley after his first sermon and fled back into the shadows. She
would be young, willing, or unwilling, passionate, terrified,
shocked by her own daring, praying him, maybe God, to stop
her doing this, to save her from her own desire. One arm would
press her against him as the other pulled up her skirt; then, in
a whirl of lust, loneliness, desperation, love, hunger, he would
topple her onto the bed and feel her nakedness, the nakedness
of her thighs, the—

"No!"

He got up from the bed on which he had been staring at the
ceiling, where he had seen it happen, all of it: the knees arching
sideways, upwards, the shriek—

He went to the washstand and splashed a handful of water

from the jug onto his face, snorting as the water went up his nose. Still, there she was: arching backwards, up, up, the shriek, the shriek of the cheetah . . .

"Liza!"

He must kill the dream, strangle these insane imaginings: they only made the loneliness worse. The loneliness was an ache, a physical pain. He had never known such loneliness in his life before ending up here in the wilderness, among these stolid, thick people, these self-righteous, humorless clods from whom came no laugh, no smile, no kind word, no look of understanding. Clodhoppers, that's what they were, bucolic morons, creatures from the abyss of this untamed land. Give them a horse and they would know how to handle it; give them a prophet, a singer of God's praises, a bard, minstrel of the Lord, and they stared at him unblinking, hostile, as they would at a theatrical performer, a salesman, a seller of glass diamonds.

Well, tomorrow another performance. Already buggies and wagons full of rural troglodytes were arriving; he would have a house full of them and their womenfolk: staid, stodgy matrons, with thighs like bears and bellies like—enough!

He washed his face again. Sat down at the school desk, a sheet of paper before him. No need to write anything down, he knew it by heart: *Where in the universe, among the stars, the moons, the rings around Saturn, the balls of Uranus . . .*

One thing was certain: in this school no trembling maiden would turn up; there was no such thing as a trembling maiden among the troglodytes from the abyss. 'Come kneel with me! Easy, now! *Not* like a stampeding herd of heifers!'

Oh, my God! If only Liza were near, if only she—

If only *he*. The folly had been his, the recklessness, the hubris, the daydream of the maiden trembling at his door. One of these days God would strike him with His lightning, the world-large whiplash of His fury. 'Away! Out into the desert with thee, fornicator! Fake! False prophet! English groper on America's frontier!' Adam, at least, had not been cast out alone; there had been a naked woman with him, shivering with cold, stunned by the fury of the Lord. 'Come, Eve, come, love, let's sit down for a moment, lie down, here . . .'

Outside, in the far distance, yet with shocking closeness, thunder rumbled, shaking the room. More blasting for the canal. More violence in the air. More despair. More loneliness.

The loneliness, that was what would get him in the end. Adam without Eve, cast out into the American wilderness. *Heavenly Smiles*. The innocence of it, when he had first made up the recipe for the liqueur-filled bonbon! The joy of creation, the delight of the first woman who tasted the sweet chocolate, still soft and warm on his finger. What had been her name? The little secretary with the huge gray eyes? Licking his finger, looking up with a hint of boldness—all that had achieved was to drive him back into Liza's embrace, that night. One more cry in the lamplight. One more cup of tea—*careful!*—not to be spilled onto naked breasts. One more bill of one shilling and sixpence for breakfast. And this man would have the temerity to rise in front of Quarterly Meeting tomorrow, in the name of God?

Another distant explosion shook the room, setting the jug clattering in the basin, the candle flame trembling. Suddenly he had a feeling of danger. Some incomprehensible, all-swallowing calamity was about to engulf him. Him and the naked Eve, fleeing down narrow trails, while fire and ashes rained down upon them.

Good ministry, that!

And so the Lord set about destroying the wicked couple—Let's write it down.

CHAPTER 7

PENDLE HILL, INDIANA

June 1833

The next afternoon, at the time of the opening addresses of
Quarterly Meeting, Lydia entered the winding lane to the wagon
trail in the forest again, and realized only then how hasty and
ill-considered this expedition was. What did she expect to achieve
with a few pieces of fruit, a handful of candy, a couple of toys,
all of which might be the opposite of comforting to a frightened
Indian child? What power did she presume to represent in the
face of angry men on horseback: a Quaker busybody with a
basket, planning to mess with 'their' Indians? Maybe by this time
they had all passed, anyway.

But she was committed now. As she neared the end of the
lane, she stopped for a moment to catch her breath. All was still
in the dappled forest. Not a sound, not the crack of a twig
betrayed the presence of any Indians. But when she turned the
corner to the trail, there they were: a soundless procession of
trudging shapes covered with dust, images of misery and despair.

Her fear was overwhelmed by their monstrous suffering; she stepped onto the trail, uncovered her basket, and proffered an apple to the first figure that came stumbling past. But the glazed eyes of the man did not notice the tempting red fruit; so she offered it to the next one, an old woman, carrying an incredible burden of junk. "Please," she pleaded, "take this, it will be so good for thee . . ." But it was like offering an apple to a creature from another world, who did not associate the succulent fruit with eating.

A family with two small children passed, the man pushing a cart with blanket rolls, mattress, pots and pans, the woman pulling; the narrow wheels of the cart plowing the dust of the track. She held out the apple to the children; when they did not respond she tried the rag doll. Any child she knew would at least have looked at it; these children just trudged past with staring eyes, like damned children in hell. She tried to hold back her tears and prayed, "God, help me—please, God, help . . ."

A voice called, "Hey, you there! Get out of the way!" A whip cracked viciously, so close to her face that she felt the wind of it.

She opened her eyes and saw a coarse, unshaven man on a dust-covered mustang among the mass of stumbling Indians, knocking them aside, pushing them over, scattering their belongings. "Get off the road!" he yelled. "No peddlers allowed! This is a government convoy, get the hell out!" He raised his whip again, this time to strike her.

A great calm came over her. She picked up her basket and said, "I am not a peddler, Friend, I am a Quaker, offering these people sustenance."

"Huh?" He did not understand. His mouth, stained with tobacco juice, showed as a dark hole in his face as he gaped at her. Then he said, "Well, you stop that. Nobody is allowed to talk to these here people. This is a government convoy. Go on, clear outa here!"

"I am sorry, Friend," she said firmly. "I cannot obey thee, I obey a higher authority."

"But the captain—"

"I do not mean the captain, Friend. I mean God."

Even as she said it, she felt she was overdoing it. Her basket with fruit and toys did not warrant the grandiose statement.

But the drover seemed impressed. He swung his horse around and loped off toward the end of the column.

She went on trying to press gifts on the Indians, without success; they did not even seem to be aware of her existence. Then she heard the labored breathing of a fast-approaching horse; the Indians moved out of the way in obvious terror. When the horse loomed over her she thought for a moment it would knock her down, but it was reined in just in time, covering her with dust. "Stop that!" an angry voice shouted. The horse took a step and pushed her over. She fell to her knees, and could not help screaming when she heard its hooves crush the basket. "Please, please!" she pleaded, struggling to her feet.

The man on the horse was an officer with a florid face, a rusty beard, dark holes for eyes under his hat. He seemed inhuman; she knew at once that he had no respect for her Quaker garb, no awareness of her femininity even, only of the fact that she was messing with his Indians.

"Move!" he said.

Frightened as she was, she pleaded, "Please, Friend. All I am trying to do . . ."

The horse stepped closer; she backed away from the hooves, the demolished basket, the squashed apples. "Move!" the man shouted, "Move!"

The horse advanced. Terror swamped the last vestige of her courage. She turned around and ran. The dust of the trail was deep and soft, she tripped on the hem of her skirt, stumbled, fell to her knees, when she tried to rise, something kept her skirt pinned down. The horse was standing on it.

She screamed, screamed, tugging at her skirt, tearing it; above her the horse shook its head with a jangle of chains, spraying her with spittle. She tore herself loose, lost a shoe, stumbled along as fast as she could; then she saw that she was bare-legged, she had lost her skirt, and her petticoat as well. Terrified, pan-icked by awareness of the temptation she offered, she ran for her life. "Move!" the voice shouted close behind her.

The jangling horse shooed her along, faster, faster, until her lungs seemed to burst, her eyes could no longer see; finally she fell headlong by the side of the trail, panting, waiting for the horse to stop beside her, for the man to jump down, grab her, turn her over. She waited for the pain.

But nothing happened. She had no idea where she was—a winding lane, like the one by which she had come. When she saw her nakedness, she burst into tears, her face in her hands. She lay there, aware only of the trembling of her body, the slamming of her heart. Disjointed images rose and sank in her mind. The apple. The black hole of the drover's mouth. The jangling head of the horse above her. The feeling of her skirt ripping away, the unspeakable fear of rape.

Finally, she recovered sufficiently to sit up. She was still trembling and had a vile pain in her abdomen, as if something had really happened, but that was nonsense. Her drawers, her stockings were in place. It was pure fright. For her to have tried to face down the cavalry acting on instructions from Congress had been insane. If only there were a man to help her! If only there were a real man at the school! But they were all weaklings, cripples, physically or emotionally, Little Will, Uriah, and Ab-ner, the vacillating weakling. Jesse was the only real man among them, but he was always hard to find, and would certainly not want to be involved in yet another concern, he had his hands full with the underground railroad. What had possessed her to think that *she* could carry yet another concern, apart from the railroad? She should go back now. Attend Quarterly Meeting. But how could she, in the state she was in? If she did not intend to walk into the meeting half naked, she should go and look for her skirt and petticoat. They must be somewhere along the trail, if the Indians had passed by now. Unless the Indians had stolen them—picked them up, she meant. But suddenly she felt deeply ashamed of herself, her delusion of being a second Gulielma

Woodhouse. 'Unless the Indians had stolen them'—that was the truth about her noble attitude toward the helpless and the down-trodden. Hallelujah.

For some reason, the realization of her unworthiness set her moving. She went back in the direction of the trail, stopping often to listen. Not a sound. Had they gone? Finally she emerged from the brush. The trail was empty. Knock-kneed in a silly effort at chasteness, covering the front of her drawers with her hands, she minced through the dust, looking for her skirt, her petticoat, and her shoe.

In the end, she did find them all. The petticoat was undam-aged, but her skirt showed a big tear at the waist. She put them back on. The shoe was hardest to find. First she found the rag doll; then the crushed basket. The fruit was gone. Had the Indians found it? She hoped so; oh, God, she hoped so. 'Forgive me,' she thought. 'God, forgive me.'

Then she found the shoe. It was undamaged, even the heel was still there. She put it on, adjusted her petticoat, her skirt, combed back her hair with her hands.

Sobered, she set out for the Meeting House.

When Friend Monk finally rose to face Quarterly Meeting for the keynote speech, despite the dire warnings from the local Meeting, Obadiah Woodhouse watched the by now familiar per-formance with sober objectivity. First, Mordecai allowed his audience to cough, whisper, rustle, and stir for a few moments after the motionless discipline of worship. He stood, eyes closed, face lifted, in total stillness; soon this created a hush. Even the restless children in the gallery were captured by the silent man standing, face lifted, hands spread, as in a bewildered question to the Almighty.

When the hall became silent, he muttered, softly, as if talking to himself, "Time? What is time, in the world of the planets, the stars, the rings around Saturn, the moons of Uranus? Time, in the mind of God, means nothing. The man who eighteen hundred years ago stood under a tree in a Levantine garden and prayed, 'Father, if it be possible, let this cup pass from me,' did so only yesterday, in God's time . . ."

As the silence deepened, Obadiah asked himself what gave this hackneyed opening its power. What was the animal magnetism in this man, who in daily life was so unprepossessing, petulant, given to sudden excesses of emotion? Again he watched, spellbound, as before his eyes the English chocolate merchant changed into something the Quaker movement had never seen before: a poet in the act of creation.

Obadiah had heard the opening many times now; yet each time he found himself caught up in the haunting reality the poet evoked, a reality entirely of the man's own making: the young Jesus praying under the tree, the sleeping disciples at the gate, the little dog peering through the bars, softly whimpering, the Roman patrol with its bobbing lantern drawing near in the night, the yapping dog, the disciples jumping to their feet, the flash of steel, the ear lying in the road, the little dog briefly sniffing it before lolloping after the soldiers who led its master away.

As Obadiah settled down for the next episode, the crucifixion, he scanned the faces in front of him. It was the one advantage of sitting on the facing bench: you could observe the audience, see their faces. They were still suspicious, uncertain, yet attentive. Farmers, small tradesmen, trappers, loggers, the face of rural Quakerism. Not one of them had any idea what would be done to their wives and daughters in the next half-hour, no one could conceivably guess.

"He was told to lie down on a cross on the ground, almost kindly, without hostility or violence, by professionals doing their job. He obeyed, meek as a lamb, showing no outward sign of fear or apprehension except for the trembling of a corner of His mouth. No sound came from the crowd, breathlessly watching, only the anguished whimper of the little dog, restrained by one of His disciples. Then, with a butcher's cold precision, the henchman with the shaven head put a nail to the delicate wrist—yes, wrist! Painters throughout the ages have depicted the nails as piercing His hands; but the soft bones of the palms cannot carry the weight of a body. But why am I telling you this? Some of you may have seen neighbors crucified by Indians."

So complete was the spell he had thrown over his audience that nobody demurred, although Obadiah was sure no one had ever seen a white settler crucified. Indians did not crucify people, the poet had taken them into a world of fable and myth. There was something unhealthy about the wide-eyed, openmouthed, horrified fascination with which the women drank it all in, mysteriously spellbound by the graphic details of the crucifixion.

" 'Ah!' Jesus shrieked, cringing in agony as the cross was raised, to the cheers of the crowd . . ."

Obadiah watched the women: lips parted, eyes filling with tears.

" 'Father! Why hast thou forsaken me!' " The howl of agony was left to die in the silent hall. "Where *was* the father? Where *was* he? Where among the stars, the planets, the streaking comets, the rings of Saturn, the moons of Uranus *was he*? Did he not hear the howl of his tortured son? Would *you* have remained silent seeing your child trussed, tortured, crucified? 'Help, Father! Help!' " Mordecai let the shout die into silence. "*Why* did the father not save his child? *Why* did he suffer Him to be lashed and spat upon, gored by a spear, taunted by jeers, left to cringe in mortal pain and terror? *Why?* God, for the sake of our peace, for the sake of our souls, answer! *Why?*"

No one stirred now, not even the children.

The answer came as always in a dreamlike whisper: "For thee . . ." Then the shout: "*For thee!*" With spine-chilling deliberation, Mordecai's finger jabbed at a woman in the first row. This time, the victim was the principal's wife. She had, so far, remained unmoved, as if frozen in secret grief; now, as she gazed up at the speaker with startled eyes, tears began to run down her face in amazing profusion. Obadiah looked away in embarrassment, as if he had been spying upon her in a moment of utter privacy.

"*Thee!*" Mordecai repeated, ramming home the harpoon.

Then, again in a whisper, "And me . . ."

Pause.

"Why thee? I do not know. Why me? That I *do* know. Because I am steeped, soaked, mired in sin! And have been, ever since my father's seed sprang into my mother's womb and sparked my life! Even in that first, red darkness I was corrupt, lecherous, devious, vain, an abomination in the face of the Lord!"

He went on extolling his own wickedness with utter conviction, a soul in the throes of damnation. There could be no doubt that he meant it, at that moment: he was a sinner, he was a lecher, and he hurled at the stunned audience the howl of his damnation.

"Let no man, no child, especially no woman dare tell me that she is *not* steeped in sin!"

Here we go, Obadiah thought with distaste, as Mordecai started the second phase of his performance, the act of seduction. Again he singled out the wife of the principal in the front row; the woman's sallow face and haunted eyes meant an easy victim. "Can *thee* face God and say, 'Father, I am without sin'? Can *thee* say, 'There is enough of God within me to free my soul of the sin which smote me before I was born'? Can *thee* say, 'There is a light in my breast that will lead me out of the midnight of the soul without the help of a Master, a Friend, a Savior, the Messiah'? It is not true, and thee *knows* it is not true, thee *knows* there is only one way: surrender! Surrender to Jesus, *now*! Give thy all to the only One, the precious One, the ultimate, final One, so He may gather thee into His embrace, *now*!"

The poor woman closed her eyes, the knuckles of her hands folded in front of her mouth went white.

"*Now!*" Mordecai persisted. "Cast off all sin *now*! Cast off thy shackles, thy earthly garments, thy self-will, thy envy, thy pride; tear off all that is furtive and afraid; surrender, *now*, to the gentle, all-knowing, all-loving Savior bending over thee! Open thy arms, open thy very self and whisper, 'Take me, Jesus! Take me, take me, do with me what Thou willst! I am Thine, Thine! I'm coming!' " The woman was trembling visibly now.

"Come! Cast aside all timorousness, thy last trepidation, be free! Free in utter surrender! Cry with me: '*Jesus, take me!*' " He closed his eyes and swayed in almost salacious rapture. "Thy soul will melt in bliss as thee throws thyself, body and soul, into the warm, all-dissolving, sin-swamping glory of His precious, saving, sacrificial blood!"

The pathetic woman began to moan, to roll her eyes. Some men in the audience rose and started to leave. Obadiah wished he could follow them, ashamed to be associated with this shocking performance. It was new; on previous occasions Mordecai had flagellated himself verbally until he cried out for help, for someone to join him in his darkness, which had moved some women to come forward and kneel with him in prayer. This shameless mating call was a scabrous innovation. How must the principal feel as he watched his wife respond to the lowing of this rampant bull, in full view of the elders, the children on the balcony? Other women began to show signs of agitation; some, mainly the young ones, were reduced to giggles and nudging their neighbors.

"Rise, now! *Now!*" Mordecai shouted. "Come forward, *now*, to the foot of the cross! Surrender, *now*, to Him without whom thy life is empty, thy heart barren, thy body dead! Rise, Sister, rise!" he cried, pointing at the poor woman again. "Rise! Surrender! And *live!*"

There she went. She staggered forward, threw herself at his feet, arms spread, raised her contorted face to him, and wailed, "I am coming! I am coming, Jesus! Now! *Now!*"

Obadiah closed his eyes. From the hall came a rumbling of seats, a shuffling of feet. A double movement disrupted the audience: a number of people, mainly men, were leaving the hall, a larger number, all of them women, were coming forward as Mordecai, in full force now, challenged them to do so. They climbed onto the platform and knelt at his feet in response to the call: "Surrender! Surrender thy all to the ultimate One, the final One, to be hurled aloft, torn asunder, thrust into the thundering surf of His power, swept along in rapturous suspension of that pinnacle of bliss—forgiveness! Forgiveness! To be forgiven! Ah! Forgive, Father! Forgive! Take me, *take* me! I am Thine, Thine alone! Now, *now*!"

Then a last woman climbed onto the rostrum. She was without a bonnet, her hair hung loose, her dress was torn—to his horror, Obadiah recognized Lydia Best. But instead of joining the others around Mordecai, she stepped over them, moved to the facing bench, and took up position in front of it, facing the remainder of the audience.

When it became obvious that she was about to speak, Obadiah's heart leapt with incredulous joy. Could it be that Mordecai Monk was about to meet his match?

After slipping into the Meeting House unnoticed, Lydia had started listening to Mordecai Monk's ministry with reluctance. Then, gradually, it became tempting to succumb to his plea, to stop agonizing over the cruel contradiction of a God of love and a dying Indian child, and throw herself into the arms of Jesus, crying, "I believe! I repent, I am sinful, save me! Save me!" Why should she go on trying to combat the cruelty, the absurdity of life with nothing but the inward light which, according to Margaret Fell, every woman carried within her in the form of love for suffering children?

The memory of Margaret Fell made the difference. She suddenly became aware of the hollowness, the selfishness of the man's appeal. She rose, walked to the podium, climbed the steps, stepped over the women lying there in prayer, took up position in front of the facing bench, and spoke, quaking. "It is true! George Fox did say all that. But he also said that God was an infinite ocean of light and love. For centuries Friends have based their conduct not just on the knowledge that God is love, but that He has no way of communicating this love other than through us, through thee and me. That has been the essence of Quakerism from the beginning: *All He has is thee!*"

Suddenly she did not know how to go on. She was shaking

like a leaf; she wanted to flee; but something forced her to continue, some power that was within her and yet not hers. The words came without thinking. "Even in the face of dying children, in the face of the cruel suffering of our own little brothers and sisters during the epidemic which broke our hearts and darkened our lives, we did cling to that concept: 'All He has is thee!' How else could God—despite all his stars, planets, oceans, storms—reach out to one soul cowering in terror?"

She found she had talked herself into a blind alley. She fell silent, faced by the same absurdity as when she had kneeled beside the dying child. How could she prove that all that God had was she?

She became aware of a commotion in the hall. People were leaving, others argued. She waited until the meeting centered down. While doing so, peace seemed to settle over her. It did not matter whether she could prove that all God had was she. She did not have to prove anything, all she had to do was tell them what had happened and leave it to that of God in each one of them to respond.

Her very patience as she stood there, waiting, seemed to have an effect. Gradually the meeting, half its original size by now, calmed down. When silence returned she said quietly, "Let me tell you what this is about. Within a mile of this meeting, down the wagon trail in the forest, hundreds of Mahanoy Indians, helpless, defeated, degraded, are being herded to the prairie by the United States Cavalry—in *our* name."

Those who had been standing started to sit down. She waited.

'Magnificent!' Obadiah thought. There was no other word for it. The women at Mordecai's feet rose, rather sheepishly, and started for their seats, or so it seemed: in fact, most of them were heading up the aisle and out of the hall. After a moment of total bafflement, Mordecai himself stepped down from the podium and marched up the aisle; many people, men as well as women, rose, forcing others to stand and allow them to pass. They followed Mordecai and the women out of the hall.

With a shock Obadiah realized what this meant: the schism had arrived in Pendle Hill. In her innocent spontaneity, fired by an experience which had deeply shaken her, Lydia had done something half the Society of Friends would never forgive her for. To say that to serve others as an embodiment of the love of God was more Quakerly than to kneel and whine about your own soul's salvation was the central issue of the schism: salvation by Christ's blood on the cross versus serving those in need and thereby turning love into a verb.

Those who were left of the audience sat in motionless silence, as if waiting with the woman on the podium for God to manifest Himself. Then, when the silence had deepened to stillness, she continued calmly, "Yesterday, I found myself in the forest and came upon an abomination: hundreds of Indians, bewildered, robbed of all their possessions, being herded along the other side of the lake toward a 'reservation' in Kansas by the United States Cavalry. In our name, men on horseback, called 'drovers,' whip them with total heartlessness. In our name, they are treated like cattle, lashed along with curses and whips, while exhausted, sick children are left to die by the roadside. The Mahanoy are the last of the tribes with whom William Penn made a pact, which still binds us. All that God has to alleviate their unspeakable suffering is us. How, I do not know. What we could possibly do to help them, I do not know. But I am certain that way will open the moment our prayer changes from 'Lord, save me' to 'Lord, let me embody Thee.' "

Obadiah became aware that he was witness to one of those historical occasions when Friends take on a major concern when, after a long silence, somewhere in the hall someone rose and called, "Let's form a Meeting for Sufferings—*now!*"

Within half an hour an action committee was formed under the ancient name of Meeting for Sufferings, this time for the care, protection, and legal representation of the Mahanoy Indians—especially the children—forcibly removed from their hunting grounds to unorganized territory.

All over the hall people rose to donate money, food, personal involvement. With every decision, every promise, the Meeting took on life. Mordecai's leaving became shameful, the elephantine pout of a demagogue interrupted in mid-oration. Obadiah was certain that the man had no idea what had happened, other than that he had been rejected.

After pledging fifty dollars as his contribution to the Meeting for Sufferings of Mahanoy children, a reckless sum of money, Obadiah left.

Abner Best waited until everyone had gone, his arm around the shoulders of Saraetta, who sat beside him sobbing despairingly, a lost soul. When at last they were alone, he made an effort to help her to her feet.

"Why did she?" she whimpered. "Why did she take him away from me?"

"Who, love?"

"I was happy!" she cried. "I was reaching out to grasp his hand, and she took him away from me!"

"Who?" He had not seen Mordecai Monk reach out to her.

"Jesus! My Savior, my Lord! From His tears, His wounds, His blood—His awful, awful loneliness on the cross! They were all mine, all mine, then she took Him away . . ." Convulsed with sobs, she leaned against him. He pulled her to her feet almost brusquely. She was in a state of collapse; he stood with her slight body in his arms, not knowing what to do next.

Dr. Rossini, who must have been watching from afar, came to his aid. "Let me take her home," he said.

"She is distressed because—"

The doctor silenced him with a warning shake of the head. "Leave her to me. This has to do with—other things. She is not well. I'll put her to bed and give her a sedative. She'll be all right."

Reluctantly Abner let go of her, feeling he had failed her. He followed them, miserably, up the aisle toward the porch. At the doors, he could no longer take it. "What *is* the matter with her?" he whispered when Saraetta, howling like an animal in pain, seemed about to collapse.

"Not now," the doctor replied, trying to keep her from falling.

"I *must* know!" Abner whispered foolishly.

"What she needs is a child," the doctor said, then he steered her through the doors into the open.

A child? Weariness struck Abner; he felt like sitting down with his head in his hands. Should he tell the doctor that she had refused all physical contact since Vestal died? She seemed to blame him for it, for the epidemic, the massacre of the innocent, all the dead who had disappeared under the harsh unforgiving grass of the burial ground without a headstone, not even a tiny cross to mark their graves. It had been fourteen years now, how could—

A loud voice on the porch alerted them, it sounded like a woman wailing. They hurried outside.

On the porch a large black woman was lamenting as only Negro women did; it took a moment before Abner realized it was Peggy Higgins, the school cook. "All of them!" she wailed. "All of them taken to jail, even the babies!"

Dr. Rossini, suddenly distracted, thrust Saraetta back at Abner. "Take her home," he said, "put her to bed. I'll be back as soon as I can." He ran toward his buggy.

"What happened?" Abner asked, his arm around Saraetta's shoulders.

"Arrested!" Peggy Higgins wailed. "Lordy, Lord! They've all been arrested and taken to—oh, Lordy! Lord, have mercy on us!"

Dr. Rossini's buggy disappeared down the pike, his horse's shoes striking sparks off the cobbles.

In the meantime, Obadiah, who knew nothing about all this, was accosted on the way to his room by Lydia, looking determined. "Friend Obadiah!"

"Yes?"

"Forgive me for jumping on thee like this, but would thee mind driving me into town? I want to go and apologize to Mordecai Monk for interrupting his sermon, and I'd rather not go alone, with all the riffraff that's out in the streets right now."

"Mordecai? But isn't he here, in his room?"

"It seems he left in a huff and moved to the inn. I feel guilty about him so I thought I should go to see him, in the spirit of love. Would thee take me there?"

"I—I'm not a very good driver but—"

"Oh? All right, in that case I'll take the reins. Would thee mind . . . ?"

"Of course not. My pleasure."

He followed her into the courtyard, where she disappeared to fetch a horse from the stable. Bats were swooping and diving, it seemed, for his hat. The horse was very noisy as she led it out; it sounded gigantic, with hooves like sledgehammers in the echoing courtyard. What tripped into the light was a delicate little mare with restless ears. While he held its head, or tried to, the animal sniffed all over him like a dog. Lydia fetched the buggy, put the rig together with practiced ease, hoisted up her skirts, and climbed into the driver's seat. "Need a hand?" she asked.

"No, no!" But he did; he missed the step and would have ended up on his chin had he not managed to grab something soft and yielding at the last moment. It turned out to be her thigh. "Er—forgive me," he stammered.

"Help thyself," she said cheerfully and clacked her tongue. Caught off balance, he was tossed backward onto the seat, as they took off at breakneck speed. She rounded the corner outside the gate without slowing down and nearly lost him over the side.

As they started to rattle down the dark tunnel of the pike, he recovered and began to mull over the reason for their journey. Her going to see Mordecai 'in the spirit of love' seemed a terrible idea. But then, presumably, she did not mean it carnally; it was just one of those Quaker platitudes that had the tendency to take on a life of their own. Mordecai, hopefully, would have calmed down by now; even so, the sight of her might inspire some symphonic prose. But she seemed capable of taking care of herself.

"You don't mind waiting in front of the inn?" she shouted over the rattle of wheels and the clatter of hooves.

"Until you are catapulted out?" She did not hear that, fortunately.

"What?!" she shouted.

"Excellent idea! Very Quakerly! Like me to go with thee?!"

"No! Can handle him! Thanks!"

They reached a roughly paved section of the pike; the racket of the wheels put an end to all conversation.

The inn was on the edge of town. The saloon sounded noisy; he did not care for the idea of her running the gauntlet of singing drunks. Handing him the reins she said, with a laugh, "Listen to that! The Methodists are at it again." Only then did he realize it was hymn singing. "They do that every so often," she continued, "to discourage people from imbibing alcohol." She jumped down with a bounce, like a gymnast, and said, "Pray for me."

He managed a laugh, and watched her stride into the inn, reticule swinging. He wished he could be a fly on the wall during her encounter with Mordecai. A high wall. The ceiling.

What ravishing lunacy! Within minutes the saloon doors might slam outward, and a projectile, skirts fluttering, might come cannonballing out. And he had thought of the Indiana backwoods as the home of boredom!

At first, when Mordecai Monk had seen the woman heading for him down the aisle, he had not recognized her. Hair loose, eyes staring—he had assumed that she wanted to join those at his feet. When she walked past him, he forgot about her, for more of them were coming, eager to join his flock. Then, suddenly, a commanding female voice issued from somewhere behind him. He turned around, bewildered, and realized who, of all people, had the gall to brazenly address the meeting over his head.

After a few stunned seconds, he was overcome by unholy rage. This was intolerable, outrageous! The creature went on and on; his little flock of mesmerized women dispersed to their seats; he was being turned into a figure of fun!

As he could not vent his wrath without engaging the unspeakable female in a slinging match, he stalked out, went to his room, packed his valise, and looked for a hansom among the carriages lined up in front of the school. When he discovered that there weren't any, he had himself driven to the inn in town by a sallow youth who had ducked meeting in order to canoodle in his parents' rockaway; the girl had fled like a startled chicken.

Now, hours later, he was still beset by waves of rage alternating with sinking lows of despondency. Fit to be tied, he was about to hurl a boot through a windowpane at one moment, only to collapse on the bed the next. No post-oratorial daydreams about faceless virgins swooning at his door; instead, he saw, in his fevered lust for revenge, the woman who had challenged him—for the second time!—being chased, cornered, raped by apes . . .

It was this accursed country! In England he had been a serene Christian widower dreaming of his late wife, with whom he would be reunited in the hereafter as two disembodied saints. His romps with Liza had not tarnished that vision; their cavorting in the double bed had been guiltless, innocent, like children playing. But in this country of vibrant energy resulting in continuous sexual stimulation, his daydreams had turned to plain lust. After Philadelphia, he had dreamed the dream of getting even with the snooty women who had smiled at him with one corner of their thin-lipped mouths; now he daydreamed about the wanton young teacher who had turned him from an archangel into an aging windbag vainly bellowing at a disappearing audience.

He crashed against the wall and slammed his head in fury.

Even as he did so, he saw in the red darkness behind his closed eyelids the naked challenger rise with sneering disdain.

He pushed himself free and resumed his pacing. He was corrupted, infected with the foul pox of doubt. Never again would he be able to dominate a crowd. The power had been taken from him. He should steal away now, before they noticed that Samson had lost his hair. He tried to picture them beseeching him to return, but he knew they would do no such thing. They were going to forget him. Before the sun rose on the prairie he would be forgotten, remembered only by some children as the evangelist with the accent who had talked about an ear lying in the street, sniffed at by a dog. Struck by loneliness, he sank to his knees beside the bed and sobbed, shoulders heaving, "Emily! . . . Emily! . . ." The image of her, staring down from heaven, brought him the opposite of comfort; he changed to "Liza! . . . Liza!"

There was a knock on the door. He raised his head.

Another knock, more urgent.

"Who's there?"

"Mordecai Monk—" He could not hear the rest. A girl's voice; must be a serving wench with a message.

He stood and put on his coat. "Come in!"

He saw the door open in the mirror. It was the wanton young woman.

After seconds of stillness, he turned slowly around.

"Please, Friend Mordecai," she said, at the sight of his face. "I come to thee in the spirit of love . . ."

The partition between dream and reality broke. "*Wha!*" he roared, and threw himself on her in one maddened bound. She darted back, he crashed on his knees at her feet, threw his arms around her thighs, buried his face in her skirts; the imagined scent of her femininity drove him mad. Passion, tenderness, rage, and lust became tangled in fury as he felt the softness of her belly; he reached up, grabbed her bodice to bare her breasts as he would have Liza's, but instead he grabbed her hands, kissed them, mumbled insane words, tried to pull her down into an embrace. She struggled free, crying, "Stop! No! Stop!" and battered him with a handbag full of hard objects. She walloped his shoulders, his head, which he shielded with his hands. They both stopped, panting. He looked up at her, she looked down on him. Then she tore herself free and fled, down the passage, without closing the door behind her.

He rose shakily to his feet. He would destroy her. He would chase her to the far corners of the earth, the way God had chased the twinbacked beast from Paradise. He would—

He slumped sprawling across the bed.

Hollow words reverberated in his mind. 'Sword of God.' 'Caliban.' 'God-tempered ax of retribution.'

There he lay, slain by a reticule, yearning for home.

Lydia saw, as she reached the door to the taproom, that her bodice was undone. She paused to button it, smoothed her hair, hurried past the singing drunks to Obadiah Woodhouse, waiting for her in front of the inn.

"What happened?" he asked, as she clambered into the buggy. "What did he say?"

She felt the urge to burst into tears, but managed to sound calm as she replied, "I'm afraid he was not open to the spirit of love."

"I didn't think he would be, quite frankly." He sorted out the reins. "Ready?"

She settled on the seat; his taking over gave her a chance to recover. She could not hold Monk responsible; before he threw himself upon her, he had stared at her the way the mother of the Indian child had the moment after it died. That was what she should remember—the rest had been sheer foolishness. She was all set to be driven back to the school when, to her utter surprise, she burst into tears, after all.

Obadiah Woodhouse put his arm around her shoulders; she shook herself free. "Let me drive," she said.

"Relax, Lydia," he said. "I'm not a good driver, but I suppose the horse knows the way."

She let him be. He started to tell her, by way of entertainment, about his fiancée, a distant cousin whom he could never marry because her family belonged to Cherry Street and he to Arch Street. He told it humorously, while the horse walked them home, calling himself and his girlfriend 'the Pyramus and Thisbe of the Quaker schism.' He meant well, but for some reason it deepened her depression.

The moment they drew up before the school, she saw there was trouble. The windows of both the girls' and the boys' dormitories were lit; from both came the sound of screaming voices, loud and strident in the summer night. Obviously it was complete chaos up there, not one child had gone to bed. Where were the teachers? She left it to Obadiah to take the horse to the stable, hurried up the steps to the front door; once inside, she ran up the stairway to the first floor. From there, the noise in the dormitories was deafening; she stood for a moment in indecision, then ran to the study. Everybody was there, including Peggy and Adam Higgins, looking as if they were taking part in a wake.

"What on earth is going on?" Lydia asked. "Why is nobody taking the children in hand?"

Abner closed the door behind her; the noise from the dormitories faded into the distance. "Tell her, Jesse."

Jesse said, "We're discussing what the arrest of the slaves means as far as the school is concerned."

"The slaves? Arrested?" Lydia asked, shocked to the core.

"Yes," Jesse said. "They were taken off the island in two boats while everyone was in the Meeting House; when they landed, the slave hunters and the sheriff were waiting. Someone must have betrayed them. The sheriff managed to keep the hunters at bay, he and his deputy took them to jail."

"And Viola?"

"They got her too."

There was a knock on the door; at Abner's "Come in!" Obadiah entered.

Jesse continued, "As far as hiding slaves here in the future is concerned, we've botched it."

"I will speak to that later," Abner said, sounding very detached. "I have a plan which is not yet ripe for discussion."

His pose of being in control of the situation while the children were running wild seemed unreal, he must be living in a dream. Suddenly Lydia's shock about the slaves turned into concern for her brother; she knew him better than anyone else, certainly better than did Saraetta; something was very wrong.

Obadiah asked, "Do I understand that the slaves have been intercepted?"

"Yes, indeed," Dr. Rossini said. "The first item on the agenda should be: What are we going to do about the prisoners? There'll be a trial. The law says they have to be handed back to their owners. As to Viola, what she needs is the best lawyer money can buy. And that, I'm afraid—"

"Who is Viola?" Obadiah asked.

"A Negro woman, an escaped slave herself, with a police record. She was the conductor on this section of the railroad. She—" He stopped abruptly. "By the way—does he know about all this?"

"He does," Lydia said. "Go on."

"Well, she's an impossible woman, violent as a bobcat, who'll have everything against her when it comes to a trial. The best she can hope for is to serve her prison sentence in this state, but they may try to extradite her to Louisiana, and we all know what that means. It's a great loss. She was the heart and soul of this section of the railroad."

Lydia looked at Obadiah in a manner that left him no choice. "I'll defend her," he blurted out. "And them!" The smile on her face made him add, somewhat lamely, "However, I'm not familiar with Indiana law, not yet. But if this were Pennsylvania she would have a fair chance of being found innocent. The courts are, on the whole, very sympathetic in these cases."

"Not here," Rossini said.

"Has she committed violence? Now, or earlier?"

"I have some documents belonging to her that you should read, if you are serious about this."

"I am serious, and—"

"And suppose they're not acquitted, what do we do then?" Jesse interrupted.

"I'll speak to that, as I said earlier." Abner rose. "But I want the whole school to be present when I do. So, Lydia, Will—please go and get the children. Assemble for meeting in the hall. I want everyone there, everybody under this roof."

"Come now, Abner!" Little Will's childish voice sounded the most adult of them all. "Has thee any idea what that means?"

"I know what that means," Abner replied, with fragile determination. "Now will you all please do as you are told? We have no time to lose. What I have to propose concerns us all, and it is urgent."

Something in his manner persuaded them; in Lydia's case, it was his vulnerability. None of them seemed to realize that all it needed was an angry push or a harsh word to make his courage crumble and leave him no protection from the world except her sheltering arms. "Very well, Abner," she said. "We'll go at once."

When she entered the girls' dormitory, it took all her composure to retain a façade of authority. The place was a shambles; bedsheets and pillows were strewn all over the floor, cots had been pushed about until they stood at crazy angles; children were bouncing on the beds like monkeys, screaming shrilly with mad glee; here and there groups of them were slamming at each other with pillows, feathers swirled in the air.

"Girls!" she cried at the top of her voice. "Girls! Listen to me! *Girls!*" She was unable to make herself heard above the din; but gradually the noise abated as a few of the girls spotted her and alerted the others. She decided to remain calm and ignore the shameful chaos. "All right, girls! Listen to me! There is to be an emergency meeting downstairs in the main hall in five minutes. Please get dressed—those of you who undressed—and get in line. Quickly now!"

Grudgingly they obeyed and started to line up inside the door. Had it not been dark, with owls and whippoorwills screeching outside, they might have been lining up for morning worship.

On the landing, they had to wait to let the boys file past.

"All right, girls, here we go!" she called when their turn came. They filed down the stairs, into the main hall, with its flickering candles.

The children sat down in their customary rows with the usual rumble, the boys to the right, the girls to the left. She saw Will go to the facing bench, but thought it better to stay with her girls to control them should the need arise. She took a seat halfway down the aisle; at Abner's request, Dr. Rossini took her place among the faculty. The only place left open was poor Saraetta's. Lydia wondered how she was, alone in her bed with all this going on; but of course, Dr. Rossini would have given her a sleeping draught.

To her surprise, Abner did not call for a moment of silence. He rose, frail and determined, in the restless light of the candle flames dancing in the draft.

"Boys and girls, fellow Quakers," he began in a strained voice. "I have called on you because of an urgent concern that burdens us all. I am talking about the slaves, captured by the sheriff's posse and taken by force to jail where, no doubt, they will be kept until their so-called owners come to claim them."

It took a few moments for Lydia to take it in. Had Abner gone insane? The children knew nothing about the slaves, or the underground railroad. But there was something about him she had never seen before, which yet seemed familiar.

Abner continued, his voice high-pitched and quavering: "To us Friends, the plight of the slaves presents a challenge to the essence of our calling. We either accept the challenge or forfeit the right to call ourselves Quakers."

She recognized now what had seemed so familiar: he was imitating Father. Father had used those same words when the first rumors of the schism had reached Pendle Hill Meeting. It had been an emergency session like this one; with his immense authority and unquestioned personal integrity he had called upon everyone to forget about 'Arch Street' and 'Cherry Street,' and never to use the words 'orthodox' or 'activist' again, only 'Quaker.'

"Our principles are familiar enough, we have mouthed them ever since we were taught to speak," Abner continued. "We are, as Friends, guided by the principle that every man and woman is unique, irreplaceable, never been on earth before and never will be again, and that this individuality is the most precious thing we have. As Quakers, we say, 'We shall never, under any circumstances, violate that individuality in our neighbors or ourselves.' Well, we are tonight confronted with an intolerable violation of that principle. Twelve individuals, unique, irreplaceable, precious to God, have been chained together like cattle and herded into prison, there to await their collection by another unique, irreplaceable individual, who in his tragic blindness considers himself to be their owner. This is, to us Friends, an intolerable violation of their humanity; not just that of the slaves, but of the owner as well. If we acquiesce in this, if we do not rise to the challenge and do whatever we can to free those slaves, we ourselves will become tainted with this sickness of the soul." He looked about him, took a deep breath, and continued: "I propose, not as principal of this school but as clerk of our School Meeting, that the setting free of those slaves shall be made a concern of the Rebekah Baker Boarding School. That all of us —children, teachers, all those present in this hall—shall unite without reservation in this concern. After a moment of silence, I will disclose my plan. But first I ask for the sense of the meeting." He sat down and bent his head in prayer.

The silence that followed should have been full of joy and light for Lydia, in honor of her brother and the spirit he embodied, but something held her back, a doubt, a sense of darkness. With a vast rustling sound, the children rose to their feet. Abner, startled, looked up and stared at them, uncomprehending. Then the teachers on the facing bench rose too.

It was an impressive moment. For meetings to rise silently to their feet was very rare, she had only witnessed it once before, in approval of her father; that time she had felt the indefinable but unmistakable presence of God. It was obvious that the others, everyone else in the hall, experienced this at that very moment.

But to her, alone among the multitude, He was not there. This was wrong; Abner should not have involved the children. But then what? Leave the Negroes to be shipped back into slavery?

She waited for the silent part of the meeting to end, for Abner to disclose the plan he had mentioned. She had little faith in whatever he might propose, for he surely was the world's worst conspirator.

But when it came, the moment of disclosure, she was struck with admiration. His plan was bold, brilliant; she could not believe that her meek, brooding brother could have come up with this ingenious, cunning stratagem. He had, in a moment of grace, surpassed himself.

Grace? Perhaps not quite that. But it held every promise of success; the slaves could never be set free without the children.

Yet, it was a call to break the law . . .

She gave up.

"Yes," she said, when asked. "I understand. I will do my part. I—I will."

The only one who read her thoughts, it seemed, was Obadiah Woodhouse, of all people. He looked very worried.

Meeting did not break until the candles guttered. Finally, the children marched back to the dormitories—disciplined, calm, composed. They seemed suddenly to have reached maturity.

They were now going completely overboard, Obadiah thought to himself. To use the children under their care to break the law could not, by any stretch of the imagination, be called Quakerly, or Christian for that matter. He was baffled by the innocence with which these thoroughly decent people had arrived at the conclusion that this was the only nonviolent way in which to help the slaves escape. Instead of turning up with a bunch of bandits firing shotguns, they were going to use children to create a disturbance in a courtroom on the day of sentencing, in order to give the defendants a chance to abscond. To spring the prisoners from jail, in their eyes, made the whole episode an exercise of love in action.

Was it innocence? Or was it, in fact, the hard, steely core of the Friendly persuasion? He had often wondered at the unruffled toughness of the Quaker princes in Philadelphia when it came to 'defending basic principles,' which meant getting their own way. This was a bucolic version of the same thing: in the eyes of God (read: Rebekah Baker School's Monthly Meeting) slavery was an abomination, no man should own another man. Therefore anything that would serve to set the slaves free and spirit them to Canada was doing God's work. All He has is thee, to blast the vitals out of the judicial process, incite children to create mayhem, and fill the streets outside with a herd of cows so no deputy could go after the fugitives other than astride a bucking steer. And he, a lawyer, should aid and abet this riot?

The only one ill at ease with her brother's Quaker version of Guy Fawkes Day was Lydia Best, it seemed. She had shot Obadiah a glance while everyone was rising to their feet to express unity; she might as well have said, 'This is awful,' in so many words. Afterwards, when everyone had left except for a few excited teachers hobnobbing in a corner, he went up to her as she stood in the aisle. "What does thee think of all this?"

She thought it over; then she said, "It's the end and the means, isn't it?"

"Indeed. And that ethical question, as I remember it, was settled quite a while ago."

"Not tonight," she said.

There was a silence; they slowly walked up the aisle.

"I don't like it," he said finally.

She stood still, then turned to him. "Thee is not involved in any of this. Thee should prepare thy case and defend those slaves as best thee can; who knows, they may be set free and the whole thing will prove unnecessary."

He smiled. "Is this how our forebears slid out of awkward situations? By praying for tunnel vision and proceeding, hands folded in prayer, in a Friendly version of the three monkeys?"

He saw she was perplexed.

"Hear, see, and speak no evil," he explained.

She frowned. She was quite beautiful, in thought.

"Let's look at the alternative," she suggested, and then fell silent.

"I'm waiting," he said, with a smile. An impish little devil in his mind whispered: 'The alternative is: let's go for a walk in the grounds.' This was no way to solve what might be a crucial problem in his life as a lawyer. The other crucial problem . . .

"The alternative is to send those people back into slavery while we indulge in the luxury of an unresolved moral conflict."

"In other words, let's all be heroes and corrupt the law?"

"We would not be corrupting the law. Sentence will have been passed, we would be corrupting the execution of the law, if I am putting it correctly."

Ah, those Quakers! Jesuits were innocents by comparison. "Let's look at it from a different angle," he suggested. "What will be the consequences for the school, and for each one of us personally?"

She gave him a heart-melting regard of stunning blue eyes. "Thee would suffer none. Thy only task is to defend the slaves. If thee loses the case, leave the rest to us."

"There is such a thing as complicity by silence."

"There is such a thing as twelve people being sent back into slavery, three infants included. Thee does understand that I'm acting the devil's advocate?"

"Lydia, my—"

The other teachers made their way past them up the aisle, casting pre-gossip looks.

"Yes?" she asked. The blue eyes were questioning now.

He took a hold of himself. "All right. Let's each of us solve this according to—what is the term?"

"According to the measure of light granted us."

"Right."

She smiled. "We'll come back to it. Now I should pay a token visit to the girls' dormitory."

"Right." But nothing of it was 'right.' All of it was wrong.

He watched her until she disappeared into the lobby. He had better go and bone up on Indiana law, and pray for tunnel vision. With his heritage, that should come easy. During the French and Indian Wars, the Quaker-controlled Pennsylvania Assembly had been forced to contribute to the military, despite the peace testimony. They had solved the problem by contributing 'wheat and other grains.' How many of them had known that the military would interpret 'other grains' as meaning 'gunpowder?' Had Great-grandpa Woodhouse known? You bet.

He had felt a great deal clearer when all he had to do was deal with Mordecai Monk's antics. Moral challenges were not his forte. He did not want to be challenged, he wanted to be comfortable.

Now who was it, who had said that before? Ah! His great-aunt Gulielma, about the Quaker establishment in Philadelphia. He wondered how Pissing Gulie would have solved this ethical conundrum. All it took was tunnel vision. Pontius Pilate had been a good lawyer. One of the best.

CHAPTER 8

PHILADELPHIA

July 1833

Charity Woodhouse, a pretty young woman in Quaker dress, read Obadiah's letter over again, seated on a bench under a tree in the Cherry Street burial ground. She thought, 'Nonsense! I cannot possibly travel five hundred miles, or whatever it is, on impulse!' The letter was romantic, adventurous, and very seductive; but to leave all this . . .

She gazed at the old Meeting House, the manicured lawn no one outside the Society would suspect of being a graveyard. Granny lay there, somewhere, and Uncle Peleg, and Uncle Joshua. She picked up the letter again and read it once more, from the beginning. Halfway, she stopped.

'The one outspoken member of the rather timid faculty is Lydia Best, a captivating, courageous, and, I must admit, strikingly handsome young woman.'

She lowered the paper. The message was clear: now, or never. Well, then, it had to be never. The price was too high.

She wished, fervently, he had never sent it. It was over, forever. She folded the letter and put it back into her reticule.

On her way home, she passed the office of the Western Transportation Company on Race Street. Just out of curiosity she went inside to ask how a lady, traveling alone, could get to a place called Pendle Hill in Indiana in the shortest possible time and greatest comfort. Before the man behind the ticket window was able to reply, a jolly voice with a heavy Irish accent cried behind her, "Pendle Hill? Dearie, that's where *I'm* going! My son is an engineer there! When are you leaving, sweetheart?" It was a fat, middle-aged woman, a cook or a midwife. "He is working on the canal, and he asked me to join him! Are you leaving tomorrow too?"

Suddenly, without knowing why, she found herself telling the woman and the unfascinated agent behind the ticket window an outrageous lie: that she was a teacher who had been offered a post in Pendle Hill, an emergency, someone had fallen ill.

"Dearie!" The woman embraced her with smothering arms. "This is God's will! I was *so* nervous of traveling all by myself, and now, behold! An angel!" She held Charity at arm's length and beamed at the ticket agent. "Book us together! I don't care when she's going, I am going with her! When are you going, dearie? I'm Molly O'Grady, everybody calls me Moll. Are you leaving tomorrow? Then *I* am leaving tomorrow! What time's the stage, sir? Where does it leave from?"

"The corner of Broad and Vine, between seven and eight in the morning. I still have room for you."

"No, no," Charity protested hastily. "I could not possibly go tomorrow!"

"Well, day after tomorrow!" the woman cried. "Whenever you say, dearie! As long as there are two of us they'll give us a separate room at the inns, but a woman alone, dear girl—those *men*!" She rolled her eyes.

"The morning coach to Columbia," the agent droned, "connects with the Harrisburg stage, which leaves at six o'clock the next morning. There, you'll take the Western Transportation

Company stage to Johnstown, change to the coach to Pittsburgh. You'll make the journey without fatigue in six days. The tables are plentifully provided, the accommodations ensure comfort and render the tour most interesting to the traveler. Only eight dollars to Pittsburgh, all found."

"And after Pittsburgh?" she asked, keeping up the shameful pretense.

"You will have to make your own arrangements in Pittsburgh. Check with the agent there, ma'am. I'm sure the trip will be comfortable, the Cumberland Road has been improved."

Charity realized to her surprise and alarm that she was actually ready to do this insane thing: throw away all she had, family, security, friends, position in society—and why? Why?

The letter was among the batch Peggy, the school cook, had collected at the coach station. "Here," Saraetta said, sorting out the mail. "Here's one for Obadiah Woodhouse."

"I'll take it," Lydia said, "I have to go upstairs, anyhow." She took the letter from Saraetta's hand.

On her way up to his room, courage failed her. For days she had been agonizing over her sudden and surprising change of feelings about Obadiah. Should she approach him boldly, never mind the feminine passivity she was supposed to show at this point? Goad him into declaring himself with the coyness she detested in other women? Even as she lifted her hand to knock on his door, she had not decided; all she knew was that it was a fateful moment. Now or never; no other man like him was likely to come her way: cultured, civilized, bright, funny, courageous . . . How *could* she sell herself that sickening stuff? She was twenty-nine years old! Even if he were knock-kneed—

She rapped on the door. Too loud. Be feminine.

"Come in!"

She opened the door and there he stood, in hat and coat, dressed to go out. As elegant as Quaker garb allowed. Smiling. God, what a catch! She stepped inside, leaving the door open.

"Thee has a letter," she said, handing it to him.

"Ah?" He looked at the envelope, turned it over and put it in his pocket.

"Is thee going out?" she asked stupidly. She had never seen a man more ready to go out.

"Yes, I have an appointment to meet the judge. He only holds court on Thursdays." He headed for the door.

"Obadiah," she said, barring his way. Too forcefully! Take it easy! "I have been thinking." Silly remark. So she had been thinking—that might have been extraordinary had she been a pig. "All night," she added lamely.

The regard of his calm gray eyes seemed to rest upon her like a friendly hand on her shoulder. She knew at that moment, as if he had spoken the words himself, that he knew exactly what she was about to say.

"Here," he said, taking a sheet of paper off the mantelpiece. "Read my arguments and give me thy reaction. While thee does that, I'll read my letter."

A sick, sinking feeling in her stomach. She had made a fool of herself. She felt as if she had lain down on the floor before him, skirts up, and he had turned away. "Thank thee," she said, and took the sheet of paper.

But she did not read it. That is to say, she read it, but not a word registered. Keeping her eyes on the paper, she watched, with the peripheral vision of a duck, as he opened the envelope, unfolded the letter, took it to the window to read. She guessed who it was from. She felt ashamed, because her body refused to accept the conclusion of her mind. She felt wildly, furiously excited. She wanted to rip that sheet of paper from his hands, tear it up, throw her arms around his neck and kiss him, kiss him until he caved in with his silly hat and his city manners and his wonderful gray eyes, and roll with him onto the bed—

"I'm afraid I have a problem," he said with a wan smile, folding the paper.

He had a problem! For a moment she thought that her body had been right and her mind wrong: his girlfriend, whatever her name was, had written to him that she loved him, but he no longer loved her.

"Tell me about it," she said. "About these arguments, by the way—they're very good. Thank thee for letting me read them." She put the paper on the bed. Why the bed? She wanted to run from the room, back to hers, throw herself on her own bed and sob, curse, beat the pillow.

"My fiancée, Charity Woodhouse, who is also a distant cousin of mine, has responded to a lighthearted letter I sent earlier, when circumstances were different."

God, dear God, her body had been right! He *was* going to propose!

"Tell me about it," she said, startled by her own bland reaction.

"I casually suggested—well, I—er—suggested she might consider joining me here, never expecting— Well, for her it meant leaving everything she had in the way of family and possessions, friends, status—I did not for a moment expect . . ."

"Pretty rash, Friend Obadiah." She managed a comradely smile.

"It now turns out, alas, that I misled her."

Ha!

"There is no post for her at this school, not under the present circumstances. Or is there?"

She looked at him for a long moment before saying, "Does it matter, Friend Obadiah? I gather she is on her way?"

"Yes," he said. "I'm afraid she is."

She took a deep breath, smiled, and said, "Well, way will open. See thee downstairs." She turned to the door. No—no more. Say no more!

She let herself out, closed the door behind her, and stood in the empty corridor, eyes closed, thinking, stupidly, 'Next month I will be thirty.'

• • •

No wonder the ticket agent had been reticent about the second part of the journey. Never in her wildest dreams had Charity imagined such ghastly discomfort as when she and the moaning Molly O'Grady were jolted, tossed, and rattled in stagecoaches that became more and more primitive and roughshod, until they ended up, in Indianapolis, in the worst contraption of all: the South Bend Stage, a six-horse Conestoga wagon; according to the coachman, a Concord was unable to negotiate the ruts, gulleys, and potholes of the rest of the road west.

And the inns! The last one, somewhere in the wilds, was so filthy, so hot, so swarming with flies, that even Molly O'Grady's indomitable cheerfulness collapsed. When they complained to the landlord about the flies on the food, the uncouth creature replied, "Why don't you quit feeding till mornin'? At breakfast there ain't no flies, they're all in the outhouse."

That night, the irresponsibility of what she had done was brought home to Charity. The horrible little room, the creaky bed she shared with the huge, smelly woman, the certainty that they would be attacked by bedbugs the moment she blew out the candle made her get up, sit on the windowsill, and gaze out at the dark, menacing forest. Alien odors were wafted toward her by the breeze. Even the fluting and ululating of birds in the woods seemed hostile. Above the forest was the vastness of the starless sky. She thought, 'I am a liar, lost in the wilderness. A liar, a liar. I lied to my parents, my family, my friends, to this woman. I lied to myself. What really brought me here were the words "*a captivating, courageous, and, I must admit, strikingly handsome young woman.*" '

Could she still turn back, at this moment? Rush home, hide her face in her mother's lap, and never again venture outside the sheltered life of her family? Below her, alien creatures chortled, whistled, hooted in mindless merriment. *A captivating, courageous, strikingly handsome young woman.* Could such a person exist in this world of open privies, bedbugs, drunks vomiting in the courtyard, and, as at that inn a week before, giggles and screams from a brothel across the street? What chances had a captivating, courageous, strikingly handsome young woman to survive among these yokels and brutes? In the stagecoach, where the stench of sweat was such that people passed out from it, one of those brutes had that morning pulled off a boot and stuck his stinking foot under her elbow, nudging her at every bounce of the coach. If she had not been protected by the presence of the huge Irishwoman now snoring behind her, heaven knows what would have happened to her. She would have arrived ravished, distraught —and to what purpose? To push a captivating, courageous, strikingly handsome young woman out of her way? What wicked nonsense! Childish jealousy! What was their future going to look like, after marrying out of Meeting, cast out by both Cherry and Arch streets, disowned by their parents? Fool! What a fool she had been!

Despite the late hour, a fiddle struck up a scratchy jig in the courtyard below, and a male voice started to bellow the indistinct words of a song. Laughter, the tinkling of broken glass. The voice fell silent; the fiddle went on scraping and chirruping like a giant cricket in the night. To her amazement, it slowly began to call forth a response in her. An awareness, slowly expanding; the opening of a door to dormant spaces within herself. She was larger, more primitive than she had suspected. Who was she, really? Who was the woman hiding behind the smiling face, the hazel eyes? Suddenly, the girl called Charity Woodhouse from Philadelphia seemed to be a pretense, a pretty picture; the true woman inside the petulant little doll began to respond to the jerky, male chirping of the fiddle, calling her, challenging her to come out into the night. Then a coarse, repulsive noise sounded behind her like the tearing of a piece of taffeta, and the bulbous shape in the bed muttered, "Bejesus—those beans . . ."

In a few days she would face Obadiah, the man the pretty, petulant Charity with the winning little ways had imagined herself to be in love with. A creature just as conventional as herself: an earnest young lawyer, sensitive and bookish, whose future depended on his family, his Meeting, his father's money. All of which he stood to lose, were they to marry.

Suddenly frightened, she crawled into bed and snuggled up to the warm bulk of Molly O'Grady, a child afraid of the dark.

In Richmond, Indiana, at Yearly Meeting, Mordecai Monk ministered with great power to a packed house. It felt different, though, from previous occasions. There was the same power, no doubt about that, the same mysterious exchange of energy between himself and his audience, growing into an ever faster spinning vortex of emotion, ending in a spiritual consummation of almost orgiastic ecstasy. But this time, instead of flaring joy, a sense of triumph, his ministry had a strange undercurrent of melancholy, an edge of loss. For the first time, he dwelt on the grief of the small band of disciples left behind after the crucifixion, the emptiness of their lives, the bewilderment, the incomprehension, the sense of guilt. 'Am I to blame? Did He die because I failed Him?'

The words came, as always, by magic, from nowhere. Words he had never used before, phrases that had, so far, never occurred to him, emotions he had never articulated with the same haunting realism. Yet, even as he moved people to tears, he became aware that he had not been speaking about the disciples mourning Jesus, but about himself mourning little Rebecca, Emily, his mother, even—bewilderingly—Liza, whose nature, looks, and generosity he borrowed to describe Mary Magdalene. He even went so far as to mention how, at the depth of their heartbreak and sorrow, Mary Magdalene had made them a cup of tea. The meeting swallowed it without a murmur: the crushed little band of disciples had been consoled by a prostitute making them a cup of tea.

Only later, in his room at the inn, did he conclude that what happened at Pendle Hill had dealt a blow to his mastery, maybe his innocence. The wanton young woman who had twice silenced him and made a hall of spellbound listeners forget about him proved unforgettable herself. The feel of her hips in his arm, her thighs when he embraced them, the softness of her bosom, the scent of her loins, haunted him, obsessed him, troubled his dreams. Liza, rolling over on the bed, her breasts, thighs, cries, were less real in his memory than those long seconds during which he had actually held the Quaker maiden in his arms, before she had started to batter him with whatever it was she had had in her hand. Alarmingly, the memory did not bring thoughts of love or tenderness, but a violent vision of rape, which made him wake up with a sense of horror to the real nature of his musings. He must forget her, put her behind him, carry on: new Meetings, new faces. But Richmond was the end of the line; after this, no more visits to outlying Meetings were planned. After this, he would go home to England.

After the sermon, he was physically exhausted and longed to lie on his bed, arms flung out, to recover from the usual draining of his vitality. But the clerk of Yearly Meeting and its school committee wanted to hear his impression of Pendle Hill and his report on what had occurred at the Rebekah Baker Boarding School on Founders' Day. Was there any truth to the rumor of a stage play, or a theatrical event, being performed by the pupils of the school? Was it true that Pendle Hill Meeting had made the removal of the Mahanoy Indians their concern? It had made him aware, again, that Richmond Yearly Meeting belonged to Arch Street.

He wanted to change first, his undershirt and shirt were soaked with perspiration; but there was no time for that, he had to join them, now. The members of the committee were gathered in a side room, four somber, worried men. They had more questions. Was it true that the schism had now reached Pendle Hill? That half the Meeting had walked out in protest after a call for repentance, had refused the Sacred Fount of Salvation—Christ's blood, shed on Golgotha—in favor of a social concern? Talk, talk, talk, talk—finally, they wanted to hear his version of what had happened at Pendle Hill. At the school.

He spoke slowly and carefully, trying to be objective, feeling totally drained. He wished people would realize how exhausting it was to pull along an audience of hundreds, to cause an upheaval in many individual souls which made them rise and come forward, why afterward he was merely an empty shell. He gave as sympathetic a picture of the faculty as he could, but, alas, there was no doubt: a teacher *had* organized a historical pageant acted out by children.

When they asked if the same woman teacher had been the instigator of the Meeting's decision to form a Meeting for Sufferings of Mahanoy children, he felt he had said enough. "I really don't know, Friends. When the deliberations started I left the gathering. As an outsider I felt I had no business there."

"But is it true that the woman actually said: 'Individual salvation through Christ's atonement is self-indulgent,' or words to that effect?"

"I would not know."

"And that to come to the aid of those who suffer, the Indians, without vocal ministry, was the true way of embodying God's love?"

"I cannot confirm that. By then I had left."

After more probing they finally let him go. He left, feeling dirty, soiled by betrayal. He did not really care what the wanton young woman believed, or anyone else, for that matter, as long as they listened to his sermons. For his sermons were glorious, with lots of excitement and love and heroes, and a little dog.

Oh, that damn little dog! Bet you anything it was all some of the children would remem— For God's sake! Not *again!*

A bosomy young woman showed him to his room. But hers were not like the breasts that haunted his dreams, his thoughts, his ministry. Could he? Could he dare to say, at the height of the ecstasy, as the women lay twitching at his feet: 'Bare thy breasts for thy Savior?'

No. Definitely: *no*. Even so . . .

Just to be rid of the thought, he wrote it down and slipped it inside his Bible, which was full of little notes like this one. Better be careful; to hear him sing, at the height of his peroration, 'Let His love penetrate thy soul, thy very womb' was quite enough; to have these slips flutter down from his Bible, to be caught by some stranger like falling snowflakes—

Snowflakes. Gaslight.

Homesickness for Liza made him bury his face in his pillow and howl. The howl of the lone wolf in the prairie.

Good, that. Better write it down.

Chapter 9

Pendle Hill, Indiana

August 1833

The morning of the trial, just after sunrise, the school's vegetable garden was fresh and wet with dew.

"Was that the bell?" Himsha Woodhouse asked.

Boomer McHair, her cousin from fourth grade, climbed on the workbench and peered into the garden through the window of the potting shed. "Don't think so. Don't see anybody moving."

"Well, we'd better go." Himsha turned to Bonny Baker. "Come, Bonny, we're leaving."

"Just a minute," Bonny replied, squatting in front of the cage with his mice. "I'm not through feeding them."

"Thee and thy mice!" Boomer scoffed. "They've had enough fodder to last them a week! Come on, or they'll be too fat to move."

"No," Bonny said, "you go ahead, I won't be a minute. I still have to give them water."

Himsha grabbed Boomer by the arm and pushed him to the

door. "Leave him alone," she said with an authority that even her cousin found it risky to flout. "Move!"

"Take thy paws off me! One of these days I'll grab *thee*!"

She ignored him and turned back to Bonny. "Don't be long. The bell's about to go."

"Don't be long, sweetie!" Boomer mimicked. "Don't be long, pussypie!"

She pushed him out; Bonny heard him cry angrily, "Stop that, Himsha Woodhouse!" and then them racing off to the school, down the path between the runner beans.

In the sudden silence, the twelve mice squeaked and rustled in their cage. All these weeks, days, nights he had worried about them being hurt in that courtroom. He closed his eyes and prayed to God to protect them.

The mice were not their old selves this morning. They had not scurried toward his open hand but scrabbled up the sides of the cage in an effort to get out. Did they know what was going to happen to them? Or was it the explosions at the canal? They had been very loud last night. He filled their dish with water; not too much or they might be sick. He was so engrossed in what he was doing that Himsha speaking behind his back made him jump.

"Come along, Bonny," she said gently. "Thee'll be in trouble when the bell goes again." She stood, tall and dark, in the open doorway.

"They're scared," he said. "I wonder if they know. Look how jittery they are."

She came and squatted beside him to look, her braids dangling. "Thee loves them, doesn't thee?"

He had never thought about them in those terms. They just were separate mice to him, like people became separate as you got to know them better. He would have worried about them less if they had been merely a dozen white mice; now they had each become different from the others, each with its own character and personality. He had even given them names. "Oh, I don't know," he replied.

"It is wrong," she said. "Thee should not love animals as if they were people."

"I just don't want them to get hurt."

She straightened up and said, "It is wrong, Bonny. They won't get hurt today, thee will. Don't squander thy love on mice."

"Why not?" he asked defiantly. "Who else is there?"

"That's unfair, and thee knows it."

"We're different."

"I should hope so!"

"I—I love thee, Himsha," he said, trying to explain. "But thee does not need me to stay alive. Thee can look after thyself, everybody is afraid of thee. But if I'm not around, the mice—"

"That has nothing to do with love! Love has to do with that of God in the other person. There's nothing of God in a mouse."

"How does thee know?"

"Animals have no souls. Come along! The second bell will go any minute." She took him by the arm.

"What about John Woolman's chickens?" he asked, as she pulled him toward the door.

"What about them?" She pushed him outside and closed the door of the shed behind her.

"When John Woolman went to England, he had a concern about the chickens, cooped up on the deck of the ship. He went to see the captain about them."

"If thee thinks that thee is like John Woolman . . ."

He did not hear the rest; she was crawling through the gap in the hedge. He crawled after her.

"I'm not saying I am like John Woolman," he said, once on the other side. "I mean: he didn't want those chickens to get hurt, even if they didn't have that of God in them. What about God, anyway? Doesn't He worry about the fall of a sparrow?"

Somewhere a whippoorwill struck up its mournful tune.

"Bonny," she said, so close to him that he had to look from one eye to the other, "those mice are going to die to set fifteen human beings free, three of them babies. Does thee understand that?"

"I know," he said miserably. "I wish God would open another way."

She put her arms around his neck and kissed him. She did not startle him, he was used to it; she was like his sister. She let him go, took his hand, and said, "Come, I'll race thee."

He ran with her toward the school as the second bell began to clang in the distance.

Before the trial, Dr. Rossini took part in the final deliberations of the faculty in the principal's study. He disapproved of the involvement of the children, even though he was impressed by the thoroughness of Abner's planning. He wondered what an action like this would do to the children's respect for the law; once again he was confronted with the mystery of the Quaker character, seemingly so meek and forbearing. Even after years of dealing with them, their ultimate toughness remained an enigma.

Lydia Best seemed subdued this morning, possibly because her part in the plot was the most difficult: she was in charge of the babies. "Let's hope they won't cry," she said. "Has thee brought their medication, Doctor?"

"Yes. I'll give it to the mothers in prison. I'll have to see them before the trial anyhow, to check their scars and birthmarks with the owner's list. It should be administered ten minutes before the verdict."

"How long will it keep them drowsy?"

"About an hour. I could not make it more potent, because of their age."

"But can it be given to the babies in the courtroom, in view of everybody? Won't that alert the slave catchers that something's in the wind?"

"I have prepared three sops containing the drug. Their mothers will give them to the babies. I need to have some idea how long Obadiah's plea is going to take. Does anyone know?"

"He's upstairs working on it," Abner said.

"I'll go and see him. Anything else I should know at this point? We won't meet again until after the trial."

"Thee'll tell the slaves what to do?" Little Will asked.

"I will. One thing isn't quite clear, though. Where do the cattle come in?"

"Never mind, Doctor," Jesse McHair said, "that's no concern of the niggers. All they have to do is head for the wagon and get in as fast as they can."

"All right." Rossini rose. "I don't know if it's un-Quakerly, but keep your fingers crossed."

As he closed the door behind him and faced the empty corridor, he was overcome by a sense of foreboding. What if the marshals used force? What if the slave catchers, who were certain to be present in the back of the courtroom, tackled the schoolchildren and started to kick them out of the way? He did not share the Quakers' faith in a benevolent Providence; someone was bound to get hurt, most likely the children. There were also long-term implications: whether they failed or succeeded, their relationship with the townspeople would never be the same again.

He climbed the stairs and knocked on the door of the second-floor guest room. A voice called, "Yes!" He found the young lawyer in shirtsleeves at the table by the window, a stack of open books before him.

"Sorry to interrupt, but I need more information before I see the prisoners. Give me an idea how long your plea will take. I must tell the mothers when to give their babies the sedative."

"Good heavens!" The young man looked strained. "I have no idea. Ten, fifteen minutes? From what I hear, this judge can be long-winded, especially if he gets on his hobbyhorse: federal law versus state law. How long does it take your sedative to work?"

"In the case of children this young, ten minutes."

"And it lasts how long?"

"About an hour."

"In that case, let the mothers give it to them as soon as the judge starts his summing up. He'll certainly not take less than ten minutes."

"Thanks. See you in court. Good luck."

"Likewise, Doctor."

The rain which had been threatening all morning was coming down with a vengeance by the time Rossini arrived at the courthouse. He tethered his horse and went to the sheriff's office.

"Morning, Sheriff. All right if I go and have a look at their identification marks? I have to check them before the verdict."

The sheriff, feet on desk, handed him the list of names and drawings and tossed him the master key. "Help yourself, Doc. Downstairs, first cell on the left. Need any help?"

"No, thanks."

"I needn't tell you, the whole thing is a pain in the ass to every decent man in town." The sheriff took his feet off his desk. "The law's the law, but—well, I'm glad it's not a bunch of slave catchers getting them."

"Have you seen the owner?"

"He asked me over to the hotel. Looked like a real gentleman. He has a little boy with him. As humane, I'd say, as you can expect of any slaveowner."

Rossini went to the door. "I won't be long. I'd appreciate it if you could keep your men away till I'm through. I'll have to ask some of the women to bare their buttocks; I don't want to turn it into a peepshow."

"Don't worry, Doc," the sheriff said, with feeling. "Jake's down there; send him on up. Hell, he'd as soon stay around to see those nigger wenches in the raw as leer at his own daughter."

When Rossini pulled open the heavy door that led to the cellar, the stale air that came up was like that of a morgue. A man's voice called from the bottom of the stairs, "That you, Sheriff?"

"It's me, Dr. Rossini." He went down the stairs. "I've come to check on the prisoners."

"Oh, Doc!" The deputy seemed relieved. "They're right over there. Hope you can do something about them."

"What's wrong?"

"Well, Jesus! They know what's going to happen to them. How would you feel? It's the babies that get to me, and their mothers. I don't mind the men, but the mothers—"

"All right, Jake," Rossini said. "Go and have a cup of coffee with the sheriff. I have to examine them."

"Sure, Doc, sure . . ." He seemed eager to leave. "I'll just open the cell for you. Holler when you're through."

"I will."

The man went down the dark passage between the cells; Rossini heard the sound of a key turning. "All yours, Doc. Here's the key. Lock up when you're through, will you?"

The cell was darker than the passage. The Negroes, standing motionless at the bars, watched him approach like horses in a stable. A tall, middle-aged man with prominent front teeth stood in the doorway.

"I am Dr. Rossini. I'm here to give you your instructions."

The man moved aside; Rossini entered the cell. They all simply stared at him. They were a sad lot, browbeaten and totally demoralized after all these weeks in prison. Even so, you never knew. They had escaped once, from their masters; they might have the gumption to do it again. But not by the looks of them.

"I have a message for you from Viola."

"Yassah," the tall man said.

"Your escape has been arranged. If the verdict goes against you, we won't have much time, and I have instructions for you. Who do I speak to? You?"

"Yassah," the tall man said.

"You will be defended by a Quaker lawyer, but chances are, the judge will order you to be returned to your owner."

"Yassah."

The others went on staring at him. Their stillness was unnerving.

Rossini opened his bag and took out the three pacifiers. "These contain a medication meant to keep the babies quiet. Give them these the moment the judge starts his summing up.

That means: when the judge responds to the speech by the Quaker lawyer. The drug won't harm them, even if an escape should turn out to be unnecessary." He tried to hand the pacifiers to the women holding babies, but they refused to accept them. The tall man took them and put them in his trouser pockets.

"Don't squeeze them, the medicine is inside."

"Yassah," the man said.

"You'll be asked to rise for the verdict at the end of the trial; then the marshals will want to take you back to your cell. What we are counting on is that they will not walk ahead of you when you leave the courtroom, but wait until the last of you has left the dock. When you move up the aisle, toward the exit . . ."

He continued his instructions, uneasy at their lack of response. None of them so much as blinked. They just stood there, motionless, staring at him. Then a baby started to cry in a corner of the cell; one of the women waded through the straw toward it.

"When you arrive at the farm," he concluded, "you'll be moved to a loft in one of the barns. You're supposed to stay there until after dark, when you'll be taken to the next station. Any questions?"

Silence. Then the tall man asked, "Does Viola know about this?"

Rossini felt a twinge of irritation; they would never trust a white man, even if he risked his livelihood for them. "Viola is in prison too," he said, as if they didn't know; she was in a cell a few doors from theirs. "I'll visit with her. If she does not agree with the plan, I'll come and tell you."

"What's this stuff we's to give our children?" a woman asked.

"A mild sedative. All it will do is make them drowsy, so they won't give you away by crying once you are in the wagon. I'm a doctor, I promise you it is safe."

The woman said nothing. The tall man said, "Yassah."

Rossini looked around the circle of staring eyes. "I'm supposed to check on your identification marks, but I suppose you all are—were—the property of Mr. Armand Delatour of Morning Rose Plantation, Louisiana?"

"Yassah," the tall man said.

"All right, then, this seems to be all. Goodbye, good luck, if all goes well, I'll see you at the farm." He turned away, opened the door of the cell and stepped outside. He was about to close it again when he became aware of the tall man staring at him with an odd look. "Sorry," he said, "but I'm supposed to lock this door. We must not arouse their suspicion. All right?"

"Yassah," the man said.

He pulled the door shut and locked it with the key. He hesitated for a moment; his next assignment was a tough one. The other cell was at the far end of the corridor, where it was darker, and the air more dank. He peered through the bars but could not discern a thing in the gloom.

"Viola?" he asked, his voice low.

"Well, well," the hateful voice sneered. "Look who's here. Want my confession, boy?"

Rossini looked over his shoulder; the corridor was empty. He opened his medicine bag and took from it the master key the locksmith had copied. "I'm not coming in, Viola," he whispered, "it's too risky, the deputy may come down at any moment. I'll give you your key now." He did so, relieved for some reason when she took it.

"Well, well," the voice said, unimpressed. "What you want me to do, boy? Run out and get myself lynched by the paddyrollers?"

"In about an hour there will be a disturbance in the court-house upstairs. The sheriff will be in the courtroom, the deputy upstairs will run out to see what's going on. There'll be a lot of confusion. You have two alternatives."

"I have what?"

"There are two things you can do, depending on how it works out. If all goes well, the slaves will run from the courtroom and climb into Farmer Ely's covered wagon, parked right in front of the main doors. If you can get outside in time, join them. If they are on their way by the time you get out, turn left and walk away. Nobody will notice, for—here . . ." He took from one of the pockets of his coat a tightly folded thin skirt, from the other a blouse, and from his medicine bag a Quaker bonnet. He pushed them through the bars. "Put these on. Leave what you're wearing right here."

The straw rustled, a shadow moved and disappeared. Not a word of thanks, that was not her nature. But if she got away this time it would be a miracle.

"Anything else I can do for you? Do you need medical attention?"

"Do I need what, boy?"

"Did those brutes hurt you? Are you wounded? I'd like to know what your condition is."

"My condition is fine. I'm dragging one leg, and I was lucky they didn't rape or bugger me before the deputies arrived. Maybe if I do this they can make up for lost time."

"Maybe," he said. "Good luck, Viola."

"Same to you, boy. See you in heaven."

There was more rustling of straw. Then, suddenly, terrifyingly, a ghoulish mug loomed through the bars. It took him a second before he realized it was she, wearing the Quaker bonnet.

He could not discern her face, only the grin of yellow teeth. "Purty?" she asked.

"I have seen prettier," Rossini said. "Godspeed, Viola."

"Godspeed yourself." She made it sound obscene.

He hurried up the stairs. In the office, the sheriff and the deputy were waiting.

"All through, Doc?" the sheriff asked, taking his feet off the desk.

"Yes." Rossini handed back the key and the list. "Thanks. See you in court. See you, Jake."

"See you, Doc."

"Be good now," the sheriff called after him.

When Lydia saw Obadiah enter the courtroom, he appeared shaken by the sight of the unruly crowd. He obviously had no experience with raucous trials; in Philadelphia they were conducted with more decorum. Here, the spectators were divided into two camps, those in favor of helping slaves escape and those against. It was that simple; neither party showed any inhibitions when it came to making clear which side they were on.

Obadiah looked so disconcerted by the whistles and boos directed at him by some rowdies in the back that Lydia rose and went up the aisle to meet him. His face lit up the moment he saw her. She put her arm through his and said, "Don't worry, it's just noise. Would thee like me to sit by thee?"

"Yes, please!" he said with such enthusiasm that she felt like kissing him. But she had made enough of a demonstration as it was; already the rowdies were yoo-hooing and whistling lecherously. Most of them were Irish laborers from the canal, out for entertainment; but there was a sprinkling of slave hunters among them. In the plaintiff's bench sat an elegant, stern-looking gentleman with a child by his side, a boy of no more than eleven, in a velvet suit.

"Come, sit down," she said.

"All rise!" the bailiff bellowed at that moment.

There was a huge noise of shuffling and grunting as the crowd rose to their feet. The islands of children on either side of the aisle looked prim and virtuous in their Quaker garb. The judge entered.

"Well," Lydia whispered, "this is it. God be with thee, Counselor."

"The Court of Baker County, Indiana, is in session!" the bailiff bellowed. "Judge Ezekiel Saunders presiding! You may sit down!"

The many-headed beast sat down, growling.

In her mind, Charity had pictured her arrival in Pendle Hill many times: a sunny little town in the hills, helpful people to show her the way; hire a hansom; Obadiah stunned by the sight of her in the lobby of the school . . . Reality proved to be a drab roadside shelter in driving rain; only one person was waiting for the stage to arrive: a hairy, coarse-featured man, hat and coat sodden with rain, calling, "Mother!" Molly O'Grady descended the wagon steps backwards, jabbering, "Tom! Tommy! Tommykins!" and fainted in the man's arms. She had fainted before, it was something she did well.

No one else, apart from a hansom and an empty buggy, the horse of which was kissing the nose of its opposite number.

Noisy Irish laborers spilled out of the Conestoga wagon with jeers, shouts, drunken curses at the rain, clamoring angrily for their luggage off the roof, answered in kind by the angry coachman, who flung grips and valises at them with a vengeance. Then Molly O'Grady, back among the living, smothered her face in wet kisses, wept, and was led away by her son to a waiting buggy. That was it.

Charity walked through a drenching rain to have a look at the hansom. She opened the door and was met by a smell of whiskey, which she had come to recognize during the journey. A sozzled old man, slumped on the seat, leered at her. "Hansom, miss?"

"Are you spoken for?"

"No, miss."

"All right. Take me to the school."

"School?"

"The Quaker boarding school."

"Ah, but there won't be anyone there, miss."

"I don't understand what you are saying."

"Everyone will be in the courthouse, miss, for the verdict. I'm going there meself."

"What *are* you talking about, man? What verdict?"

"On slaves, miss! The whole Quaker school will be there. They should be, it was them that hid 'em."

"Hid who?"

"The slaves, miss! They'll all be there. Every blessed one of them."

"But, surely, there must be someone left at the school? The children, for one thing?"

"Like I told you, the children are there too. They've been there every blessed day since the trial started, last Thursday. How would it be if I took you to the courthouse, miss? We'd go in together, you could leave your valise in the cab. Drive you to the school after the verdict. I aim to hear what the Quaker lawyer has to say. Placed a small bet meself."

"Bet?"

"Aye, the whole town's been wagering. You can get five-for-one on the Quakers. I'm betting on that fellow Woodhouse."

"All right," she said. "Take me there at once. Now!"

"Yes, miss—excuse, miss, while I get out—thank you, miss. Would this be your valise?"

"Yes! Yes! Hurry!"

"Sure, miss . . . Mind the door, miss . . ." The door slammed. He heaved her valise onto the roof, climbed into the driver's seat, and they set off.

Obadiah in court! The rain started up again, drumming like hail on the roof of the carriage.

When they arrived at what had to be the courthouse, there was no place to park the cab. Sulkies, carriages, and wagons were jammed side by side all along the curb, restless horses were nibbling each other's necks, and rain, rain everywhere, flailing the roof of the hansom, blown by the wind into gusts whirling down the pavement and soaking her as she stepped out. God! This was awful . . . "I go inside! I'll see you later!" She made a run for it under her umbrella, leaving the coachman behind.

Inside, the courtroom was stifling hot. The crowded hall reeked of sodden clothes, tobacco smoke, sweaty bodies. There were a lot of children in Quaker dress who must be from the school. The majority of the audience was made up of rough men in an angry mood. Where was Obadiah? The judge, a bewigged old man, brooded on his bench; in the dock huddled a row of Negro men and women, some with babies. There was no counsel for the defense to be seen. She looked around for the prosecutor, he was not there either. All she saw were children, some Quaker women, and rowdy, vicious-looking men, shouting, stamping their feet, laughing. She found a seat in the back row; then she spotted Obadiah.

He was sitting in front of the dock, a woman beside him. Charity knew at once who she was, even though she was not 'strikingly handsome' but a thin-faced, blue-eyed person in her thirties watching the crowd with an expression of defiance on her beaky face. Next to her, making sheep's eyes as he whispered in her ear, sat Obadiah in a wig that was too small, his shoulders sprinkled with dandruff, or so it seemed, his cravat awry. His gown looked as if he had slept in it.

The judge gaveled and cried, "May we hear the case for the owner, please?"

A fat man, who must be the bailiff, bellowed, "Silence in court!"

A rake-thin gentleman in wig and robe rose and approached the bench. Somewhere in the crowd a coarse voice yelled, "Let him have it!" The judge gaveled. The bailiff, like a giant frog rising on its hind legs, bellowed, "*Silence in court!*"

"Your Honor," the thin man began, in a tone of indifference, "these endless procedures have been a parody. The ownership of the slaves is incontestable, proven by documents, birthmarks, and the testimony of sworn witnesses. The fifteen slaves were apprehended looking for the person or persons meant to further their escape, one of whom was apprehended. When approached by officers of the law and representatives of the owner, they resorted to violence and had to be forcibly placed in custody. If it please Your Honor, having deposited with the court exhibit number one, the list of names and full description of the slaves, and exhibit two, a drawing of their identification marks, followed by the testimony of the witness Leon Rossini, physician, who identified . . ."

As the man droned on and on, naming each of the slaves as 'male' and 'female,' Charity observed Obadiah with mounting anger, directed not at him but at herself. What had possessed her to burn all her bridges behind her and make this insane expedition for a man who sat there smooching with another

woman, shoulders dusted with dandruff, a cravat like a hang-
man's knot, his wig a bird's nest? The elegant, debonair young
lawyer she loved had turned into a tramp. What in the world
could have happened to him?

There followed more dry, legal parleying about ownership
and the circumstances of the prisoners' arrest as the prosecutor
continued his deposition; finally, Obadiah rose to make his plea,
reading from a brief. His discourse was carefully worded and
spoken with dignity and composure, but Charity soon lost confidence, and so, it seemed, did everyone around her on the back
row. It was wrong to read from a piece of paper; even though
he appealed to Judge Ezekiel Saunders 'as a man, not the impersonal representative of the law,' he never actually looked at
the man. The judge listened politely, nodding occasionally in
approval, which Charity found disconcerting. "I plead with thee
to shed thy robes," Obadiah intoned, changing to plain speech;
the suggestion might have interested the judge had it not been
read from notes. "I challenge thee to remove thyself from thy
awesome seat of office and consider the human plight of these
miserable slaves, not as an official of the state but as a man." It
seemed a foolish suggestion; to ask a judge to act as a private
person was to ask him to step out of office. "Here they stand,
Friend Ezekiel, about to be handed back into bondage. Passing
judgment, thee will be passing judgment not on the fate of these
Negroes alone, but on thy own Christianity."

The judge's nod seemed to say, "Well put, young counselor."
Charity began to suspect that Obadiah was walking into a trap.

"I have the temerity, Friend Ezekiel, to compare thy pre-
dicament to that of Pontius Pilate . . ."

Charity stopped listening. Did Obadiah realize that by challenging the judge, he was in some obscure way serving the man's
purpose? He ended, saying, "I know, Friend Ezekiel, that from
a purely legal point of view my plea is an exercise in futility. All
I plead, standing before thee as a representative of the Least of
these His Brethren, is Christ's plea for mercy, the only key to
our deliverance from evil. It is in thy hands, Ezekiel Saunders,

to relieve not only our friends in the dock from the fear of that most ignoble condition to beset man, the fear of bondage, but to deliver us all from evil." He gathered his notes and sat down, welcomed with a smile by the middle-aged woman. He obviously was totally smitten with the creature. Well, Charity decided, she might as well get out now and go home. What was she doing here? She did not know this man. She had no desire to know him. She was totally clear in her own mind, in an icy, terrified way, that she had made the biggest mistake of her life. What she should do now was disappear as fast as she could, go to an inn, and take tomorrow's coach back to civilization, back to Philadelphia, back to the Charity she had been all her days, who would marry an upstanding, solid young man who shared her views.

The judge started his summing up in an almost conversational tone. "Let me start by thanking counsel for his moving plea in behalf of these unfortunate people. I am grateful, and so should all of us be, that at this moment, in this courtroom, the voice of humanity and mercy has been raised in such an admirable manner. Counselor, not only the bench but all of us present are indebted to you for speaking in behalf of our consciences. Be assured: as a private person, I would rejoice if I could now say to my dark-skinned fellow men in the dock, 'Go free, and may God go with you.' Therefore, I will now address the plaintiff."

He turned to what must be their owner, a stern, prosperous-looking man at the plaintiff's bench, and continued in the same conversational tone: "Armand Delatour, would you at this solemn moment join in the sentiments and the wishes of this community, as expressed by counsel for the defense, and retract your request that the defendants in the dock be handed back to you in slavery?"

The urbane owner patted the shoulder of the little boy beside him, who looked very worried. He rose, bowed to the judge, and said, with a French accent, "Your Honor, I too was impressed by the eloquence and sincerity of counsel for the defense. However, this is a court of law, in which all men, of necessity, act as symbols, whether they like to or not. I cannot set a precedent that will harm a cause which overrules my personal feelings in this matter. The slaveowners of the southern states have been increasingly subjected to injustice in courts north of the Ohio. Their growing indignation at these breaches of laws passed by Congress will have grave consequences for our country, unless our grievances are heard and redressed. So, much as I may regret this personally, fate wills it that I stand here as an instrument of the law on fugitive slaves, voted by Congress and duly signed by the President of the United States." He sat down, welcomed by an adoring expression of the face of the little boy.

The judge cleared his throat, arranged the papers in front of him, then said, still in that conversational tone, "Because of the unusual nature of this case, I will not rebuke the plaintiff for reminding the bench of its duties—as I did not rebuke counsel for deviating from normal procedure when addressing the bench. We are faced, as a community, with an insoluble conflict. The citizens of this town and this county would like nothing better than to turn down the plaintiff's request—"

Some men among the audience booed; the bailiff rose, but the judge gestured him to sit.

"To consider one man as the owner of another man," he continued, "is abhorrent to us all. But, alas, the law knows no emotion. Dr. Leon Rossini has checked the identification marks of the defendants; these leave no doubt that under the law, as it stands, the plaintiff is entitled to apply for the restitution of these people as his property. So, in the fervent hope of nobler times to come, I, Ezekiel Saunders, Justice of Baker County in the State of Indiana, hereby order and direct the bailiff to restore to Armand Delatour of Morning Rose Plantation, Pointe Coupée Parish, State of Louisiana, the following individuals, at present aligned before me . . ."

He began to read out the names of the slaves; Charity did not stay to listen.

She hurried up the aisle to the doors of the lobby, passing a young girl—from the school, no doubt—who stood with a kerchief pressed to her mouth; outside, beyond the carriages and the wagons jammed together, sounded the lowing of cows.

She stood on the courthouse steps wondering if she should wait inside the hansom cab for the driver when she heard behind her the angry shouting of men, the high-pitched shrieks of children.

In the courtroom, at teacher Will's signal, Bonny Baker had released his mice. As arranged, Himsha Woodhouse started to scream, "*Mice! Mice!*" The slaves, in a stunning burst of speed, sprinted from the dock to the doors; the moment they passed, Bathsheba Tucker threw herself in the aisle, in the way of the marshals going after them. She rolled on the floor, screaming, kicking, showing black stockings and white knickers; other girls threw themselves on the floor, climbed the backs of benches, screaming, "*Mice! Help! Mice!*" The women in the courtroom ran squealing into the aisles, blocking them totally as they stood there yelling "Mice! Mice!" holding their skirts around their ankles.

The Negroes reached the street, piled into Farmer Ely's wagon; the farmer's wife whipped the horses, the last of the escapees barely made it.

A small band of slave hunters from the back of the courtroom reached the street, wanting to run to their horses tethered across the road, but to their fury and confusion they found themselves confronted by the chaos of a milling herd of cattle. It looked as if hundreds of cows, lowing, bellowing, tails raised, were crowding the street outside the courthouse.

It was quite a while before the men, joined by the sheriff and his deputies by then, could gallop off in pursuit of the wagon which, someone shouted, was racing down Martin Street toward the pike. The crowd from the courtroom was now streaming outside; inside, teacher Abner called the children to order. They rose to their feet, dusted themselves off, and started to leave.

Instead of joining them, Bonny Baker went down on hands

and knees between the benches to try and recapture his mice. During the trial he had peeked at them often in the box at his feet, secretly; each time, they had turned their little faces up to him in mute supplication, especially Plumpy, the friendliest of them all, who had seemed frantic with fright. Now Bonny crawled along between the benches, making sucking noises as he always did when he came into the potting shed with food. "Plumpy! Spotty!" Then he saw Plumpy.

It was she; she was the only one with three white socks on her feet. All that was left of the rest of her was a blotch of bloody pulp and dirty fur. He pulled his handkerchief out of his pocket, tried to scrape up the filthy mess; it was wet and sticky, so he spread the handkerchief over her and crawled on. But although he called and whistled, peered under the benches in all directions, he saw no fleeting little shadows. Fervently hoping not to find other horrible blotches, he crawled on; then a boy's voice asked, "What are you doing there?"

He rose to his knees and saw, standing at the far end, the little boy who had been sitting next to the slaveowner. The boy was white as a sheet, his face was wet, as if he had been crying.

"I'm looking for my mice."

"*Your* mice?"

"Yes . . ."

"*You* brought them here? With you?"

"Yes."

"Why?"

"Because they told me to." He felt like crying himself.

The little boy's face became ugly with anger. "You did it on purpose? Let those mice loose on *purpose*?"

Bonny did not reply; he wished he had not told him.

"Those slaves were my father's!" the little boy cried, his voice thick with tears. "He worked for them all his life! You are a thief, a *thief*! You are all *thieves*!"

A voice called from the lobby, "George! Where on earth—"

"Coming, Father!"

Bonny ducked between the benches, waited a while, then straightened up and found himself face to face with the slave-owner. The man looked down at him sternly. "My son tells me you are looking for your mice."

His voice was pleasant enough, but his eyes made Bonny turn on his heels and run as fast as he could down the narrow gap between the benches, up the aisle, and out into the lobby.

He stopped running only after he had reached the street. It was full of cows; in the distance, he saw the children march down the sidewalk in a single file, pressed against the houses because of the cows. He leaned against the wall to catch his breath, heard angry men's voices, and saw a bunch of irate slave hunters headed straight for him. Terrified, he ran.

A stunned Charity had watched the chaos of the slaves' escape with pure astonishment, which changed to unease when she realized that the children had played a crucial part in what had clearly been a planned operation. When the angry deputies, or whatever they were, gave up trying to force their way through the herd and turned around, she felt she had better get out of their way. Looking for the hansom, she heard shouts behind her, screams of pain. On the steps of the courthouse, the angry men were now flailing sticks and fists, beating up somebody. A woman screamed, "Stop! Stop, you monsters! Stop, in the name of God!"

Charity caught a momentary glimpse of a woman kneeling beside the man, her hands uplifted, trying to stop the beating; when she recognized who it was, she realized, sick with the shock, that they were beating up Obadiah.

She did not stop to think. She ran up the steps and fought her way through the rowdies, kicked, shoved, used her elbows, battled her way to where the woman sat. There he lay, bleeding, covering the back of his head with his hands, face down; they were beating him, kicking—

Before she knew what she was doing, she threw herself on top of him, sheltering him with her body. Blows hammered on

her back with searing pain, the like of which she had never felt
before; but she managed to get hold of one of his hands and
whispered at the back of his head, "It's all right! It's all right!
I'm here, it's me!"

By the time the sheriff's deputies got to her she was lying
quite still, only her mind alive in a body that no longer felt pain.

The first Rossini heard about the beatings was when Harlan
Tucker accosted his buggy, in Baker Street, while waiting for
Farmer Kowalski's cows to pass.

"Thee had better go and have a look at them, Doctor," the
dour old Quaker said, peering up at him from the sidewalk.
"They took them to the school."

"What's that?"

"The Philadelphia lawyer and some city woman. Reckon
she's his wife, by the way she behaved, she's too young to be
his mother. Where was thee? I thought I saw thee in the
courtroom?"

It did not seem wise to tell the old buzzard more than he
already knew; he was an arch-orthodox who disapproved sternly
of the underground railroad. "I was called out to see a patient,
before the verdict." In effect, he had gone to the sheriff's office
to make sure that the deputy would run to the courtroom when
the riot started.

"Well, thee has two more waiting for thee at the school.
Badly bruised, I reckon." He said it in a tone implying that it
served them right.

"Who did it?" Rossini asked.

"The slave hunters," the old man replied. "Ten more seconds, I'd say, and they would have kilt them, at least the woman.
She got the worst of it. Well, there thee goes."

The cows had passed, and Rossini took off for the school at
a fast clip. A city woman shielding the Philadelphia lawyer? So
far as he knew, Obadiah Woodhouse had no wife. Well, he'd
soon find out.

He did indeed. The school was in a state of great agitation, part triumph, part outrage. Children's voices as well as Lydia's welcomed him as he entered the lobby.

"Well, who do I see first? I gather the woman took the brunt of it. Is that so?"

"Yes, Doctor," Lydia said. "I'll take thee to her. She was unconscious when we carried her up there. I hope she's going to be all right."

"Who is it?" he asked as they climbed the stairs.

"Obadiah Woodhouse's fiancée," Lydia replied, in a tone that made him look at her.

"You don't say," he said.

They went the rest of the way to the hospital room in silence.

On the bed nearest the window lay a still form. Himsha, the Indian girl, sat stiffly in attendance beside her.

"Thee can go now, Himsha," Lydia whispered. "The doctor is here, he'll take care of her."

The girl rose; Rossini addressed her: "Thank you. Is she conscious?"

"Oh, yes," the girl said calmly. "We talked."

"Talked about what?" Lydia asked.

"I told her I was Uncle Obadiah's ward. She said they were going to be married."

"You don't say," Rossini said. "Now leave us to it, will you?"

The girl turned around and left the room.

"Miss—er—" He looked up and asked, "What's her name?"

"I believe it's Woodhouse," Lydia replied. "They are cousins."

"Miss Woodhouse?"

The still form, lying on its stomach, grunted. There was a dark patch on the back of her head where blood had coagulated in her hair. What he could see of her face seemed unbruised, but was distorted in agony.

"I'm Dr. Rossini. I would like to have a look at you and see what I can do."

She grunted.

He signaled Lydia on the other side of the bed to help him remove the blanket. The woman had been put to bed in her gown, which was sticky and discolored with blood.

"I'm afraid I may have to cut your gown, Miss Woodhouse," he said.

No reaction.

He took the surgical scissors from his medicine bag and was about to start cutting from the collar down when Lydia said, "There's no need for this, Doctor. I can unbutton it."

She did so deftly; when she was through, her fingers were red with blood. The undergarments, however, had to be cut, and when finally he bared the girl's back, he shook his head in anger and concern. That hooligans could bring themselves to so cruelly beat a helpless woman! He could only hope they had not damaged any vertebrae, or ribs.

It took a bit of gentle probing and questioning, which she answered in grunts and moans, before he could conclude that there was no internal damage; but the skin was broken in several places. For that to happen through a layer of clothes, they really had had to apply maximum force, the bastards.

Finally, he said, "Well, she seems to be basically all right. Now get me some warm water, will you, and some bandages; meanwhile, I'll give her a sedative."

Lydia hurried out. When the door was closed he asked softly, "Can you hear me, Miss Woodhouse?"

The young woman grunted without opening her eyes. The wound on the back of her head was the most serious. He hoped the Indian girl had not told a lie when she said that she had spoken to her and received a reply. It was important that he find out. "I don't want to press you for answers, but I would like you to just tell me how you're feeling."

"All right . . ." she said thickly, her eyes still closed.

"Which part of you hurts most? Your head? Your back? Your neck? Can you tell me?"

"Neck," she said.

"Could you open your eyes for me?"

She was lying on her right eye, but at last she opened the left. It was blue and young, and bloodshot.

"Mind if I lift the eyelid for a moment?"

He did so. "Could you roll your eye for me, please?"

She did. "I'm sure you're in pain," he said, his hand on her shoulder in a gesture of reassurance, "but I don't think it's serious. You'll just be very stiff for a while."

She grunted.

"That was a very courageous thing you did, Miss Wood-house."

She did not answer. Then the eye opened again and gazed at him. She grimaced, in an effort to smile.

Lydia came in with hot water.

"Well," Rossini said, "let's give her a wash-down. Have you got the bandages?"

"Yes, Doctor, here . . ."

Ten minutes later, he had done all he could and gave the patient a sedative. "Now, where's the other one?"

"Thee means Obadiah?"

"So I gather."

"He is in the large guest room, one floor below, number fifteen."

"Get some help to change her into a nightgown, or whatever. It may be best if you just cover her with a sheet and leave her for now. Once the medication takes effect, it will be less painful to change her into a nightdress."

"Yes, Doctor. May I come and see thee after thee has seen Obadiah?"

"Certainly," he said.

Too bad. They would have made a good couple.

In the guest room he found Obadiah fast asleep, but looking hale and healthy. The young man barely woke while Rossini examined him. His bruises were superficial; the only really pain-ful location was his left knee. He screamed dramatically when Rossini tried to bend it; nothing seemed broken, so the doctor decided to let it be and covered him up again. The young man asked drowsily, "How is she?"

"She'll live," Rossini said, irritated as usual by male antics. Compared to the girl upstairs, who had truly saved him from serious injury, his performance was like that of a husband in couvade. One of the first discoveries any family physician makes is that the attributes men ascribe to themselves are, in effect, those of women: courage, constancy, loyalty, stoicism under pain. All the female faults agreed upon by men are typical of their own sex, down to histrionics under pain and the inability to keep a secret.

Faintly disgusted, Rossini closed the door, to be met in the passage by Jesse, who was in a state of great excitement.

"Doc!" he cried. "You know what? Viola has escaped! She managed to get out of prison while the slaves were running away! The whole town is full of it, the sheriff is spitting with rage."

"You don't say," Rossini said. As he crossed the lobby to the front door, the Indian girl stopped him.

"Doctor?"

"Yes?"

"Is he all right?"

"He is very much all right," he replied. "The one who took the beating was—isn't she a relative of yours?"

The girl said coldly, "A distant aunt."

"Well, if any laurels are to be distributed, they should go to her. She has the courage of a lioness."

"I should hope so," the child said, much too adult for her age. "Gulielma Woodhouse was her great-aunt." She turned her back on him and walked away.

A few hours later, in bed at the school, Obadiah finally found a position in which nothing hurt any more. Not much, at least, on condition he did not move. In that forced stillness, eyes closed, he was drifting back to sleep when he heard the door open, the rustle of skirts; his eyelids darkened when someone moved between him and the window. He opened his eyes and saw it was Lydia.

"How is thee?" she whispered.

He tried to answer, but his jaw was too painful, all he could do was smile with his upper lip, which must make it look like a snarl. "Tha—ee." Impossible to make it sound like 'Thank thee.' "

"Don't talk," she said, stroking his sweat-soaked hair.

But he should say more. What she had done was heroic, magnificent. What other woman would try to shield a man from kicks and blows with her own body? He remembered the weight of her body on his back, he remembered thuds, as if they were beating him through a mattress or a thick carpet. He gazed at her silhouette in the window. How come she was so calm, unscathed? They must have stopped kicking and beating virtually at once after he passed out. Even so—what a woman! "How's—" he could not get out 'thee,' it hurt too much.

"She's all right," Lydia said. "Dr. Rossini has been to see her. She—well, she is hurt, but he does not think there is permanent damage."

Who was she talking about? He wasn't interested. One of the children. Oh, God! That would be serious. That was exactly what he had foreseen when he warned them against involving the children. The parents—

"Who wah't?" he croaked.

There was a pause, as if she had to think. Then she asked in an odd voice, "Thee doesn't know?"

Stupid question to ask of a man who had been lying with his face squashed on the courthouse steps while they beat the living daylights out of him. "No," he said. Smiling turned out to be painful in a different way. Why had the doctor been so casual? He might have a broken jaw!

"It was Charity."

"Chee—*hoo?*"

"Thy Charity. Charity Woodhouse. She came to surprise thee."

He froze. "Huh? *Huh?!*"

"She was the one who shielded thee, not me. I just sat there and yelled at them."

"*Huh?* Huh?"

"She arrived on the Richmond coach, while the trial was in progress. A cabby took her to the courthouse. When they were beating thee, she was there all of a sudden, and threw herself on top of thee. They really let her have it, the swine."

"No—*ee?*"

"Sorry, not me. She's a plucky girl, all power to her. Thirsty?"

"Huh."

"Meaning what?"

"Huh."

"She's upstairs, in the hospital. Don't worry, she—"

He tried to get up; it was like trying to lift a tombstone. Maybe he was dead, and all this was a dream.

"Don't move!" she warned. "She's all right. She's fine! The doctor is with her. Don't move, thee'll hurt thyself."

He wanted to say: 'Thee was wonderful. I remember thee trying to keep them away. I remember thinking: What a glorious woman.' Now it turned out to have been Charity. Damn the mail! It was too damn slow between here and Philadelphia! What a mess! Charity throwing herself on top of him? Without thinking, straight from the coach? Marvelous, terrific; but what a mess!

"Don't cry," she said. "She is fine. Thee is fine too. You'll be fit to pass meeting in no time. Don't cry."

Stupid woman! Please, God, give me time! Make me pass out again!

He did pass out. Almost. He stayed passed out until he heard the door close. Then he wept some more, at his ease.

At dead of night—at least it felt like night—he could stand it no longer. He was as stiff as a plank, every movement hurt like blazes, but he had to go and see Charity if he had to crawl on all fours.

It almost came to that: if he had not been afraid of waking people behind the closed doors along the passage, he would have screamed with pain. He made it to the hospital, where he presumed she was; he had seen it once before: a high-ceilinged room full of white beds smelling of mothballs. He did not remember which door; he found the right one at the third try. It was indeed a high-ceilinged white room, looking bright with the light of the full moon. In the bed closest to the window lay a still, slight form; the other beds were empty. He tiptoed—ouch!—to the foot of the bed, still not sure that it was indeed Charity. But who else could it be?

The small, slight form gave a surprisingly masculine grunt. Was it a man?

It was not. He tried to kneel beside the bed, but could not manage because of his damaged knee; he just lay, one leg outstretched, one elbow on the bed, in a bizarre ballet stance. The girl's face in the moonlight opened one eye and said, "O—"

Was it 'O' for Obadiah, or 'Oh' for 'Not *him* again'?

"Hallo, love . . ." he whispered, or tried to. It came out as 'Ah-oh.'

"Grr."

Was it a groan? Was it . . . He peered closer, to check if she was really awake or whether they had sedated her; then an arm came from under the blankets, reached around his neck, and pulled him down screaming, smothering his yowls with a kiss.

After a moment of stunned shock he threw himself into an irrevocable future by climbing, wincing, onto the bed. He threw an arm around her; this time it was her turn to scream, and his to smother her scream with a kiss.

Himsha Woodhouse, who had been delegated by teacher Lydia to keep an eye on her aunt and to sound a warning the moment there was any change in her condition, woke up with a start in the armchair in the anteroom where she had been sleeping.

From the sickroom came agonizing screams. Startled wide awake, she was about to run to warn teacher Lydia when she decided to go in there and have a look first, for the screams had sounded desperate.

She rushed to the room, opened the door and saw, in the moonlight, Aunt Charity, twice normal size, struggling and thrashing under the covers. She thought for a second that the woman, insane with suffering, was wrestling with death, then she realized there were two people in the bed. Far from wrestling with death, Aunt Charity was bundling with what could only be Uncle Obadiah.

Deciding that teacher Lydia should not be alerted but kept away, Himsha closed the door and went back to the anteroom.

She sat upright in her chair, staring at the moonlit window, wondering what Aunt Charity would look like. For some reason, this was the moment she decided not to marry Bonny Baker after all.

CHAPTER 10

RICHMOND, INDIANA

September 1833

The morning before his departure for Philadelphia—and thence home to England—Mordecai was called upon to attend an emergency meeting of the school committee of Indiana Yearly Meeting. The latest news from Pendle Hill was that something utterly scandalous had taken place: children under the school's care had been used, without the knowledge, let alone permission, of their parents, to create a disturbance in a courtroom, as a result of which fifteen slaves had escaped. Now this had nothing to do with theology or differences in the interpretation of God's love, this was a gross abuse of parents' trust, not to mention the disrespect for the law this action must have fostered in the children.

The committee was unanimous in its condemnation; those among the faculty who had hatched the plot and taken an active part in its execution must not only be dismissed from their posts but read out of Meeting. It was decided that four committee members would visit the school forthwith to announce this decision.

They proceeded to discuss arrangements; Mordecai had just closed his eyes when he heard someone ask, "Would thee, Friend Mordecai?"

What had the question been? He looked around the table, saw their expectant faces, and realized they were waiting for his reply.

"I would like to hear more," he said evasively.

The chairman explained to him: "We feel thy presence would make our confrontation with the faculty less impersonal, introduce an element of caring. Would thee accompany us, perhaps act as our spokesman?"

"I? Why should I? I am an Englishman, not even a member of this Yearly Meeting!"

"Thy eloquence would help explain to them the essence of their failing."

"And what would the essence be?"

"That whatever Friends may think individually about Quaker involvement in the underground railroad, to use children in an unlawful act without their parents' permission is a betrayal of trust."

"No eloquence is needed to make that clear, I would say."

"There are so many personality conflicts involved, we would be most grateful if thee would speak for us."

He looked from one to the other. It was a trap. He was being drawn into a situation that did not concern him.

"It seems thy erstwhile companion was involved, not only as lawyer for the defense, but as a fellow plotter," the chairman said.

"Well . . ." He was struck by a thought that unnerved him. This would mean he would see the wanton young woman again.

"Would thee, Friend?"

He knew it was a momentous decision, but he could not make out why. "As you wish," he said.

They closed the meeting with a period of silence.

• • •

Early in the morning, Jesse entered the principal's study without knocking and said, his voice low, "The sheriff and Harlan Tucker are downstairs. They want to search the school."

Abner went to the window. In front of the school a dozen horses were hitched; deputies were standing around, chatting. Why so many? With his back to Jesse, he said, "Ask Harlan and the sheriff to come up."

Harlan Tucker, chairman of Pendle Hill Monthly Meeting's school committee, was the first to enter. A tall, gloomy man in his sixties, he looked even gloomier now, as if visiting a house in mourning. The sheriff followed, taking off his hat.

"Good morning, Abner Best," Harlan said gloomily. "Thee knows Joshua Standing?"

"Of course," Abner replied. "Good morning, Joshua Standing." He would have to take care during this conversation not to call the man 'Sheriff'; Harlan Tucker was a stickler about the testimony against titles.

The two sat down in front of the desk, Abner behind it. "What can I do for you?"

"Joshua Standing has a warrant to search this school," Harlan Tucker said. "Before he does, I wish to put thee a question. Are there any slaves hidden in this school?"

"Not to my knowledge."

"Very well, Joshua Standing. Do thy duty."

Despite his martial bearing, the sheriff appeared uncomfortable, like a pupil sent to see the principal. "I needn't tell you people that I hate to do this. I've always thought highly of you Quakers—"

"Yes, yes," Harlan Tucker said dourly. "We know all that. Now let us see thee put that sentiment into practice."

This seemed to restore the sheriff's self-confidence. "But let's get one thing straight," he said. "I do not intend to give you people preferential treatment. I am investigating a serious offense. I—"

"Thee has a warrant to search this school," Harlan Tucker interrupted. "Get on with it."

"Allow me to run this investigation my own way, Mr. Tucker!" The sheriff was angry now; Abner wondered why wily old Harlan had thought it necessary to goad the man. "To start with: was it you, Mr. Best, who arranged for mice to be let loose in the courtroom?"

Abner hoped the sudden wave of nausea that overcame him did not show. He had not slept all night, worrying about this question.

Harlan Tucker replied for him. "What does thee mean, Joshua Standing: 'arranged'?"

The sheriff looked from one to the other, his jaw set. "I see," he said. "It's going to be like that, is it? In that case, I might as well stop now and leave you two to the judge."

"Meaning what, may I ask?" Harlan Tucker became more formidable by the minute.

The sheriff replied grimly, "I've been dealing with you people for sixteen years. I would sooner question a riverboat gambler than a Quaker."

"Explain thyself," Harlan Tucker requested.

"You people are supposed to speak the truth at all times, aren't you?"

"So?" Harlan Tucker answered.

"Then why do you answer every question with a question? Dealing with you is like—like groping for a needle inside a feather pillow."

"I have no idea what thee is talking about, Joshua Standing," Harlan Tucker said grandly. "Why not do thy duty instead of sitting here making small talk?"

The sheriff seemed to consider taking him on, but thought better of it. He turned to Abner. "Did you or did you not release those mice in the courtroom?"

"No," Abner replied firmly.

"Think carefully now," the sheriff continued. "The owner of the slaves is going to lodge a complaint, and Judge Saunders is as mad as a wet hen. So think carefully before you reply."

"Friend Joshua," Harlan Tucker rumbled, "thee put Abner Best a straight question, he gave thee a straight answer. Now shall we get on with it?"

The sheriff looked from one to the other, then shrugged his shoulders. "As you wish. But you would do well to realize who your friends are in this community." When there came no reaction to that, he continued, "Did the wagon the bounty hunters were chasing belong to this school?"

"No."

The sheriff sighed. "Very well," he said, rising. "We'll search the building. Would either of you gentlemen care to come along?"

"That will not be necessary," Harlan Tucker replied. "We trust thee."

Without another word, the sheriff left.

The moment he was gone, the old Quaker turned on Abner. "Pray explain thyself, Abner Best," he said ominously. "I know thee did not release the mice in person, but who did?"

"A little boy, pupil of this school. He brought them with him into the courtroom; at a given moment they got away. That much I can affirm."

Harlan Tucker stared at him. "This school has become part of an organization known as the 'underground railroad' without being liberated to do so by the Meeting. True or false?"

Abner wavered. Harlan Tucker was a harder nut to crack than the sheriff. "Is this an official inquiry, Harlan Tucker?"

The old man regarded him without tenderness. "Abner Best," he said, "I warned thee months ago that the way thee and thy sister were running this school created a sense of unease in Indiana Yearly Meeting. Instead of heeding that word to the wise, thee has acted in a manner that has now resulted in law-breaking and scandal. Surely thee does not expect me to protect thee from the school committee of Yearly Meeting, the way I protected thee from the world a moment ago?"

"I understand," Abner said, feeling goose pimples rise on his arms.

"In my capacity as chairman of the Monthly Meeting's school committee, my advice to Yearly Meeting will be that thee, thy sister, and all others among the faculty involved in this illegal action shall be dismissed from your posts. Until then, thee is suspended."

They sat facing one another for a moment in silence. It was a fateful moment, yet it made no impression on Abner, for his mind was a blank. He became aware of the breathless wigwagging of the clock on the mantelpiece. Then he asked, "When does this go into effect?"

Harlan Tucker replied, poker-faced, "The school committee does not have the authority to suspend anyone without a sense of the Meeting, in this case, Indiana Yearly Meeting. Until then, go ahead." The canny old eyes watched him unblinkingly.

"I do not understand . . ."

"Whatever thee or others do until then will make no difference. Your goose is cooked." He rose arthritically. Once on his feet, hand on his hip, he said, "So go ahead. Help any poor devil who might come to this school asking for shelter, for as long as thou canst."

"Thank thee, Harlan," Abner said, trying to sound equally stolid, but overwhelmed by the childish urge to cry.

Harlan Tucker said, "Good day."

"Thank thee, Harlan."

The old man went to the door and closed it behind him without looking back.

When Dr. Rossini returned to the school, he found it in the process of being searched by the sheriff and his deputies. Everyone was in a state of utter dejection.

Its days as a station on the underground railroad were definitely over; still, Viola, with a brazenness that was either heroic or fatalistic, had contacted him less than twenty-four hours after her escape. She needed two nights' shelter for a batch of twelve passengers, urgently. Rossini had agreed to pass on the message, but he hesitated as he stood before the door to the principal's study. He knocked.

"Come!"

Abner Best behind his empty desk looked even sallower than usual. "Yes, Doctor?"

"How is your wife?"

"God knows."

Never before had he reacted with callousness to anything that had to do with his wife. Was it rebellion, or part of his state of despondency? The progress of the sheriff and his crew through the school was far from orderly. Overexcited children were running about unsupervised, the faculty was steeped dramatically in gloom; the whole town had turned against them, as had the elders in Richmond. Abner looked as if he heard the wheels of the tumbril turning; Rossini hesitated to hasten his moment of execution. "I'm afraid we have another emergency on our hands, Abner," he said with an apologetic smile. "Viola urgently needs shelter for a dozen passengers, for two nights."

Abner, with startling calm, replied, "Of course, Doctor. For when would that be?"

"Tonight, until day after tomorrow, in the afternoon."

"Any special requirements?"

Rossini could not believe his ears. Well, better forge the iron while it was hot. "That afternoon, you would need to call a general meeting, or something, to get everyone off the grounds, children included. Some event in the Assembly Hall. I'd need two hours, say."

"Very well. A meeting for marriage. Would that do?"

"That would do."

"Starting at two o'clock? That would give you your two hours, with the reception."

"Splendid. Who'd be the happy couple?"

"Obadiah Woodhouse and his cousin."

"But she can barely walk!"

"She'll walk for the cause," Abner said with uncharacteristic humor. He turned out to be one of those who thrive on crises.

Either that, or sheer panic had caused a dissociation from reality.

"Many thanks, Abner."

"Any time, Doc!" Abner crowed, alarmingly.

The meeting for marriage in the school's assembly room had been gathered in silence for twenty minutes when the doors in the back opened and the bridal couple walked down the aisle. They both looked like fresh casualties of war, the groom limping with the aid of a stick and sporting two ghoulish black eyes; the bride, whose normal appearance no one as yet had seen, like a young actress trying to impersonate an old woman: shuffling, stiff-limbed, with the glassy stare of those who dare not move their heads. To Lydia, she looked like a very tough cookie indeed, far too tough for sensitive, delicate Obadiah—well, meow, et cetera. There they went, for richer, for poorer, in sickness and in health, come slave hunters or sheriffs, till violent death would them part, if the ravishing little battle-ax had a taste for adventurous Quaker concerns. Meow indeed.

Two seats were reserved for the couple on the facing bench; Lydia, at the corner, rose to let them pass. The meeting resumed its silent worship. The children, well trained, relapsed into motionless torpor after the momentary diversion. After ten more minutes of silence, Lydia felt Obadiah rise beside her. Charity must have done the same, good for her.

"Friends," he started, in the solemn voice befitting the occasion, "in the presence of God and of this assembly, I herewith take my Friend Charity to be my lawful wedded wife, and promise to be unto her, with divine assistance, a loving and faithful husband for as long as we both shall live."

Then Charity spoke, almost inaudibly. "In the presence of my Friend Obadiah—I mean God—I promise to be unto him—" She realized she had left something out; after a moment's hesitation, she resumed, ". . . be unto him with divine assistance a loving and faithful wife for as long as we both shall live." Luckily, the wedding certificate, prepared before the event, carried after each vow the rider 'or words to that effect,' or she might have run into some stickler on some future committee for Ministry and Worship who would have frowned at her mixing up her husband and the Almighty. Meow, meow, a chorus of cats. Shame on thee, Lydia Best.

The meeting was supposed to continue for another half-hour; Lydia expected someone to rise and minister as was the custom after an exchange of vows. But no one did, and Lydia found her mind wandering. What would she have to say to the happy couple, if she were to rise and speak her mind? The two had a normal life ahead of them; she herself and most of the others were certain to be fired. If God was love, how could He desert them after what they had done in His name? How could their involvement in the railroad have ended in this disaster for themselves? But that was water under the bridge, they had known what they were doing before they did it.

She glanced briefly at Obadiah beside her. He looked as radiant and flushed with happiness as a man could with two black eyes. A honeymoon, and then they would move to some large city—

She saw the back door being opened. Five strange men in Quaker garb came in. She had no idea who they were, until she recognized Mordecai Monk. The sight of him made her go rigid with alarm. The slaves! Twelve escaped slaves were hidden in the cellar, to be collected any moment now! She looked about her; no one else on the facing bench seemed to have noticed as yet that they had been joined by strangers. The bridal couple were sitting with their eyes closed, the rest of the elders were probably asleep. What to do? Where was Jesse? She dared not look around too obviously.

The five men, after a brief hesitation, sat down in the last row and joined in meeting for worship; Mordecai Monk lifted his face heavenward in a theatrical demonstration of devotion. Immediately she was overcome by loathing for the man. She *loathed* the rapist, hypocrite, gasbag, mellifluous blatherskate! Her mouth turned bitter with the bile of hatred as she stared at him. There he sat, face uplifted as if sunning himself, radiating devotion, a giant toddler gazing up at Daddy. What was he doing here?

She became so worked up about what he might be up to that she closed her eyes, though not in worship.

After the signing of the wedding certificate, Harlan Tucker invited faculty and newlyweds to join him and the five representatives of Yearly Meeting in the principal's study. Charity Woodhouse was tired and went to lie down for a rest; Obadiah was collared by Mordecai Monk. The man must have exerted superhuman self-control not to minister during the meeting for marriage; now he got his own back. The moment the introductions had been completed he started to minister—there was no other word for it, as no one could get a word in edgeways—about 'the sad, sad fall from grace when teachers, especially Quaker teachers, abused the time-hallowed sacred trust of parents who placed in their care the harmless, innocent souls of their little, little children, of whom Christ had said—'

It was a rather bewildering speech, Obadiah thought. As always, the man phrased it sonorously, came up with analogies and images which, if their heads had not been on the block, they might have admired. 'Transforming the dove of peace into a bird of prey' was what they were guilty of by disturbing the court proceedings, and they had 'made off with the innocence of children, like eagles with struggling silver fish.' They also had 'turned the Shining Light into a will-o'-the-wisp,' it was not clear where or when. Actually, the mere fact of the man's presence on this painful occasion was bizarre, for what in the world did a traveling English evangelist have to do with Indiana Yearly Meeting chastising the faculty of a rural boarding school? He had not been present at the trial, he had not even been aware of the school's being a station on the underground railroad; he had marched out in a huff when Lydia had interrupted his peroration, he had packed his bags, moved to the inn, and left the next morning for Richmond.

Could he be responsible for this visit by the Quaker Inquisition? Had he egged on the hotheads of Indiana Yearly Meeting, who fulminated against any involvement by Quakers in the escape of slaves 'because it did not minister to the owners'? The more Obadiah observed him standing there, sounding off like a harmonium with the vox humana pulled out, the less sympathy he felt for the self-obsessed poet. Three cheers for Quaker Art; but Quaker artists were a different matter. In America the man had turned from a minstrel into a demagogue.

Harlan Tucker, chairman of the local school committee, and not a poetic soul, finally interrupted Mordecai's peroration to ask, "May we now hear what Yearly Meeting has decided in this matter?"

Mordecai, winged in mid-flight, sat down pouting. One of the four strangers, the chairman of the Yearly Meeting's school committee, brought out a piece of paper, cleared his throat, and read aloud the recommendations of the committee. Abner Best, William Martin, Jesse McHair, and Lydia Best should be dismissed, Uriah Martin, Adam and Margaret Higgins suspended. Whether Abner Best, Jesse McHair, William Martin, and Lydia Best could be maintained as members of the Society of Friends was up to the committee for Ministry and Worship of Indiana Yearly Meeting, but the committee's recommendation was that they should be read out of Meeting.

This, Obadiah thought, was excessive and vindictive. He was about to speak when Lydia asked, in her unfortunate imperious manner, "And what are we supposed to do with ourselves after this, Friend? Commit hara-kiri?"

The committee chairman obviously did not know what 'hara-kiri' meant, only a history teacher would, or a salesman of Oriental geegaws. Abner rose unheroically and excused himself, presumably to be sick. The silence that followed his departure seemed a good opportunity to state a few home truths.

"I hope that Friends will allow me a few words," Obadiah started, smiling to establish his harmlessness. "Considering that both my wife and I have been beaten like gongs in connection with the school's action, and that we are not part of the faculty and do not intend to be, it might be helpful if I were to present a point of view slightly different from yours."

The committee looked pained. Mordecai Monk, despite himself, was interested. Drama, that was what he lived by: masterscenes. Maybe this would present him with new material for his ministry, which was in dire need of refreshment.

"During the past few weeks," Obadiah continued, "I have come to the conclusion that the problem of slavery is more important to the Society of Friends than meets the eye. We have all lived with lip service to abolitionism since we were babes in arms, so have our parents and our grandparents; but Philadelphia Yearly Meeting took ninety years before it finally accepted a minute against slavery. We are victims of a delusion if we believe that abolitionism is merely a spiritual concern; slavery is an economic necessity. The Southern States cannot survive without slavery, Friends' plantations there would all go bankrupt without slavery. Boniface Baker, patron saint of this school, proved as much by donating his plantation to his slaves, with dire results for all of them: their plantation was stolen, and they were resold in the open market. I am a scion, I think the word is, of a family of so-called Quaker princes. They consider anyone who says that slavery must be abolished to be a fool, although they will not say so openly. They pay lip service to abolitionism as a time-hallowed ideal, but anyone who becomes involved in helping slaves escape risks being read out of Meeting." He smiled, despite the obvious discomfort of the committee. "I am raking all this up because you are, in actual fact, trying to silence the challenge facing all Christians—what is described in the parable of the king in St. Matthew: 'I was ahungered, and ye gave me meat; I was thirsty, and ye gave me drink—' "

At that moment the door was pushed open by Abner, as white as a sheet. He said to a shadowy group of people behind him in the hallway, "Come in, please!" Then he addressed the committee. "Friends, here are some people I want you to meet." Slowly, hesitantly, twelve Negroes filed into the room. They were clad in rags, demoralized by terror and lack of sleep; one woman was holding an infant. As they shuffled in, the committee was clearly at a loss as to how to react. Mordecai Monk rose to his feet; one by one, the others followed suit. The slaves facing them, ill at ease, uncomprehending, averted their eyes.

"Friends," Abner said in a voice shrill with stress, "these are guests of the school who arrived unexpectedly, a few days ago . . ." He seemed to falter on seeing the anger in Harlan Tucker's eyes, but continued bravely, "Let me introduce them to you: Jonathan Curry . . . Henry Washington . . ."

It was obviously an act of desperation, typical, to Obadiah, of the muddleheadedness of these good people. It might be a splendid gesture to introduce slaves the school was hiding to the committee; it was the death knell for the slaves themselves. The moment this splendid demonstration was over, the four gentlemen from Richmond, not to mention Mordecai Monk, would be on their way to town, and chances were that one of them would alert the sheriff, which meant a posse in the courtyard within the hour.

Abner must have realized that his ploy had failed dismally; after the introductions were over he muttered something about 'each of these people being unique, irreplaceable, never seen on earth before, never to be seen again,' but the five men were impervious to Quaker platitudes. Suddenly, in obvious desperation, Abner turned to the black mother, took the sleeping infant from her arms, and proffered it to Mordecai Monk, as if for inspection. It was a ludicrous moment of bathos; in a last lunge of folly he cried, "Take her! Take her, Friend Mordecai! Hold her! Thee is not dealing in abstractions, this is a matter between thee and she! This is Rebecca McCauley. Will *thee* send *her* back into slavery? Will thee? Can thee? *Look at her!*"

To his astonishment, Obadiah saw a look of panic on the face of Mordecai, who, dumbstruck, had taken the baby. For a few moments the Quaker poet stared at the black infant in his hands as if he had been given a boa constrictor to hold; then, in a gesture of exquisite irrelevance, he deposited the child on Abner's desk and hurried from the room, whether in flight or in protest was unclear.

The others stood about in embarrassment; finally Lydia

picked up the baby and handed it back to its mother with a gesture of tenderness. The baby, in the meantime, had slept through all this; most likely Dr. Rossini had sedated her for the journey.

After the slaves had been led out of the room by Abner, Lydia joined the others as they silently made for the landing. They dispersed in some confusion; no one quite knew what to make of the theatrical event.

On her way downstairs to the lobby, she realized that she had nowhere to go. She was no longer allowed any contact with the children; her career as a teacher was at an end, not only in this school, in any Quaker school. She would be excommunicated from the church that had sustained her all her life. Obadiah was married. She no longer had any future, any future at all.

Downstairs in the lobby, innocent Lizzie Dowding, who had not been present at the wedding and knew nothing of what had happened upstairs, accosted her and told her in an excited whisper that a new convoy of Mahanoy Indians had been sighted by Farmer Kowalski, who had alerted Maria Winslow, who had, in turn, alerted her.

With practiced efficiency Lydia set the wheels in motion: food baskets, toys, warm clothing, blankets. She drummed up the three other members of the Meeting for Sufferings, and an hour later six women set out by rowboat for the Indian trail across the lake. At the last moment, before pushing the boat off, Peggy Higgins said to Lydia, "By the way, there was a letter for Mordecai Monk among the mail. What do I do with it?"

"Hand it to him," Lydia replied. "What else did thee have in mind?" Without waiting for the answer, she gave her the sign to push them off. Peggy waited until they were out of sight before turning away.

CHAPTER 11

PENDLE HILL FOREST

September 1833

Blindly, without awareness of where he was going, Mordecai Monk blundered down the lane around the lake in a state of shock. Little Rebecca . . . the perfect little white body . . . All the years since her death it had haunted him; now he had been handed a perfect little black body, fast asleep, and he had been on the point of sending this little Rebecca back to the hell of slavery.

He roamed on, not caring where he went. The truth was inescapable: his mission, which had started in an illusion of love, had ended with his holding in his hands an infant like the daughter he mourned, and he had been about to send it back into slavery. Exhausted, he sat down by the side of the road. Sweat stung in his eyes. He groped in his coat pocket for his kerchief and felt something hard, crackling: the letter the Negro woman had pressed into his hand in the lobby as he left, saying, "This came for you, a week ago." He wiped his eyes with the back of his hand and tore open the letter. It was from Warthell, Croydon, Croydon and Havers, Philadelphia.

'Dear Sir,

'*Pursuant to our conversation dd September 12th of the present year, we are pleased to send you the information you requested. Some of it has been rather difficult to obtain, hence the tardiness of our response, for which we present our humble apologies.*

'*BASIL LEONARD GOODLOVE was born in Earth, Virginia, on the 2nd of the 4th month AD 1749, to William Bernard Goodlove (father) and Maria Willemans (spouse). In April '68 he entered Haringer's Theological College (no denomination) in New Orleans, where he received a license as Minister of the Gospel in July of the same year, the college being of a commercial nature, i.e., little more than a printing press for diplomas. He started his career as traveling minister (no denomination) almost immediately. The first record of his encounter with the civil authorities (as a result of a complaint lodged with the judiciary in Nashville, Tennessee) dates from September 18th of the same year. The complaint concerned "carnal assault on a female member of (his) congregation" and was not pursued by the plaintiff because, an official footnote states, "the defendant had left the State with tent and entourage." The documents concerned will be available to you in our office at your next visit, this letter being a preliminary report to give you a general impression of the Rev. Goodlove and his activities during his lifetime.*

'*From the above it becomes apparent that the Rev. Goodlove carried on a traveling ministry with a tent, without fixed abode. No documentation as to the nature of his ministry could be obtained other than that he announced it as "The Christian Church of Love." It would appear that Rev. Goodlove was its only representative.*

'*The following twenty years present only an occasional official reference to the Rev. Goodlove's activities and peregrinations. Among the incidents we have been able to trace are: a complaint lodged about his management of "The Rev. Goodlove's Fund for the Suffering Poor" which, according to judicial records, was in fact entirely used for his private financial support. Another complaint, "assaulting a female member of his congregation," was lodged with the board of elders of several Protestant*

churches, all of whom publicly denied having any ties whatsoever with
Mr. Goodlove; a letter from the Baptist Convention in Atlanta, Georgia,
of June 1770 calls him "a thorough scoundrel, well known to us by
reputation, who travels the countryside with his own brand of evangel-
ism, leaving a trail of unpaid debts, widows swindled out of their savings,
and numerous seduced, assaulted, or raped female followers who are,
without exception, abandoned together with eventual children fathered
by him."

'In January 1787 Rev. Goodlove crossed the ocean to England, a few
days ahead of a posse of citizens of the village of Washington Crossing,
New Jersey, who had set out to lynch him for the impregnation of three
members of the same family, two sisters aged 17 and 21, and an aunt
aged 42. In March 1787 the Rev. Goodlove arrived in Liverpool, where
he started a "crusade of love" which lasted one year, of which no record
has been made available to us; we have, however, lodged a request with
our correspondents Hobson, Sturgeon and Jones, solicitors in London, for
information and documentation. Five years after his return to the United
States the Rev. Goodlove ran into serious difficulties in Georgetown,
Maryland, where he was forced to go through a marriage ceremony with
one Belinda Walker. He cohabited with his bride for three months, then
absconded without leaving a forwarding address; a posse was organized
by the parents, joined by other individuals whose female relatives had
consorted with the Rev. Goodlove. They made common cause with the
relatives of the three women in Washington Crossing, New Jersey, and
sent a circular to all Baptist congregations in the Eastern United States,
asking for assistance in tracing "the scoundrel." They caught up with
him in the village of Pokoanoke, Virginia, where he was cornered in the
yard of an inn called "The Boar and Stag." As he tried to escape, the
horse he had appropriated at random shied and threw him, and he broke
his neck.

'Basil Goodlove was buried in a pauper's grave in the community of
Pokoanoke, January 3, 1794, aged 45 years.'

Mordecai lowered the letter, folded it, put it back in his
pocket, rose to his feet, and wandered on, oblivious of his surroundings. It was all proven true, at last. When he had risen to

speak during the meeting for burial of his mother, he had not spoken in the power of the Lord, but in the power of Basil Goodlove. And on that evening of his first lecture, when for the first time women had come forward to join him on the podium in spiritual ecstasy, in response to his call, it had not been his call but Basil Goodlove's. Basil Goodlove had been reborn from his own evil seed after it sprang into foolish Hannah Monk's womb, where it grew from fish into tadpole into mouse into monkey until it was expelled, bleating, as a homunculus christened 'Mordecai.' The homunculus had been received by the cuckolded husband, tears running down his face; how the poor man had loved the son squalling in his arms! All the while his mother had lain in the birthing bed smiling, sweat-soaked, exhausted, dreaming of the rapist who had besotted her with blather about truth and love. And forty-five years later, at exactly the same age when he had been cornered in the yard of the Boar and Stag, thrown by his horse, and broken his neck, he had returned to claim a new body, a new mind, by overwhelming the law-abiding, colorless personality of his bastard son. As 'Mordecai Monk' he had proceeded to garner the old familiar harvest: women, women, rape-ripe women, swooning, eyes rolling, mouths slack with lust, kneeling at his feet. He had resumed his waiting, night after night in lonely hotel rooms, for a Quaker maiden to knock on his door, an innocent like Hannah Monk, who would stagger into his arms to be mounted and put with child and—

No! No, no! God help me: to blame it all on the ghost of a satyr who had taken over the soul of his son was too easy! He himself was to blame! He had done it by using his heritage of words!

Words, words, words, words—glorious, glowing words of love: 'Throw thyself upon the mercy of Christ, the Only One! Surrender, totally, utterly, to His all-swamping, all-consuming love—"

It had been he, Becky's father, who had been about to sacrifice the black infant on the altar of blarney, not Basil Goodlove; though damned, damned, damned be his feral name!

Now what?

There was only one answer: stop the words. Stop preaching, stop the blarney. He had no hope of ever exorcising the evil spirit of his father as long as he remained a word-lecher, besotted by bombast, lusting after willing women mewling kitten-cries of ecstasy, yet trapped by his own cowardice in blather, a randy cherub ranting in a golden cage.

H'm. Pretty good, that. Must remem— No, no!

Silence! That was how simple it was: be silent. Stop being a sewer disgorging putrid poetry. Shut up, not for a week, a month, a year—forever. Words had drawn him into this labyrinth; he would never find his way out unless he cast out words. *Silence.* One word, and his father's ghost would leap at him again, screaming, 'Surrender! Surrender to his all-swamping, all—' One word, and he might find himself holding another little black sleeping body, not to put on a desk this time and flee, but to hand back to its 'owner.' God, help me never to speak again! No more ministry besotted with language! Please, God, from now on, make me minister with *deeds!*

Deeds? He did not even know where to start. He was a singer of the Lord, not a doer. Where, what could he *do?* For that matter, where was he? A narrow footpath, along a lake . . . Where did it lead?

To a rutted cart track, coming in from the prairie, leading into a forest, it turned out. Somewhere nightingale-like birds were warbling. He sat down again, not knowing whether to turn left or right, and not caring. Then he heard, in the forest, on his left, the soft, smothered whinny of a horse. He was sure it had come from the left, down the cart track disappearing among the trees. For some reason he rose and stepped back into the shrubs.

A horse was approaching. A growing sound. More than one horse, several. Dark shapes detached themselves from the shadows and came toward him, slowly, down the track. A transport? Laborers, working on the canal?

The sound grew. Massive creaking. Rustling, shuffling. A host of people on foot, five abreast, heading in his direction. A

guard, on horseback. Prisoners? When they had come close
enough for him to discern their features, he saw they were
Indians.

He watched, fascinated at first, then with a feeling of outrage.
Women, babies on their backs, bundles on their heads, staggering
under the load. Children dragged along by their parents, stumbling, falling. Eeriest was the silence: no one groaned, cried out
in pain; the children did not whimper. Creaking of wagons,
muffled hoofbeats, that was all. The silent ranks exuded such
utter desolation that, without thinking, he left his hiding place
to walk along with them, asking, "Who are you? Where are they
taking you? What is happening?"

No answer. No one seemed to notice him. A feeling of un-
reality came over him; he had become invisible.

A horseman came loping out of the forest, a cowboy-like
individual with a floppy hat and a coarse face, brandishing a
whip. "Can I he'p y'all?" he asked, threateningly.

"Who are these people? What are you doing to them?"

There was no answer. The horse swung around and loped
off, back down the cart track.

Then he saw an image that stood out even in this tragic
procession of misery, an old Indian woman dazed with exhaustion, carrying an infant. He caught up with her and cried,
"Please! Let me carry the child for thee!"

The woman did not respond. Behind him, hoofbeats approached at a fast clip, the clanking of metal. Then a voice rang
out, "Stop that! At once! Come here, you!" A different voice,
harsh with authority. It was a man with a red beard on a huge
black horse. He was wearing an officer's hat. "Answer me! What
are you doing here?"

He did not know what to say.

"Get out of there!" the officer commanded. "You have no
business here! Go home!"

He faltered, saw the old woman with the child draw away.
He hesitated, then went after her again, taking off his coat as he
went.

"Jake!" the voice behind him shouted. "Stop him!"

As he put the coat over the old woman's shoulders, a whip lashed his back. He felt no pain, but the skin on his calves tightened with shock. Again, the whip hit, this time with a sharp pain. He suppressed the urge to flee and moved closer behind the old woman, to protect her. When the whip bit into his back for the third time he cried out in pain, but in a strange, dreamlike state of grace. He stumbled on, shielding the old woman. The whip went on flogging him with savage fury, the pain increased until his back seemed to be on fire, but the state of grace in which he stumbled along deepened: 'No more words! No words! Deeds!' he thought, in growing ecstasy. Then, as the whip went on lashing, another voice screamed, "Git, you bastard! Git! Git, you goddamn Indian-lover! Git! *Git!*" A blinding pain struck his right eye. He shrieked, covered his face with his hands, tripped up, dropped to his knees. The whip went on lashing, lashing; blinded, he could no longer bear it. The pain was too much.

He heard a woman cry, "Stop! Stop!" and fell headlong in the dust.

Hearing the strident sounds of an altercation—a man's voice shouting obscenities, the cracking of a whip—Lydia had hurried down the column, holding on to the slips of her apron full of apples.

A drover on horseback was viciously flogging someone lying in the road; when she reached them she realized it was a white man in shirtsleeves, lying face down, protecting the back of his head with his hands, bloody smears on his shirt. "Stop! Stop that!" Without thinking, she let go of her apron; amidst cascading apples she fell on her knees beside the man to protect him. She expected to be hit by the whip; but a harsh voice bellowed, "Column, halt!" and she was roughly pulled back to her feet.

It was the red-bearded officer, the one who had pushed her over with his horse last time.

"Sorry about this," he said above her. "Sometimes, these civilian drovers get carried away."

She gazed up at the red beard, the cruel blue eyes, and said nothing.

"Let me have a look at him," the captain said. "Jake!"

The drover dismounted, turned the man over with his foot for the captain to see. Lydia stared at him in disbelief. Mordecai Monk? What on earth— She knelt by his side. A fierce red welt, oozing blood, crossed his cheek and his forehead; his right eye, puffed and swollen, was closed. He must be in agony.

The captain dismounted to have a closer look. "That's a nasty bruise, mister," he said. "You'd better have that looked at by a doctor. Who is this man, anyway? Your husband?"

She shook her head, speechless.

"All right, I'll get you an escort back to your village." He looked at the women who had gathered around them, their Quaker bonnets, their aprons full of toys. "How did you folks get here? On horseback?"

Suddenly Mordecai Monk rose to his feet, swaying. "Thank thee, Friend, but I intend to stay with these people."

"Of course. I'll have you all escorted back to your village together. You take it easy now, hear?"

"No, no," Mordecai said, eyes closed, swaying. "I don't mean these women, I mean the Indians. I intend to stay with the Indians." Despite the welt on his face, his clothes, smeared with blood, he seemed to be serene, at peace. The transformation was baffling.

The captain looked at him the way he had looked down on her when he had pushed her over and his horse had trampled the basket of toys. "Say that again?"

"I will stay with the Indians."

"Stay? What do you mean, stay?"

"I will remain with them wherever they are going."

"Why, for God's sake?"

"Because it is God's will."

The way he said it was so unlike the man she knew that

Lydia wondered if the blow on his head had affected him. The captain, when he spoke, sounded calm, almost courteous, but she knew what would happen; it had happened to her. "What purpose would that serve," he asked, "apart from your personal gratification?"

Mordecai Monk tried to smile, the welt turned it into a grin. "I want to join them as a witness."

The captain said, "Obviously, you know nothing about Indians. I've taken six convoys to the Mississippi, and I came to know them intimately. Let me tell you, they'd sooner cut their throats than as much as look at a white man. So make no mistake: you'd join them for your own sake, not theirs."

Lydia could not remain silent. "Can't thee see? He is moved by that of God in him! There's that of God within thee too, trying to be heard!"

The captain was not interested. "Okay, Jake," he said to the drover, "go get the chief." The man got on his horse and made off.

Mordecai Monk looked as if he were about to fall; Lydia put an arm around his shoulder to steady him. But despite his suffering, she could not help feeling an instinctive revulsion. She might have misjudged him spiritually, but physically he remained the man who had tried to force himself upon her. The hands now covered with blood had tried to tear her bodice, the mouth now smiling in eerie bliss had covered her face with slimy kisses. She should take him to their boat with the help of the other women, row him to the school, call Dr. Rossini. He might be getting a fever; if he persisted in this, he would fall by the roadside before long.

A tall Indian, two feathers dangling from his crest, was pushed toward them by the drover called Jake.

"Chief," the captain said, "this man wants to join you by way of a sort of protest, God knows why. I have no say in this matter, as it concerns your internal affairs. Do you want this man to join you, or don't you?"

The Indian did not respond.

"If you allow him to join you," the captain continued, "he'll be an Indian as far as I'm concerned. He'll be your responsibility."

Mordecai Monk began to tremble, and said, "Chief, I am a Quaker. I want to honor the treaty between William Penn and thy people. I want to join you on your journey as a witness to our brotherhood."

The Indian did not seem to hear him, or even see him. He stared into the distance for a long moment, then turned his back and walked away.

"What did I tell you?" the captain said with satisfaction. "To him, you don't exist. He wants no part of you, and neither do I. Go home." He climbed back into the saddle, raised an arm, and cried, "Column! *Move!*"

The mass of silent Indians was slowly set in motion. Mordecai Monk shook himself free and stumbled along with them.

Lydia caught up with him and pleaded, "Why? What could thee *do* for them? Please, Friend Mordecai! Tell me!"

He did not face her. "No words," he said. "No more words." He stumbled, was about to fall; she took his arm to keep him on his feet. He tried to shake her off, even though it was obvious now that he was blinded and would fall on his face if she were to let go of him. "Please!" she urged. "Don't do this, thee is in no condition to do this!"

"I must do it, I must," he said. "This is my concern. Go home."

"I can't leave thee like this! I—where's thy coat? Did thee lose it somewhere down the road?"

"I gave it to a woman, an old woman, with a child."

"Save thy strength, sit down for a while. I'll go and get it for thee." She let go of his arm and walked ahead. When she looked back she saw he had not sat down but was walking, unsurely, along with the slow-moving column of Indians.

She did spot an old woman with a man's coat around her shoulders; when she caught up with her, she realized the woman was carrying an infant in her arms. She could not bring herself to take the coat away, and made her way back against the tide of shuffling Indians. She said to the other women surrounding him, "We can't leave him like this. I'll stay with him until help arrives. Go back to the school, now. Tell them Mordecai Monk has been wounded, blinded by a whip. That he needs medical attention, must see the doctor. And do get some of the men to come here and force him to go. Quick!"

The women seemed reluctant at first, but Lizzie Dowding took the lead. "Let's go!" she said, and to Lydia, "I'll be back!"

After they had left, Lydia said to Mordecai Monk, who was stumbling along, like a sleepwalker, "Come, let's sit down for a moment, please! I'll bandage thy eye."

"Not now," he said, "not yet."

All she could do was let him have his way. She walked along with him, out onto the prairie, thinking, 'But this is absurd! Mordecai Monk, of all people! Was he suddenly in the power of the Lord? He must have been. Like Saul, hunter of Christians, who was blinded by God on the way to Damascus, who fell off his horse and turned into Paul the apostle. But how odd of God, to choose this—well, mountebank, this would-be rapist, who had not only split the Meeting but complained about them in Richmond, with the result that—'

A horse came snorting down the ranks. "Keep moving!" a voice bellowed. "*Move!*" A whip cracked; she felt him cringe. "Don't worry," she said, "he's just making a noise, not hitting anybody."

"Go home," he said wearily.

"Don't be ridiculous. Suppose I were to walk away? Thee'd fall flat on thy face. Then where would thy witness be?"

"Go home," he persisted. "God will protect me."

"Even God needs help," she said. "At times. But it *would* help if one knew what He had in mind."

Night had fallen when the urgent call from the school finally reached Dr. Rossini. He was exhausted, had missed two meals, lost a patient, and had been dogged all day by Farmer Kowalski, whose wife wasn't due for another week. The message, garbled and emotional, was that Mordecai Monk, for some reason, had joined a convoy of Indians, had been manhandled by the drovers, and needed medical assistance. A party had left to bring him back; Jesse saw to it that the four members of the committee from Richmond went along with them, so the coast was clear for moving the slaves to the Ely farm.

This seemed to be the second urgent call from the school, there had been one earlier. He was tempted to send an excuse; presumably, the man had been put to bed, and if he had managed to survive this far he would live till morning. But that was not how physicians were supposed to think; what was more, the school was close to his heart, even though he detested that English windbag. So, in the end, he hoisted himself back into the damn buggy and clippety-clopped through the night to the damn evangelist.

Abner Best, pale and pinch-faced, was waiting for him in the lobby. It turned out to be about his wife, not the evangelist. Saraetta was in bad shape. The party had come back with the news that Mordecai had been blinded by a whip, but refused to leave the Indians whom he had joined as a witness; Lydia Best was staying with him until he received medical attention. As a result of all this, Saraetta—

"Well, come and see for thyself, Doctor."

There she lay in the marital bed, moaning and gasping, drenched with perspiration. She must have been thrashing dramatically; the bed looked like a dog's nest. She really was an impossible woman; Rossini was tempted to send her husband out of the room, lock the door, and have it out with her. 'Saraetta, let's face it, you reject your husband because for some insane reason you blame him for the epidemic and the death of your child. You are a full-blooded woman with normal carnal urges, you have fallen in love with a windbag who aroused you by spouting religion. It's time you realized that you are not answering a call to come to Christ, but a mating call.' But no, that would only make matters worse.

The moment she saw him, the woman wailed, "It cannot be true! Not he, not he! Oh, Doctor, Doctor!"

"Hush, Sara." Rossini put an arm around her; she was trembling like a reed. Much too thin. Her husband stood by in embarrassment.

"Please, Doctor!" she wailed. "Please go to him! Bring him back!"

"Would someone tell me what exactly—?"

"He's covered with blood! He lost his coat, his hat, all covered with blood! And he's blind! They blinded him, with a whip!"

"You don't say," Rossini said neutrally.

"Yes," the miserable husband affirmed. "One of the drovers—"

"Flogged! They flogged him!" the woman cried. "Now he's blind!"

Rossini could take no more of this. "All right. Do you know where they've made camp?"

"On the edge of the forest, where the buffalo hunters used to have their bivouac."

"Very well, I'll go and see him first thing tomorrow morning. Now, please, get a hold of yourself."

"Go now, Doctor! I beseech thee! Go now, he may die!"

"Saraetta, pull yourself together. I cannot make my way through the forest at dead of night. What's more: Lydia is with him, he'll keep till daylight." Actually, she was right: ten years ago he would have saddled his horse and set off at once to minister to the sick. But since he had taken to driving the buggy, he no longer made visits on horseback and had sold his sorrel horse. The old mare wouldn't take a saddle, and he was damned if he was going to venture into the pitch-dark forest on someone else's horse and be thrown into the brambles, or decapitated by a branch when the brute took off at the screech of an owl. Moreover, that man Monk was a born actor. As was she.

"Don't come back without him!" she wailed. "Promise me, Doctor! Promise!"

"I promise I'll do whatever I can."

While his wife went on moaning and sobbing, Abner, deathly pale and looking somehow elongated, stood helplessly by.

"You went with the posse, Abner?"

"Yes. We caught up with the convoy and—and spoke to him."

"When was that?"

"Eight, eight-thirty this evening."

"Then what happened?"

"The Friends from Richmond labored with him for a long time, trying to dissuade him; but he refused to leave the Indians, so we came back. Lydia insisted on staying with him until thee arrives. She will have to spend the night in the open, and—"

"All right, I'll go there at first light. Now for God's sake give me something to eat, I haven't had a bite all day. Here is a potion for your wife . . ." He rummaged in his bag. "Here you go: one tablespoon twice a day. Give her two now. Let her sleep! No food, just sleep. Now, where do I go for that bite?"

An entire escort had gathered outside the door: the women of the Meeting for Sufferings. They accompanied him to the kitchen and sat down with him, talking, following his every bite with round-eyed drama. These Quakers! He loved them, they stuck their necks out for his slaves, but even so. Now an English tragedian had taken it into his head to give a one-man show in the prairie, an hour's ride away. Two hours in the saddle there and back. Leave at the crack of dawn. God help us all.

"No, thank you, Peggy, no more potatoes. I'll have a bit of that pie over there, though, if I may . . ."

Lydia had been shocked beyond words when the men had made off without them. Surely they were not going to leave her alone in the prairie with a wounded man? Without blankets or food? She stood gazing after them incredulously when she heard the jingling of spurs. The captain, red beard stuck out, hands clasped on his back, was standing behind her.

"Good evening, miss. Would you two do me the pleasure of being my guests at supper?"

His sudden gallantry surprised her. She was about to accept when Mordecai, whom she had thought to be numbed by exhaustion, said, "No, thank thee, Friend Stewart. Lydia Best will prepare a meal for us, the way the Indian women do."

The captain seemed about to say something intemperate, but restrained himself and strode back to his horse, spurs jingling. Impulsively, Lydia ran after him.

"Friend Stewart!"

The man turned around.

She asked, her voice low, "I—I wonder if I could have a word with thee? In private?"

"Certainly. Join me in my quarters."

"Quarters?"

"I have a tent, with a porch. We can sit outside. Look: over there, away from the crowd."

She hesitated, glanced at Mordecai who had slumped back into his own world and sat huddled on the ground. "Well— thank thee . . ."

"My pleasure, Miss Best. Allow me." He led the way through the crowd, which parted for him at the sound of his spurs. The tent turned out to be a square edifice made of tarpaulin with a front porch, beside it a small shelter without roof. On the porch were a table and two folding chairs.

"Please take a seat." He helped her up the steps, and waited until she did before sitting down himself. A Negro servant appeared in the doorway. "What do you fancy, Miss Best? Lemonade, tea, a mint julep?" He was a different man; she wondered what had brought this about.

"Nothing, thank thee."

He said to the Negro, "A double."

"Yes, sah." The man disappeared inside the tent.

"What can I do for you?"

"I wanted to talk to thee about Mordecai Monk. As thee can see for thyself, he is in a bad way. One of his eyes is hurt, he seems to be in considerable pain, yet he refuses to leave. I think thee would be doing him a service if thee would arrange for him to be taken back to Pendle Hill."

The captain looked at her with a slow smile. "Those friends of yours made the same request earlier on."

"So they should!"

"Now, let's get this straight, Miss Best—are you suggesting I use violence?"

"Pardon me?"

"You know he will not leave of his own accord. His coreligionists have been unable to convince him that he should return. The only way open to me, if I want to respond to your request, would be to have him trussed like a pig and carted back to your village—what's it called?"

"Pendle Hill."

"Well, I'm afraid I cannot do that. Much as I resent his presence among my Indians, I cannot use force to remove him. He is a free man in a free country."

"But he is not an Indian!"

"As I had occasion to say before, Miss Best, an Indian is anyone who says he is."

The Negro came with a glass on a tray, the captain took it without thanking him, the man withdrew. The captain lifted his glass, sipped, and wiped his mustache with the back of his hand. "Let me ask you something, miss—" Suddenly, his face went hard. "Not now!" he snapped.

Startled, she looked around and saw an officer walk away.

"Let me ask you something, Miss Best. Are you familiar with the prairie?"

"As children we picnicked here, once in a while."

He took a long draught from his glass and wiped his beard. "These plains, in which we'll disappear tomorrow, reach from here to the Mississippi. Between us and the river is nothing but emptiness. We'll be provisioned by the Illinois and the Osage Indians, contracted to deliver four buffalo a day. When they can turn the money into alcohol, they don't turn up, sometimes for days on end. During that time my own Indians do some hunting, but as they are Woods Indians it doesn't amount to much. In a few weeks we can expect the first frost, after that the first blizzard. This convoy moves at the speed of the elderly, if we make it to the Mississippi in five weeks we'll be on schedule. Someone like yourself, without the practice of walking for hours at a stretch, without a layer of callus under her feet as the squaws have, simply could not make it. Within a week you'd no longer be a civilized young white lady, devoting herself to the well-being of savages, but a limping squaw."

"But there is no question of my even considering such a thing!"

He ignored it, she wondered why. "Squaws on the prairie are treated—well, differently," he continued. "We, the cavalry, are merely a token force, the actual herding is done by civilian drovers. I would be unable to protect you against them, certainly after dark. So, with your permission, I have to tell you that you'd be insane to try it."

"But, my dear man, there is no question of my doing it! I'm simply staying with Mordecai Monk until the doctor has been."

"If he comes."

"Of course he will come! As soon as he gets word, he'll be on his way."

"Very well." He rose. "You are the mistress of your fate. I just want you to realize what it would entail, should you decide to stay with Mr. Monk. He, I'm sure, is determined to act out his version of the Passion of Christ, with bells on."

She gave him a cold look, rose, and was about to go down the steps when his voice stopped her. "I'll instruct my servant to provide you with the wherewithal to set up a shelter for the night, and bring you some food."

"Thank thee."

"Food rations are distributed daily by the chuck wagon. As your Mr. Monk seems to prefer the Indian way of life, you'll have to cook your own meals from now on, I'm afraid."

She set out toward Mordecai Monk in a state of bewilderment. Why was the man so insistent that she would end up staying with the Indians? It was almost as if he willed her to do so . . . Suddenly, she remembered the words of the young officer who had taken her home on his horse that first day: *I would not want for one of my sisters to have any truck with Captain Stewart.*

She did not feel like facing Mordecai Monk quite yet; instead, she wandered for a while among the Indians. The encampment was not really worthy of that definition; there seemed to be only one teepee, it must belong to the chief. The rest of his tribe, which the young officer had said was not really a tribe but a herd of five hundred head corralled at random by the cavalry, had to make do with flimsy shelters made of sticks and bits of cloth. That was to say, couples and families huddled together under shelters, others must have dropped wherever they found themselves when the convoy halted. Some of them, rolled in blankets, already seemed to be asleep. Cooking fires were lit here and there; there seemed to be one big communal one not far from the chuck wagon. Chuck wagon! She had better hurry back to Mordecai Monk; the captain had promised to have food delivered to them.

She made her way back to where he was sitting as fast as she could, difficult with all those sleeping Indians. She had to walk around them; in the end, she followed the example of other Indians and jumped over those who were asleep. It almost became a game, shame on her; but it brought back memories of hurdle races, at which she had been very good as a young girl, better than most boys.

How odd of God to choose her too.

CHAPTER 12

THE PRAIRIE

September 1833

The next morning, at dawn, Dr. Rossini found himself on a borrowed horse following Jesse McHair down the footpath through the forest. Presently they reached the prairie, a misty immensity under a young mackerel sky. His horse trotted along behind Jesse's, which cleaved the man-high grass without hesitation, surefooted and bold. A flight of starlings, flushed by their passage, swooped overhead with the sound of a whirlwind. As the mist dissipated in the heat of the rising sun, the horizon widened, distant hills emerged. Without warning they suddenly found themselves on the edge of what was once the buffalo hunters' campground, a clearing in the tall grass trampled bare by Indians and horses. They set out looking for Lydia and her companion, then a raucous voice yelled, "Halt! Who goes there?"

Jesse replied, "Take it easy, Friend. We've come to have a look at the injured man and the girl. This man is their doctor."

"Let's see your faces!"

Rossini saw the silhouette of a horseman with a gun across his saddle, a civilian, not a soldier.

"I can't give permission," the man said. "Go see the captain in the command tent, over there."

"Thank thee, Friend," Jesse said. "Come on, Doc. Let's go, I've met him before."

They made their way across the campground, careful not to step on one of the many sleeping Indians lying all over the place like corpses on a battlefield. Here and there the embers of a cooking fire glowed. Somewhere a child was crying.

They dismounted before the front porch of the command tent; a Negro orderly appeared in the doorway. Jesse said, "A doctor to see the captain."

The Negro was pushed aside and an ill-tempered man with a red beard came out, buttoning his tunic. "What's going on?"

"We'd like to visit with the two Quakers, Friend. The guard won't let us through without thy permission."

The captain beckoned, crooking a finger. "Come here."

Jesse obeyed. Rossini followed more slowly, stiff-legged and sore after the ride.

"Weren't you here yesterday?" the captain asked Jesse.

"Yes. I have with me a doctor to check on them."

"Rossini, Leon, ex-medical officer, U.S. Cavalry," the doctor said, saluting.

The transformation was magical. "Doctor? Have a seat! What may I offer you? Boy!"

"Yes, sah."

"What is your pleasure, Doctor? Julep, whiskey? Never too early for a military man, eh?"

"Whiskey, please." Rossini saw Jesse and his horse leave, picking their way among the sleeping Indians toward the edge of the clearing.

"Make it two doubles," the captain told his servant. "Doctor, make yourself comfortable. Is the man a patient of yours?"

"No. His companion is."

The captain gave him a searching look. "A lot of things have changed in the cavalry, Doctor, since your time."

"How so?"

"Look about you! This is not a cavalry job. Any officer worth his salt feels ashamed escorting these people. Rounded up in one of the large camps in Ohio, without regard for family ties, to break any organized resistance from the outset. Cut up into convoys of five hundred without their own chiefs or medicine men, and it didn't matter—"

The servant arrived with the drinks. Rossini smiled his thanks, but the Negro withdrew without having looked him in the eye.

"That's why I allowed the man Monk to stay," the captain continued after a sip from his glass. "It came as a relief to see somebody doing something, however unworldly, to redress the balance. Last night a bunch of elders from his church came to ask me to chase him off, but I told them he's a free man, if he wants to be treated like an Indian, I'll treat him like one. That's what I told them."

"What if he wants to persist in this?" Rossini asked.

The captain ignored it; he obviously liked to hear himself talk. "The young woman is a different story. I talked to her last evening and didn't mince my words. For her to come along would be lunacy. The civilian drovers may have a shot at raping her out there in the grass, they do it to squaws routinely. Even if I tell them that the first to touch her will have his balls shot off; if they grab her after dark—"

"Cheers," Rossini said.

"Cheers. The man thinks he can live among the Indians as an equal, but that's bullshit," the captain continued. "Take them away from the graves of their ancestors, force them to abandon the spirits in every tree—to the Indians it's like taking away their soul. Separate an Indian from his tribe, his family, and you break his will. All that has been done, on purpose. What you see lying around are not braves any more, but hoboes. Some politician in Washington worked it all out, then locked his desk and went home to kiss his wife, hug his children, and stroke his dog. I have fought Indians, and came to respect them; now I've been ordered to do the politicians' dirty work. Castrated, that's what they are, those people." He emptied his glass. "The politicians would have a fit if they heard I gave a Quaker permission to join the Indians. But shall I tell you something? A secret? In my heart of hearts I take my hat off to that man. He is, I'm sure, going to milk it for all it's worth, but in my heart of hearts: hats off." He belched. "Excuse me. Hats off, especially after those elders tried to force him to give up. I'm telling you, just in case you might be planning to drug him and cart him off unconscious: he's not sick."

Rossini said, "All I'll do is check him over. He's injured, I'm told."

"That man is as sound as a bell!" the captain said, with a throwaway gesture. "Last night I thought: he's only doing it for the good of his soul. But since then, I've decided it's not just for his own soul, but for mine as well, and yours; the soul of this country. So, as far as I'm concerned he can stay. But I'll treat him like an Indian, as I told him."

"Well," Rossini said, "let me go and have a look at him."

"Hey!" the captain cried, with tipsy surprise. "Not yet, Doc! We've a whole morning ahead of us! Here, have another. Boy!"

"Yes, sah."

"Same again! And bring us something to eat with it. Hot sausages, bacon—something savory."

"Not for me," Rossini said.

"Okay, just for me," the captain said. "Doc, you and I are going to talk about the old days, when to be with the cavalry meant to be a man of honor."

He pointed to Rossini's glass; the servant obeyed.

A voice called, "Lydia! Lydia!"

Lydia emerged from under their shelter among the sleeping Indians and answered, "Here!"

"I've brought thee something," the voice said, then he stepped into view.

"Jesse!" She threw her arms around his neck and kissed him

on both cheeks. "What is thee doing here? Where's the doctor?"

"He's with the captain right now. Could I have a word with thee in private?"

Before she had been able to reply, Mordecai Monk said, "Of course! Take thy time. I'm all right." He spoke, eyes closed, in the direction of Jesse's voice; but Jesse had stepped away by then, taking her hand. "I hope thee'll succeed in convincing her," Monk added.

"Of what?" Jesse asked coldly. He could not stand the man.

"That this concern is not suitable for women. Not even this woman." He smiled.

Jesse led her away, out of earshot, to the edge of the tall grass. Then he asked, "Is thee ready to come back with us?"

"No," she said, "not unless someone else is prepared to take over from me. He cannot fend for himself, not for the moment."

"Why thee, Lydia?"

"Nobody else has volunteered. Would thee?"

"Me? I'd strong-arm him onto a horse, tie him down, and take him home to be looked after. What is this nonsense? He's off his rocker! Why should thee—"

"Because I happen to believe in his witness. I gather I'm the only one. I'll stay with him until he can look after himself, then I'll ask the captain for an escort to take me home. Where is the doctor?"

"Does thee believe in his so-called witness to the point of risking thy life?"

"Don't talk nonsense. Discomfort, yes. But danger? With the cavalry in control?"

"Here." He took her hand and pressed something cold in it. She stared at it, horrified. "A pistol?"

"Hush! Make sure thee doesn't show this to anyone. If thee's going to stay with the convoy thee'll be needing this."

The object in her hand was so blasphemous that she could not find any words; all she could do was stare at him, aghast.

"I'm serious," he said. "Drovers are like slave hunters: catching niggers or herding Indians, it's the same thing. Put that gun somewhere inside thy clothes, and be sure to take it with thee whenever thee needs to—well, move out of sight. If thee hears anyone following thee, shoot. Don't try to frighten him with that thing, shoot. And don't aim at the head, it's too small. Aim at the body."

The fact that Jesse, a Quaker, tried to force this monstrous thing on her was a fall from grace. "I—I can't possibly accept this." She wanted to give the pistol back.

He refused to take it. "Lydia, listen. Thee can do more for the underground railroad than thee can for these lousy savages, much more! Believe me, Indians aren't worth it. They are blood-thirsty, conniving—"

She threw the pistol away and covered her face with her hands.

For a moment he stood motionless, then got down on his knees to grope for the weapon in the grass. He found it, stuck it in his belt, and said, "Goodbye, Lydia."

She cried, her voice hoarse with tears, "How *can* thee! How *can* a Friend talk like this about people?"

"They kept slaves, and bred them like cattle. Good luck." He walked away.

She stood, her hands on her mouth, staring after him as he made his way among the Indians, toward his horse. She wanted to run after him, grab his arm, let him take her away; then a kindly voice said, "Good morning, Lydia. How are you?"

"Doctor!" she cried. "Oh, Doctor . . ."

He put an arm around her shoulders. "Let's go and have a look at Mordecai Monk, shall we? How has he been?"

"Oh, Doctor! He's badly hurt! I—I . . ." She needed all her strength not to burst into sobs; his presence gave her such a feeling of security that she blurted out, "I am afraid! I can't help it, I'm terrified! But I must go with him!"

"Why?"

"I can't let him go by himself! He's blind!"

After a moment's silence, he asked, "How come?"

"A drover flogged him and hit his left eye with the whip.

The other eye must be damaged too, because he can't see a thing any more. Doctor, he *cannot* go alone!"

He hugged her and said, "Calm down, Lydia. I'll have a look at him. Maybe it's not as bad as you think."

"It is, it is! I have been with him all night long, he can't see a thing any more . . ."

"All right," he said. "I'll go and have a look. I'd better go alone. Wait here, I'll be right back."

She watched him as he walked over to Mordecai Monk, who was waiting.

"Good morning, Mr. Monk, I am Dr. Rossini. We met briefly, on Founders' Day."

The man looked up with a smile. A remarkable change had taken place in that face since Rossini had last seen it. Despite the bandaged eye, the welt, and the bruises, it seemed to radiate serenity. "Let's have a look at that eye." Rossini cautiously took off the bandage. "Looks pretty angry," he said. "Would you open your other eye, please?"

The man obeyed and blinked.

"Try to look straight ahead, please. That's right."

Rossini covered the sound eye with his hand. Then again. And again. No doubt about it: the pupil contracted and expanded normally. He repeated the test a few more times; suddenly he stabbed at the eye with a finger, without touching it. The man reeled back. "Thank you," Rossini said. "Now let me have a look at your back. I hear they whipped you badly."

The man lay down on his stomach, his head on his arms. Why had he made Lydia believe that he was blind? He would not have backed away from the stabbing finger if he were.

The shirt was soaked with blood, the lacerations on his back were real enough. They must have thrashed him savagely. Could a man be a malingerer and a martyr at the same time?

While Rossini treated the wounds with Peruvian balsam and applied a dressing and a bandage, he reflected upon the enigma.

Maybe it was the enigma of human nature itself: two-faced Janus, good and evil, compassion and selfishness mysteriously intertwined. The man was obviously trying to lure Lydia into accompanying him. Rossini's first impulse was to warn her that he was a trickster and to run for her life; but something held him back. Something the captain had said. *It's not that he's saving just his own soul, but mine and yours as well. The soul of this country.*

He decided to let it ride for the moment, patted the man's shoulder, and said, "Well, this will do for now. I won't bandage your eye again, the open air is better for it."

The radiant face beamed at him; something—the sanctimonious grin?—made him change his mind. "I think you and I should be frank with one another, friend. For some reason, Lydia is under the impression that you are now totally blind. She'll be much relieved to know that your condition was a temporary one and that your vision has now been restored to normal."

The man seemed stunned. "Blind? I did not say I was blind! I close the other eye from time to time because it hurts! What gave her the idea I was blind?"

"Well, we had better reassure her, hadn't we? Would you like to do it, or shall I?"

"By all means, go and tell her! I had no idea! I was just sitting here, basking in the peace of the Lord . . ."

Rossini rose to his feet. "I think you should return to Pendle Hill with us. There is nothing basically wrong with you, but you are not in a fit state to walk the three hundred miles, or whatever it is, to the Mississippi. Someone will have to look after the wounds on your back, or they'll become infected. And you are likely to have a reaction. You cannot suffer that kind of trauma without any aftereffects."

The man looked up at him with the beatific smile, which, on second thought, might be a symptom of shock.

As Rossini made his way back to Lydia he wondered what would be the best way to tell her, for tell her he must.

"How is he?" she asked when he joined her. "Is he going to be all right?"

Rossini put his hands on her shoulders. Her face was haggard with worry and fatigue; she too was in a state of shock.

"Lydia," he said, "he may be sincere in his convictions, but in one respect he was not."

"What does thee mean?"

"He is not blind."

The expression on her face was enough to break a man's heart. Then she said, "I see. Is he otherwise fit to travel?"

"Not really."

"What if I were to go with him to look after his wounds? Until someone else takes over, perhaps?"

He did not understand the workings of her mind. Or was it her soul? He had known her since she was a small child; he had seen her survive, by sheer force of will, the loss of her entire family in the epidemic—leaving only her much older brother, who at the time had been even more dependent on her than he was now. He thought he had understood why the cruel bereavement at that tender age had turned her not into a victim, but a challenger of life. At this moment, she was a closed book to him.

"If you have any sense, Lydia, you'll come back with us. He will too, if you make it clear to him that he would be on his own. He may want to, but he cannot make it by himself. Not in the state he's in now."

"I don't know about him, Doctor, but I cannot go back," she said with a sudden, disquieting detachment. She seemed a different woman, a fallback to the dissociated calm of the child in the epidemic.

"Would you mind telling me why not? I don't mean to pry; I just want to understand."

She became her present-day self again, at least outwardly: firm, in control, daring him almost. "Doctor dear, use thy brains. There's nothing left for me in Pendle Hill. I've been fired as a teacher for corrupting the children. I'm to be read out of Meeting for the same reason. I—I have no personal prospects either, and I am thirty years old. I want to go with the Indians because I want to make my life count."

"Doing what, Lydia?"

"Who knows? Way will open. Teaching their children, for one thing. Seeing this man through his present state of weakness. I may not like him, but that's not the point. I respect his witness. I expect thee, of all people, to respect mine."

"Why I of all people, Lydia?"

"Because," she said with the daredevil smile he knew well, "of the two of us, I seem to be the one to take the rap for the underground railroad. Or are they about to arrest thee?"

"Not that I know of."

"Are thy patients abandoning thee in droves?"

"Lydia, listen—"

"No, Doctor. I'm through listening. I presume that God, if He is a God of love, wants to express His love for these Indians. Tough luck on His part, but all He has right now is me and that—that enigma over there. An odd choice, but there we are."

He saw in her eyes that the die was cast. "So be it," he said. "I'll leave these dressings with you. They should be changed daily. Now, are you sure—"

"Goodbye, Doctor. Be well."

She turned away and did not wave when, later, he and Jesse left. They did not even see her; her slight elegant figure was lost among the Indians.

Mordecai Monk, shocked out of his dreamlike state of bliss by the doctor's accusation, asked himself if it could be true. Had he indeed pretended to be blind in order to make sure the wanton young woman would stay with him? His first reaction was, 'No, no, absolutely not!' But after spending all those months in thrall to his father's ghost . . . It might be true.

For some reason, the thought shattered his state of inner peace. If he had managed to hoodwink himself to that extent, what about his decision to give up preaching? What about the very nature of his witness? Had his decision to share the fate of the Indians, come what may, been divinely inspired, or was that too a delusion?

It shook him to the core of his being—whatever that might be. If the way he had carried on after being whipped had given the impression that he was as blind as a bat, then his witness of joining the Indians might belong to the same theater. Looked at soberly, the notion of marching along with the convoy in his present state, with only the clothes he stood up in, no practice of walking any distance let alone hundreds of miles, was ludicrous. Could the key to his *imitatio Christi* be the Quaker maiden, so tender, so concerned? *Is thee all right, Friend Mordecai?—A root in thy path, Friend Mordecai!* It had been dreamlike, ecstatic. He could happily stagger on till doomsday, blind eyes squinting heavenward, supported by his latter-day Mary Magdalene. If he had been Basil Goodlove, this would have been his way of making sure that Mary would not go home: who would leave a blind man to his fate?

He had to face it: he might have shut up for the time being, but that did not mean he had shaken Basil Goodlove. Even to think of it as a state of possession by his father's spook was another piece of rustic theater; simple heredity would do. Bulls were bred so that calves might carry their characteristics; if he were a liar, a fraud, a word-slinger, any cattle raiser would put as his first question, 'Which bull sired this one?' He had better treat all forms of ecstasy, godliness, and spiritual delirium with suspicion. What would Basil Goodlove have done? Would he have joined the Indians as a witness? If there had been an audience, yes. Was this woman his audience? In the case of Basil Goodlove, she would have been his prey; he would have enacted Paul on the road to Damascus, fainted by the roadside: 'Lydia! Lydia! . . .' Next thing she knew, she would have found herself in his bed, or sleeping bag, or whatever.

The Indians slept under blankets on the naked ground; they just dropped wherever they found themselves when camp was made, pulled their blanket over them, and fell asleep as if felled by an ax. Would he be able to do the same? An English businessman astray on the prairie, without so much as a change of underwear, a piece of luggage? A spoiled, pampered—

He decided to put it before God. "God? Am I insane? A fraud? A lecher?"

A voice in his mind said coldly, *Yes to all three.*

"Father, if Thou still want me, if Thou hast a plan—"

The voice within—not God's, surely—asked, *Which father are you addressing, boy?*

"No!" he cried in anguished fury. "Get out of my prayer, Basil Goodlove!"

He grabbed his hair. He was lost! Lost, far away from home . . .

The empty hall of his mind echoed with the sound of slow clapping.

Roaming aimlessly among the Indians, Lydia asked herself what in the world had made her decide to do this. She had said it herself, to the doctor: she was at the end of her tether and might as well do something to make her life count. But was this the way to do that? At home, she could return to the underground railroad—

Could she? As a station on the railroad, the school was finished. She could be of use only as part of a station, an organized group. And who would take her in? She would stand out like a sore thumb anywhere else except as a teacher. And what school would hire her now?

Well, there were other concerns, such as . . . She waited for the other concerns to reveal themselves, and discovered there weren't any, not really. Distribute fruit and toys among the occasional Indian convoy to pass the village? This made more sense. But what was 'this'? She had made her case for the doctor, but what could she really do here, other than hobble along with the herd, handmaiden to the latest Quaker saint self-elected to represent the Lord among the suffering masses? And what was *his* contribution to be? Unfair to ask that now, while he was still recovering from his wounds; but once he was hale and healthy again, what could he *do* for the Indians, other than be a symbol of unity with the Mahanoy on the part of the Quaker movement? Ha! That was all they needed: a fat white man enriching his soul by 'sharing' their deprivation, waited on hand and foot—

Stop it! She should not break down his witness just because she herself was overcome by doubt. What on earth had made her suddenly strike that splendid pose for the benefit of the doctor? Yet she had meant every word of it, at the time. Well, so too—she was sure—had Mordecai. *'It is God's will.'* It had been very impressive when he said it, but now, a day later . . .

She heard a child crying somewhere and went to see what was the matter. But there was no child, only a small shadow disappearing in the crowd. Children ran away at her approach. Sad, because there were so many children, children of school age, in the convoy. Most of them were with their parents, but many, she was sure, were orphans or abandoned children just tagging along, like the stray dogs that also ran away at her approach. Well, maybe after a few days they would get used to her presence and be willing to be rounded up each time the convoy made its bivouac. She had worked it all out in her mind overnight: she would pull them together into one big class, divide them into sections according to age, like a small village school. She was not quite sure what she would teach them, once she spoke their language. The children were as wild as monkeys; no point in coming at them with the three R's. It would have to be picture-book teaching; they would have to draw the pictures themselves—

Suddenly, out of the blue, a trumpet blared just behind her. She swung around and saw, on the captain's porch, the black orderly, pigeon-chested, standing to attention, blowing an ear-splitting staccato command. The sound flushed birds from the grass, startlingly close. The drovers on horseback began to move among the Indians, who rose as from the grave. "Git! Git!" they shouted, cracking their whips. "Git, ya bastards! Git! Git!"

Oh, my God—Mordecai Monk! She hurried to join him.

• • •

Weary beyond words, hurting, exhausted after his emotional self-searching, Mordecai stood up. All around him Indians were doing the same; some humps he had taken for part of the prairie were rising too. Where should he go?

Thank God, there she was. "Friend Mordecai!"

Needlessly, he cried "Here!" The relief at her appearance was such that he almost sat down again. Maybe that was all he would be able to do; he suddenly felt stiff and unstable. The mere idea of having to walk—

"I see," she said, out of breath. "Stiff, eh? To be expected. Try walking, just a few steps."

He tried manfully. Too manfully; he was a fraud. But even as a fraud he winced and stumbled. "Pity we let the doctor go," he panted. "I'm afraid I can't hack it . . ." The panting was overdone, but he wasn't going to make it all the same.

"Just for a few days," she said, "it's likely to get worse. But it will pass. Wait! I'll see if I can find an army wagon with some room left . . ." She disappeared.

He felt quite faint. Giddy. And whatever the doctor had done to his back, it had made things worse.

"Come," she said.

He felt her hand on his arm.

"I found a wagon belonging to the army with some room left in it. Come, I'll help thee get inside."

"They—they won't let me . . ." The mere idea of one of the drovers spotting him and using his whip made him feel sick.

"Don't worry, I'll fix it with the captain. Easy now . . ."

He let himself be guided. Supported. Held close.

"Easy!"

How good it was. If it was going to be like this, he'd rather — "No," he said, and stood still.

"What? It's only a small distance from here—"

"No. I will not be driven in a wagon when my witness is to share the fate of the Indians. They aren't given preferential treatment when they are footsore." It was true—and not true. It *was* his witness, but at the same time, he relished being succored, supported.

"Right," she said, after a moment. "I can unite with that. Luckily we must have left late because of Jesse and the doctor. It's past midday, it can't be long before we stop for the night. Come."

He let himself be led back to where their bedrolls were, together with the tarpaulin and the shelter they had been given, compliments of the army. The Indians didn't get those issued either. The whole thing was a fraud.

Lydia picked up the shelter, tarpaulin, and bedrolls. Pity Mordecai Monk had refused to ride in the cook's wagon, she could have put it all in there with him. But good for him. He was going to stagger on for the sake of his witness despite the pain; the least she could do was carry their bundle of belongings like the rest of the women. Some of them pulled whole carts stacked high with stakes and hides; others walked bent double under their load, like exhausted beasts of burden. The image of Lydia Best carrying two bedrolls, a shelter, and a tarpaulin was not likely to be added to the lithos of the Quaker saints on schoolroom walls.

They joined the slow-moving herd. Its progress was determined, the captain had said, by the elderly; and the human cart horses were by far the worst off; she should take turns with some of them if she were worth the trumpet voluntary of her self-sacrifice. Not a sound came from the Indians as they shuffled along, not a whisper. Obviously no one wanted to be singled out by the drovers, still yelling their moronic chant, "Git! Git! Git, ya bastards!" The only other noise was that of the stray dogs, racing around the convoy at top speed, yapping at the horses, yelping when a whip stung them.

The sun, now high in the sky, lit up the faces around her, harsh with shadows. She seemed to be surrounded by people in a trance staring fixedly ahead. The dazzling sky was empty of birds, except for a flight of buzzards circling lazily overhead. The convoy was moving slowly up a slow rise in the endless plain. She looked behind her and saw a long procession of people with only here and there a horse or a wagon. At the horizon, a platoon of horsemen brought up the rear; she saw a glint of gold, that must be the captain and his soldiers. There were only a few of them, compared to the number of civilian drovers trotting up and down the column, cracking their whips, shouting curses.

After the first hour or so, she began to feel tired. Her feet started to hurt; when she looked down, she saw her shoes were scuffed bare, like a beggarwoman's. The sight of them suddenly threw her into a panic. What was she doing? What had possessed her to think that she could make a difference to the fate of these people? She and the man by her side were being carried along by a river of humanity in which they were no more than bobbing corks. And those shoes were not going to last another day!

For the first time in her life she had the eerie sensation of losing her identity. She saw, as she looked down at her shoes, the person she was turning into: a ragged scarecrow, with dangling hair, cracked lips, expected to squat, like the squaws, by the roadside to relieve herself. She would never be able to do that, not with all those leering men around—

Suddenly Mordecai Monk staggered and fell to his knees. She hauled him up, untenderly. "If thee starts doing that," she heard herself say, "thee had better ride in the cook's wagon."

It changed her concept of herself as a strong but gentle Quaker woman. How shameful, to turn into a harridan on the first day of a journey that was supposed to take weeks! Now was the time to be loving toward the Indians, to approach that of God in Mordecai, try to break through their staring remoteness . . .

But one could not 'love' all by oneself. Even the baby in its basket on the back of the woman trudging ahead of her seemed to look straight through her with its tiny black slitted eyes. Stumbling in her unsuitable shoes, she panicked. She was not going to make it. She had taken on this insane thing not out of a motion of love but because she had been at the end of her tether. Those shining Quaker women from the past had set out in the unshakable certainty that God was with them, that all He had was them; she had simply run away from an empty future. The captain would have to delegate someone to take her back to Pendle Hill, he—

With a strangled cry, Mordecai Monk fell headlong in the grass. She tried to help him back to his feet, but he seemed heavier than the last time. "Lydia!" His open eye roved sightlessly, his trembling hand touched her arm, "Lydia!" He was like a child, three times life size.

She managed to hoist him upright. Dusted him down. Put an arm around his portly waist. "Come," she said. "I'll take thee to the wagon."

"No—no! The Indians must walk, so must I! But what about thee? Thee must go back, Lydia, thee must go back! This is not for a woman, this will kill thee, it will kill thee . . ."

"Hush," she said. "I can go on like this for months, if need be. But how about thee? Please, let me take thee to the wagon!"

"No," he whispered, lifting his face to the sky. "No."

Suddenly it seemed very familiar—she had seen this many times in kindergarten, after a toddler had fallen flat on his face and decided to whoop it up. His back might hurt, but this dramatic collapse was a childish put-on. To have a useless male on her hands was one thing, a playacting male was unacceptable. But her instant decision to ask the captain to ship him home that night did not survive.

By herself she would never make it; with him to look after, stumbling, collapsing, she might. Why? Motherly instinct? Nothing of the sort. What she felt for him was not the feelings of a mother. She remembered something that George Fox had said about someone, 'I love that of God in him, but very little else.' That summed up her attitude toward Mordecai Monk.

"Come on," she said, supporting him. "It won't be long before we make camp. Then I'll find us something to eat."

"Thee must go back," he panted, "thee must go . . ."

She smiled indulgently, trudging along on blistered feet, leading the monster toddler in the power of the Lord.

It all seemed to be part of a dream. Who was he? Mordecai or Basil? Whoever he was, he was being mocked by God, in a landscape like hell, prisoner of a woman who detested him. She treated him like a child, but there was no love for him, not even contempt; she took him along with her just for moral sustenance, as a spiritual pig for the road.

But that was nonsense. He was clinging to the wreckage of his belief that God had a task for him, that he had been sent among the Indians for a purpose other than to serve as a female weightlifter's emergency rations. What could conceivably be left after his spiritual and emotional castration? If only he could free himself from his fatal addiction to words, experience life's vicissitudes like everyone else, without turning them into bombast! Oh, for a lyre, an audience! A singer needed listeners; had David, God's best friend, been a posturer too? A songster, an entertainer?

"God," he started, but that was as far as he got. God had left and gone home, bored with his boring bombast. There he went, led like a pig. Nothing left of beauty, music, imagery, passion; no joy sweeping through him, no poetry. *Then the Romans came, gently almost, with the inner security of having been the sole power on earth for five hundred years.* Bombast! No more than foam, thrashed in the soapy water of banal emotions. What could God possibly have had in mind to send him, of all people, as His messenger among the damned? What possible purpose could he serve?

"All right?" she asked, with a firm grip on his arm. The pig grunted. Another loss: suddenly all carnal desire was gone. If only he were fired by lust! If only he could have trod this trail brandishing Priapus's lance! But nothing; not a shiver of desire for the Quaker jailer now guiding him in chains. Why had even

sin been taken away from him? Because the hunted do not copulate? God had reduced all love, poetry, beauty, promise, tenderness, to ashes.

"Look where thee is going, Mordecai!"

He looked, and saw the ground rise, then fall away, like
waves. Waves on the sea of grass. Was he dreaming all this?
Would he wake up in his comfortable bed in Birmingham? Or
in Liza's? *Cup of tea, love?* Please, God, wake me . . .

As if in response to his prayer, the trumpet blared behind
him, a shattered signal partially blown away by the wind. The
last trump! But instead of rising from their graves, the dead, or
near-dead, dropped where they stood, drew blankets over their
thin bodies, and fell asleep.

"Well," his jailer said, "this seems to be the end of another
day. How is thee? All right?"

"Ready to join the dead," he said, not meaning it dramatically, just a visual observation.

"Easy does it," she said coldly. "Let me get thee something
to eat, before thee descends into thy ornate tomb."

The day's march had ended earlier than Lydia expected. She
was amazed at her own resilience; she could have walked on
much longer, preoccupied as she was with her plans for organ-
izing classes. When the column halted, she first settled Mordecai
under the little shelter, then made a tour of the camp on her way
to the chuck wagon, counting children.

They were finally showing themselves. Including strays, she
counted sixty-eight, ranging from first to seventh grade. She
could commence with one class a day, to start an hour after
bivouac was made and they had had their evening meal. They
seemed to have nothing to do at that time but just sit around,
too tired to play after the long walk.

As she moved among the Indians, anxious to communicate,
she was met by their now familiar refusal to acknowledge her
presence. The children followed the example of their elders;

when she sat down beside a couple of small girls, they looked through her, as if she were invisible, a ghost. Was this how these sad people retained their self-respect? Surely, the approach to conflict after the manner of Friends would be able to get through to them? But first she should be able to speak their language; at least some words and phrases. It was time to go and see the chief.

His teepee was the only one in the camp, a high triangular edifice of hides, its entrance screened with strings of beads. She stood in front of it, mustering up courage, when she became aware of a change around her. All movement had stopped. The Indians, who had been scurrying around like ants, had suddenly come to a standstill. She looked at them; those whose eyes she met instantly looked away. Yet she was sure everyone was watching, waiting to see what would happen.

She tried to knock, but there was nothing to knock on. So she approached the screened doorway and called, "Chief? Friend Chief!"

No answer. The tent seemed empty. Yet she sensed the presence of someone behind the screen.

"Chief?"

No answer.

"Friend Chief, there is something I must discuss with thee! I am a schoolteacher, I—" Suddenly the beads parted.

The stony-faced Indian with the two feathers emerged, followed by a woman with heavy breasts; clinging to her skirt was a child of about two, lip and chin wet with snot. The woman eyed her malevolently; the chief stared fixedly at a point above her right shoulder.

"Good evening, Chief."

No response.

She drew a deep breath; it was time for Quakerly bluntness. "Chief, I am burdened by a concern about the children. I am a teacher from the Quaker school in the town you have passed. The school was founded for Indian children, we still have a number of them among our pupils. I am well acquainted with their needs."

The woman stared at her venomously; the chief remained fascinated by the point above her right shoulder. Maybe 'Indian' had not been the right word; she should have used 'Mahanoy.' Well, no point in being delicate; either they wanted an education for their children or they did not. Now was the time to find out.

"I would like to remind thee of the fact that we are united by the treaty between our ancestors," she continued. "I intend to make this journey with you. I propose to organize the children by age, in two groups, to teach them reading, writing, and arithmetic, or play games with them, depending on their ages. In order to do so it is essential that I speak your language. Would thee be so kind as to appoint someone from thy tribe to teach me some basic Mahanoy, so the children may understand what I say?"

No reaction. Surely, she was entitled to *some* response from the couple she was addressing? The woman went on staring daggers at her, the man refused to look her in the eye in a pitiful display of hostility. The snotty child could not resist, it peered from behind its mother's skirt with one pitch-black inscrutable eye. When she smiled at it, however, it withdrew at once. Then she felt someone standing behind her.

She turned around and saw it was the captain, arms akimbo, legs apart.

"Madam, you are wasting your time."

"In that case, I would like to have a word with thee, Friend Stewart."

"With pleasure," he said. "My name is Ebenezer. This way, please." He gestured toward his tent across the clearing.

She said, "Thank thee, Chief," and headed for the captain's tent, chin high, ignoring the Indians ignoring her as she walked past. Mordecai would have to wait for his supper.

If she had not seen the captain's headquarters being put up earlier, she would have thought it had never moved. The view of the prairie was the same, and likely to remain so for the next five weeks.

On the front porch stood the table and two chairs. "Have a seat, please." The captain helped her up the steps and waited until she was seated before following suit. The Negro servant appeared in the doorway.

"What is your pleasure, miss?"

"Nothing, thank thee, Ebenezer Stewart." She felt on edge, but was determined not to show it.

"In that case, allow me to order for myself." He turned to the servant. "The usual, boy. And take care of the others."

"Yes, sah." The servant withdrew.

If there were other officers around, she had not noticed them.

"Well, Miss Best, what can I do for you?"

She tried to read the cold blue eyes. They gave her the shivers, but she shrugged off that un-Quakerly reaction. "Thee must have overheard the proposal I made to the chief. Perhaps thee could help me get through to these people?"

"My dear Miss Best—"

She did not let him finish. "I know it looks like I'm wasting my time, but I am not. The moment they realize that I am serious about teaching their children, that I honestly want to serve them, not use them for—"

The servant returned, carrying a tray with a glass of yellow liquid and some sprigs of mint. The captain took it without thanking him; the Negro went back inside.

He raised his glass to her, took a draught, and said, "I respect your courage, Miss Best, but it is my duty to tell you that the truth—" His face hardened and he said, "Well, well, look who's here."

She looked. Jesse McHair was heading for the command tent, leading a packhorse loaded with what appeared to be supplies.

"Hello there," Jesse touched his hat. "I brought some stuff, Lydia, for thee and fatso over there."

"Who?"

Jesse and the captain exchanged male glances. "I have most of what thee asked for. The women sorted out thy clothes. Obadiah did the same for Mordecai Monk. He didn't have anything of much use in his luggage, but I brought him a change of underwear and my second pair of boots. I don't know if they'll fit him, but all he seems to have in the way of shoes is what he's wearing."

"How kind of thee," Lydia said, for some reason suddenly close to tears.

"Well, where shall I dump all this, Captain? Would there be room in one of the wagons?"

The captain said, "I'll find a spot. Just unload it all where Mr. Monk is, right there, across the clearing."

"Thank thee," Jesse said, and turned around.

"Well, Miss Best," the captain resumed, with a smile, "you and I will have to postpone our little tête-à-tête. After supper I'll send my orderly with another invitation."

"Thank thee, Ebenezer Stewart."

"You know where to collect your rations, don't you? At the chuck wagon, over there."

"I know," she said.

Mordecai Monk watched his measly valise and Lydia's trousseau being unloaded at his feet. The mere thought of having to carry part of that, even a small part, made him consider joining the uncouth Jesse on the road back to Pendle Hill, and never mind his female jailer.

He felt better than he did a few hours ago, as if the walking had done him good. His eye still hurt, and the wounds on his back had begun to suppurate, or maybe the fluid dribbling down his spine was sweat. Anyhow, Lydia would look after that. Otherwise, his mind was clear, the feeling of being caught in a nightmare had dissipated. All that was left, for some reason, was a sense of dull resentment against the bossy woman. 'Ornate tomb' indeed! What about food? Where, for that matter, were they?

He looked about him: the same scene as when they had left: grass, grass, waving and undulating, a darkening blue sky, and buzzards. Always the buzzards. They were part of the nightmare.

He gazed at his worldly belongings stacked at his feet. Well, 'stacked' was too grandiloquent: one valise, looking as if a stage-coach had driven across it, and a pair of boots sure to be too large for him; he had his mother's dainty feet. That was all, for a hike of hundreds of miles across virgin prairie. But, soft! There came the maiden, ready to unpack her hope chest. Indefatigable, talking about classes for the children, unpacking school books, dictionaries— "Ha! There's the abacus!" She made him feel useless, a drone with a valise full of unsuitable clothes, like nightshirts and a nightcap with tassel.

For some reason, or for no reason at all, he was moved by her determined activity. Poor soul. To say something nice, he came up with, "I hope, in time, to be able to follow thy example."

She looked down on him with raised eyebrows, and asked, "Am I to understand that thee is planning to teach the children? Or are we going to have sermons?"

For a reason he could not fathom, her waspish response pacified him. It made her sound young, and frightened, and lost. Well, so was he. A chocolate merchant and a schoolteacher, lost in the Stone Age. What in the world could God have in mind, if He was involved in this at all?

"I wonder," he said aloud.

"Ha!"

She had been rummaging in her hope chest and now hauled out a purple dress. "Now what in the world would thee say Saraetta expects me to do with *this*?" She turned it around; in Quaker terms it was quite 'brittle,' something to associate with barn dancing. Only he had no idea what barn dancing was; just a word he had picked up somewhere along the road to nowhere. "Maybe they visualized a weekly officers' ball on the prairie," he suggested.

It brought her back to his contemptible presence. Dress in hand, she contemplated him, as if he had just slithered down from the apple tree in Paradise. "Why?" she asked.

"Why what?"

"Why did thee fool me by pretending thee was about to collapse today?"

He had no idea what she was talking about. "When?"

"I see. We're going to have amnesia, are we?" She folded the dress and put it back in the chest.

"I honestly don't remember," he said, sincerely. "As a matter of fact, I remember very little of this afternoon, other than feeling, well, a bit giddy."

She rose. "It's time I went to find us something to eat."

She gathered her skirts and strode off in the dusk full of Indians and horses. Neither of them had any business here, except maybe the Lord's. But the Lord remained silent, and mysterious, and vast, like the prairie itself.

The young man Jesse intercepted her and embraced her, in slow motion. Mordecai watched him mount his mustang and lope off, leading the empty packhorse behind him, the horse he himself should have been riding, back to the real world. Why hadn't he?

"Well," she said chirpily. "How about thy taking a nap while I get the food?"

A nap. In the midst of a tribe of Indians hopping around in a frenzy? Without having had anything to eat?

"I might as well," he said, to be rid of her.

He turned on his side, pulled a blanket over his aching body, placed his hat on the side of his head, and observed her horizontally as, to his astonishment, she wriggled out of her dress, let it drop in a heap around her feet, and prepared to put on the one she had just put away. He caught a glimpse of bare shoulders before she pulled the new one over her head. The glimpse made his mouth go dry.

"Lord," he thought, staring at her youthful figure, "despise me. Despise me! I am despicable. I am an abomination to Thee."

God did not respond.

Lydia, in her ridiculous purple dress, defiantly joined the squaws lined up in front of the chuck wagon to collect her ration of meat from the sergeant in charge. After he had dumped it into her cooking pot she joined the next queue, the one for the communal cooking fire. As she stood waiting among the other women, she became conscious of their body odor, enough to knock you over sideways. But where and when could they wash, poor dears? It surely was only a matter of time before she would be adding her own personal bouquet. Finally, her turn came to roast her meat. She squeezed herself in between two hefty squaws, who stolidly ignored her. They went on talking to each other across her, most insulting; their language sounded high-pitched and chittering. Squatting by the fireside, holding the cooking pot by its long handle—quite a balancing act—she came to the conclusion that they were giggling about her, saying things to one another like 'Look at that silly female! Look at the way she cooks her meat! She pretends to know everything, but she's only copying what we are doing. And what in the name of Manitou is she *wearing*?'

Their rejection became so oppressive that she went back to Mordecai Monk before the meat was quite done. He was peering in her direction with a look of expectancy. He sat up at her approach, greeted her with childish delight, and wolfed down the half-cooked meat. Only after he had eaten did he worry about her having so much to do after a grueling day's march: put up their shelter, cook a meal, dress his wounds, wash his feet . . .

"Sorry," she said, "but I am not going to wash thy feet. Thee has two hands, thee was able to move them from the pot to thy mouth, thee should be able to reach thy feet. I will do thy bandage, but first let's talk about how we can get through to the Indians. They don't want any part of us. I wonder if that will change."

"Oh," he said airily, "they'll accept us in the end."

So she did his bandage for him; the wound on his back looked angry but no more so than before. She did wash his feet for him, as an act of contrition for wondering why the captain had not sent his servant with another invitation for a tête-à-tête. She unrolled her pallet and made sure the awning was securely fastened, that it might not be blown away overnight. Finally she undressed, lay down, pulled up her blanket, and rested her head on the bundle she had carried all day. By then, darkness had fallen.

Exhausted, about to fall asleep, she was shocked awake by rustling in the tall grass behind them. It sounded as if someone was slinking about there, surreptitiously peering at her. In the stillness, in the darkness, the prairie suddenly became a world full of menace, of men inflamed with lust by the mere fact of the presence of a white woman.

Well, she would have to deal with them as way opened. And they were not really the problem. The problem was: Why? Why had God arranged things so she would end up here, alone with a man she disliked among five hundred disoriented Indians in the prairie? If there was a divine plan, what could it be? Her teaching the children depended on her knowing their language. How could she learn it without help, without communication?

Suddenly life was full of mystery, and fear, and farewell. Farewell to all she had loved despite everything, the old Lydia, so happy and gay, with so many friends. True, there had been sadness, unspoken, unremembered by an act of will: the epidemic, the dying children, the slaughter of the lambs. It had changed Saraetta; it had changed her too. It had set in her once radiant soul a core of darkness.

Was it all part of the plan? Was there a plan?

The darkness within grew slowly, like a shadow, until she was touched by its chill.

She did not sleep much that night; finally morning came, blue and rose, with small clouds like sheep, lit from below in the vastness of the sky. To her amazement she felt rested. She put on the high-button boots Saraetta had packed for her; they were a blessing. Her feet, though painful, did not prevent her walking.

She fetched some gruel from the chuck wagon; while Mordecai sat slurping it, she rolled up tarpaulin, shelter, and bedrolls. Presently the bugle sounded, the drovers began to rouse the Indians. "Git, git! Git, ya bastards!"

The mass of Indians began to move. She helped Mordecai up.

Then, as a godsend, there was the captain's servant, sent to collect their luggage and put it in a wagon. Bless the captain! "Thank thy master for us, please. Thank *thee*!"

The black man said, "Yas, ma'am."

Together, Mordecai and she joined the herd; soon she resumed walking in the rhythm of the march. This time she deliberately entered a world of daydreams. Cool water. Crisp bedsheets. The smell of lavender. In her mind, she opened her wardrobe full of clothes; pretty dresses, delicate and silky. Stockings, warm, soft, like friends first thing in the morning. She recalled the day she had tried on the dress she was wearing now: the feel of it, its elegance despite the risqué color and rather daring cut. And how she had loved these high-button boots when she first wore them! Yet she had never realized how precious they were, not even the first day she wore them: symbols of refinement, of human dignity.

As she trudged along with the herd under the wind-swept mares'-tails in the autumn sky, she was less distressed by the brutal heartlessness of the drovers than by the angry bickering of the squaws around her. In their alien world there seemed to be no room for tenderness or loving kindness; it seemed a world of anger, deprivation, violence. She tried to evoke the Presence, but all she could evoke was cool water, the smell of newly baked bread, the beauty of the little mirror her mother had given her on her twelfth birthday. *'Now, Lydia, don't give in to vanity!'* Tiredness, she discovered, was not merely a physical thing; she had walked this far before. Now, homesickness for the past sapped her strength. Mordecai, to the contrary, had marched all day with the steady pace of an elephant. No theatrical crises, for once. Well, thank the Lord for small mercies.

When, at last, the convoy made camp, she was exhausted, but headed for the chuck wagon before the line of squaws had a chance to grow. Yesterday the sergeant and his soldiers who dealt out the meat had acknowledged her as one of their own with bashful smiles; now they treated her like the rest, just another pushy female reaching through the bars for her food.

She managed to be among the first at the cooking fire and

made no bones about pushing others aside to get to it. She roasted her meat with the same egotism as the rest of the squaws; this time when she brought Mordecai his meat, he could sink his teeth into it. A couple more days, and she would have mastered the trick of roasting meat without burning it. The mashed potatoes and the vegetable slop the soldiers ladled out were foul, but that no longer seemed to matter.

When night fell, she fetched water for them to wash with, pulled off Mordecai's boots, helped him out of his jacket, rolled it into a pillow, and covered him with a blanket. He was so grateful that he managed to grab her hand and kiss it. He had hot, wet lips; it gave her the creeps. "Stop that!" she said sharply. "Go to sleep."

"Could we have meeting first?" he asked.

"No," she said. But to make up for her snapping, they had a brief one. At least, that was the idea.

But soon she sat gazing at the stars instead of centering down, daydreaming once more about freshly laundered sheets, and the silk nightgown she had almost bought but which Saraetta, who was with her, had considered too worldly. Saraetta had a witness against frivolity, she had even covered—

There was rustling in the grass behind her.

The drover with the squint? . . .

She listened; but it had stopped. That afternoon, after looking about her to see if the coast was clear, she had hurriedly squatted a short way off in the grass, and had the fright of her life when, right behind her, she heard a heavy thud and a snigger. As she ran back into the ranks, looking over her shoulder, she saw it was the lanky young drover, unshaven, as cross-eyed as a Siamese cat, who had been leering at her all day; he had jumped off his horse, right behind her. His name, she had gathered from shouts addressed to him by the others, was 'Two-tone,' or 'Boots,' maybe both. She had noticed when he trotted past, which he did frequently, that he wore scuffed boots that at one time had been black and white.

As she sat there, tense, listening, staring at the night sky, the thought occurred to her that 'Two-tone Boots' might dominate her life from now on. The rest of the day after the incident she kept an eye on his whereabouts at all times. Even now, listening, she was disturbed because she thought it might be him. How had he managed? The moment she had squatted in the grass, there he had been, leering at her with his Siamese cat's eyes, stretching his stringy neck as he tried to get the full picture.

No more rustling. It must have been birds, or grasshoppers, or whatever it was that filled the night with their monotonous chirping. Yet she was sure she was being watched. She angrily tried to shake the obsession, for what could the man do? Nothing, absolutely nothing other than gawk at her during the miserable seconds that nature forced her to squat in the grass. She would certainly not be so foolish as to back out of sight of the column.

Suddenly she knew: this is how it will end. When nature forces me to back deeper into the grass, he will pounce. She would scream bloody murder—no, she wouldn't. A calloused hand would smother her cry. The other hand would rip her dress, as she struggled when he forced her legs apart.

Again! A slithering sound! He was there, somewhere in the grass, right behind her! She concentrated all her awareness on listening. She heard panting. Pant, pant, pant . . . A dog? Had he a dog? It took minutes of motionless, terrified listening before she realized that what she heard was not the panting of a dog, but the pounding of her heart in her own breathing. When she closed her mouth, it stopped. When she opened her mouth, it started up again.

She tried to get a hold of herself by thinking about the godly lives that had gone before: Margaret Fell, Gulielma Woodhouse. What had Margaret Fell done to protect herself against rape in those hellish prisons of the seventeenth century? In London she had organized a volunteer corps of women to go into the dungeons, and dressed them in green and red so they would be recognized in the 'perpetual gloom of the dungeons,' as the teacher had put it in First Day school. And what about the prison in Lancaster, when she had been all alone among the children about to be hanged? What strength had she found within herself to stop the rising panic growing into terror? What had she done, in that dungeon, when she had to relieve herself? Gulielma Woodhouse, who had worked as a doctor all alone among the Indians deep into Mexico, had made no bones about it. Any time now, nature would force her to back further into the grass. She would have to absent herself, however briefly, unless— Ah! That was an idea! The captain's necessary! The little shelter beside the command tent! Dare she ask him?

James Stewart— No, wait, the man's name was not James. What was it—Nebuchadnezzar? Ebenezer! *Good evening, Ebenezer Stewart. Could I have a word with thee?*

Of course, Miss Best. Have a seat. Boy! The Negro servant would bring a glass of lemonade.

Ebenezer Stewart, I know it is a delicate subject, but let me be frank. That little shelter by the side of thy tent—am I mistaken? Is that a—a necessary?

No, she would never be able to ask so boldly. More delicate, circumspect. *Ebenezer Stewart, what is that interesting little building I see beside thy tent?* Phooey! That was worse, it turned her from a prude into an idiot. Why not be blunt? Quaker bluntness was always the answer in the end. *Ebenezer Stewart, forgive me for being blunt, but one of thy drovers, the one with the squint, I think his name is Two-tone Boots, is dogging me wherever I go, even when I—I have to retire for a moment. No, no, I don't want thee to do anything about him, it's fine with me, let him peep his fill and good luck to him, but there will come a moment when I must absent myself a little more substantially.* Substantially? Say that to a man? *Ebenezer Stewart, as thee knows I have joined the Indians as a witness, to start classes among the Indian children . . .* That was a long, blathersome way to get around to his privy. What if she borrowed, tomorrow evening, Mordecai Monk's breeches, put on his hat, and swaggered into the grass after darkness had fallen? Ha! Two-tone Boots might be stupid, but as he was aware of her whereabouts at all times, he would no doubt be lying in wait for her. Interesting: to strong-arm a woman into submission and have to cope with a man's breeches first.

Good evening, Ebenezer Stewart. Could I have a word with thee . . . ?

The one she should have a word with was God.

She tried. She tried to address Him as she would a father, but she would not have confided this anguish to her father either. As a friend? *Dear God, sooner or later, sooner rather, I will have to have a—*

She could not mention 'bowel movement' in a prayer. If only she could ask Margaret Fell! *Maggie? How did thee do it? I am terrified; was thee too?*

But whereas Catholics could pray to the saints of their Church, to pray to a Quaker saint did not work, at least not if you expected an answer.

Maggie? . . . Gulie? . . .

Of course there came no answer; she was not in their class. What those formidable women had done, they had done in the power of the Lord, as a motion of love, not because they had landed themselves in a hopeless mess as a result of disillusion, fear, unrequited love, stupidity. She was not in the power of the Lord. She was not driven by a motion of love. She was—

Mordecai stretched out his hand to her; they broke meeting. She went on trying to formulate what she was, in comparison to the saints, while she undressed, lay down on her pallet, pulled the blankets over her, and fell asleep, exhausted.

The next evening, after she had put up the shelter, collected their rations, elbowed her way to the cooking fire, roasted the meat, and made her way back to Mordecai with their supper, she saw the captain being served his meal on the porch, his black servant in attendance.

"I'll be right back," she said to Mordecai, handing him his plate.

He mumbled something; she headed straight for the command tent. Forgetting about her dusty dress and scuffed boots, she said, in a tone too regal by far, "I wish to have a word with thee, Ebenezer Stewart."

He rose. "Of course, Miss Best. Please . . ." He dabbed at his mustache with his napkin and pointed to the chair opposite.

"Thank thee." She lifted her skirts, exposing the wrecks of her boots, and stepped onto the porch. The table was decked with fresh linen, silver, china, a glass half-filled with red wine; on his plate a juicy steak, a crumbled biscuit beside it. At his signal the servant pulled out the chair for her.

"What may I offer you, Miss Best? Coffee? A glass of liqueur?"

"Nothing, thank thee. I will not stay. I came to ask a simple favor."

"You have not eaten yet?" the captain exclaimed. "How stupid of me! May I invite—"

She cried, "No, please! Don't offer me anything. I—I have had my meal."

To her dismay she could see that he knew she was lying; he spread his hands in mock surrender. "All right. Boy, clear away, I'll have my coffee later."

Deftly, the servant made plate, cutlery, biscuit, and crumbs disappear, leaving only the glass. He returned with another glass and a jug, which he put on the table, then disappeared again.

"At least share a glass of wine with me," the captain said.

She shook her head.

"Surely, one glass? A cup of coffee, then?"

"I do not want any special favors." She realized too late that this was hardly in accord with the reason for her visit. No Indian squaw would take it into her head to ask the captain if she might use his privy.

The man must have read her thoughts. "Surely you are no longer under the illusion that those people care about you one way or another?" he asked. "I would have thought you had learned your lesson by now."

"These things take time," she said.

The captain had the good grace not to smile. "Well, what is the simple favor, Miss Best?"

She took herself in hand. She had decided to think of him as a doctor. "I would not make the request if thee had not shown thyself to be a gentleman," she began, then lost heart at the thought that this too was a lie: he had pushed her over with his horse and made her flee half naked into the bushes.

He picked up his glass. "This may be the moment to remind you, Miss Best, that in order to survive you'll have to turn into an Indian squaw. Remember?"

"Of course."

"However, I have given the matter some thought. You have a second choice." He took a sip of wine.

She watched him with a frown. Something had gone wrong.

"It will take us a while to reach the Mississippi. You've spent only three days with us, and look at you. No civilized white woman is up to this. You will fall ill. Something untoward may happen to you at any time. Unless—"

"Yes?"

"Unless you were to avail yourself of the sanctuary of this command post. I offer you my hospitality for the rest of our journey."

She did not know how to react. All she could think of was flight.

"I do realize," he continued, "that in the world we left behind this would be a shocking proposition. But we are on the prairie now, the world we left behind is as remote as the moon. So, please: avail yourself of the civilized amenities of my quarters."

When she did not reply, he raised his glass to her and emptied it. She saw his Adam's apple move under the red fur on his throat as he drank. His brazen maleness filled her with terror. She rose. "Good night, Ebenezer Stewart." She sounded self-possessed, but as she swept off the porch she tripped on one of the steps and nearly fell on her face. Dropping all pretense, she ran toward the shelter as fast as she could. She saw Mordecai Monk sitting under the awning, suddenly a beacon of security.

'Thank God,' she thought, 'thank God for that man! What would I do without him to protect me? I would be lost in a nightmare . . .'

In the far distance sounded the grief-stricken howl of the first coyote of the night.

"Thank God!" he said as she appeared beside him.

"Thank God for what? Thee hasn't finished thy food."

"I was afraid," he said.

"Thee? Afraid? Don't be silly. Give me thy jacket, I'll make up thy pillow."

"I thought thee was asking him—"

"Asking who?"

"To be taken home . . ." he said, tears in his eyes. It was a bit much, all the same. She had forgotten what a showman he was.

"I would never do that without telling thee first," she said.

"But thee might?"

"Mordecai," she said firmly, "if thee does not stop this, I have half a mind to tell him to take *thee* home. I trust God had a purpose when He sent thee here; but occasionally a person cannot help wondering what in the world it might be."

"I know," he said, hanging his head in exaggerated shame; he should go home and join a traveling theater.

"It is time we both faced facts," she said. "Here." She put down his pillow. "Lie down."

He obeyed.

"What facts?" he asked almost eagerly, as if expecting a bedtime story. Saraetta had been right: in their hearts all men were seven years old.

"The fact is that neither thee nor I have the faintest idea why God sent us here. That is, if we really, honestly believe He did."

He did not respond, he seemed unhappy with the turn of the conversation. He would have preferred Little Red Riding Hood.

"One of these days," she said firmly, "thee and I will discover what He had in mind, and we had better be prepared for a surprise. It may be totally different from what *we* had in mind. Is thee following what I'm saying?"

"Let's have meeting," he pleaded, eyes already closed. An astute move. He was, on reflection, an extraordinarily nimble man. She wondered who he would ultimately turn out to be, for eventually their true selves were bound to be revealed. Not something to look forward to.

"I am serious," she said. "Neither thee nor I are what we have appeared to be for most of our lives."

This was his cue to say 'Speak for thyself,' but he had closed his eyes and folded his hands.

"We must stop fooling ourselves," she persisted. "I was deeply affected by the Indians when I first saw them, but it never occurred to me, not in my wildest dreams, that I would throw in my lot with them. So, why did I do it?"

"Thee was moved by me in my affliction," he said, eyes closed, hands folded.

"Don't preach to me, Mordecai," she said coldly, "and above all, don't preach to thyself. Whatever anyone else may think, both thee and I know that we find ourselves here because we were not intelligent enough to get out while the getting was good."

"God may need us," he intoned.

"Well, good luck to Him. Maybe He is just stuck with us, after the way we blundered into this situation. What are we going to *do*, Mordecai? What earthly use are we to them? We don't speak their language, we—"

"That reminds me," he said, opening his eyes.

"Of what?"

"I found something among the clothing and toiletries they sent me." He sat up. "Where is my valise?"

She stopped herself from saying, 'Get it thyself, thee lazy slug,' went to fetch it from the wagon, and dropped it by his side.

He rummaged among the contents and came up with a dog-eared sheaf of papers. "Here," he said. "Have a look at this."

"What is it?"

"A dictionary of the Mahanoy language—well, more like a list of words. Made up by a Friend. Someone at the school put it in my suitcase."

"Why didn't thee show me this before?"

"Look at it," he said. "Take it to bed with thee."

She did. Snuggled down inside her blanket, she looked at it in the faint light of the dying day: twenty handwritten pages, crudely sewn into an exercise book. Heaven knows what the name of the Friend was who had composed this list of words; one thing was obvious: he must be dead. The list had to be at least a hundred years old, maybe more.

'*M'mitzi: I eat. M'gáuwi: I drink. M'wachpacheli: I awake. M'menne: I think.*' Just go ahead and try to pronounce that—

Behind her the grass rustled. She lowered the pamphlet.

Rustle. *Rutsch.*

In the distance a second coyote joined the first. The grass had fallen silent.

'God,' she thought. 'Oh, God, have mercy on us.'

'Not intelligent enough to get out while the getting was good.' What a fascinating thought! She was, really, quite an original, not the standard Quaker maiden of past dreams.

But was she right? Should they have got out while the getting was good? And if so, why hadn't they?

The stars were brighter than he had ever seen them in England. The Milky Way was a white smear across the sky. Never before had he felt so close to nature, so overwhelmed by sheer space. Gazing at the stars made him feel close to all creatures huddled together on this one small planet, in the immeasurable space that was God. Under the world-large arc of the Milky Way it was ludicrous to think that the Creator of this vastness could be presumed to have any part at all in their finding themselves here. They were here because they had not been intelligent enough to get out while the getting was good.

If that were so, what was there left in the way of hope, trust, faith in a heaven-ordained destiny? How tiny they were. How evanescent.

As he lay there, staring, he became aware of a soft animal sound, small and harmless in the vastness. It took a while before he realized it was her, snoring.

For a reason beyond comprehension it made him feel furious with God. Look at her! Look at her, Thou man-eating, star-squandering monster! There she lies, with her courage, her fear, her loneliness, her hunger for love, snoring in Thy universe! Hear her! LOVE her, damn Thee!

No response came from the stars. And no wonder.

CHAPTER 13

THE PRAIRIE
October 1833

The hornets came a week later, as camp was being made. They descended in hungry swarms, stinging like sparks from a fire, lusting for blood. Everywhere Indians were slapping their faces, arms, necks; dogs spun round and round, snapping, then tried to flee with their tails between their legs. Horses, exhausted and footsore as they might be, burst from the corral and galloped through the crowd, whinnying and kicking.

Mordecai was fighting off the vicious insects when he heard a thunder of hooves storming past, and a piercing scream.

A child had been hurt by one of the horses. Without thinking, he ran toward it. It was a terrified little Indian boy holding his leg, screaming, screaming. Mordecai tried to calm him down, but the child shrank away from his touch and tried to crawl out of his reach. Still, he managed to grab hold of him and take a look at the leg. There was no wound, no fracture, yet the little boy went on shrieking, holding it.

On impulse, Mordecai started to make the passes with his hands that Nanny Maple used to make when he had hurt himself as a child. It was a silly pretense, more like a game; even as a child he had realized it was Nanny Maple's own invention. But for some reason it had worked, at the time.

The assault of the hornets had abated; the little boy calmed down as Mordecai stroked the leg with both hands, without actually touching the skin, in long slow passes; after each pass he shook his hands to throw away the pain. He remembered the accompanying rhyme. Nanny Maple had probably made it up herself:

Hoopla! Hopla! Feel how it mends?
Stroke—and stroke—and shake your hands.
Froggy, piggy, baby bull,
Grab the pain and pull, and pull.
Hopla! Hoopla! There it goes!
Little boy back on his toes!

When the little boy scrambled to his feet and ran off, Mordecai became aware that a small crowd had gathered, watching the proceedings. He gave them a wave, said, "Hello! That's what my nanny used to do. Have a good day now," and returned to the shelter. There was Lydia, staring at him with what looked like awe.

"That was the first time!" she said.

"First time what?"

"The first time they actually *looked* at thee!"

"Ah?" he turned around, but the crowd had dispersed. "Well, they could hardly do otherwise, could they? Luckily the boy wasn't really hurt. Just a fright, I presume."

"What was that magic rhyme?" she asked.

"No magic, just something I remembered from my childhood. If there was any blood, Nanny Maple had another one, something about a toad. 'Hop and skip and grab a toad, chase the pain out of the road.' 'Out of the road' is Yorkshire. Thee would say 'out of the way.' "

She seemed to want to ask more, but the line of squaws was forming in front of the chuck wagon; she hurried off with her pot to be among the first.

They had their meal. The meat was on the tough side, and it had a faint odor he was not keen to inquire about. He was lying on his back, gazing at the first star in the deepening blue, when he heard her say in a tone of warning, "Mordecai!"

"Huh?" He rose on his elbows.

She pointed, discreetly, at something behind him.

He heaved himself into a sitting position and saw that a new crowd had gathered a few yards away, a row of staring Indians, gathered for some ominous purpose.

"Good evening," he said with a smile, wondering what was going on.

An old squaw slowly advanced on him, cautiously, as if approaching a fire. She kneeled and stared at him with black expressionless eyes. He was uncomfortable; he had no idea what she wanted. He was about to ask when she slowly raised a hand and tapped on her forehead.

"I do agree," he said heartily. "Sorry about that. Anyone outside the family who heard Nanny Maple chant her incantation must have thought she was barmy. At least the boy managed to run afterward."

Her face expressionless, her eyes those of a different species, the old woman tapped her forehead again.

"I *am* sorry," he repeated. He did not know what else to say.

Another squaw, a younger one, detached herself from the crowd and approached slowly, warily, until she stood behind the old one, who was still on her knees. The young one rocked her head with both hands, as if in a demonstration, and rolled her eyes, uttering moans. Mad? Madness? Was the old woman insane?

"I think she means the old lady has a headache," Lydia whispered behind him.

"So?"

"Maybe they want thee to—to do something about it."

"Me?"

"Whatever thee did for the little boy . . ."

He gazed at the old woman in disbelief. She just sat there on her knees, staring at him, her face a mask. The young one made a stroking gesture in the air with both hands and then shook them.

It was an important moment. For the first time the Indians had made contact. Now they were expecting something of him. He could not repeat the silly rhyme while stroking the old woman's head. It was something for children, not for grown-ups.

"Recite from the Bible . . ." Lydia whispered over his shoulder.

"Think I should give her the King's Touch?" he asked.

"What's that?"

"English kings used to, once a year, as the sick passed in front of them."

"Do what?"

"Touch them and say, 'I touch thee, may the Lord cure thee.' "

"Do it!" she urged. "Touch her . . ."

But he decided not to. "Dutch King William the Third of England refused to do it, he thought it was superstition. So he touched his first patient's head and said, 'I touch thee, may the good Lord give thee more sense.' "

Something stopped him from laughing, something in the face of the young woman: a desperate plea.

"Must be her mother," Lydia whispered.

Her mother. If someone had been present when his mother lay in pain, and had laughed . . . ?

Out of sympathy, not expecting it to have any effect, he reached out, touched the old woman's hair, recited the poem again, making the passes, throwing away the pain by shaking his hands, the way he had done for the little boy. As he did so, something extraordinary happened. He felt, coming from the small crowd that was watching, the same power that had come to him from those halls full of people in the past. The power was there, he felt it surge through him, so strong that it made him quake. He felt a sermon coming on, but the power would have to stand by itself. 'God,' he prayed, 'have mercy on the soul of Basil Goodlove.'

Now what on earth made him pray that? The power drained away; he awoke as from a spell. Something had been given to him and all he had known to do with it was to speak a prayer for the soul of his evil father. He took the hand of the old woman in his. It felt like a dead object, but he kissed it. Just as a gesture; it made no sense. "Thank thee," he said.

The old woman looked at him. There was now something in her eyes that had not been there before. A question? Amazement? Her face slowly changed. It was alarming; with all those wrinkles it looked as if a clay pot were slowly disintegrating in front of his eyes. Then he understood it was a smile. She rose with a surprisingly young movement, turned to her daughter, and said something. The daughter stared at him with a look of awe, then put her arm around her mother's shoulders and led her away. The crowd moved aside to let them pass. Then they turned away and left. He saw they were all women.

"Well," he said, "how about that?"

Lydia looked at him with an expression he could not interpret.

"As I remember it," he said, "each time, after the King's Touch, the monarch had to wash his hands."

Without a word, she picked up the pot and went to fetch the water.

Lydia had no idea why, but after the first impact she reacted to this development with anger. She was filling the pot from the spigot of the water wagon when she decided to have it out with him. She went back to their shelter, prepared for the showdown.

Mordecai lay yawning on his litter, knees pulled up, hat over his eyes, not a suitable posture for a man who had just been granted the power of healing.

"Here," she said, putting down the bowl. "Wash thy hands. Then we must talk."

"What about, dear heart?" he asked, yawning.

"What is thee going to do if they bring in more people? Has thee any idea what thee is playing with? This is not a sideshow!"

"Hey," he said, and lifted his hat to look at her. "What brought this on?"

"Thee has been given the gift of healing," she said, hearing herself how shrill her voice had become, "and thee treats it as if it were some childish magic!"

He looked bewildered.

"It is a gift from God! But I did not for a moment have the impression that thee was involved in a religious ceremony. All I heard thee say was 'Good, love'; and then thee kissed her hand."

"I don't get this," he said, sitting up. "What exactly is thee trying to say?"

"It was terribly important! The first time the Indians sought contact with us! The first time they acted as if they were *seeing* us! Where was thy prayer? Was this a laying-on of hands in the name of Christ?"

He thought it over, head bent, then he looked up and said, calmly, "Lydia, it is none of thy damn business."

She gasped. "That's right," she said, "throw in a couple of blasphemies! Does thee not realize what is happening? If they come back, and thee gives another performance like that one, thee will not become their Christian healer but a medicine man! A magician, washing his hands like a monarch! And I will find myself reduced to the role of a magician's moll!"

It made him laugh uproariously. She turned away and strode off, leaving him hee-hawing like an ass.

Alone in the dusk, at the edge of the encampment, she stifled a scream of anger and exasperation. Dear God, what was happening to her? The image she had built up of herself was crumbling: the strong-willed, calmly determined frontier woman cheerfully caring for a lazy, infantile man who depended on her for everything. She was returned once more to the truth of her condition: a pampered creature plagued by constipation, scratching her armpits, her hair a tangled mess, her second pair of shoes in shreds, beset by terror of a man with a squint called Two-tone Boots.

Tears began to flow. The pampered creature was crying because the malingerer she had relied on to sustain her self-image had shaken off the spell and acquired power of his own.

Nonsense! He was still the same old Mordecai Monk, posturer, blatherer, stricken with the fantasy that he was now a healer, not as representative of Christ, as the apostles had thought of themselves, but like a snake-oil salesman using a nursery rhyme for a magic formula. That little boy had obviously suffered a fright, easy to take away with some mumbo jumbo and sleight of hand. The old woman's headache had not been a headache at all, she had just wanted consolation, encouragement.

"Stop it!" she cried aloud.

What was she doing? Was she so weak that she saw no means of restoring her sense of superiority other than by slandering the man? Diminishing what he had done, calling it humbug? He had broken the ice, the Indians had at last looked them straight in the eye. Now *she* should move, corral the children and form them into classes. Where was her faith, her inner strength, her belief that, maybe, she might come to know Christ by doing His work? Some work!

At the bottom of it was the fear. Twelve days now without a bowel movement. She scarcely dared eat any more. She had begun to feel sick. A person could not go for this long without falling ill. Unless she managed tonight, at the latest tomorrow, she would be in real trouble. She should force herself, now, this minute. Disappear in the grass . . . But even as she stood there, tarrying, she heard him. Crackle. *Rutsch!* Two-tone Boots was peeping.

She ran back to the shelter. To Mordecai. Maybe Mordecai could put his hands on her stomach. 'Hopla, hoopla—'

She found him lying on his back, knees still drawn up, hat over his eyes, and felt the crazy urge to give him a kick. Choked with emotion, she kneeled in the darkness, and prayed to God for guidance, like all those women who had gone before, in whose lives her faith was founded.

The next morning, just before setting out, another patient was brought to the white medicine man for consultation. Another old woman, on a litter this time, exhausted and confused by the dramatic change in her life. She was revived, probably temporarily, by the now self-assured Mordecai, who was loving it all. After the trumpet had already blared its command to depart, a child was brought to him by its mother. It was a spindly little girl with a boil in her armpit. She was given Nanny Maple's 'hoopla' treatment and sent back to the fold. At least, Lydia concluded, the Indians now fully acknowledged their existence.

Alas, as it turned out, only his. To the squaws, she remained invisible. She dutifully provided water for the circus magician to wash his hands in, but was not even granted the humble status of the girl sawed in half. To them, she remained the insubstantial ghost she had been all along, the limping, stringy-haired ghost of the former Lydia whom everybody had loved so much.

Her constipation became an obsession. As she stumbled along with the herd that day, visions of death haunted her, agonizing death, poisoned by her own intestine. Would she be buried, or tossed, like the Indian dead, in the tall grass by the drovers, for the buzzards to feast on? And her soul, where would that go? Floating overhead with the buzzards? Or would it sprout wings like a chrysalis and wing through the dark valley of death to where the saints were? How would they receive her? What would Margaret and Gulielma have to say to the scolding harridan who turned up expecting a welcome? Oh, what childish, degrading nonsense! 'God, dear God—what is to become of me?' Self-pity turned out to be of no help either. If only something would happen!

If that had been a prayer, it was answered promptly. After the column had climbed another rise that seemed to go on forever, she caught the first glimpse of other human beings on the prairie. On top of the next ridge, sharply silhouetted against the sky, a row of motionless horsemen was ranged, observing them for a while before disappearing.

That evening, when they were making camp, a party of strange Indians on horseback emerged from the prairie, different from the Mahanoy, naked and wild, with feather headdresses. They dragged two dead buffalo into the bivouac. Ululating squaws threw themselves onto the beasts and started to stab and hack away at them, each trying to tear off a piece of the best meat. The drovers turned up with their whips to force them away from the carcasses, one of which was dragged across the clearing to the cooking fire, the other somewhere else. Then the screaming assault of the squaws resumed.

Lydia could not bring herself to join in. Only after everyone else was through hacking and tearing did she approach the bared skeleton. Nearly all the meat was gone, dogs were tearing and gnawing at the bones. She spotted some left near the hump of the skeleton, too high for the dogs to reach; but a rangy one with a patch around one eye, with whom she had had a run-in before, was waiting for her. As she stood with a blood-dripping hunk in her hand, she was prepared for his attack; and when it came, she dealt him a ringing blow with her cooking pot. The yelp attracted the attention of the squaws around the fire, but they turned away at once when they saw who it was.

'Damn them!' she thought. 'Damn! Damn!' She strode toward the fire, elbowed her way between the chief's wife and another hellion; their body odor was stronger than the stench of frying fat and smoke. But she should probably take herself down a peg, her fragrance must outstrip theirs by now.

While cooking the meat, she looked at the women around the fire. Her arrival had stopped their conversation; they could not have clammed up more thoroughly if she had been Two-tone Boots himself.

Suddenly she decided she had had enough. She put the pot down to reserve her place and ran to the shelter. Mordecai was lying on his back again, hands behind his head, hat over his eyes; when he heard her unroll her pack to take out the dictionary, he lifted his hat and smiled, thinking she had come to feed him. She leafed through the dictionary. *Constipation* was not listed. She felt her eyes fill with tears again as she flicked the pages; then, under *H*, she found the word *Pusil*. '*Help (help me): Pusil.*' That would do! She walked away; Mordecai called after her, "Where is thee going?"

The pot was still there. She squeezed between the two smelly women again, turned to the chief's wife on her left, and said, "*Pusil!*"

The woman went on staring stolidly at the fire.

"*Pusil!*" she repeated. "*Pusil! Pusil! Pusil!*" and she shook her by the arm. The touch of the soft feminine flesh became her undoing. She burst into sobs.

She sat there, bawling like a child, unable to stop. Then someone touched her shoulder.

For a moment she thought it was the captain coming to her rescue. She looked up and saw it was the chief's wife. All the other women were staring stolidly into the fire; the chief's wife was not looking at her either, but it was her hand on her shoulder, a motherly hand.

"*Pusil*," she said, trying to master her tears. "Constipation. Stomach cramp."

The hand was taken away, leaving such feeling of abandonment that she grabbed it and put it on her abdomen. "Ouch!" she cried. "Ouch! *Pusil!*"

The woman slowly turned her head and looked at her; the black eyes were as expressionless as pebbles.

"Help me!" she cried. "*Pusil! Pusil!* Please! I am in pain!"

At last, the stony face relented. The woman frowned, trying to understand.

She let go of the woman's hand to make a bulging gesture in front of her belly.

The woman smiled.

She thought she was pregnant! The other squaws had turned their heads now too and stared at her, fascinated.

"No, no, not pregnant! *Ouch!*" She must make them understand, but how? Sign language! She pressed her hands on her stomach, wailing "*Ouch!*" She made the gesture of pregnancy and vigorously shook her head. "No, not pregnant! *No papoose!*" She tried to think of a gesture that would express intestinal blockage; all she could come up with was one fist above the other, like wringing out a dishcloth. They remained fascinated, but uncomprehending. The face of the chief's wife now expressed concern, but no understanding.

She pointed at the pot with meat, mimed taking a bite of it, chewing, swallowing, following the food down to her stomach, into her belly; then she clenched her fists, wrung out the imaginary dishcloth again, and cried, "*Ouch!*" Surely now they would understand.

They did not. But now she had got this far, she might as well see it through. She squatted on her heels, lifted her skirts, proceeded to act out as explicitly as she could an effort to relieve herself, then cried, startled, "Two-tone!" and jumped, to evoke the drover who had flushed her time after time. She ended with the desperate cry, "*Pusil! Pusil*, please!"

The chief's wife talked to the others. They all started talking at the same time; Lydia looked anxiously from face to face, trying to understand what they were saying. Then one of them pointed at the sky, at the circling buzzards waiting for the dogs to abandon the carcass. The squaws all looked up, and shrieked with laughter.

Her hopes were dashed. She was about to pick up her pot and leave before she burst into tears again when the chief's wife took her by the hand and pointed. At what? A person? A place? "*Teepee*," the woman said. Her husband's teepee? She proceeded to pull Lydia to her feet.

They walked toward the chief's teepee through a crowd of staring Indian men, who, she now realized, had been watching her embarrassing performance from the start. The woman stooped through the bead curtain, leaving it swinging. Lydia waited, expecting her to come back; but a hand appeared through the beads and beckoned her.

The inside of the teepee was dark; the stuffiness was stifling. She heard the woman speaking rapidly, but when her eyes adjusted to the gloom, she saw that they were alone. The woman took her to a stack of hides and made her lie down. The soft, springy mattress gave her a sense of luxury; she yearned to stretch out on it. The woman, chattering all the time, offered her a beaker. Lydia sniffed at the liquid, it smelled foul. Rotting leaves? The woman made a drinking gesture, rubbed her stomach, screwed up her face, cried, "Ow!" and then, with a gesture that could not be misinterpreted, "Poof! Ahh!" It was a laxative.

She was reluctant to take it. If it worked, it would make her the helpless prey of Two-tone Boots. She stared at the woman, who smiled, shook her head, and pointed at the sky. Heaven knew what that meant, but she had to trust somebody. She took a deep breath, closed her eyes, pinched her nose, and swallowed the evil liquid. It tasted better than it smelled: a strange, nutty flavor.

She handed back the empty beaker; for some reason the woman heaved a sigh of relief. When she went to get up, the woman held her down. *"Ono, ono! Kakiwale aneeko!"* Presumably it meant, among other things, 'Wait for it to work.' Lydia relaxed and sank back onto the hides. The woman kneeled at her feet and began to unbutton her tattered boots.

"No, please! If I take those off I'll never be able to put them back on again!"

The woman held up a pair of moccasins, invited her to feel them. They were soft, made of supple deerskin, they felt like sheer luxury. The woman finished taking off the boots and started to massage her feet. It was pure heaven. She was beginning to relax when the doorway darkened. The chief! Only after she had half risen did she see it was the woman who had been sitting on the other side of her, pointing at the sky, hooting with laughter. The woman kneeled beside the chief's wife, unrolled a bundle of cloth she had brought with her, and held up the contents for Lydia to see: a squaw's skirt, a blouse made of deerskin decorated with beads, a headband. They pulled her to her feet and took off her dress. Then her petticoat and camisole. Then her drawers. Now everything had come to an end, she had never shown herself naked before, not since she was a child, not even to Saraetta.

The chief's wife poured oil on her chest, dollops of it, and started to smear it out on her naked skin. It felt lovely but stank the place up. She now realized that their smell was not body odor but this Indian lotion. She was obviously supposed to love it, so she said, "H'm . . . h'm. Nice! Lovely!" closing her eyes to demonstrate her delight.

Now that they had brought her this far, they proceeded to give her the full treatment. The chief's wife produced another bottle and doused her hair with its contents. The liquid stung her scalp: they must have known she had lice. It was Indian hunting water, bless them.

The sensuous feeling of having her scalp massaged made her drowsy. There she lay, stark naked, in an Indian teepee, worked over by two grunting women, pervaded by a sense of peace and well-being. They rolled her over, oiled her back, kneaded and massaged the muscles of her shoulders, her spine, her buttocks, her thighs, her calves. Finally, as limp as a rag doll, she was pulled upright into a sitting position. They braided her hair, put on the headband, the moccasins; she had to put on the clothes herself. Despite the fact that they were made of leather they felt warm and comfortable. She wanted to hug the two women, then bawl on their shoulders. But she was too limp, too groggy; they had drawn all tension, tiredness, and terror from her body and her mind. "Thank you," she whispered. "Thank you, thank you." She fell asleep.

She was awakened by the first warning twinge in her insides. Women's voices sounded outside. She was pulled to her feet again, the women pushed her out through the bead curtain; she emerged in a blinding sunset. The first person she recognized, after blinking in the sun, was Two-tone Boots on horseback, staring at her, mouth open, tobacco juice dribbling down his chin. Then his attention was diverted by the distant squealing of women.

All the squaws were rushing toward some spectacle near the buffalo carcass. They ululated, clapped their hands, advancing and retreating in what looked like a tribal dance. A huge bird was lying on the ground, helplessly flapping its wings. She wondered what on earth they were doing; suddenly, she doubled up in a violent spasm.

The chief's wife was by her side in a flash, took her arm. The distant cheering and stamping increased in volume; Two-tone swung his horse around and cantered off to investigate. With her arm around Lydia's shoulders, the chief's wife took her into the tall grass, deeper than she had ever dared venture alone; then, after a pat on the back, as if encouraging a child, the woman vanished from sight.

What followed was plain torture. It felt as if her body was being torn apart. The pain was such that she finally had to cry out in agony, but no pain could dim the relief she felt. When it was all over, she must have passed out, for she came to, lying on her back in a man-high basket of grass, looking up at the sky. A huge buzzard wheeled into view. Its wings were trailing colored streamers fluttering in the wind, like a living kite. Then the bird soared out of sight.

In the distance she heard the cheering of women.

After Lydia had been gone for over an hour, Mordecai became worried. What could have happened to her? And to his dinner? Then he heard women cheering and applauding in the distance. They were flying a kite which, he realized after a few moments, was a bird decorated with streamers. Had Lydia been caught up in whatever was going on there? A young squaw turned up with an armful of twigs—not another patient! He must get it through to them somehow not to turn up at suppertime. Rather touchingly, she built a fire for him with kindling, lit it, and said, "Sorry I'm late. I was held up by the kite-flying."

It was Lydia! Dressed as a Mahanoy squaw! What in the world—

She started to rummage among the contents of her backpack. "I'm afraid a dog got hold of our meat while I was gone. It will have to be biscuits tonight." She brought out the Mahanoy dictionary again and started to flick through its pages in the firelight.

"What happened?" he asked. "Why is thee dressed like that?"

"A long story," she said, then she seemed to find the word she was looking for. "How about that! In the English–Mahanoy half of this thing it says that *pusil* means 'help me'; in the Mahanoy–English half it says, 'Embark! All aboard!' No wonder they thought I was raving mad. I was crying for help, but in fact yelling, 'All aboard!' "

She tossed the dictionary into the fire.

"Lydia!" he cried. "What is thee doing? We needed that!"

"We need it like the pox," she said.

Her transformation disturbed him. Her face in the firelight was that of a half-breed; she suddenly was no longer an alien among the Indians but one of them. Her eyes seemed to have become lighter in color now that her skin had become darker, burnished by the sun and the wind.

"That dictionary was our only link with the Indians! How are we going to communicate without it?"

"By listening to them," she said, poking the fire. "By pointing at things and asking. They have accepted me now. Tomorrow I'll start rounding up the children. Now that I look like their mothers, instead of a witch on a broomstick, maybe they'll let themselves be caught."

"But what *happened?*"

"As thee can see, they turned me into a squaw."

"Who did?"

She turned away to put some more wood on the fire; he now

saw that her hair had been braided, Indian fashion. Then she said, "I think we're in real trouble."

"It certainly looks like it."

"We are in the process of losing our identity. What does thee think happens to two drops of water falling in a lake? I have been accepted by the women, they dressed me up, they were very kind to me, they made me one of them. Thee is going through a different process, but in the end the result will be the same. In the end we'll disappear. Not die: simply disappear, like the drops of water."

"Lydia, tell me what happened."

To his amazement her eyes filled with tears. "I'm afraid," she said.

He was tempted to take her hand; for this tower of strength to be afraid of disappearing was rather touching. "I think I understand thy distress," he said, "but I think also that, as long as we stay together, our losing our identity seems unlikely."

She shook her head, and stared grimly at the fire. "I am not strong enough, Mordecai, neither is thee, to handle this, other than in the power of the Lord. But did the Lord burden us with a concern? Did He tell us: All I have is thee? We may tell ourselves so, but did He really? I, for one, was at the end of my tether. I had lost my job. I was about to be read out of Meeting. The man I cared for married someone else. For me to say that I joined this convoy in the power of the Lord would be a lie. And we must no longer deal in lies, Mordecai, or we'll be lost. I'm not going to say this again, it's difficult enough as it is, but I am *not* in the power of the Lord, Mordecai. I am *not* embodying Him. I am a thirty-year-old spinster without a job who lost her man and fled among the Indians." She picked up a stick, but instead of poking the fire she stared at the flames, dejected.

He did not know what to say to her, other than "I am not in the power of the Lord either, Lydia. But if whatever power I do possess can be used to heal people, to give them heart, I want to do it. It may not even be my power, but their own."

"Whose?"

"The Indians'. Those who are there when I do it. In the past, when I first started to minister, I soon found out that the power with which I seduced them came from the audience itself. Maybe it's the same with my healing."

She said nothing. The coyotes wailed in the distance. Among the sleeping Indians a dog answered with a long, drawn-out howl.

Then she said, "Please, let's have meeting. Or try to."

He bent his head, folded his hands, and centered down. Or tried to. It was not easy. Then he became aware of a different power. Maybe 'power' was not the word—a different vibration. No, that was not right either. A strange, yet familiar feeling of inner security that had nothing to do with God, but with the earth, the sleeping Indians, the coyotes on the horizon. An inner security that needed no words, but simply was. Only it had nothing to do with Mordecai Monk the English merchant, or with his real achievement: Heavenly Smiles. It had to do with —nature?

It was bewildering. Maybe Lydia was right, maybe they *were* losing their identity and on the way to becoming Indians. Maybe it was their ancient, mystical civilization claiming him as its instrument. For the power was his, and not his. Theirs, not theirs.

Could it be God, after all?

That night, the moment he had fallen asleep, or so it seemed, Mordecai was running down a narrow street with a woman—Lydia? Liza?—holding a crying baby in his arms. They were running for their lives, in utter terror; behind them flames roared, buildings crumbled, burning timbers came crashing down. It could not be! It could not be the end! His whole life was still ahead of him! With a shattering explosion, the world erupted in flames. He tried to hold on to the baby as he reached for the hand of the woman, but she turned out to be a man, screaming, "*Mahónink! Mahónink!*"

Mahónink? He woke, still terrified, confused, and looked

about him. The real world was dreamlike too: stark white in the light of the dawn, everything covered with hoarfrost. The tall grass, the sleeping Indians, his blanket.

"*Mahónink!*" the voice urged. "*Mahónink!*"

He turned and saw the silhouette of an Indian against the sky. "What's the matter?"

"Man! Old man! Him die! Quick!"

He recognized the chief. The man had never looked at him before, as that would have lessened his prestige among the tribe, who were not a tribe but five hundred Indians cut away at random by the cavalry. Probably not a real chief either, more likely just a male picked by the captain because he knew some English.

"Excuse me—what was it thee said?"

"Man," the chief repeated, "old man. Him die. Old man ask for medicine. Up! Old man. Quick!"

Mordecai threw off his blanket and rose. Lydia's still form, covered with hoarfrost, lay with her back to him. He found his coat; half of it was white, like a Pierrot's costume. Still groggy, he put it on. He combed his hair with his fingers and found it covered with hoarfrost too. "All right," he said, "let's go."

He followed the chief, who weaved his way among the white humps of the sleeping Indians, occasionally stepping over one. He still could not shake that dream. Whose baby had it been? What woman? Was the disaster an earthquake? Had it been Pompeii?

They reached a flatbed cart; on it lay a body rolled in a blanket, white with frost. A puppy dog that had taken to following him stood up against the wheel in an effort to join him when he climbed onto the cart.

In the misty light, the old Indian in the blanket looked like a member of a different species. His triangular face with its high cheekbones was deeply wrinkled; a hooked nose jutted out like a beak; the eyes were closed. Yet he must have seen Mordecai, for a gnarled hand reached out to him, but dropped with exhaustion.

"What does thee want me to do?" Mordecai asked the chief.

"Him dying. Release him."

"Of what?"

"Free him. Set him free."

The old man's lips moved, he uttered some guttural sounds. The hand reached for Mordecai again.

"Him say: 'Rain,' " the chief said. " 'Children playing in rain.' "

The slitted eyes opened and focused on Mordecai. A startling grimace cracked the surface of the ancient face. The clawlike hand made a feint toward him with unnerving playfulness, then he muttered something.

" 'Children play in rain,' " the chief repeated.

The old man squealed eerily; his face, despite the wrinkles and the crows'-feet, took on a childlike glee.

"Little boys say: 'Eee-eee.' " the chief explained.

"I see."

Mordecai did indeed begin to see: a clearing in the forest, torrential rain, a pack of naked little boys gamboling in puddles, chasing one another, throwing mud. On impulse, he took the gnarled hand, now waving erratically at the sky. It felt alien, like an animal's paw. The moment he got hold of it the old man gave a hissing sigh, ending in a whistle.

Mordecai said, "Play, old friend. Play, play, let it rain. Join the little boys. Squeal. Throw mud."

The black slitted eyes gazed into his. The cracked smile returned.

Staring at the old man, Mordecai saw the naked little boys dance in the rain, screaming with glee, rolling in the mud, ecstatically scared by the thunder booming in the caverns of the forest. He realized that the old man must be a Woods Indian lost in the prairie, dreaming of his childhood.

He stroked the alien hand. "Play . . . play in the rain . . ."

"Eee-eee . . ." the old Indian squealed. "Eee . . . eee . . ."

The slitted eyes closed slowly, the smile froze on the wrinkled face. The hand became heavy; Mordecai gently put it on the man's chest and was moved to say softly, "Free. Thee is free now. Free . . . free . . ."

Squatting beside the body of the old man, he went into worship. He had no idea whether his reaction to the challenge had been pagan, Christian, or Quakerly. Maybe by identifying with the dying old Indian's last dream of children playing in rain, he had managed to relieve the man's loneliness, that was all.

He sat, eyes closed, hands folded, until the bugle shattered the silence. The Indians rose like the dead at the last trump. A horse whinnied, answered by the braying of a mule. He came to a decision. He looked up and said to the chief, "Stop the convoy. We must bury him first."

The chief gazed at him without expression.

"Tell them to wait," he repeated. "This man must be buried."

"No stop," the chief said. "Cap'n never stop. Him—" he made a gesture of tossing something away, and looked over his shoulder at the rear of the column, where the captain and his soldiers were taking up position. "Never stop," he said.

Mordecai was well aware of this, but his decision was made. He rose and stared at the captain in the far distance, now swinging into the saddle. The first rays of the rising sun flashed in the gold of his epaulettes. When the cart started to move, he shouted, "Stop! In the name of God! *Stop!*"

With a jolt the cart stopped. He lost his balance but managed to stay upright. The convoy drew slowly to a halt.

Drovers came riding down the column, shouting, brandishing their whips. "Git! Git, ya bastards! Git, git!"

The Indians did not budge. They stood staring fixedly ahead, in silent defiance.

"Did *you* do this, you bastard?"

Mordecai looked up and saw it was the squinting drover, glaring at him from his bit-chewing horse.

"We must bury this man," he replied. "He has just died. Go tell the captain."

"You goddamn old billy goat!" The drover was about to lash

out with his whip when suddenly, four, six, ten Indians leaped at him with chilling agility, dragged him off his horse, yanked the whip out of his hand, and threw it in the tall grass.

"Don't hurt him! Don't hurt him!" a woman cried. It was Lydia; Mordecai had not seen her coming. Her warning was not necessary; the Indians gave the drover's horse a slap on the rump that made it gallop riderless toward the head of the column. Then they turned away and vanished in the anonymity of their ranks.

The other drovers saw what had happened; they made for the spot where their comrade had fallen. But before they reached him, there was a rumble of hooves, a shouted command. The red-bearded captain on his horse loomed beside the cart. To the drovers, who had come yodeling and shrieking to the aid of their fallen comrade, he called, "Leave this to me!" Grudgingly, they reined in their horses.

The captain gazed at Mordecai kneeling by the side of the dead Indian. "Is this your doing, Mr. Monk?"

"We must bury the dead," Mordecai replied, feeling small. "He just died."

"We do not stop for burials," the captain said calmly. "And please do not incite the Indians to rebellion. I would have to shoot you." He said it without animosity, simply as a statement of fact.

Mordecai suddenly felt a powerless nonentity, about to be overwhelmed. For the first time, he experienced what it meant to be an Indian: he responded instinctively with a rudimentary hatred, a helpless fury. The fury and the hatred made him do the first thing that came into his head: he stabbed at the man above him with two fingers, hissing, "Pestilence! Pus! Pus! Pustules!" The motionless silence of the Indians was so charged with hatred that he carried on, fueled by their fury. "I curse thee! Curse! Curse! Curse!"

"Well well," the captain said. "Quite a conversion." Then he shouted, "*Convoy*, march!"

After a long moment, the huge mass of Indians began to

shuffle forward. Within minutes it seemed as if the incident had never occurred; the mule drawing the cart trotted ahead, the chief had vanished among the ranks, the drovers rounded up the loose horse, and the fallen Two-tone was helped back into the saddle.

"How could thee?" Lydia asked aghast, walking alongside the cart. "That was awful! What got into thee?"

He did not respond. The cart lunged, making the dead body slide. What had caused him to do this vicious thing? The power, which for a brief time had seemed to be godly, had been sullied beyond redemption.

Two drovers dismounted, picked up the corpse by its arms and legs, and tossed it into the grass by the side of the trail. A brief rustle and it disappeared from sight; but not from the buzzards'.

For Lydia, all was lost. Their mission, if ever there had been one, had ended in violence. After hissing that obscene curse at the captain, even Mordecai himself could no longer pretend that they embodied God's love. Whatever he had embodied when he put the hex on Captain Stewart, it certainly was not divine love. She could only keep herself from despising him by recognizing the naughty child. Nanny Maple must have been familiar with the fat little boy who yelled naughty words when thwarted in some childish impulse. But this had been no childish impulse. He had risen in fury at being thwarted and had cursed the captain with spine-chilling power. She could not shrug it off as a childish prank. Lucifer was now his God, not Christ.

As she walked alongside the cart on which he still sat, head in hands, she rued the depth of their failure. She had finally been accepted by the Indians, though not really. They tolerated her skipping along with them, braids bobbing, occasionally losing a moccasin, that was all. Mordecai had appeared to do better with his voodoo, but had been given the name *Mahónink*, which he had mentioned to her with the modest cough of the newly knighted, assuming it meant 'Great Healer' or 'Luminous Hands,' or something like that. The chief's wife, the only one with whom she communicated verbally, had told her that it meant 'Deer Lick' because of the way he licked his plate after finishing his meal. Well, 'All Aboard' was no crown of laurels either. All Aboard and Deer Lick: the Indians clearly considered them to be a couple of nuts who had joined the convoy like the stray dogs they were unable to shake, two harmless village idiots living in cuckoo-land.

She had had illusions about teaching the children, but the only ones who responded to her were the *sopsus*, 'the naked ones,' children separated from their families by the cavalry at the round-up. The *sopsus* had got their name because they had not a thing to call their own, not even clothes. About a dozen of them now tagged along with her, she fed and tried to clothe them. They, on their part, taught her the language by naming the words for things she pointed out or did. *M'mitzi*—I eat; *Mgáuwi*—I drink; *puff-puff-puff*—I smoke; and, with realistic retching and rolling of the eyes, *m'paisi*—I am being sick. They had nicknames which they had given themselves or one another: *Ilau*, Great Warrior, and *Lachpi*, He Who Runs Fast. One boy, with huge eyes and a frail, almost girlish body, had a name he clearly had not chosen himself, *Tscholéntit*, Little Bird. He was a lost soul, but shrank from her hand; when she reached out to him he ran away.

The women who had been so kind to her, she now suspected, had done so out of a sense of fun: white squaw shouting 'All aboard!' and asking for help because she was constipated, what a hoot. Massaging her, giving her a potion, and dressing her up as one of themselves had all been part of a joke, culminating in the decoration of the buzzard, a way of cocking a snook at the drovers. Afterward, they had turned their backs on her again; she had the feeling she would become the focus of their attention only if she were to provide the opportunity for another practical joke. She had heard that Indians made prisoner by another tribe feared, most of all, being handed over to the squaws for torture. She could well believe it now. She and Mordecai should have introduced an element of love and tenderness into this world of elementary cruelty, but when Mordecai put a hex on the captain by poking two fingers at him and hissing 'Pustules!' that chance was lost forever.

That evening, she was putting up their shelter when the chief turned up with a handful of bloody entrails from a buffalo carcass. He threw them at Mordecai's feet and said, "Tomorrow."

Mordecai was perplexed; but Lydia knew at once what this meant and her heart sank. The chief wanted to turn him into a soothsayer as well.

"Will I and wife live in new land and leave to sons?" he asked.

Mordecai stared at the slimy offal at his feet, then said, to her horror, "Thee and thy wife will share the fate of us all." The chief seemed satisfied and stepped aside; instantly, his place was taken by a young squaw who hawked and spat at Mordecai's feet. It startled Lydia, even though she could identify with the woman's sentiments.

The chief said, "Tell squaw tomorrow."

"From her spittle?" Mordecai asked. It seemed too much even for him. He grimaced at the phlegm in the dust, then said in a tone of exasperation, "Tell her to beware of horses." A sensible piece of advice; thank God, no future-mongering. When someone else stepped forward to take the squaw's place, Mordecai said firmly, "No! No more! Enough! Finished!"

The chief translated it; the Indians dispersed and left them alone.

"What in the name of God came over thee this time?" she asked, her voice unmelodious.

"Oh, it means nothing," he said evasively.

"Nothing? Thee tells the future from entrails and spittle and calls it 'nothing'?"

"I said whatever came into my head, only to be rid of them. Are we going to have any food tonight, or what?"

"I have no words for this!"

"Dear heart," he said with infuriating superiority, "when in Rome, do as the Romans do. What they expect from me is what Roman soldiers expected from their haruspex."

"Haruspex?" she cried. "Snake-oil salesman!" She turned away.

He cried, "What about the meal?"

"Get it thyself!" she shouted. "Put a hex on one of the squaws and let her fetch it for thee!"

The Indian orphans hanging around her were fascinated. The one calling himself Great Warrior called after her, *"N'dellenowi, Pusil!"* That was all she needed: an urchin telling her she was a 'real man.' As she walked away, on the brink of tears, she realized they were lost. The Indians had engulfed them, like the lake the two drops of water.

Someone slyly slipped a hand in hers as she walked over to the chuck wagon. She suppressed a scream; it was Little Bird, naked as a stick. What had the child done with the shirt she had stitched together for him? "Where's thy shirt? *Shirt una hono i'agna?"*

"Peewo!" he sang, skipping. He had given it to a dog.

She let Little Bird carry the pot, to have a hand free to scratch with. It occurred to her, as she scratched and the child skipped along with the upturned pot on his head, that Pissing Gulie would have loved this. Margaret Fell might have frowned, and Boniface Baker have sunk his teeth in her neck to make her scream like the cheetah—if that had indeed been his practice.

Rum lot, Quaker saints, she thought. The salt of the earth, of which only a pinch is needed every other generation. Thank God.

CHAPTER 14

PENDLE HILL, INDIANA
October 1833

Obadiah Woodhouse thought his wife had discarded the hare-brained notion of following Lydia Best and Mordecai Monk into the wilderness, but that morning she brought it up again.

It was First Day. They were dressing to go to Quarterly Meeting and he was fumbling his way up the row of minute eyelets on the back of her dress. Suddenly she said, "I can't help it. I find myself thinking about Lydia and Mordecai all the time. Doesn't thee?"

"Can't say I do," he replied, with more honesty than diplomacy; he was too busy concentrating on the infernal little hooks.

"Not at *all?*" she asked, aghast. "Not even *once?*"

"Of course!" he replied, irritably. "More than once. Stand still!"

She obeyed, but her back expressed disapproval. "*Must* thee breathe so dramatically?" he asked. "Those hooks are tight enough as it is without thy puffing thyself up with indignation."

"I'm not indignant," she said. "I'm disappointed, that's all."

"Why? Because I spend my time trying to make a decent living for us, instead of meditating on Lydia Best and Mordecai Monk? They are minding their light, I am minding mine. Or trying to, at least. Keep still."

There was a short, thoughtful silence, in which he managed to hook her up as high as the collar. Then she said, "I thought at one time that thee was in love with her."

"Huh?"

"That's why I came. Because of what thee wrote about her."

"When?"

"A captivating, courageous, and strikingly handsome young woman. That's what thee wrote about her, Obi."

"I did? Oh, well . . ."

"Oh well what? Is thee now trying to tell me that thee has not given a single thought to that captivating, courageous, and strikingly handsome young woman since she vanished in the wilderness?"

He sighed. He loved her, marriage had worked out better than he could have dreamed, but he would never get used to this feminine parlor game of tricking a man into saying something and then calling him to task for it. She was a ravishing, passionate creature, she made him forget all other women to the point where he even didn't care whether Lydia Best would ever return. Yet—"If I haven't given her a thought, it was because of thee," he said and kissed the nape of her neck with its curling tendrils of hair.

But the gallantry fizzled. She turned around scornfully. "How like a man!"

"Hark, hark, the voice of experience," he teased, trying to hide his exasperation by picking up his boots.

"All right," she said. "I might as well tell thee, here and now, that I have been weighing thy argument in my mind and found it wanting."

He gazed at her, boots in hand. "What argument, for God's sake?"

"I'll thank thee not to blaspheme in my presence," she said. "If thee's going to behave like that, I'm not going to discuss it with thee. I will simply inform thee of my decision when the time is ripe."

He suddenly felt the overwhelming desire to give her a piece of his mind, but managed to keep the violence out of his voice when he replied, "Anything thee says, dear heart. It would help if I knew what thee was talking about." He sat down to pull on his boots, wishing they could start this conversation all over. He hated conflict, it always made him feel miserable and for some reason sorry for himself.

"My idea of founding a school for Indian children in unorganized territory is not harebrained, it's the very way in which this school was founded. Boniface Baker and Cleo Baker went first, the way Lydia and Mordecai Monk are going. They were followed by a wagon train full of young Friends, and older ones with supplies and building materials, and—"

"I know all that," he said tersely.

"Let me finish! Thy point was that I might be—in a delicate condition, and that therefore our going was untimely."

"Well?" He looked at her nonplussed, his hands at his boot straps. Then a sudden thought occurred to him. "Does thee mean to tell me that—that—"

She frowned. "Don't be ridiculous! We've only been married three weeks! We'll have to wait at least—well—" She stopped, obviously embarrassed, for he saw her blush, which always made her look delectable. This time it bewildered him a little. She was so complicated, so mysterious, her reactions were so unpredictable. Maybe she *was* pregnant; he had heard that women in that condition always became irritable and emotional. "I meant to say," she continued, "that should it be the case, I would consider it all the more reason for joining them."

"I *beg* thy pardon?"

"I would rather give my child an example than security, if that security is bought with cowardice. I want my child to be proud of its parents, not ashamed—the way I am."

He looked at her, aghast. It was as if suddenly, from within the childlike, tempestuous creature he adored, a woman had emerged whom he did not know at all, strong and distressingly mature. He was overcome by a feeling of betrayal. "Darling Charity," he said, with judicious calm, "I think that is a lovely, noble thought. And it leads me to believe, whatever thee may tell me, that thee *is* with child. This whole ridiculous argument is typical of a woman in—in thy condition." He pulled on his other boot, rose, and straightened his waistcoat.

"What exactly does thee mean, Obadiah dear?" she asked sweetly. "That I am unstable?"

"For heaven's sake!" He reached for his coat. "Merely emotional." He put on his coat.

"Why is it," she asked, "that all our lives we pay lip service to saints like Margaret Fell and Gulie Woodhouse, and that the moment someone wishes to follow their example we call them 'emotional'?"

"Don't be ridiculous!" He buttoned his coat. "Thee is not following anybody's example. Thee is suggesting that we remove ourselves from civilization, all medical help, to go and live on an Indian reservation. Sooner or later thee *will* become pregnant, thee might as well suggest having thy child on the moon. Our child! I'm responsible for him too! I'm his father; I'm not going to permit thee to put thyself and him in jeopardy for whatever reason, I don't care if it's a school or—or a three-ring circus!"

To his amazement she suddenly turned back into the sensitive, delicate person he knew and loved. "Oh, Obi . . ." she cried in the little girl's voice that signified surrender; she rushed toward him, threw her arms around him, and rested her head on his chest. "Forgive me, forgive me, I know I'm impetuous, but I *must* tell thee that they are terribly, terribly much on my mind. I can't forget them, I can't!"

"I know, dearest, I know." He stroked her hair, experienced enough now as a husband to do so gingerly, for fear of mussing it before meeting. "I understand. But we have to use our heads as well as our hearts. Even if I were to accept thy argument about where to have our child, thee has a certain responsibility toward this school, in its present state of disarray. Thee cannot walk out on that responsibility on the harebrained pretext of starting another school! I have an office in town now, I can't walk out on that either. The first thing people expect from a counselor at law is stability."

She made no reply. It gave him a feeling of relief; yet he felt a nagging unease. "Come, dearest." He kissed her hair. "We'll be late for worship."

"Oh, Obi . . . where would I be without thee?" She looked up at him with eyes full of love.

"Philadelphia," he said with a smile, hoping she would not see the weariness in his eyes.

"Good evening," Captain Stewart said, rising from the table. He patted his lips with a napkin. "Kind of you to come, Mr. Monk. Won't you sit down?" He indicated the empty chair; the Negro servant pulled it out.

"Thank thee," Mordecai Monk said.

The table, the napkin, the tiny civilized world in the heart of the wilderness seemed a hallucination. An hour earlier they had halted near the fire-scarred ruins of an abandoned farm, like others they had passed; ageless ruins, remnants of walls, broken wagons, vegetable plots run to seed. This one had a windmill, starkly outlined against the red horizon, which turned now and then with a skeletal rattle in the evening breeze.

As Mordecai sat down he heard a whimper and saw, level with the floor of the porch, the little snout and pointed ears of the puppy that had attached itself to him. "Ksht!" He tried to wave it away.

"Oh, let it be," the captain said, "I don't mind."

"No, no," Mordecai said irritably. "I want nothing to do with the animal. He's a pest."

The captain smiled. "A little dog bothering a powerful person like yourself?" The question carried a hint of irony.

"He licks my face in the middle of the night," he replied lamely. "Well, thee sent for me?"

The captain, with a wince of discomfort, pulled the napkin out of the collar of his tunic. "I want you to have a look at this boil on my neck." He unhooked his collar. "I have tried medicating it, to no avail. I thought, as you may have put it there, you might be able to take it away."

"I?" Mordecai was so amazed that he momentarily lost his composure.

"That time I refused to stop the convoy for the burial of the chief's father, and you put a curse on me: 'Pus and pustules.' "

"His father?"

"Do you think the chief would have called on you for any old man who happened to be dying?"

"I had no idea . . ."

"Here, take a look." The captain stood up, unbuttoned the rest of his tunic, and turned around. His neck and the top of his shoulders were covered with curly red hair, like fur; on the left side of his neck was an angry abscess. It looked revolting. "Sorry, Friend," Mordecai said. "There is nothing I can do."

The captain showed the beginning of irritation. "Are you saying you are prepared to act as a faith healer for savages only?"

"If I'm able to do something for the Indians, on occasion, it is by sheer suggestion."

"Your patient needs to believe in you before you can cure him? Is that what you're saying? Well, I do. Go ahead." He proffered the revolting abscess again.

This might become unpleasant, Mordecai decided. He was about to give the man the King's Touch when it occurred to him that he should not pass up this chance to bargain.

"I'll do what I can . . . on condition that from now on thee allow the Indians to bury their dead, instead of having the drovers toss them into the grass."

The captain stood quite still, for so long that Mordecai thought he had not heard. Then he said, "Very well, but only after bivouac has been made. I cannot stop the convoy every time one of them dies."

"Good," Mordecai said with a heady rush of triumph. He lifted his hands, held them some distance away from the hairy neck, and said, "*I touch thee, may the good Lord cure thee.*"

"I don't feel any touch," the captain said suspiciously.

"That is not necessary. I felt the power pass into thee."

The captain turned around. "You're not putting me on, are you, Mr. Monk?"

"Why should I? We had an agreement."

The captain stared at his mouth, for some reason; then he said, "I want the works, just as you do it to the Indians. Nursery rhyme and all."

"As thee wishes," Mordecai said, purse-mouthed. Then he recited, with gestures, in genteelly accented English, like Nanny Maple's:

Hoopla! Hopla! Feel how it mends?
Stroke—and stroke—and shake your hands.
Froggy, piggy, baby bull,
Grab the pain and pull, and pull.
Hopla! Hoopla! There it goes!
Little boy back on his toes!

After each line he made a gesture of stroking the neck, and shook his hands to disperse the pain or the infection, or whatever the hell it was.

"Thank you," said the captain when it was all over. He buttoned his tunic. "Glass of wine, Mr. Monk?"

"Thank thee, no," Mordecai replied. "Now, if thee will excuse me, I have to arrange a funeral."

"Ah! You have a customer, eh? Who is it?"

"An old squaw."

"The one carrying the papoose? The one you gave your coat to?"

Mordecai stared at him, astonished.

"Don't look at me like that," the captain said. "I know everything that goes on in this convoy, that's my job. I have given you a lot of power, Mr. Monk, by asking you to perform your voodoo on me. You will find you are now the most powerful man in the convoy, bar one." He smiled. "Off you go."

"Thank thee," Mordecai said, stepping off the platform.

"I hope you get your coat back!" the captain called after him, in high spirits. He must be pleased with his end of the bargain.

"Go away! Ksht!" The little dog ran around him in circles, yowling with joy.

Halfway to the chief's teepee, Lydia caught up with him. Her transformation was now so thorough that he had difficulty recognizing her in the dusk. Behind her hovered a shadow, the frail boy with the huge eyes, Little Bird, now their constant companion. He shared their meals, slept with them, a few yards away at first, then a few feet; now he was lying between them every night under her blanket, part of the family. It seemed only a matter of time before he would be joined by the little dog.

"What did the captain want?" she asked.

"He wanted me to cure a boil on his neck."

That stopped her in her tracks. "He *what?*"

"In exchange for the promise that the Indians may bury their dead when we make bivouac."

He expected her to be impressed; when he got no response he looked around and to his surprise saw her striding toward the command tent, where the captain was dining on the porch in splendid isolation. Little Bird flitted after her; the dog was torn by indecision, then decided to stay.

"Miss Best? This is a rare pleasure! Please, join me." The captain indicated the chair Mordecai had occupied a moment ago.

Lydia climbed the steps reluctantly, not knowing how to explain her presence. The black servant pulled out the chair for her, she sat down. Little Bird hovered in the shadows, not daring to cross the invisible line that separated headquarters from the rest of the world.

"A glass of wine, Miss Best? Ah, but you don't drink alcohol, do you? May I offer you anything else?"

"No, thank thee, Ebenezer Stewart," she said primly. A bit too primly, perhaps.

"Your company, Miss Best, is a balm in this wilderness, as always." He noticed her glancing at his neck and said, "I gather Mr. Monk told you I called him in for consultation?"

"He did indeed," she replied with sudden firmness.

"You must be asking yourself why I share the Indians' superstition?"

"I am glad thee understands that it is a superstition."

He smiled. "I am delighted you do not, Miss Best. This may sound odd to you, but it is as important for you not to believe it as it is for Mr. Monk to do so."

"I'm afraid thee is talking in riddles, Ebenezer Stewart." She now wished she had never let herself in for this, but it was too late. Now she had to stand her ground and voice her repugnance. Mordecai had, again, betrayed their witness.

"I gather that you disapprove, Miss Best."

"The Society of Friends has a testimony against spirit healing and all other forms of superstition."

The captain said lightly, "You must forgive me, but the fact that your church has decided to deny a phenomenon does not mean to say it does not exist."

"Let me make this clear, Ebenezer Stewart. Our founder, George Fox, did perform feats of healing that have never been denied. But he did so as a representative of Christ, just as the apostles did."

"Then who, pray, does Mr. Monk represent? Satan, perhaps?"

She suspected she was being mocked. "I can assure thee it is certainly not the power of Christ. Friend Mordecai is in error."

"I'm glad to hear you say that." The captain smiled. "As I said: it is important that you stick to your guns, if you'll forgive the unsuitable expression. Would you like to know why?"

"Please," she said without enthusiasm.

"Mr. Monk is indeed not acting in the power of Christ. He is acting in the power of the Indians."

She frowned. "I don't understand."

"People may think they are browbeaten, powerless, destroyed, as individuals and as a race, but that is a fundamental error, Miss Best. The Indians are not defeated. They are indefeatable, like the wind. You have to know them intimately, both as enemies and as prisoners, to realize that Mr. Monk may *think* he acts in the power of his own tribal god, but he has, in effect, been appropriated by theirs. The power of healing he possesses is not his, but theirs." He read her thoughts. "I am sure that comes as a surprise to you. Why do I harbor such fancy theories? Like the Roman centurions on campaign, officers in my position are avid students of philosophy, religion, native customs, anything that exercises the mind." He made a gesture at the compound. "The brutish reality in which we are forced to live would otherwise get the better of us. I have had many discussions on shamanism with older colleagues, and read up on it whenever I had the chance to visit an academic library. The powers possessed by a shaman or witch doctor are derived from the communal energy of the tribe, of which he becomes the tool. Am I being obscure?"

"I think I understand," Lydia said, impressed despite herself. This was a different man from the one she had assumed him to be.

"That is all there is to it, Miss Best. Of course, it needs an individual who is receptive to these impulses. Mr. Monk, obviously, is one of those. In his healing, he is as much a prisoner of the Indians as if they had him in chains."

"I see . . ."

"I'm telling you all this, Miss Best, to impress upon you how important your firm stand is. Now that Mr. Monk, through circumstances beyond his control, finds himself enslaved in spirit, you are, one might say, the only civilized person left in our midst, the keeper of our souls. We do want to come out the other end as Christians, do we not? Despite the fact that, during our journey, we may have called upon black magic? I expect the boil in my neck to be cured in a matter of days, by the way. Confusing, isn't it?"

"I don't think so, Ebenezer Stewart," she said, getting to her feet. "Frankly, I think thee is trying to have thy cake and eat it. I wish thee success. Now, I'd better get back." Somewhere on the periphery a little shadow rose with her, expectantly.

"Miss Best, you are an admirable woman," the captain said gallantly, with a little bow. "If there is anything I can do to make your life easier, do not hesitate to let me know."

"I will," she said, and hurried back toward the security of her own world. The shadow joined her; she put her arm around Little Bird's narrow shoulders and pressed him against her in a gesture of protection.

In front of their shelter Mordecai and the puppy sat waiting by the fireside.

"I have a funeral after dinner!" Mordecai said peevishly. "Where's the food?"

She looked at him as he sat there in the firelight: a spoiled old cherub; the ringlets over his ears had gone lank and gray. "I'll go and get it," she said, turning the other cheek. "Come, Little Bird. Thee may carry the pot."

The little dog knew where they were going, and stood quivering with excitement. "Stay!" Mordecai said; a change from 'Ksht!' So the beast had been admitted into the medicine man's family circle.

You are the only civilized person left in our midst. Men and their illusions! Another month of this, and the shaman would barter her for a set of female twins, one to take off his shoes while the other massaged his shoulders.

Panting, the little dog overtook them on their way to the cooking fire.

In the vain hope of preventing the body from being disturbed by scavengers after they left, the Indians had dug the grave in a plot enclosed by a broken-down picket fence, which at one time must have been a vegetable garden.

A small crowd of women, lit by a single torch, had gathered around the grave. As Mordecai approached, the puppy at his heels, Lydia detached herself from the crowd and joined him. In the background hovered the shadow of Little Bird. Together with Lydia he sat down in front of the squaws, facing the grave.

He had given it all a good deal of thought. Some sort of nondenominational ritual seemed indicated; he could not allow them to just dump the old woman unceremoniously into a hole. The squaws were clearly waiting for him to take the lead. After a respectful silence, he intoned, "Friends, we are gathered together to commit to the earth from whence she came the mortal remains of our Friend—?"

"Sedpook," Lydia whispered.

"Sed Spook, who departed from this life today. Before we bid her soul farewell on its journey to her eternal home, let us evoke the Great Spirit, who is the Father of us all, in silent prayer."

They entered the silence of worship. The red dusk on the prairie, the primitive creatures squatting around the grave, the rattle of the windmill whirling intermittently in the gusts of wind provided a dramatic setting befitting the occasion. A flock of birds whooshed overhead on their mysterious flyway, descending to settle for the night. In the distance, coyotes howled at the moon. The grave and the shrouded body seemed to be part of earth, of cloud and sky, setting sun and rising moon, the wind, the surge of the birds. Then he became conscious of someone staring at him; it was the puppy, ears cocked, head to one side, gazing up at him adoringly. As soon as it sensed he had become aware of its presence, it began to wag its tail. "Ksht!" he whispered. But it lifted its head and gave a high-pitched yap, provoking an instant response from another creature near the grave.

"Yap! Yap!" the puppy barked, shrill in the silence. It started to prance in front of him, begging him to throw a stick. "Yap! Yap!" The small creature near the grave squealed in response; the holy silence was suddenly filled with their yelping.

It took a while before it dawned on him that the creature was an infant, not another dog. It lay at the foot of the shrouded body, a small, dark form wrapped in a blanket. That must be the papoose the old woman had been carrying all these weeks. What a barbarous thing to do, to put an infant at the foot of its grandmother's grave! Or its great-aunt's, or whatever she was. Were they planning to bury it with the corpse? The infant went on screaming, the puppy yapping. He whispered to Lydia, "*Do something!*"

She rose to her feet, walked toward the squalling bundle, and picked it up; suddenly, as if by prearranged signal, all the squaws in the circle, who so far had been frozen in silence, began to ululate in high, keening voices and clap their hands. The abrupt change was bewildering; the applause and ululations continued until Lydia returned to her place beside him, the child in her arms. Then the chief's wife rose to her feet, the others followed her example. Their ululations mounted in fervor, they started to clap once more, this time in unison. Before he knew what had happened, the women were dancing around the grave, bowing, throwing their heads back, ululating, clapping their hands in ecstatic rhythm, a mysterious celebration. Suddenly, the answer struck him: according to some Indian tradition, Lydia had adopted the infant by picking it up!

He looked at her; she was staring at the dancing squaws with a strange look on her face. The child in her arms started to scream, to struggle; instead of protesting against this responsibility thrust upon her by subterfuge, she cuddled it and kissed its little face. At that, abruptly, the screaming ceased. She turned to him with a radiance in her eyes he had not seen there before.

From the moment old Sedpook died, Lydia had wondered who was going to care for the little waif she had so fiercely protected; not for one moment had she considered the possibility of taking on the infant herself. Now, as the clapping, dancing women began to make her the center of their ritual, the implications of her innocent act dawned on her. The first thing that occurred to her was: 'How can I do it, alone?'

She was not given time for reflection. The squaws crowded

in on her and touched her, a gesture she had come to know as a rare sign of approval. They hauled her to her feet, ululating, hand-clapping, and danced her through the gathering dusk to the chief's teepee. The shrouded body of the old woman was abandoned by the side of the grave.

The baby was squalling and struggling wildly in her arms. The poor little mite had to be frightened out of its wits, away from the old woman who had cared for it for so long. Close up, it seemed an ugly child, with a huge red mouth and puny fists that waved frantically.

Once she had been led inside the teepee, she was forced to sit down on the couch of buffalo hides. The squaws pressed around her, at least twenty of them, who had squeezed themselves into the small space, chattering, giggling. The baby became more frantic by the minute.

She knew them well enough by now to conclude that to them the whole thing was a lark, another practical joke pulled on the unsuspecting Pusil. But as she pressed the baby against her breast and kissed and hugged it in order to comfort it, she realized that she didn't give a hoot.

Then the chief's wife turned up with a bowl. The similarity to her first visit was reassuring until, suddenly, two of the women got hold of her, took away the baby, and started to pull her jerkin over her head. She reacted by crossing her arms over her chest to protect her nakedness; the child shrieked in the other woman's arms. Then both women pulled her arms away, exposing her breasts; the chief's wife dipped two fingers in the bowl and began to smear her nipples with some ointment. Then the baby was stripped of its swaddling clothes; it screamed bloody murder, as if it were about to be slaughtered. The chief's wife took it and handed her the naked little body. It was a boy.

The feeling of the little boy's naked body touching hers was overwhelming. Instantly the screaming fell silent, the little boy's hungry mouth searched for the nipple of her left breast. When he found it he started to suck frantically, painfully, and she winced. The women applauded, but as the utter helplessness of the child, his pathetic vulnerability dawned on her, she forgot her surroundings. There was now nobody to whom this little boy could turn for love and protection except herself; she had suddenly become the center of his world. She looked down at the shock of black hair, the tiny hands kneading her breast like a kitten feeding, and a well of tenderness opened within her, a sense of fulfillment she had never known before. But after only a few moments the chief's wife took the child away again, setting him screaming like a banshee; she made a lunge for him, but the women forced her arms back and put her jerkin back on. The moment they had done so, however, they put the frenzied, struggling little body inside, then proceeded to tie a belt around her waist, leaving only the top of the child's head exposed, as was the practice among Mahanoy nursing mothers. The chief's wife stuck her hand inside to smear some more syrup on her nipple, the little boy began to suck again with amazing, agonizing strength. She was only dimly aware of being helped to her feet and guided to the door; they had to push her head down as she left the tent.

Outside, a large crowd of women had gathered; they accompanied her, slowly, across the camp to where Mordecai was squatting by the fire.

He looked up at her with, it seemed, total bewilderment. Not so Little Bird, who sat pressed against him, huge dark eyes shining in the firelight; all he did was put his thumb in his mouth.

She sat down opposite them, whispering to the baby inside her jerkin, and turned away from Mordecai in an effort at prudery. The women left at last; the warm little body finally became still in her arm. The hungry mouth let go of her nipple; the little boy fell asleep with a suddenness that seemed alarming. But when she peeked, his face was at peace. What about real food? What could she give him to eat, once he had calmed down and become accustomed to her? Well, the squaws would know.

She heard Mordecai get up beside her. "Back in a moment, Lydia. Take thy time." She forgot about him when the baby suddenly jerked awake and started to wriggle inside the jerkin. The hungry mouth groped for the nipple again; she saw the women had left the bowl, dipped two fingers in the gooey liquid, smeared some of it on her other breast, and helped him find it. Instantly, his mouth closed over the nipple, his little fists started to knead; he tugged at her with such power that it hurt, yet at the same time it filled her with an all-pervading joy.

She bent over the child and kissed his hair. It felt soft and fluffy, not as hard and alien as it looked. He sucked, sucked; her eyes filled with tears, she threw her head back, and gazed at the stars. The tears transformed them with brilliant colors. She knew a moment of exultation, sensuous and religious all at once, a euphoric moment of love. Then she saw Little Bird, squatting on the other side of the fire, staring at her intently, sucking his thumb.

She wondered where Mordecai had gone.

Mordecai had observed the touching image of motherhood in the firelight with growing disquiet. Something alerted him, filled him with alarm. A danger, deadly danger; only he had no idea what it was. Jealousy? So far, he had been her sole companion in this alien world. Her initial hostility had gradually changed into acceptance, then dependence, with lately a hint of a growing affection, which had evoked a surprising lack of response on his part. *The hunted do not copulate.* If so, who was the hunter?

He was no longer the lecherous son of Basil Goodlove, the preacher who mesmerized women. The other self, which he had first become aware of that night during meeting, after his first healing, had now taken over: Mahónink, medicine man, fortune-teller, haruspex to a random herd of Indians. Mahónink was now his dominant self.

Suddenly he was overcome by longing for Liza. Not for the sensuous rapture of her embrace, but the security he had felt in her arms. She seemed his last handhold, last link with the portly widower content within his limitations, living with no lurking inner danger other than the occasional fantasy of deflowering Hodgkins the parlormaid. The realization that he might never see Liza again filled him with panic, a sudden sense of abandonment.

He stared from afar at Lydia going through the motions of feeding the baby. Gradually, the cause of his sense of abandonment revealed itself. It had to do with the child—*he* was no longer the center of her world, but that Indian brat. Until now, he had been the anchor keeping her from being swept away into the Indian world. She had been the same to him, keeping him from being swept away and turning into Mahónink entirely, irrevocably. Now he had lost her. What was to become of him? Of her? And all that for the sake of a smelly, slit-eyed—for one unfortunate moment he felt like jumping up, grabbing the little cuckoo, and tossing him out of the nest. Then he understood it was not the baby who was challenging him, nor the foolish virgin in her solitary rapture while suckling, empty-breasted, someone else's child. The one challenging him was God.

He felt the desire to confront God, now. To meet Him, like Jacob, in the wilderness, and cry, '*I will not let thee go except thou bless me.*' He must do so away from this scene of imaginary domesticity. Lydia, the dauntless one, the embodiment of the incorruptible soul of Quakerism, had fallen into a trap set for her by the Indians. She was no longer like the great Quaker women who had saved the Society over and over again during the past centuries, she had become a squaw, with no other message than that women love babies, even if they are not their own. He had to get away, confront God Almighty in solitude and clearness, to ask Him: 'What art Thou doing to me? What dost Thou want of me, Thou man-eater?' But where? Indians, Indians everywhere, especially squaws, waiting, watching, preparing to waylay him with headaches, blisters, pustules, and the unfathomable sufferings of their alien souls. Where could he be alone with his mischievous God?

The one place least likely to be invaded by squaws seemed to be the graveyard. At the gate, he came upon a group of them leaving. He let them pass, then closed the gate behind him, locking out the little dog. It protested with shrill, desperate yapping, but he said, "Shut up!" and "Stay! I say *stay!*" Alone in the darkness, he approached a mound that had not been there before; the body had been buried.

The grave was covered with a dark cloth. His coat! It had been the old woman's most fiercely defended possession. It was the first part of himself that he had given away. How long ago it seemed! Now here he was, about to give up the last part.

"God," he said, "I am in danger. Help me."

He was about to kneel in prayer when he heard the dog yapping behind him. He turned around and saw the squaws, wrapped in their blankets, huddled outside the gate. This was the very scene he had so often described in his Goodlove sermons: the gate to the garden of Gethsemane, the huddled figures of the apostles, the little dog waiting for its master to return.

It was a coincidence, of course. It would be demeaning to assume that the Almighty spent His time imitating the theatrical fantasies of rogue evangelists. But what could the purpose be of his finding himself, as in a hallucination, confronted with a scene that had been the most effective part of his ministry? Was he supposed to draw some conclusion now? Was he being mocked? If so, why? His sermons had been theatrical extravaganzas—so what? They were things of the past; his present ministry was real enough. He was actually *healing* people. His healing the captain had brought about that the dead were now being buried instead of tossed into the grass by the wayside. His protest had brought about cohesion among this disorganized, despondent band of homeless Indians. By joining them as an equal, sharing their humiliation, he had given them humanity in the eyes of the drovers. The result was right here: the first grave. The first burial, after a dignified ceremony; the hoopla of the squaws dancing around the grave was, of course—

Hoopla. *Hopla. Feel how it mends? Stroke, and stroke—*

It was all nonsense. More theatrical self-aggrandizement. Anyone could have done it: put a hex on the gullible captain.

Cure minor ills with the aid of Nanny Maple's ditty. Any ditty.
Read from a blob of spittle that you should be careful around
horses. As a shaman he was a fraud, as much of a fraud as he
had been when he preached his sermons, ogling the women about
to kneel at his feet. Only as an English chocolate manufacturer,
lover of a whore, could he stand before God and say, 'Lord, here
I am.'

He lifted his head and gazed at the sky. Fleeting clouds veiled
the stars. The full moon was ringed by a halo of haze. The old
windmill squealed and clattered in the moonlight, like a living
creature of the night.

'Father, if it be possible, let this cup pass from me.'

The hackneyed words came to him with a sense of shame.
How dare he impersonate Christ at that terrible moment when
he first saw what awaited him? He asked the starry void, "Father,
what am I doing here? What is happening to me? Is this all part
of Thy plan?"

Alas, this too was pure theater. Even if there had been Divine
Intent in his healing, putting a hex on the captain had taken care
of it. The way he sat there, gazing at the sky, captive of the
Indians of his own volition, must be the way Adam had sat on
the first night after being banished from Eden, cast out into the
wilderness with stunned Eve . . .

The dream! That was the dream: cast out, terrified, running
for his life, together with a woman holding a child, the erupting
volcano, the narrow street of crumbling houses—"Yap!"

A wet snout was pressed against his hand, a tongue licked
his thumb; the little dog had managed to worm its way through
the picket fence. "Good boy," he murmured, stroking its fur. It
was unpleasant to the touch. Would Christ have thought the
same? 'Piss off, little bugger'?

Hardly. That too was make-believe: Christ had never had a
little dog following him everywhere. He was incurable. A liar,
a fake, a ballyhoo man, Basil Goodlove redivivus. *Hymns! Testimonies! Laying on of hands! Speaking in tongues! Glimpses of the
future!* Exactly, but exactly what had been promised in that

advertisement for an afternoon of prayer and worship by the Reverend Basil Goodlove he had found in his father's concordance. Admission three pence, all proceeds to go to the Reverend Goodlove's Fund for the Suffering Poor.

There was no hope, no mercy, no 'mission.' Only the blind, irrevocable fate of the bloodline.

On the way out, he retrieved his coat from the grave.

CHAPTER 15

THE BANKS OF THE MISSISSIPPI

November 1833

The convoy reached Indian Landing on the Mississippi on the afternoon of a very cold day. Lydia had expected to see houses, streets, a fort; she had looked forward to seeing white people again, wondering what her reaction would be after all these weeks as a Mahanoy squaw. The vision of the little town with its white clapboard houses and tree-lined streets, buggies and hansoms and bakers' shop windows and warm, warm parlors and bedrooms with featherbeds became a sort of life buoy to her after, suddenly, winter had hit the plains. Rainstorms, hailstorms, blizzards, and hoarfrost that turned the prairie into a beautiful picture and a veritable hell to slog through: freezing, wet, shivering, endless, hopeless, deadly. There had been burials virtually every day, and not just of the old. Many of them had been children, and her main fight these last weeks had been with death stalking little Obadiah, relentlessly. Little Bird had survived, but only because he slept in Mordecai's bed and rode on Mordecai's shoulders when the snow was deep, or the sludge treacherous, or homesickness for a lost world rendered him vulnerable. She had even promised him the warm, welcoming little town full of kind people in warm, hospitable teepees—luckily, he had not quite understood, for the reality proved grim.

Indian Landing was no more than a clearing of dirty trampled snow on the bank of an enormous river, without even the humblest of shacks. It was strewn with the wrecks of wagons; a crude dock jutted out into the slow, sliding river; tied up to it lay the steamer that was to take them to Kansas. In her imagination she had seen a twin-funneled river steamboat with tiered decks and decorated paddle-wheel boxes, pictures of which she had seen. The ugly contraption awaiting them did not look like a ship at all. What there was in the way of a hull was dwarfed by a huge superstructure, a blank wall of peeling paint like the side of a dilapidated barn. Above that, two decks supported by posts, the railings broken in many places; perched on top of the contraption was a single black funnel without decoration, belching black smoke that smeared the autumn sky. At the forward end of the deck was a hutch with windows, which probably housed the steering wheel; there were no paddle-wheel boxes, only one huge wheel at the stern that ran the width of the vessel, its spokes tangled with refuse. Her apprehension deepened when she caught a glimpse of the crew: a bunch of coarse white laborers, who at the sight of her shouted words and suggestions to each other that made her blush with indignation. Because of the papoose in the carrying basket on her back they must have taken her for a light-skinned squaw who could not understand what they were shouting; even so, some of the words were unknown to her, although their meaning was clear enough.

It was a frosty day with a wind that cut like a knife. The sunlit river had a dull glint, like pewter; the empty landscape was bleak and desolate. She was setting up their shelter as a windbreak for Little Bird and the baby when the Negro servant came to tell her that Captain Stewart sent his compliments and wished to see her. She hesitated; then she told Little Bird to stay where he was, slung the baby in his basket onto her back, and followed the man through the desolate crowd of Indians guarding their meager belongings. It had to be a frightening time for them; the squaws were gathering their children together, casting terrified looks at the louts waiting for them on the deck of the riverboat.

The command tent had already been erected; the captain received her on the porch with a stiffness in his bearing that puzzled her.

"Sit down, please, Miss Best."

"Thank thee, Ebenezer Stewart."

He waited until she was seated, then sat down in the other chair. He was wearing a different uniform this time, gaudier than his usual one; it contrasted oddly with the dismal surroundings: the clearing strewn with refuse, the terrified Indians staring at them in motionless desperation, the gawking ghouls on board the ship.

He cleared his throat and said, "The time has come for us to have a serious conversation, Miss Best. Er—may I offer you some refreshment?"

"Thank thee, Ebenezer Stewart, nothing right now." With a practiced movement she swung the carrying basket with the baby off her back and put it on her lap. The little boy did not stir; he had just had his meal of mashed beans and gruel and fallen asleep; he would go on sleeping until wakened by hunger.

"Something for the child, perhaps? A mug of malt?"

She looked at him, surprised. He had never mentioned the child before. "What did thee wish to see me about, Friend?"

For a warrior decked out with gold tasseled epaulettes, lacquered bandolier, and a sword in an ornate scabbard, he was ill at ease.

"Miss Best, what I am about to say may startle you, so let me take the bull by the horns. Er—" He sounded as if he had lost track, then he continued, in a formal tone, "I have the honor to ask you for your hand in marriage."

She gaped at him, speechless for once.

"Your hand, Miss Best. In marriage."

He could not be serious! She wanted to say something joky, lighthearted, to break that awkward formality; but his discomfiture was so obvious that she simply had to take him seriously.

"I—I am deeply honored," she said; but the bright look in his eyes made her add hastily, "but I must decline. Regretfully," she added.

The eyes narrowed. "Tell me why."

"Because—because I am committed to stay with these people—"

"You cannot stay with them," he said brusquely. "Look at the brutes on that ship. Just look at them! That's the kind of man you'll find waiting for you in unorganized territory, with no cavalry to protect you."

"I know," she said. "I—"

"Has it occurred to you that it is only owing to my protection that you have, so far, been spared the fate that awaits any presentable squaw from the moment that ship casts off?"

"Fate?"

"Forgive me, it is too late for niceties." He scowled at her. "You know what rape is, I trust?"

His gruffness could not hide his embarrassment. She suddenly saw that had she moved in with him at the beginning as he had suggested, she could have managed him without any problem.

"Yes," she said.

"Well, that will be your lot, Miss Best. Look at the brutes! They can hardly wait. To them you will be what you pretend to be: an Indian squaw. And Indian squaws—well, need I say more?"

She tried to read the truth in his eyes. Was he exaggerating to serve his own purpose? "Is thy proposal intended to prevent my being—molested?" she asked, demurely.

For some reason the question appeared to restore his confidence. "I propose to you, Miss Best, because over the past weeks I have become impressed with your sterling qualities, both as a woman and as a Christian." The 'sterling qualities' rendered him innocuous, despite his resplendent garb, which he clearly had put on for the occasion, complete with a pair of white gloves tucked under his belt.

"Thank thee for the compliment," she said, "but thee is idealizing me, Friend Ebenezer."

"What do you take me for?" His tone probably was intended to be mortifying. "I'm not one of your city slickers, proposing to any presentable lady who happens to come their way. You are the first woman for whom I have true admiration. The first woman, as a matter of fact, to whom I have ever made a proposal of marriage. I would be proud to have you for my wife."

One thing was clear: her witness had spoken, at least, to him. "I am very touched, Friend Ebenezer," she said sincerely, "but I cannot accept thy offer. I am committed to these people. That is what God wants of me."

"I fail to see how God could want you to submit to rape for His sake. It makes no sense, and it troubles me that it seems to make sense to *you*. Either you are less intelligent than I surmised, or incurably innocent. Forgive me for being blunt."

She rose and swung the carrying basket onto her back. He watched, his face set in a scowl, his eyes full of hurt and anger. At the very least, she owed him a kindness, a word of appreciation. "Under normal circumstances I would have seriously considered thy offer, Friend Ebenezer. But, alas, I am burdened by a concern. That may be what thee seems to have seen in me; what attracts thee is not my person, but my commitment."

He looked at her with an expression she could not interpret. "As I cannot stop you, will you do me a favor?"

"Certainly, if I can."

"Before going on board, take off those Indian clothes and put on your own Quaker dress."

"But it is all crumpled!"

"It is your only protection. Dress as a Quaker, not an Indian. In fact, this is not a request but an order."

"And what about my son?" She used the word for the first

time, and realized at that moment how ludicrous his proposal had been. A man like him would never accept an Indian child as his own. To her surprise he replied, "I would have been happy to give him my name and be a good father to him."

For a moment they faced each other, then she said, "Thank thee, Friend Ebenezer, in behalf of us all. I do wish thee could come with us."

He gave her a wry smile. "I never thought the day would come when my captives would invite me to stay."

She resisted the impulse to kiss him.

On her way back to join Mordecai, she wondered if he might be right about the Quaker dress. But it was important for her to retain her identity as a squaw; only after having become one of them had she been able to do something for the Indians, however little it might have been, and she was not done yet.

What she had turned down was a good, decent husband, a father for her boy. But there was no doubt that she must stay. For the first time since the day she joined the convoy, she accepted the possibility, the remote possibility, that she might be in the power of the Lord.

Mordecai, Little Bird, and the puppy watched Lydia's approach after her visit with the captain; but before he could question her he was accosted by the Negro servant himself.

"Captain Stewart sends his compliments, sah, and wishes to see you at once, sah."

"What is this all about?" he whispered to Lydia.

"I don't know why he wants thee," she replied, "but he asked me to marry him."

"He *what?*"

The orderly urged him, "Sah?"

Mordecai set his jaw and followed the man, the puppy at his heels. When he saw the captain waiting for him, in parade uniform, he had still not recovered.

"Good afternoon, Mr. Monk. Please sit down. What may I offer you? Gin? Whiskey?"

"Thank thee, nothing."

The captain waved the servant away. "Mr. Monk, I have been trying to dissuade Miss Best from boarding that steamer. I wonder if you would convince her that it may be a matter of life and death."

"Why?"

"Have you any idea what awaits her in Kansas? Even on board that ship?"

"Well—" Mordecai began, preoccupied with what Lydia had just told him.

"Obviously not, so let me enlighten you. All unorganized territories are beyond the law. People who settle there do so without the protection of the army. A male settler can do pretty well what he likes, unless he runs into somebody quicker on the draw. The Indians, however, will be at the mercy of whoever is waiting for them when they arrive. The miscreants preying upon them can only be described as human vultures. Some of them haven't set eyes on a white female for years. These men are not given to courtship; what they want, they take. Congress may have granted the territory to the Indians as a reservation, but the white men you'll find there have no intention of accepting that. It may become necessary after a while for the government to send in the cavalry to protect the Indians' rights; until then, they have none. I don't know what exactly you are planning to do, Mr. Monk, it's your life; but Miss Best must not go. It is our duty to stop her from committing suicide. I have tried. Now it is your turn."

"I'm afraid I am as powerless as thee is, Friend. I don't think there is a man alive who could stop Lydia Best once she sets out to do something out of conviction."

The captain set his jaw. "In my capacity as commandant of this convoy I cannot allow anyone to commit suicide, whether out of ignorance or religious zeal."

"But I am there to protect her!"

The captain gave him a mortifying look. "If you were to intervene, sir, those men would shoot you without thinking twice. You may have acquired a certain power among the Indians, but to white outlaws in unorganized territory you will be a figure of fun."

Suddenly it became clear: of course, the man was furious! Lydia had turned him down!

The captain continued, "No point in pulling that face, Mr. Monk." He said it as if he were addressing a malingering soldier. "You had better listen, for if you allow that woman to board the steamer, her life will become your responsibility. Your duty is to stop her and take her home. If you decide you cannot do that, then at least be honest with yourself and admit that you don't want to."

"But what could I do? No one can stop her, I tell thee!"

"All it would take is for you to say that you are going home. The moment you do that, she will follow suit. Even she will not go on alone."

"Thee is wrong," he said. "She will board that boat whether I go or not. Her heart is with the Indians."

The captain contemplated him thoughtfully for a moment. "In that case, the only solution is for you to marry her before the ship sails."

Mordecai stared at him in amazement.

"You Quakers marry yourselves, don't you? If you don't, I'll do it for you. If she has to go, at least make it known to those rascals waiting at the railing that you two are Quaker missionaries, the Reverend and Mrs. Monk. I told her she must change into her own dress; I would advise you to do the same. And put on your black coat."

"Black coat?"

"The one you took off the old squaw's grave, as I suggested," the captain said coldly.

The fact that the man knew even about this was unnerving. "Thee must have a poor opinion of me indeed," he said stiffly. "As a matter of interest, how is thy boil?"

"Sir, I have not for a moment doubted your powers. The difference between Miss Best and you is that between a Christian saint and an Indian shaman."

Mordecai could not help smiling. The poor man was besotted indeed.

"It is amazing," the captain said, rising. "You, presumably a man of God, have lived in the presence of a saint for two months without realizing it, while I, a confirmed agnostic—" He turned away. "You are under orders to marry Miss Best. You may perform the ceremony in my presence. I will legalize the wedding certificate. Do so *now*." He stooped into his tent.

Mordecai slowly walked back to their shelter through the throng of Indians. Lydia had indeed changed into her brown and gray Quaker dress, which was very rumpled; she was now pinning up her braids. Seeing her like that gave him quite a shock, she looked so unfamiliar. She bent down, picked up the basket with the baby, and swung it onto her back.

Puzzled by his scrutiny, she asked, "What's the matter?"

"Our friend the captain has been cutting quite a swath this afternoon, I must say."

"What did he want?"

"He has now ordered *me* to marry thee, for thy protection." She froze.

"He says thee may only go on board that steamer as a married woman."

"Nonsense! He talks as if all of America beyond the Mississippi is peopled with criminals!"

"Whatever the case, I am under orders to put on my black coat, marry thee, and announce ourselves as the Reverend and Mrs. Monk."

"The Reverend?"

"Yes, as a matter of fact. I was registered as a minister by Birmingham Women's Meeting."

"I don't care!" she cried angrily. "Do whatever thee feels thee must do! I myself will not go beyond putting on this—this dress! And I will take it off the moment we arrive at the reservation. I will certainly not call myself 'missionary' or 'reverend' or any other name for 'hireling priest.' I am a settler in the power of the Lord."

"Of course," he said, "we both are, and hope for His protection."

"Hope?" she asked. "It is a certainty. It is what enables me to face those men over there." She nodded in the direction of the decrepit steamer now belching white steam with a roar in front of its stack. The crew, chewing tobacco, leaned on the rail watching the squaws, whistling, laughing.

"We had better go on board and have a look at the accommodations, especially for the children," she said. "It is apt to be cold on the river at night. We want to make sure they will be warm. Please, be so good as to hook up the back of my collar. I cannot reach it, with the basket on my back."

She turned around and lifted her bonnet, exposing the downy whiteness of her neck. It looked young and vulnerable. He reached over the head of the sleeping baby to close the two hooks at the top of her dress, which turned out to have rusted; he had difficulty putting them through the eyelets. Suddenly, he knew that the captain was right. For her to go alone, even in Quaker garb, was suicidal madness. Her neck looked how Mary Stuart's must have looked to her executioner, when she put her head on the block.

"There," he said. "I think I did it."

She turned around. "Thank thee. Shall we go on board?"

"Lydia," he said, "I think we should do what the captain says. Our witness will end in bloodshed and tragedy, unless thee goes on board that ship as a married woman."

Her face went blank.

"Also, the two boys need parents. So, let's get it over with, marry ourselves in the face of God, and include Obadiah and Little Bird in our wedding certificate."

"But, but—that's nonsense!" she cried, shaken. "We cannot do that!"

"Why not?"

"Because it would be a lie! I have no intention of stating before God that I will be a faithful, loving wife to thee for as long as we both shall live!"

"Then make it 'companion,' " he said. "The Book of Discipline offers that formula merely as a suggestion; we are at liberty to say anything we like. 'In the presence of God and this assembly I hereby take my Friend Mordecai as my life's companion, and I promise to be a faithful and loving mother to our children, Obadiah and Little Bird, for as long as I shall live.' Would that be acceptable?"

She looked, suddenly, forlorn. "Let me think about it," she said. "Let me put it before God. Please."

"No," he said. "There is no time. Thee must decide now. Our concern is to serve the Indians wherever they go. We must do what is needed to carry out that concern. Thee need not say anything at all, leave it to me, but we must set foot on board that ship only as man and wife, parents of our children. If we don't—"

She looked up at him; her eyes were brimming with tears.

"If thee refuses," he continued, "I'll go back to Pendle Hill. With the cavalry. I mean that, Lydia. I will."

She did not answer, only closed her eyes. A tear ran down her right cheek.

"Say yes or no, Lydia. Now."

He thought she would not reply, just turn away. But she opened her eyes, gave him a look that he would never forget as long as he lived, and said, "Oh, God . . . I will."

She was shaken by her own tears. They came before she had articulated the reason in her mind: this was the end of girlish dreams, of the secret certainty she had had for a long time, that one day there would come a man she would love above all others, a man for whom she would go through fear and fire, a man who would unlock her womanhood and free her of the burden of physical loneliness that had begun to weigh more heavily with every passing year. She had thought, at one time, that Jesse might be the one. He had never known. Then there had been Obadiah—so close, so almost there. Now God had ordained that she go through a form of marriage with this person, the mere thought of whose touch upon her bare flesh made her shiver. A total stranger, whose character changes had been like the helter-skelter images of a kaleidoscope. 'A poet,' Obadiah had called him, 'the first Quaker poet.' But she had never sensed any beauty in either his being or his utterances; the images in the kaleidoscope she knew had been of a loudmouth, a bully, a lecher who had almost raped her, a mad demagogue who threw spells over countless women, a petulant monster toddler, a healer of Indians by means of a nursery rhyme, a fake fortune-teller—but he was right. Or rather, Captain Stewart was right: she could not go it alone.

From the moment she stepped ashore in unorganized territory, not to mention the steamboat itself, she wouldn't stand a chance. The child on her back would be no protection, but as the Quaker wife of the Reverend Monk it might be a different story.

But, oh—the dreams! The dreams of a lifetime!

Farewell, great lover, mysterious prince waiting beyond the horizon. Farewell, nights, days, years of rapturous love, and laughter, and little secrets, years of children and—well, the children were real, and she was all they had. They were all *she* had. Better accept her fate and turn her back on girlish dreams. Better to dream of what it would be like: the school, Little Bird playing with his younger brother, the class full of attentive children, the Meeting she—they—would start. Mordecai Monk, of all people! The 'Reverend' Monk!

God saved her from pointless anger and frustration by making the baby cry like a whelp that had lost its mother. The swinging of the basket off her back brought her back to reality. The mother who lifted the child in her arms for a cuddle and a kiss was Pusil.

Forget Lydia, sweetheart. Forget her dreams. Who knows, baby Obadiah and Little Bird may be just the beginning. Thee may end up as the old woman who lived in a shoe.

Goodbye, love. Goodbye.

• • •

Stony-faced, Captain Stewart observed the most bizarre wedding ceremony he had ever witnessed. The two celebrants, looking like tramps in their crumpled clothes, appeared before him solemnly. The bride, press-ganged into marriage, looked ready to run for her life before the deed was done. The child the Indians had foisted upon her was bouncing on her back; the little orphan boy who had attached himself to them squatted behind the couple, picking his nose. In the background, the ghouls on the deck of the riverboat watched the proceedings like a row of buzzards.

If they needed hymns, his porter would play the mouth organ. But as it turned out, they married themselves, without frills and in record time. They simply stood before him against a background of curious drovers, took one another by the hand, and intoned, in turn, a formula that proved to be virtually inaudible as the ship at the dock started to blow off steam with a deafening roar. The noise was so intrusive that he waved at the sailors, managed to attract someone's attention, pointed at his ears, and made a gesture of slitting his throat. It took a moment before the man understood what he meant and went to turn off the deafening roar. Too late, as it turned out; all he could hear was the bride whispering, '. . . *as long as we both shall live.*' There was no ring, of course; they shook hands as if in parting, then the groom handed over a piece of paper, which turned out to be a wedding certificate. It was a coldhearted business, like a commercial contract.

The captain signed the certificate after the two parties had affixed their signatures; one witness was insufficient for legal reasons, so the servant attached a cross to which the captain added, '*This is the mark of PFC Washington McDonald, witnessed by Capt. E. Z. Stewart II, US Cavalry.*' The wine he had set aside for the occasion remained unopened; the bride looked pale and in shock, the bridegroom beamed like—well, the less said about him the better.

In the meantime, the crew of the riverboat had started to

herd the Indians on board. The captain escorted the bridal couple toward the gangway; ahead of them, a demented brave who had walked the whole way like a sleepwalker leading an emaciated pony was trying to take his horse on board with him. The animal stood precariously perched on the gangplank, a line of squaws behind it; then the brutes loading the Indians let out a yell, panicking the horse. It backed away, pushed over one of the squaws, and trampled her underfoot. There were screams; the horse stampeded out of sight; both bride and bridegroom hurried to the aid of the stricken woman. But the squaws were ahead of them and carried her on board. The chief turned to Mordecai Monk and said, "You told her! She should have known better!"

"I did?" Monk asked, amazed.

"Yes!" the chief said. "You told her: beware of horses!"

For some reason this seemed to upset the couple deeply; they stared at each other, mouths open, as if some horrible truth had been revealed to them. It was time to go on board, certainly for those children of theirs; the little boy clung to her skirts, hiding his face, the baby screamed like a piglet in her backpack.

Impulsively, in a gesture of sympathy, the captain did something foolish: he took out of the side pocket of his greatcoat the rabbit's foot he always carried for good luck; it had a silver cap on one end with his initials engraved in it, given to him by a sentimental godmother years ago. He fastened it onto the baby's bindings by one of the tapes. The little boy looked on with envy and was given a cigar. After that, the new little family hastened on board.

Half an hour later, ropes were cast off and the ship began to move away from the riverbank. Captain Stewart stood among the abandoned wagons and stray horses and scattered belongings, watching the crush on the decks, looking for the two Quakers. The sun set in a blaze of orange, adding to the drama of the slave ship's departure. On previous occasions, the captain had left as soon as the last Indian was on board, relishing the prospect of returning to civilization at a fast clip, unencumbered by his sad herd. This time he stood watching with a sense of outrage at the sight of the lumbering vessel, almost a wreck, manned by ruffians known to help themselves liberally to the squaws and young girls on the voyage downriver. By the time they reached St. Louis, there wouldn't be a virgin aboard. As for Lydia, he had done all he could to ensure her safety; even so, he felt as if he had delivered her to her executioners. What were her chances of survival in unorganized territory? Even before she arrived at the Indian reservation, outlaws might make short shrift of her; she was determined to return to Mahanoy dress, and a white woman gone native must be a delectation for those roughnecks after a steady diet of Indian squaws. Even in the best of circumstances, if she were to arrive unmolested and start life among the Indians, who merely tolerated her, what was her future? Those people were unsentimental; already, behind him, a band of Plains Indians had started to pilfer the horses and wagons left behind.

He scanned the decks of the ship, now swinging downstream, and spotted her on the foredeck, taking the baby off her back and putting it inside something that looked like a coil of rope. The river was afire with the reflection of the sunset; the vessel, belching black smoke, slowly gathered speed. The captain, on impulse, was about to salute when, suddenly, there was a blinding flash, a shuddering blast. Bodies, planks, bundles were hurled upward by the explosion; a shower of wreckage came tumbling down into the river. Captain Stewart stood petrified; clearly, the worn-out boiler of the vessel had exploded; he realized, with a heart-stopping sense of horror, that after his request that the safety valve be turned off, no one had thought to open it again.

He ran to his horse, swung into the saddle, galloped down the river's bank looking for survivors, followed by his men. For hours he rode up and down the bank, calling, looking for Lydia among the debris that drifted slowly downstream. Behind him, the Indian scavengers calmly went on picking over the spoils left by the dead.

Finally, desolate and heartsick, he turned his horse around and headed back to his command tent. Then someone called,

"Captain! Over there, sir! Over to your right! Can you hear it?"

The captain halted. Indeed: a thin, high sound, the yapping of a dog.

"Where?" he shouted.

The sergeant on his horse in the shallows, near a clump of reeds, shouted, "Over here, sir! Over here!"

On the river's edge, caught up in the reeds, the sergeant had spotted a round leather coracle. "Listen, sir!" The captain listened. There it came, indeed: the distant crying of a baby, a dog yapping. He wheeled his horse around, forced it into the ice-cold water, and made it wade in the direction of the sound.

When he reached the coracle, he saw, in a nest of bedrolls and blankets, a frantic puppy tied up and an Indian baby in a carrying basket. He attached a rope from his saddle to it and turned his horse back to the shore, towing the coracle. When he reached dry land the little dog jumped out and the sergeant picked up the child. He held it up for the captain to see. Just a papoose. "See if you can find someone among those Indians over there prepared to take it on," the captain said. "I'm going to change before I catch my death."

He was toweling himself down, his orderly standing by with a hot toddy, when there was a knock on the doorpost. A voice called, "Captain, sir!"

"See who that is," he said. "Put that glass down, I'll get it in a minute." The orderly obeyed. There followed some mumbling in the background, while the captain was toweling his hair. At a given moment, he realized that the servant was waiting for him to finish. "What is it?" he asked irritably.

"Sah, this is what they found on the baby, sah."

He held it out on the pale palm of his black hand. It was Aunt Dinah's rabbit's foot.

"Jesus Christ," the captain said. "Where is the child now?"

"I don't know, sah."

"Ask! Ask, goddammit! Go find out where it is! Bring it back! I want it back, *now*, before those savages make off with it!"

The servant ran off.

The captain was dressed by the time the man returned, trailed by the little dog and holding the baby in his arms. It did not look any different from all the others he had seen since he started this foul assignment, but it had to be the one. For a moment the thought crossed his mind that he was honor bound to take care of it himself, after his assurance to Lydia Best that he would have accepted this creature as his son after marriage. But he said, "You take care of it, boy. Know how to feed a baby, change it, and so on?"

"Yes, sah," the Negro said, with the slightly condescending obedience that, at times, made the captain want to give him a sharp kick.

"We'll return it to the school in the village where they joined us—what's its name?—Pendle Hill."

"Yes, sah."

"Now get me a double, straight up." As the man turned away with the child in his arms, the captain added, "And take that dog with you."

Lydia Best . . . Professional training and battlefield experience had taught him never to mourn the fallen, but this one was tough. This one was a swine. This one broke his goddamn heart.

He changed his mind. "Come here!" he called after the dog. "Like some bacon?" To his orderly he said, "Okay, leave him here. I'll take care of him. You take care of the baby."

My God! Why did she have to *die*?

Why this, why that. No sense in asking questions. She was dead.

"Here," he said. "Try some cheese."

But the dog needed time. Well, hell, so did he.

Chapter 16

Pendle Hill, Indiana

December 1833

Abner the stableboy was giving the horses their evening feed; this humiliating position had been the only one offered to him after he was read out of Meeting. When he heard the clatter of hooves on cobbles, he wondered who it could be; he had to be careful to whom he showed himself now that Saraetta had been made principal.

He started for the door and was almost bowled over in the gloom by Adam Higgins. "Abner! Abner! The cavalry's here! An officer with a baby who says it belongs to thy sister!"

Lydia? A baby?

Abner went outside; a group of cavalrymen were hitching their horses to the posts in front of the school; among them was an officer carrying a basket with a baby. Abner accosted him, forgetting about the rule of secrecy Saraetta had insisted on. "Yes, Friend? What can I do for thee?" Then he recognized the man; it was the red-bearded captain who had been in charge of the Indian convoy.

The captain did not remember him. "I need to see the principal. Where do I find him?"

"I—my wife—what is this about a baby belonging to my sister?"

The child, thin and solemn with two pitch-black eyes, gazed at him from the basket.

"Lydia Best was your sister?" the officer asked, eyebrows raised.

"Yes. I used to be the principal of . . . *was?* . . . You don't mean . . . ?" He was unable to continue.

"I'm afraid so. The boat she was on blew up as it left the landing. There were no survivors. I'm sorry."

"I see . . ."

He did not see at all. What did the man mean? There must be some mistake. He looked about him. "Let's—let's go in here . . ." He indicated the stables.

The officer followed him, spurs jangling. While the hungry horses whinnied and snorted in their boxes, the man told Abner what had happened. Lydia had adopted a Mahanoy waif. The riverboat's boiler had exploded at Indian Landing. The baby and a little dog that had belonged to Mordecai were the only ones to come off alive. The dog must be around somewhere, it had followed them all the way from the Mississippi.

Numb with shock, Abner could only guess at what Mordecai's death would do to Saraetta. She had started an official concern for the blind in an effort to give a purpose to her hero's suffering; now she had to be told the man was dead. "I—I think I should go tell my wife," he said to the officer. "I mean, before she hears it from someone else. You will stay with us overnight?"

"No, sir," the officer said. "I only stopped to deliver the infant. We have to be moving on."

"Please! Please don't go yet! Just let me take the child to my wife—I'll be right back."

The captain, aware of Abner's distress, nodded and handed him the basket.

Abner entered the lobby just as the classes were on their way to the dining hall. He was stopped by a crowd of chattering children, asking why the soldiers were there, who the baby was, could they see it. Scores of little hands reached out toward the child who, frightened by the noise in the echoing hall, started to bellow with a strength that was somehow reassuring.

"Careful!" Abner cried. "Quiet, please! Let me through! You stay here!"

Peggy Higgins came waddling toward him from the kitchen; he fled up the stairs, the baby screaming in his arms. He nearly tripped, regained his balance, slowed down as he entered the dark corridor leading to their apartment. The baby went into a paroxysm of shrieks; it sounded as if it were choking.

Suddenly his courage, or whatever it was, failed him. He could not see it through: facing Saraetta, her reaction to his news, handing her the baby.

He turned around in desperate indecision and found Himsha Woodhouse standing right behind him, the only one from the crowd of children who had dared to follow him. "Here," he said. "Hold this baby. Take it to the kitchen, while I—I go and call the doctor."

He fled, there was no other word for it. As by magic, the baby fell silent behind him. Maybe it had recognized Himsha's Indian face. He started toward the children on the landing, but found he could not face them, not just yet. There was only one way to avoid them—he opened the door to the attic and climbed the narrow stairs.

Standing in front of the window, overlooking the barren treetops and the distant prairie, he wept, struck by a grief he had never known before. Lydia . . . Lydia!

He did not know how long he stood there weeping; but gradually he grew calmer. He should go downstairs now, back to the captain who was waiting below.

He opened the attic window, breathed the frosty air, gazed at the prairie. A flock of geese heading south drew an arrowhead across the wintry sky. The horizon was clear and white.

Beyond that horizon Lydia had vanished forever. It was unimaginable that the goodness and strength she had squandered on people like himself and Mordecai Monk should have been wiped out. It could not be that this was all there was to the miracle, the irreplaceable marvel of courage and love that had been Lydia. If she were anywhere at all right now, if there were anywhere for her to go, she must be with Margaret Fell, Gulielma Woodhouse, Becky Baker, all those women on whose godly lives the Quaker witness was founded.

But as he gazed at the sea of grass, all he had to hold on to was the Friends' old belief that love was eternal, life immortal, and death a horizon. And a horizon was nothing but the limitation of our sight.

Dr. Rossini was hauled out of his first sleep by his Cajun housekeeper, who, as always at this ungodly hour, looked like a voodoo priestess with her head full of paper curlers. "*Docteur!*" she called. "*Docteur!*"

"*Oui, Hélène,*" he groaned, "*qu'est-ce qu'il y a?*"

It turned out to be another call from the school. Rossini was of half a mind to tell the messenger he would be there first thing in the morning, but when he questioned the man, a vague shadow in the night outside the doorway, he was told it was a matter of extreme urgency, something about Saraetta having a child.

Suddenly wide awake, Rossini dressed with practiced speed, while Hélène prepared his buggy. He ought to have a manservant to do that, but Hélène might eat him.

Saraetta, a child? As he drove through the night, he could not repress the irreverent thought that it must have been an immaculate conception. To father a child on that snow queen was a triumph—but as her doctor, he would have known about it. It had to be a false alarm. If anyone seemed predestined for a phantom pregnancy, it was Saraetta Best. What a curse to be married to a woman like that! And now poor Abner had been demoted to some menial job . . .

He reached the school and handed the reins to the stablehand in the courtyard. The man started to brief him in the dark, but Rossini wanted to hear it firsthand from the Bests themselves. Then he remembered who the stablehand was. Poor Abner was virtually in hysterics: the cavalry had turned up with a baby, an Indian baby Lydia had adopted, but Lydia herself was dead, also Mordecai Monk and all the Indians, the boiler of the ship in which they were being transported to Kansas had exploded—

Lydia dead? Rossini made his way to the glass doors of the lobby, struck by unprofessional grief. Lydia had seemed the most enduring of them all. It simply did not seem possible—a glorious life of courage and gentleness, snuffed out as if God had trod on a beetle, crushing His own creation.

He was not often personally affected by a death this way; he was almost grateful when, on his way up the dark stairs, some child stepped in his way from the shadows, saying, "Here he is, Doctor."

It took him a moment to realize it was the Indian girl Himsha, holding a baby.

"You didn't give it to her yet?" Rossini asked, surprised.

"No, Doctor, I—I didn't dare go in."

"Why not?"

"Listen . . ."

He listened, and there it was again: the familiar sound of hysteria, this time with trumpets, cymbals, and temple bells. Not even Madame Guijon, whom he had seen, and especially heard, in New Orleans as a student, had managed to fill the stage all by herself quite as fulsomely as Saraetta Best when she let it rip.

"All right," he said. "Come with me. Is the child all right?"

"Yes, Doctor. He was crying, but we fed him and he's asleep now."

She really was going full tilt, old Sara. He wondered what exactly had brought about this gargantuan demonstration of operatic grief; she and Lydia had not been exactly bosom friends. Then, just before he opened the door, it struck him: it was not

Lydia she mourned, but her idol Mordecai Monk, the holy demagogue.

He opened the door and there she lay, Medusa strangled in her own coils. My God, to turn a bed into a nest of vipers all by yourself was quite a feat unless you were insane. Maybe she was. She howled and heaved, gasped, beat her breast and tore her garments in the most Biblical fashion. He felt like giving her a potion that would poleax her into silence but thought, in the words of Will Penn, 'First let us try what love can do.'

"Saraetta?" he said, approaching the bed. "Look at me, I am Dr. Rossini. There is someone I want you to meet."

She swung around with such violence that he stepped back involuntarily. "He's dead!" she shrieked. "They murdered him! He has been crucified!"

Rossini beckoned the Indian girl who hovered on the periphery. "Give him to me," he whispered, and took over the little papoose in its tight swaddling clothes, an ugly child with motionless features, old before its time.

"Here, look at this," he said, in a moment of silence amidst the shrieks. "This is what Lydia wanted you to have. This is . . ." He was forced to wait until more howling had run its course. "This is the baby Lydia adopted a few weeks before she died, a motherless infant she made her own, now motherless again. Unless you—" With perfect timing, he put the baby in her arms as she sat, mad-eyed, struck with stillness at the height of her passion. God, what the right man would be able to do with this smothered volcano!

"He is yours, Mrs. Best—if you want him, that is."

"Lydia's?" she asked, stunned for once.

"Yes. You are his only hope now, ma'am." The 'ma'am' was a bit much, but she looked at the child in her arms, cradled it, and at that moment God performed a miracle by making the baby cry.

"Come now, come now . . ." She took over the crying child with the tenderness she had waited all her life to spend, comforted it, kissed it, hugged it, said, "Hush baby, hush little

beastie, hush, it's all right, it's all right, thee's safe now, all is
well . . ." She kissed the black hair, pressed the child's face
against her bosom. After a while, Rossini said, "I'll go and order
some milk. Shall I leave him with you?" A reply was unnecessary, she was now totally wrapped up in the child.

"Come." Rossini put his arm round the shoulders of the
Indian girl. Outside, in the corridor, he said, "Keep an eye on
him, will you, Himsha? It seems you have a new brother. He
may need help."

"I will," she said. "He has a little dog too. It's in the kitchen.
Come and have a look," and she led the way downstairs.

Well, another foundling had joined the flock. 'Little Beastie'
would need a lot of resilience and personality to withstand the
storm-tossed waves of his adoptive mother's emotions; but what
Rossini knew of Indian babies was reassuring. And this one
looked as if he were made of drop-forged steel. 'Who knows,' he
reflected as he followed Himsha to the kitchen, 'one day this
may be someone to be reckoned with in the Quaker establishment: an Indian Friend. They haven't had one for a long time.
Talk about landing on your feet!'

CHAPTER 17

PENDLE HILL, INDIANA
January 1834

After the Christmas holidays, everything returned to normal. The school resumed its daily schedule of work, play, and worship. Charity taught fourth grade. Obadiah scribbled away at his desk in a corner of the room that was now their home: an essay about 'Law on the Frontier.'

The first meeting for business of the new year was held separately by the men and the women in the old Meeting House, with the partition lowered between them as usual. It was a humdrum affair, concerned with dreary minutiae like covered-dish lunches to be given to neighboring Meetings and the rota of those taking charge of First Day school during the coming months. Within half an hour, Charity noticed, everyone was getting drowsy; then Amanda Tucker, cochairman of the school committee, rose to make her report.

She started by eulogizing Mordecai Monk, out of the blue. "Saintly, selfless Friend who, despite his cruel blindness, joined the Indians as a testimony of Christian love." She did not mention Lydia Best at all; Charity felt the urge to take issue with her. But as the youngest member of the Meeting she had better hold her peace. The paean of praise for Mordecai Monk continued, and she waited in growing distress for someone else to rise in protest, but no one did. The old woman on her right, who must be at least ninety, had fallen asleep soon after the start of meeting and now sat peaceably snoring. The woman on her left, a gruff-looking farmer's wife with calloused hands and hairy chin, grunted in disapproval but did not speak up.

Then Charity found herself beginning to quake. It had never happened to her before; it took a while before she realized that was what it was. The trembling started in her hands; she folded them tightly. Then the rest of her body began to quiver, until she sat there shaking like a leaf. With a feeling of reluctance she gave in, found herself on her feet, and cried, interrupting Amanda Tucker, "Please, Friends! Let's not pretend that Lydia Best never existed! Not only Mordecai Monk joined the Indians as a witness, but Lydia did too! And she was a member of this Meeting! I know I am the youngest among you, but I beseech you: let us rise, all of us, as a witness that we unite with her. Let us rise and express the wish, in prayer, that somehow God may give us the power to turn Lydia's witness into a testimony of our own! We can either kill her memory forever, or rise where she fell. The choice is ours. *Now!*"

Whatever the power was that had forced her to her feet stayed with her. She gripped the back of the bench in front to keep herself from swooning; then, to her utter astonishment, the meeting rose to its feet.

After a stunned silence, Amanda Tucker asked, "Has our eloquent young Friend any constructive suggestions to make? If so, would she please come forward and submit them to this meeting?"

Charity understood too late what she had done. All that was weak and insecure within her wanted to let the meeting decide for itself what to do next, not take the lead. But she had no choice now but to respond. To the dozing old woman by her side she said, "Excuse me," and tried to pass her, but a hand grabbed her skirt. The old woman gazed up at her with rheumy eyes and a cracked voice and whispered, "Don't do it!" The hand tugging at her skirt urged her to sit down; for a second she stood in doubt, then said, "Sorry," detached herself from the hand, and walked down the aisle, knees shaking, while the meeting sat down again. On the rostrum, Amanda Tucker stood waiting for her. 'God,' Charity prayed as she walked, 'please don't make me! Please, I didn't mean it! It was just a thought, an idea . . .' She climbed the steps to the rostrum, whispered, "Thank thee," to Amanda Tucker, and confronted the meeting, a sea of silent white faces. She folded her hands tightly to hide their shaking and said in a firm voice, "Lydia Best was the one who started among the members of this Meeting a motion of love that resulted in the Meeting for Sufferings of Mahanoy Indians. I was not here when it happened, but my husband has told me of it in such vivid terms that I feel as if I had been a participant. She, and others among you, expressed our common concern by distributing food and clothes, care and attention among the people in a passing convoy. But it became clear to her that this was not enough. A Meeting for Sufferings, the oldest expression of a Quaker concern, is not just an instrument for the distribution of food parcels and the odd discarded garment. To be worthy of its name, a Meeting for Sufferings, being an expression of the love of the Meeting, has to do more, set itself a loftier goal."

All this was an articulation of her thoughts as they had developed over the weeks, by now months, since Lydia's departure. Yet she felt suddenly as though she were expressing not only her own thoughts but those of many others in the hall, as they sat listening in a deep, almost scary silence. She continued bravely: "Lydia Best joined the Indians as a witness, in behalf of us all. In doing so, she was following the example of Becky and Cleo and Boniface Baker, who founded this school in what was then unorganized territory, as the Indian reservation in Kansas is today. We heard from the captain of the cavalry who escorted her convoy that Lydia was planning a class for Indian children when—when she died, together with the children. We cannot know the mind of God, but one thing is certain: He did not call her home to Him because He does not want the Mahanoy children to have an education. Maybe she was called home to Him because no one can possibly undertake this momentous task alone." She paused, then, taking a deep breath, said, "I therefore propose that Pendle Hill Meeting liberate those of its members who feel called to do so to follow Lydia Best's example. Complete her task, start a branch of our School for Indian Children in the Mahanoy reservation in Kansas . . ."

So far, it had come out firmly, calm, controlled, the articulation of the plan she had mulled over for months; now she suddenly stood tongue-tied. The meeting, silent, white-faced, stared up at her.

Beside her, Amanda Tucker's voice asked, after a silence, "Any particular Friends in mind, Friend Charity?"

Charity threw all caution to the winds and said, "Myself and my husband, for a start."

In the stillness that followed, she suddenly felt a sense of uncertainty. Obadiah was going to be furious. But something, maybe sheer panic, made her continue.

"I propose," she concluded shakily, "that a Mahanoy branch of the Rebekah Baker School for Indian Children be placed under the care of Pendle Hill Meeting, to—to benefit from Friends like—like Amanda Tucker . . ." It had been a sudden inspiration; to her alarm, the meeting roared with laughter, and somewhere someone started to applaud.

She looked around for help and saw Amanda Tucker stare coldly at her before asking in an acid tone, "May I invite comments from the meeting?"

None was forthcoming.

She continued, "Let me state, as cochairman of the school committee, that touched as we are by our young Friend's proposal, we must consider the practical aspects of her suggestion, not the least of which is the matter of financing such an undertaking." She again waited for a reaction from the meeting; when no one spoke, she continued, "I propose that we appoint Charity Woodhouse, together with two other Friends, to go to the Men's Meeting next door with the request that they appoint an equal number from their midst to labor with them on this concern. We need action, Friends, not words!"

'How was it possible?' Charity thought. Was this the way it happened? Had she, miraculously, reached that of God in Amanda Tucker?

After her failed effort to stop the child rushing toward her doom, Abby McHair decided that she must speak up. The girl had been struck by the madness of God, just as her own father and sister Becky had been. She herself had been dragged into the wilderness as a child of ten; this girl had no idea what that meant, no idea of the hardship, the loneliness, the terror, the heartbreak. All she saw in her exaltation was the fact that God had chosen her to do His work for Him. *'All He has is thee.'* It was the most bloodthirsty slogan in Quaker history.

Amanda Tucker intoned, "As cochairman of the school committee, I will accompany Charity Woodhouse to the Men's Meeting in that capacity. May we have one more Friend, please, to make up the required number?"

Abby rose unsteadily to her feet and said, "I will."

She was conscious of the silence she created. Amanda Tucker replied, with reverence, "The meeting will be honored, Abigail McHair. May I have the sense of the meeting on the delegation as proposed?"

Someone called, "I unite!" followed by a chorus of approval.

Abby set out up the aisle on her way to the Men's Meeting; someone rose to support her. She acted more fragile than she was; her power resided in the fact that she was ninety-three years old, last surviving member of the founder's family, all of which had, of course, nothing to do with today's reality.

"Careful, Abigail McHair," Amanda Tucker warned, as she opened the door in the partition. "Mind the step!"

"Step?" she croaked, overdoing it.

"Here—"

"Ah! I see . . . Thank thee." Smiling vacuously, she staggered into the Men's Meeting like a drunk. Nobody was aware that in her better moments she remained a woman of thirty-five, tough as nails, who knew intimately the validity of the old Quaker adage that if you cannot have violence, you must have slyness.

Obadiah wondered what was going on when he saw Charity, Amanda Tucker, and Abigail McHair turn up at the back of the hall. The old woman shuffled down the aisle to the rostrum supported by the two others; when they reached the facing bench, Amanda Tucker spoke briefly to the clerk, then turned around and cried, "The Women's Meeting has delegated us to present to you a concern of great urgency!"

Harlan Tucker had no choice but to invite his wife to present to the meeting whatever it was that had made them interrupt their deliberations. Amanda Tucker took Obadiah's breath away by saying, "Our young attender, Charity Woodhouse, has informed the Women's Meeting of a concern with which she and her husband are burdened. They feel moved, in the spirit of love, to follow Boniface and Rebekah Baker's example, and that of Friend Mordecai Monk and Lydia Best, by setting out for the Mahanoy reservation in order to start a branch of the Rebekah Baker School for Indian Children under the care of Pendle Hill Meeting."

Obadiah could barely contain himself. There stood Charity, looking pious, clearly avoiding his eyes. What had got into her? How dare she! He waited with rising fury for the impossible Amanda to end her monologue, so he could rise himself and announce publicly that he had no knowledge of the insane plan and was dead set against it.

Then old Abigail McHair started to speak. Obadiah had assumed she was there merely as an ornament, to lend weight to the women's message; the fact that she spoke at all came as a shock. She spoke in a slow, hesitant, croaking whisper that hushed the meeting to dead silence. At first, Obadiah was intimidated by her venerable age; but as she continued, gasping for breath after every few words, frequently pressing her breastbone, he became convinced that the ninety-three-year-old woman was dissembling. Nobody could be that feeble and be heard in the back row.

She asked for the partition to be raised so that she might address both meetings; her whispered wish was reverently obeyed. She waited until the creaking and squealing of the hoisting had stopped, then she addressed the full house, and Obadiah's suspicion became certainty. She seemed about to keel over, but her breathy whisper was audible in the furthest row; she was as adept at voice projection as Mordecai Monk had been.

He was overcome by contempt for the old woman, and for Charity. Both were arch manipulators; when one of the men dared to pose a question, Abby McHair went through a near fatal attack of exhaustion. In a dramatic swoon, pressing both hands on her chest, she closed her eyes. As a result, the meeting hushed the man with an outraged "Sssh!" and the old witch continued her performance.

What she said only deepened Obadiah's scorn. She even went so far as to exploit the gruesome death of her sister Rebekah to make a point. "We must not let these children go alone, the way Philadelphia Yearly Meeting allowed us to go, eighty-three years ago!" she croaked. "We must forbid them to go, for their own sakes, and for the sake of their future children—unless we decide to make up a wagon train of able men and women in sufficient numbers to turn this reckless witness into an organized, responsible concern, as was done by Philadelphia Meeting after the gruesome death of my sister Rebekah."

To Obadiah's amazement, a score of people rose from the body of the men's meeting to cry, "I unite!" men whom he would never have expected to do such a thing: Little Will, Adam Higgins, Farmer Kowalski, Cletus Brown. After ten minutes of communal insanity, the combined meetings approved a minute in which the founding of '*a branch of the Rebekah Baker School for*

Indian Children in Kansas Territory' was made the official concern of Pendle Hill Monthly Meeting and placed under its care.

After that, madness took hold. Spontaneous contributions of startling generosity were made to the Mahanoy School Expedition. Farmers donated horses, gear. A tailor offered to furnish clothes for the first contingent of Indian children in the school, then decided he might as well go himself and asked if somebody present was interested in taking over a fully equipped tailor's workshop. A carpenter, a blacksmith, a wagoneer, three buffalo hunters, all offered their services. One man donated a mule team, if someone else would offer the wagons. A builder offered materials for a schoolhouse. Two grocers, in a frenzy of competition, promised to stock the wagon train with food for two months. The climax came when Harry Bascombe, owner of the Pendle Hill Inn, a wet Quaker if ever there was one, pledged bedding and blankets not only for the expedition but for the entire school itself.

Everybody seemed to share in an orgy of generosity, with the exception of Abner Best. Deathly pale, obviously under stress, he remained seated. Amazing, really; having been dismissed and disowned, he seemed a natural for the expedition. Uriah Martin seemed tempted to follow his brother Little Will, but Abner grabbed his pudgy wrist; the fat man obeyed the silent command and stayed down.

That silent interchange suddenly opened Obadiah's eyes to what was actually going on: he was witnessing another demonstration of the schism in Pendle Hill. The orthodox members were satisfied to contribute; those who actually joined this harebrained expedition were all activists. The Meeting was ridding itself of dissent, in the spirit of love.

Then it struck him what the true challenge was. By joining this expedition—insane as it might be, ludicrous as the concept was of a city lawyer setting out for an Indian reservation—he himself would help relieve Lydia's death of its pointlessness. Then, in part thanks to him, it could be said that if Lydia had not died the way she did, the Quaker school for Indian children in the Mahanoy reservation would never have come about. But was he prepared to throw away his years of education, his professional future, trotting along behind his wife into the wilderness?

He was standing alone in the aisle after meeting had broken when Charity threw herself against him, collapsing, her head on his shoulder, crying, "Obadiah! What have I done?"

As if she didn't know. "Let's go home," he said. "We need to talk about it."

Home was the poky room on the fourth floor. A covered wagon could be no smaller. The only thing smaller would be a coffin.

"Thee knows thee is crazy?" He took her hand and sat down on the edge of the bed. "We had a whole life ahead of us—"

"We have!" she whispered. "We have! Kiss me!"

And so, in their confusion, they made love, as if that were the answer to everything.

'Today, at eight o'clock sharp, there will be a meeting of the participants of the Mahanoy expedition in the Meeting House.'

Eventually, they found the note under their door. Someone must have put it there while they— "Oh, no! Does thee think they *heard*?" she cried.

He smiled a wan smile. "They'll say that I sank my teeth in thy neck, causing thee to shriek like the cheetah."

Suddenly, there he was, awesome and ludicrous even in death: Mordecai Monk, who had started all this by interrupting the children's pageant with his monstrous ministry. But for him, none of this would have come about.

"God works in mysterious ways," he said.

She groaned.

As the first meeting of the participants got under way, Dr. Rossini, listening in the back row of the sparsely filled Meeting House, concluded that the Mahanoy expedition was like a children's crusade. Speaker after speaker rose to make impractical suggestions; when Baker Jenkins suggested taking along one hundred copies of William Penn's *No Cross, No Crown*, to be distributed among the outlaws in unorganized territory, Rossini realized that none of the forty participants had any idea what awaited them in that lawless world. To them, Indians were a homogeneous race full of friendship and tenderness for their old friends the Quakers. Apart from the handful of women who had distributed food to the convoys, they had never set eyes on a real Indian, only on tame ones. Nobody here had the slightest notion of the differences between the tribes, between Plains Indians and Woods Indians. Plains Indians, in their natural habitat, had no idea who Quakers were; they would scalp, rape, and murder any isolated band of whites like this wagon train the moment they spotted easy pickings.

At a given moment he could no longer resist raising his voice as their physician, to try and restore sanity among the Pentecostal dreamers.

"Friends!" he started; the moment they saw who was calling for their attention, they fell silent; the doctor should be listened to.

"Come forward, Doc!" Baker Jenkins called. "We all want to hear what thee has to say."

Rossini walked down the aisle to the rostrum and faced the child crusaders. "Forgive me if I mention a few facts from my own experience. First off, to venture into Indian territory with a wagon train, unarmed or restricted in the use of arms by your peace testimony, is to invite disaster."

"I don't agree!" a man shouted from the body of the meeting. "In many instances in the past, the peace testimony—"

"Let him finish, Harm," Baker Jenkins interrupted. "Let the doc have his say first, then thee can sound off. Go on, Doc."

"Peace testimony or no, you *must* travel under the protection of the U.S. Cavalry at least as far as the river, possibly further. But that means you must ask for it."

There was a rumble of protest.

"In order for you to acquire army protection, the government has to issue an order to that effect—"

"Which they will never do!" someone shouted.

"Which they may do, if you, as a religious body, have some clout in Washington."

Hearty laughter was his response. The mere idea appeared hilarious to them; then Obadiah Woodhouse rose and said with unexpected authority, "I happen to know that there are individual Friends who carry a lot of weight with Congress and the Senate. Both Philadelphia Yearly Meetings, especially Arch Street, have influence in Washington—"

Baker Jenkins interrupted. "Surely Arch Street would be the last to support this concern?"

"Not necessarily. They may, under certain conditions, be persuaded to do so."

"How does thee know?"

"I was a member of Arch Street Yearly Meeting myself at one time," the young man replied, smiling.

In the silence that followed, Rossini asked, "What are those conditions, counselor?"

"To begin with, it must not cost any money."

They laughed; the baker called, "Silence!"

"Secondly, it must not involve their having to *do* anything. Thirdly, and most important: they must be pressured."

"By whom?" the baker asked.

"By their wives."

There was more laughter.

"This is where Mordecai Monk comes in," the young lawyer continued soberly. The name brought an uneasy silence; Mordecai Monk had become the darling of the orthodox part of the Meeting. "If we can present this concern as a continuation of Mordecai Monk's inspired and inspiring mission, there is a fair chance that Quaker women on the Atlantic seaboard will urge their husbands to give us their support."

"How could we achieve that?" Baker Jenkins asked.

"I could write an essay," the young lawyer said, poker-faced, "in which I describe Mordecai Monk's Calvary and ultimate crucifixion in inspiring terms."

"Would it be the truth?" someone asked.

The young man hesitated before saying, "Yes, if speaking truth to power means speaking in power's own terms."

"Explain!" someone called.

"When Arch Street accepts and approves of ministry that says, 'I give my heart to Jesus,' it is generally accepted that the speaker is not about to have the actual organ removed from his chest as a sacrifice. When Arch Street vociferously adheres to the principles of the Sermon on the Mount, it does not mean that the owners of large shipping companies and the princes of commerce are going to distribute their wealth among the poor. It so happens that they are caught in the snares of traditional verbal ecstasies which bear no relation to the reality of daily life. I would write on Mordecai Monk's life and death in terms which, in other, less verbally oriented Meetings, might sound like hypocrisy. I hasten to add that I would *not* be misleading them, all I would do would be to say, 'Mordecai Monk was crucified on the road to Golgotha,' rather than 'Mordecai Monk paid for his convictions with his life.' It's a matter of identifying with the adversary, as the approach to conflict after the manner of Friends advises us to do."

There was an uneasy silence, but no one demurred.

After the meeting, the rest of which was devoted to a discussion of practical preparations, Rossini accosted Obadiah. "Are you seriously considering doing that?" he asked.

"Well, yes, I'd like to have a shot at it," the young man answered. "I don't know if I can. It will take—well—a certain effort."

"Now let me get this straight," Rossini persisted. "You *do* accept that any wagon train may only travel under the protection of the cavalry?"

"Yes."

"And to that end you want to prevail upon the Quaker establishment to turn the man Monk into a saint?"

"Something of the sort."

"You know that he wasn't?"

"I don't, frankly," the young man replied with unconvincing innocence. "For all I know I may have traveled in the company of a saint without knowing it."

"Well, I can tell you that he was not," Rossini pressed on. "The man was a humbug and a malingerer who pretended to be blind."

"It's all a matter of interpretation," the young man said with a smile.

It was easier said than done. Obadiah, seated at the tiny table in the corner of their bedroom, faced the blank page feeling—there was no other word for it—unclean. He was about to smuggle an unworthy character into the gallery of Quaker saints, on whose godly lives the spiritual edifice of the Society of Friends was based. Having no dogmas, no creed, no liturgy, no paid clergy, Quakers had to find guidance and inspiration in the godly lives that went before. There weren't too many of them as it was; to infiltrate their sparse ranks with an impostor might bear momentous consequences.

On the other hand, who was to say whether Mordecai Monk had fallen from grace when he allowed himself to be turned into a medicine man by the Indians, as the captain had reported? Curing ailments with a nursery rhyme? George Fox had performed healings and miracles; he had even, on one occasion, reputedly raised the dead. It certainly was not new to have a Friend perform the laying on of hands, or any other form of spiritual healing; whether he sang 'Hosannah!' or 'Hoopla, hopla!' while doing so might be immaterial. Presumably, it was God Himself who effected the healing; no one must think himself an authority on the musical tastes of the Almighty. His wondrous ways might include nursery rhymes intoned by charlatans, if that was all He had available at a particular moment.

Musing about it, Obadiah eventually convinced himself that his firing the first shot in the battle for the sanctification of Mordecai Monk—to coin a phrase—would not require a gross violation of the truth. Mordecai had shown a childlike quality which had been endearing, and, after all, his witness was there for all to see. How many godly Friends had had themselves blown to Kingdom Come for the sake of the Least of These Their Brethren?

But would the Quaker princes in Philadelphia fall for it? That was the crucial question. And if they did not, would their wives? How about England? Should English woman Friends be included in his—well—efforts? What had been the name of that majestic woman in London Yearly Meeting, the one with the cloth bonnet *à la* the French goddess of Reason? She had made mincemeat of the males on the facing bench, who wanted to give Mordecai a traveling minute to America; how about enlisting her spiritual artillery when it came to convincing old diehards like his uncle Woodrow to pull out their wallets for a saint? This, alas, was what it all came down to: money. What he was engaged in, if truth were told, was a hold-up of the Philadelphia princes in the spirit of love.

"What is thee doing?" Charity asked. He had not heard her come in.

"I'm supposed to write an essay on Mordecai Monk's witness that will move my aunts and uncles to support thy concern."

"*Our* concern, dear heart."

"Our concern."

"Surely, thee is not going to write about Mordecai Monk alone? What about Lydia?"

"Ah, Lydia . . . Alas, she would be a source of uneasiness, as the saying goes."

"Thee means thee is going to write about Mordecai, but *not* about Lydia?"

"Dear love: Lydia was read out of Meeting for involving the children in the slaves' escape from the courtroom. Then she took part in a brittle—that's the appropriate Quaker word—marriage ceremony with Mordecai Monk."

"I don't understand. What was brittle about it?"

"Never mind, I'll explain it to thee later. What I want thee to do now is tell me which title thee thinks will speak most to the condition of the women who have been Mordecai's main audience. 'Blinded on the Road to Damascus'?"

"Terrible."

" 'The Last Enemy Is Death'?"

"No."

" 'The Last Enemy,' just by itself?"

"How about 'Love in Action'?"

He smiled. "That, I'm afraid, would have a mixed reception in Philadelphia."

"Thee asked me what women would respond to. Well, his life was love, and love is a verb."

Lydia had said that on one occasion, he could not remember when. It gave him a sudden, agonizing stab of grief; for the first time she was, to him, really dead. How strange. How terribly, terribly sad. What a waste! And here he was, about to eulogize—

"Well," he said, "let me do some writing first; we'll decide on a title later." He turned his back on her and dipped his quill in the inkwell. What it boiled down to was the old problem of the end hallowing the means. If the Mahanoy were to have a school, their only hope was the canonization of Mordecai Monk.

He opened with: *'God's ways are mysterious. There are instances in which man, confronted with an act of God, reels back in horror and disgust at the wanton destruction, the cruelty, the violence, the pointlessness of it all. If Friends have one message to give the world, it is this: It is not up to God to justify the apparent senselessness of some of His most shocking acts. It is up to us, individual men and women, to relieve our brother's or sister's cruel fate of its apparent pointlessness by turning it into a beacon that will shine through the ages.*

'One of God's most shocking acts of destruction in recent history has been the tearing, limb from limb, of Mordecai Monk in the explosion of a Mississippi steamboat. It is up to us to relieve his death of its apparent senselessness by completing the labor of love he set out to perform but was not allowed to complete. God needs people—and "people" is thee, dear reader.'

'H'm,' he thought, 'not bad. Could have been written by old Mordecai himself.'

But who was going to eulogize Lydia?

A troubling thought: the only Quaker poet to do her radiant life justice would have been Mordecai Monk.

CHAPTER 18

❧

PHILADELPHIA

January 1834

A headline article in the *St. Louis Sentinel,* forwarded by a helpful Missouri Friend, created a stir in Philadelphia. BATTLE CORPSES HEADING FOR OUR CITY, it ran; INDIANS DISGUISED AS QUAKERS.

According to the article, a major battle had taken place upriver between the cavalry and a band of marauding Indians. The Indians had been defeated; hundreds of corpses had been about to float by the town's waterfront in full view of the city's women and children. The mayor had ordered the snagboat *Petunia* to sail upriver, scoop up the bodies, and deposit them ashore for mass burial. But *Petunia* had not succeeded in catching them all; some of the corpses, which may have been floating below the surface, did reach the city's waterfront, causing shock and dismay. The proverbial perfidy of the redskin was demonstrated once more by the fact that some of the cadavers were disguised as Quakers.

310 • *The Peculiar People*

Shortly after this, a firsthand report of the tragedy reached Philadelphia in the form of an essay written by Obadiah Woodhouse, scion of the well-known Quaker family, entitled 'Love in Action: The Life and Death of Mordecai Monk.' It described how the English evangelist had joined, as a witness, a herd of dejected, despairing Mahanoy in the process of being removed from their ancient hunting grounds to a reservation in Kansas by the U.S. Cavalry. Mordecai Monk, stirred by the fate that had befallen the tribe—once William Penn's partners in a treaty of peace—had turned himself into an Indian, been beaten, flogged, and eventually blinded by a whip at the hands of civilian drovers; but he had persisted, thereby turning his life into a classic Quaker testimony of peace, mercy, and identification. He and the Indians had reached their Golgotha on the Mississippi: the boiler of the dilapidated riverboat about to transport them to Kansas exploded after leaving the dock. There had been no survivors; his must have been the body 'disguised as a Quaker' spotted as it drifted past the St. Louis waterfront.

On the face of it, his had been a pointless death. But, inspired by his example, a group of Friends in the Indiana town of Pendle Hill were planning to send a wagon train of forty hardy souls to the Kansas reservation, with the intent of starting a school there for Indian children, in memory of Mordecai Monk.

The essay spoke to the condition of Philadelphia Friends, especially the women, and resulted in the acceptance by both Arch and Cherry Street Meetings of the Quaker school in the Mahanoy reservation as an official concern, demonstrating the truth of Margaret Fell's observation: 'Service unites, theology divides.'

The Quaker princes of commerce did not demur; when Women's Meetings were on the warpath, no man in his senses would even imagine trying to face them down. If the man Monk had not had himself killed by that boiler explosion, none of this would have happened; now, as always, it was they who had to foot the bill.

For, in an accompanying letter, young Obadiah Woodhouse

stated blithely that the school expedition could not hazard the voyage from Pendle Hill to the Mississippi and beyond 'without protection.' This meant 'escorted by the U.S. Cavalry,' which meant the penny-pinching senators of the Armed Services Committee, which meant a sizable financial contribution, recorded in the minutes of the meeting with the phrase: *'in order to promote government recognition of a school for Indian children in the Mahanoy reservation.'* In fact, it was a contribution to the army; but because of the peace testimony, this was not so stated.

It needed expert political footwork and persistence, but in the end the Mahanoy school expedition was granted government recognition and scheduled to join the next convoy of Indians in transport to the Mississippi and beyond. The words 'and beyond' were the ones that counted; the wagon train had Simon Weatherby, clerk of Ministry and Worship of Arch Street Yearly Meeting, to thank for them.

"How would the American people react," he had asked the chairman of the Armed Services Committee, "if these good farmers and grocers with their noble cause were massacred after entering unorganized territory? Might this be the inspiration for a new fort in Kansas? As long as it is not referred to as 'fort,' and its peaceable purpose is stressed, a sizable contribution on the part of influential Philadelphia citizens can be expected. Who is going to be the political genius to reach the unreachable, by coaxing a monetary contribution out of the Quaker establishment for a military installation?" History had seen several examples of such genius; but then, politicians never read history, other than that of the Roman Empire.

After solemn reflection and consultation with 'key figures,' the secretary had obliged. Simon Weatherby should have been flushed with success, but a small sense of uneasiness remained with him. Why had he cast himself as the champion of that school expedition, an activist concern if ever there was one? Guilt, because he had been material in spiriting Monk and his 'rutting mammals' away to the Far West? No, that had been a sane and necessary decision. Then why go so far as to advocate the building of a fort? It had all been handled *sub rosa*, but what had tricked him into this Byzantine political maneuver?

Outside the window, a mockingbird taunted a crow, by cawing its mating call most realistically. Vanity, vanity, all is vanity.

CHAPTER 19

THE PRAIRIE

May 1834

One warm afternoon in spring, the seventeenth Mahanoy Indian convoy emerged from the forest, escorted by the cavalry, to find a train of twelve covered wagons waiting for it, on the site of the old buffalo hunters' campground.

The prairie had changed color during the morning hours. The sky was clear and bright; a warm wind swept whorls across the shimmering sea of grass; birds warbled in the shrubs, whole flights of them swept the horizon like fleeting clouds. The vast emptiness of the prairie seemed filled with life and the joy of living.

The herd of Indians, as they came shuffling out of the forest, seemed an alien element in the abundance of renascent vitality. Rossini had never seen them on the march before, only encamped, the day he had visited the man Monk in his so-called blindness. He had not paid much attention to them then, preoccupied as he had been with poor Lydia Best, determined to 'follow the light.' A wasted life, it had seemed; now here was this wagon train full of enthusiasts. Mysterious breed, Quakers. It might seem a suicidal enterprise, a lemmings' rush toward probable extinction by rape and manslaughter in the Wild West; but Pendle Hill itself had been founded as the result of two crazies blazing a trail in the wilderness, followed by a wagon train like this one. That, ultimately, seemed to be the secret of the elusive Society of Friends and its record of good works: its actions all appeared to be based on precedent, history repeating itself. There must be a God for innocents; either that, or Pendle Hill, even Philadelphia, were the outcome of outrageous luck.

"Well, well, if it isn't our medico!"

Startled, Rossini looked up and saw the copper-bearded convoy commandant loom over him on a huge black horse. "Good afternoon, Captain," he said. "Nice to see you again."

"Likewise," the man said. "In a minute my quarters will be up, then let's have a drink on my porch."

"Thank you. I'd be delighted. I'll introduce you to the members of this expedition."

"Later," the captain said. "Let me settle down these savages first. Sergeant!"

An NCO came trotting through the crowd on a placid horse. Any other but a cavalry horse would have shied and foamed at the mouth with wildly rolling eyes when forced to make its way through this dense throng of Indians. They were a sorry sight; the captain and his men managed to sort them out in record time. Teepees sprouted on allotted plots of prairie, horses were corralled, wagons ranged in an orderly manner. Meanwhile, the commandant's quarters were raised with surprising speed; within half an hour, the captain was holding court on the steps of his porch, being introduced to all forty members of the expedition by name and having a private word with each one of them. Within the hour, Rossini and he were sitting on his porch in camp chairs, with glasses of bourbon beside them. The captain yelled for bacon and sausages. The orderly took it in his stride.

"Well, Doctor," the captain said, raising his glass, "nice to have you with us. I'm looking forward to making this a daily ritual. Cheers."

"Cheers. But, I'm sorry to say, I'm not part of the expedition. I have a practice in town to look after."

"I see." The captain looked as if he were pouting behind that copper beard. "Well, sorry about that. None of these good people drink alcohol, I presume?"

"I'm afraid not. Quakers have a witness against alcoholic beverages."

"Not even that lawyer, whatever his name is?"

"Obadiah Woodhouse? He may, eventually. He's a city Quaker, member of one of the founding families. I've been told they drink like troopers—rum and sugar pot on every hall table. But it may just be one of those stories, you know. There are enough of them about."

"Telling *me*," the captain grunted, drinking. Then he wiped his beard and said, "But having known—er—Miss Best, I have no truck with any of them. If ever there was a saint, it was she."

He had obviously been much affected by Lydia's death. Well, let him think of her as a saint, it might help her successors. That was another Quaker secret: none of their saints had been saintly, except in one respect: if they preached at all, they had preached what they practiced. Except for that gasbag Monk, whom Saraetta Best was in the process of sanctifying as 'the blind Friend of God.' Some friend. Or some God. "How about the man Monk," he asked, "in retrospect?"

The captain took a long draught from his glass, slammed it down empty on the table, and bellowed: "Booze! And where are my sausages and bacon?"

"Coming, sah," the orderly answered from inside the tent.

"A con artist," the captain continued. "A snake-oil salesman. But he had the touch."

"Of what?"

"Healing. Those wily Indians turned him into their shaman, and it paid off. It was not his own power, of course; it was theirs. He was just their instrument. He put a hex on me one time and, by God, next thing I knew I had a boil in my neck. Which he later cured."

"How?"

The captain grinned. "You won't believe this. His magic formula was a nursery rhyme. *Hoopla, hopla, feel how it mends?* And then, a bit further, *Froggy, piggy, baby bull, grab the pain and pull and pull.* At least, he didn't pretend he was an emissary from God."

"Maybe he was at that, if God has a sense of humor."

It became too sophisticated for the captain. He grunted and yelled "Booze!" again. The orderly emerged with a tray with two full glasses and a plate of sausages and bacon. No mean feat, in a tent that had just been erected.

The captain did not see fit to thank him, but grabbed a sausage which he stuck in his beard before passing on the plate. "Help yourself," he said.

"Thank you." Rossini helped himself to a slice of bacon, bit off a piece, and washed it down with bourbon. It was salt enough to pickle a fish. "Having this many Quakers in your convoy won't faze you?"

"Nah," the captain waved the thought away with the remaining half of his sausage. "They'll help to keep my drovers in line. Those jokers have the tendency to overdo it sometimes; forty beady-eyed Quakers should do the trick. Two were enough, last time. They even got my drovers to bury dead Indians instead of tossing them in the grass."

"You don't say."

"They've been burying them ever since, as if those two were still looking. Maybe they are." He masticated the rest of his sausage. "If it takes a couple of ghosts to keep those brutes from helping themselves to my squaws, I'm all for it. On the way back, last time, one of them hauled a squaw into the grass and had his prick stung by a wasp. Talk about a sun dance! He yelled the place down. That's when they decided those two Quakers must still be hanging around. No more feeling up and bedding down since, for God knows what the spooks might do. Well, peace and quiet, that's what I like. With forty Quakers, chances are I'll get it."

Listening to the monologue as an experienced family practitioner, Rossini was struck by the change in the captain since they had first met, months before. Then he had been civilized, austere, none of the coarseness he displayed this time. He brought to mind the syndrome of the widower unable to handle the loss of his beloved wife, who hides his emotional disarray behind incongruous tough talk. Rossini understood he was in the presence of grief, clumsily disguised, and wondered if he should speak to it. No, the captain was a lonely man with one of the loneliest assignments in the army. A man like that would resist any effort to make him reveal himself; drink was the usual answer. In this case too.

"Well, Captain," he said, "thanks for the drinks, but I must be on my way. I want to say goodbye to everyone here, and I still have rounds to do back home. Thanks again, and good luck."

"The luck should be theirs," the captain said, rising, "although things could have been worse."

"How so?"

"My orders are to take this convoy all the way to Kansas and establish a fort there. The Quaker school will be built within the confines of the fort, which should solve a lot of problems."

"Glad to hear it," Rossini said. "Any name yet?"

"Excuse me?"

"For the fort?"

"No. That's left to my discretion once we get there."

Rossini turned to go; then he asked casually, "How about Fort Lydia?"

The knowing eyes in their lair of beard and eyebrows froze. Then he said, "It's sure as hell not going to be Fort Monk. Goodbye, Doctor."

"Goodbye, sir," Rossini said.

• • •

When Rossini reached the circle of Quaker wagons, he was struck by the silence. He found all forty Quakers sitting on the ground in the center of the space. They had gone into meeting.

He considered joining them, but thought better of it and sat down on the back step of one of the wagons, waiting for them to finish. As he surveyed the double row of bowed heads, the men and women no longer separated, he was reminded of the gathering on Founders' Day when it had all started: the children standing motionless on the stage in their Quaker and Indian costumes, Lydia Best among them; the silent pupils in the audience, girls on the left, boys on the right, and in the first row Mordecai Monk, about to hurl his bomb into their peaceable kingdom. Now Monk was dead as a result of his intervention, so was Lydia, and here was the ultimate outcome: a wagon train on its way to start a school for Indian children in the Mahanoy reservation in Kansas, the very heart of the lawless world of the unorganized territories.

He looked at the well-known faces. Jesse McHair, the roughneck. Little Will, the dwarf. Obadiah Woodhouse, henpecked husband in the making. His wife, Charity, as gallant as they come. Black Adam and Peggy Higgins.

He looked along the rows of bent heads and felt a paternal pride. At least a third of them, now heading for sainthood or martyrdom, or both, or neither, might have been in their graves by now without his care. Well, say a quarter. All right: a fifth.

Bargaining with himself over the number of lives he had saved, he was overcome by the feeling of an unseen presence. It was nonsense, of course. Just the sentiment of the occasion. Even so, someone *was* there. Lydia? Mordecai Monk? Maybe it was the phenomenon they occasionally spoke of among themselves: 'a sense of the Presence.'

Meeting broke, they all shook hands and rose. Rossini said goodbye to them, moving among them with admonitions and farewells. He was kissed by some of the women, Charity Woodhouse and Peggy Higgins among them. Then he mounted his borrowed mare and, turning slowly, headed for the forest.

One hour and he would be home. Back to civilization. He spurred the horse to a canter, for there was work to be done: babies, terrified of the unknown, to be coaxed into the world; the dying, terrified of the unknown, to be coaxed into leaving it. It was a good life, serving humanity. But as he approached the forest, he could not escape the thought, 'I should have gone with them.'

Why? He was not a Quaker, and there were only forty of them. His practice numbered seven hundred. He was needed where the need was greatest.

Wasn't he?

The horse and its rider disappeared into the forest.

About the Author

JAN DE HARTOG, born in Haarlem, Holland, the second son of a Calvinist minister and a Quaker mother, ran off to sea at the age of ten. At sixteen he entered Amsterdam Naval College, ending up as a junior mate in the Dutch oceangoing tugboat service. When war broke out in 1940, and Holland was occupied by the Nazis, de Hartog was trapped in his native country. During this time he wrote and published his first major novel, *Holland's Glory*, which became an instant and historic bestseller and a symbol of the Dutch Resistance; the German occupying forces banned the book in 1942, but it went on selling in large quantities in the underground market. When he escaped to London in 1943, he was appointed war correspondent for the Dutch merchant marine. There he gathered the material for his postwar novels *The Distant Shore*, *The Captain*, and *The Commodore*.

In the late sixties de Hartog, himself a Quaker, undertook the ambitious project of a multivolume novel on the history of the Religious Society of Friends. *The Peaceable Kingdom* was the first book, followed by *The Lamb's War* and *The Peculiar People*.

De Hartog has written many plays, among which the most famous is *The Fourposter*, which won a Tony in 1951 and was later turned into the musical *I Do! I Do!*, and several volumes of essays, the best known being *A Sailor's Life* (memories of life at sea before World War II) and *The Children* (a personal record for the benefit of the adoptive parents of Asian children).

In 1983, de Hartog was nominated for the Nobel Prize for Literature.